# THE FALL LINE

# Praise for *Aspen in Moonlight*

"A sweet lesbian debut romance book with a paranormal twist. Both main characters are extremely likable, so it's easy to root for them and hope for a happily ever after. If you are interested in a feel-good romance, this book would be a good choice. The setting in Colorado also shined, so if you are a nature/wildlife fan especially for bears, I would also recommend this."
—*LezReviewBooks*

"The storytelling is imaginative and engaging. The descriptions are splendid. The language is fluid and magnificent. Wacker is impressive; she knows how to bring the words to life in 3D Technicolor…Wacker pulled me in and held me there with her lovely storytelling; I was captivated. She writes with such grace and intelligence. Her word building is finessed marvelously, giving the story depth and dimension. It truly highlights her talent as an imaginative and descriptive writer."—*Women Using Words*

"Excellent story and wonderful characters set against the glorious backdrop of the Rockies…the baddie is nasty, the wider cast are well drawn, and the whole is an excellent read."—*Lesbian Reading Room*

## By the Author

Aspen in Moonlight

Holding Their Place

The Fall Line

# THE FALL LINE

*by*

# Kelly Wacker

2023

# THE FALL LINE

ISBN 13: 978-1-63679-205-7

THIS TRADE PAPERBACK ORIGINAL IS PUBLISHED BY
BOLD STROKES BOOKS, INC.
P.O. BOX 249
VALLEY FALLS, NY 12185

FIRST EDITION: MARCH 2023

---

**CREDITS**
EDITOR: SHELLEY THRASHER
PRODUCTION DESIGN: STACIA SEAMAN
COVER DESIGN BY INKSPIRAL DESIGN

# Acknowledgments

While the city of Oberon and its surroundings in this novel are fictional, they are inspired by real places, like once-thriving mining company towns that no longer exist today and the university where I teach that has rich ghostlore. Personal experiences have also flavored this story. While walking across a campus quad one night many years ago, I caught a peripheral glimpse of a woman dressed in yellow seated under an old oak tree. When I turned to look, nothing was there. Weeks later, I heard about the ghost known only as "the woman in a yellow dress," an almost unknown specter on the historic campus. I've always wondered about her story.

The Cahaba River and its ecology are very real. When I moved to Alabama twenty years ago, I initially experienced the nearby river as a nice place to paddle a kayak and play in the water on a hot summer's day. Over time I became aware of its historic and increasingly fragile ecological importance. Often accompanied by my enthusiastic dog, Chip, I explored the tributary rivers and creeks near my home and learned how they all interconnect. I'm indebted to many people for helping me to understand the local ecosystem. Randy Haddock, Field Director Emeritus of the Cahaba River Society, a passionate naturalist and gifted teacher, led the guided canoe trip I was fortunate to take years ago. While writing this novel, I team-taught a course on art and zoology with my colleague, biologist Jill Wicknick. I had the wonderful opportunity to learn many things from her, including developing a nuanced understanding of ecotones and fall lines. My exceptionally supportive wife, Amy Feger, loves rivers and creeks as much as I do. Being an artist, she helped me to better understand plein air and studio painting practice. While working on this novel, I often accompanied Amy and our friend Gaby Wolodarski on their landscape painting excursions. While they painted, I explored, observed, and made notes. Gaby, also one of my beta readers, graciously shared her thoughts on the story as it unfolded. I am grateful for the generosity of her time and criticism as well that received from my other beta readers, Michele Lisper and Sallyanne Monti. My dear friend and fellow author, Karen Williams, accompanied me on the journey of this story, from a kernel of an idea, through brainstorming, writing, and editing. She also kept me well supplied with thoughtful and spooky stories along the way. This story is enriched by her presence in countless ways.

Finally, this novel wouldn't be in your hands without Bold Strokes Books publisher Len Barot; senior editor, Sandy Lowe; and my expert editor, Shelley Thrasher, whose gentle guidance has helped polish every page.

A portion of the proceeds from this novel will be donated to Cahaba River Society and Cahaba Riverkeeper, the guardians of my watershed. I encourage you to learn about and get into the natural world that lies just outside your doorstep wherever you are. Who knows what you might find?

For Amy, who always responds to the call of the river.
And for Chip, whose exuberant company I dearly miss.

## CHAPTER ONE

Jordan Burroughs gripped the steering wheel of her 4Runner with both hands. Fat raindrops pelted the windshield as strong gusts of wind buffeted the high-profile SUV, threatening to push it into the eighteen-wheeler speeding past her on the interstate. The skies had been clear when she'd left home in Chattanooga a few hours ago, but now she was running into both rain and rush-hour traffic as she drove through Birmingham, Alabama. She hunched over the wheel to get a better look at the sickly green pallor of the sky. It reminded her that it was only mid-May and tornado season still had a few weeks left. The ominous dark clouds overhead looked as if they'd been painted with aggressive strokes of a wide brush. Even more unsettling were the claw-like vaporous tendrils descending from the cloud wall, seeming to touch the top of the city skyline.

She glanced at the clock on the dashboard, thankful she'd left home early. With luck, she'd make it in time for a dinner meeting with the coordinator of the Oberon College artist-in-residence program, where she'd be working for the next month. Moving at a slow creep behind a mass of red brake lights snaking in front of her, she listened to the wipers thump rhythmically across the windshield while lightning flashed in the clouds illuminating the sculpture of the Roman god Vulcan perched atop Red Mountain to the east. She'd been to the city a few years earlier for a nature illustrators' conference and had seen the cast-iron sculpture up close while sightseeing. The brawny, bearded god of the forge, like a patron saint of the city born from blast furnaces and steel mills, stood triumphantly atop a tall stone tower, pointing the tip of a spear at the mutable sky.

Exiting the interstate on the other side of the mountain, she glanced over her shoulder at the broody storm front she was leaving behind, thankful to be moving out of its path. Guided by GPS instructions, she navigated to a narrow road that dipped and curved along the crest of a mountain ridge. Occasional breaks in the trees offered tantalizing glimpses of vistas, but with the sun low in a clearing sky, she found it difficult to see the landscape through the haze. She traveled a meandering line. If she made a 180-degree turn, the sinuous ridgeline would lead back to her apartment in Chattanooga, and, beyond that, to her childhood home in the Catskills of New York.

Forty minutes later, the City of Oberon introduced itself with a large welcome sign proudly proclaiming itself as the home of Oberon College. After passing august historic homes with lush lawns shaded by stately old oaks, she entered a quaint downtown that looked like a movie set with its brick-and-limestone buildings and their elegant cast-iron posts and balconies. Passing a block of restaurants that would appeal to cash-strapped college students—pizza, burgers, and kabobs—she spotted a coffeehouse, partly because she was always looking for a good cup of coffee, but also because of a pride flag hanging in the window. A young college-age woman with hair dyed an unnatural shade of pink walked through the door, followed by another young woman sporting a buzz cut, whose hand she was holding.

The South, as Jordan had learned from living in it, was a peculiarly conflicted place; its inhabitants could be warm and friendly, but simultaneously conservative and intolerant. It never failed to yield surprises, such as one before her right now: two hand-holding baby dykes walking down the street in the so-called Heart of Dixie.

The GPS abruptly announced that she'd arrived at her destination. She parked and took a moment to check herself in the mirror before getting out, finger-combing the curls that had come back after a recent haircut. She'd thought about adding highlights to her sandy-brown hair, but summer sun would add them naturally soon enough. Leaving the cool, dry comfort of the car, she was shocked by the air outside. While the oppressive heat of summer had yet to arrive, the atmosphere here was already heavy with humidity. By the time she crossed the street and entered the restaurant, she felt sticky.

She glanced around the upscale restaurant. A noisy crowd surrounded an elegant old oak bar, and the host's stand was blocked by people waiting for tables. She was about to text the professor that she'd arrived when a stylish older woman dressed in a brightly patterned tunic and pants caught her eye and smiled.

"Madeleine Grendel?" Jordan said, approaching her with a smile.

"Oh. I'm not Professor Grendel." The woman lifted her eyebrows and spoke with a Southern accent as strong as sweet tea. "But I just saw her. I work at the college with her."

Realizing her mistake, Jordan winced. "We haven't met in person yet. Could you point her out?"

"I'll do you one better. I'll take you to her. She was just seated."

Passing white-linen-covered tables with mason jars of cheerful bouquets, Jordan followed the woman to the back of the busy dining room to a table with a much younger thirty-something-looking woman seated at it. Her dark hair was styled in a fashionable pixie cut, and thick-framed glasses gave her an owlish appearance, accentuating large blue eyes that met hers as she approached.

"I'm not sure what you're posting on your dating app, Professor," the woman said with a playful laugh. "She thought I was you!"

"Dating app?" Madeline Grendel appeared confused.

"I'm not here for a date," Jordan said to the woman. "I mean, not that kind of date. I'm here for a dinner date—I mean a dinner *meeting*." Jordan looked to Madeline Grendel and stuck out her hand. "Hi. I'm Jordan Burroughs."

"Yes. Of course you are." The young professor stood and shook her hand. Tall and svelte, standing, she appeared less like a fluffy owl. "Nice to meet you, Jordan." She turned to speak to the woman. "Jordan is the college's new artist-in-residence."

"How nice." The woman touched her fingertips lightly to her chest and delivered the words in a tone so dripping with sincerity they seemed disingenuous. "From where do you hail, Jordan Burroughs?"

"Chattanooga."

"Lovely city, so pretty in the fall." The woman's mouth opened as if she was going to say more but then closed abruptly when a man in a suit and tie caught her attention with a wave of his hand. "That's my husband, and our table's ready. Y'all have a nice dinner." As she turned to leave, she flicked a finger at Jordan. "I hope you'll enjoy your stay in Oberon, Miss Burroughs."

"I hope so, too. Thank you," Jordan said.

"Please, have a seat." Professor Grendel gestured to the chair across the table.

The professor wasn't wearing a wedding band, and the woman had assumed that Jordan was meeting her for a romantic dinner. Was Madeline Grendel a lesbian? "I don't know why she thought I was here for a date. Not that I wouldn't go on a date with you." Jordan blurted the words without thinking. She hadn't expected the professor to be so cute, and she suddenly felt awkward. "What I'm trying to say," she stammered, "and not very well, is that…oh, hell, Professor Grendel. I've really put my foot in it, haven't I?"

"No worries. I'll take what you were trying to say as a compliment." Madeline Grendel laughed. "And please, call me Maddie. Everyone does."

"Even your students?"

"Oh, no." She pitched her voice lower in a mock-serious tone. "To my students, I am *Professor* Grendel." Two dimples, one on each side of her mouth, punctuated her grin. "I've heard I'm called Grendel the Furious. You know, like the monster in Beowulf, when I'm wielding my fiery red pen while grading papers."

"Confession—" Jordan lifted the napkin from the table and unfolded it across her lap. "I like Grendel better than Beowulf."

"Monsters are often more charismatic than the heroes."

"I read a novel that retold the story from Grendel's perspective that made me feel sympathetic for the creature. I'd never thought of him as a victim of circumstance."

"Indeed he was—a poor soul suffering the bad luck of having ancestors cursed by God." Maddie pushed a paper menu across the table.

"Do you teach *Beowulf?*" Jordan asked, perusing the menu.

"I haven't since I was a grad student. Here I teach mostly composition. My research interests are in environmental writing and contemporary fiction."

"Two of my favorite things." Jordan glanced at Maddie, whose smile hadn't flagged. She raised the menu. "Everything looks good. Thank you for inviting me."

"Thank *you* for being amenable to meeting me here. I promise I'll get you to Palmer House, where you'll be staying, before dark. As

THE FALL LINE

I mentioned in the email message, it isn't far, just outside of town, but getting there is confusing. Do you know the expression 'You can't get there from here'?"

Jordan nodded. It was a common Southernism.

"It's especially true for Palmer House. There are several sharp turns, and one of the roads makes a dogleg that GPS never gets right. Most visitors get lost the first time and end up in a panic in the woods along the river on an unmarked road in a dead zone."

Jordan wiped perspiration from her forehead with her fingertips while she looked over the menu. "It's a lot more humid down here than in Chattanooga. The house does have air-conditioning, right?" She was only partially kidding.

"Don't worry." Maddie laughed. "It might have been built in 1859, but it's been renovated since then."

"That's a relief." Jordan craned her neck to see the daily drink specials listed on a chalkboard above the bar.

"I recommend the Bee Charmer." Maddie drew out the words softly, enticingly. "It's very good—honey lemonade and Redmont gin, a local spirit—but you must be careful. Drink it too fast and you'll get stung."

"You make the sting sound worth it. Maybe I'll chance it," Jordan said.

"Good. Let's get stung together," She waved to their server to place an order.

While waiting on the drink, they made small talk about the weather and traffic. When the cocktails arrived, Maddie raised her glass.

"To inspired art-making."

"I'll certainly drink to that." Jordan clinked her glass against Maddie's and took a sip. It was refreshing and boozy. The professor was right. Only slow, controlled sipping would prevent drunkenness. The waiter remained at the table to take their orders.

"I'll have the Gulf shrimp and grits with Maxfield sausage," Maddie said to the waiter, then spoke to Jordan. "The sausage is local and made with pasture-raised pork, if that matters to you."

"It does, and I always trust the locals when it comes to food." She copied Maddie's order and gave the menu to the waiter. "Speaking of locals, you don't sound like one. Your accent sounds a little like...the Bronx? Long Island, maybe?"

"People assume I'm a New Yorker all the time. But I'm originally from the Big Easy, not the Big Apple."

"New Orleans?"

Maddie nodded. "My accent is called Yat."

"Yat? I've never heard of it."

"It comes from something we say all the time. 'Where ya't?' It means 'How are you doing?' I've trained myself not to say it unless I'm there. It confuses people anywhere else."

"I'll bet. It really does sound like a New York accent."

"It is, in a way. People from New York settled in New Orleans back in the early nineteenth century."

"It's remarkable," Jordan said, pausing to take a sip of her drink, "that people in two places, a thousand miles and two hundred years apart, could have developed such parallel accents." She looked up from the rim of her glass, catching Maddie's direct gaze. Her shadowy gray-blue eyes seemed to be studying her.

"I know you've come here from Chattanooga, but hearing you, I think you're not from the South. The Northeast maybe?"

"Good call. Yes. I grew up in the Catskills."

"Ah, so *you're* the New Yorker. How did you end up in Tennessee?"

"College. I went to art school in Knoxville and fell in love with the southern Appalachian Mountains. It's a lot like home, but not so much snow in the winter."

"I imagine that has a certain appeal."

"It does. Ashville's not so far away if I want a wintrier mountain experience. When I visit my family in New York for the holidays, it usually reminds me that I don't miss Northeast winters."

"What drew you to Chattanooga?"

"Aside from the landscape, I like the feel of the place. It's become a tech hub, and with the gig industry comes money. Where there's money, there's support for the arts. Plus, the cost of living is low, and since my commercial work is freelance, I can live anyplace with a good internet connection."

"It sounds perfect for you."

"It is for now," Jordan said. "I like it, but I don't have long-term commitments."

"Tell me about your short-term plans while you're here. I know from your application you're interested in illustrating endangered species."

"I'm here to see the Cahaba lilies bloom. I'm sure you're aware how rare they are."

"Oh, yes. They're a local natural treasure."

Jordan had first learned about the endangered flowering plants in *Smithsonian Magazine* and wanted to see them in person before she'd finished reading the article. The essay explained that the flashy, exotic-looking lilies had been common in many Southeastern states before rivers, dammed for hydroelectricity projects, had condemned many species to extinction or near extinction. Aside from the beauty of their creamy white blooms with spidery tendrils, they were special for their wildness. Resistant to domestication, they would die if transplanted elsewhere and would grow only in clean, swift-flowing water with rocks craggy enough for their roots to cling. The few remaining stands were scattered across three states, with the largest in Alabama, near Oberon.

"I'll be doing a lot of hiking and looking," Jordan said. "To record observations in notes, drawings, and paintings. I've been doing some research to prepare for this trip and have learned that this watershed is one of the most biodiverse in North America. I'll probably draw and paint lots of things besides the lilies."

"Just plants?"

"Animals and insects, too, I assume. Spring is great for observation because so much is happening. Everyone's out showing off, finding mates, and building nests. I won't rule anything out—mammals, birds, turtles, fish, invertebrates, bugs. Whatever crosses my path."

"You should meet one of our biologists. She's always happy to talk about the local ecology."

"If you could introduce me, that would be great."

The waiter returned, interrupting them with two wide-rimmed bowls, each with mounds of grits smothered in a thick red sauce and topped with grilled shrimp. The aroma made Jordan's mouth water. The first delicious bite did not disappoint—the grits creamy and sharp with parmesan, the shrimp tender, and the slices of sausage smoky and spicy.

"How long have you been here at the college?"

"Eight years," Maddie said. "I landed here fresh from grad school."

"Was that in New Orleans?"

"No. The University of Washington."

"That was a long way from home."

"At the time, it was a huge part of the appeal. I wanted to get as far away from the South as I could. My feelings eventually changed, and I was glad to come back. I like to think I help broaden people's horizons here. Fortunately, Oberon has a history of supporting diversity and progressive ideas." Maddie swirled a shrimp in the red sauce. "The residency here being a good example."

"How so?"

"The program's designed to support scholars, scientists, and creatives who work with social justice and environmental issues. Since Palmer House is dedicated to the program, it's a way of rehabilitating Palmer family history. You've lived in the South long enough to understand, I'm sure. Trace the history of a white industrial Southern family back far enough, and you'll find a story of terrible exploitation."

"But I thought a social reformer founded the college." Jordan repeated what she had read about the college's history on their website.

"She did, but the house predates the college by several decades. It was built by the founder's father, Phineas Palmer. He owned the Oberon Coal Company, though his wife, Wilhelmina, named the company. She loved literature, Shakespeare especially. Oberon is the king of the faeries in *A Midsummer Night's Dream*."

"That's such a whimsical name for an industrial company."

"Agreed, but the family believed in education, and Shakespeare was hugely popular in the late nineteenth century. The founder, Julia, and her three sisters were sent to school at Smith College in Massachusetts. And all, except Julia, came back with husbands. She returned with the audacious notion of creating a similar kind of school in the South for girls whose families didn't have the means to send their daughters to the Seven Sisters colleges up North. That was in the 1890s, and by then, the Palmers had opened several more mines and had relocated their primary home to Birmingham. They also began acquiring a *lot* of land all over the state. Their descendants are still major landholders here, mostly in timber and gas industries now. Anyway, Julia refused to marry and used her inheritance to endow the college. When the coal boom went bust, all the little company towns around here shriveled and died, except this one."

"Which seems to be thriving, from what I've seen," Jordan said. "Julia must have been quite the woman."

"I think 'headstrong' is often used to describe her."

"Where would we be without headstrong women?" Jordan asked with a laugh.

"The world would be a much poorer place." Maddie sipped her cocktail. "I, for one, am very thankful for Julia Palmer's legacy. Her spirit infuses this place."

"Speaking of spirits, when I looked up the college, I kept seeing references to ghosts." Jordan said. "Is the campus really haunted?"

Maddie nodded.

"Seriously?" Jordan widened her eyes. "You believe in ghosts?"

"Are you kidding me? I'm from New Orleans. You can hardly walk through the French Quarter without bumping into a few, or at least rubbing shoulders with a necromancer on your way to get a beignet."

Jordan laughed, but Maddie's seriousness surprised her. "You've seen a ghost?"

"I was joking about bumping into them in New Orleans. I confess I've never seen one. They say some people aren't sensitive that way, and I guess I'm one of them." Maddie shrugged. "But I do believe in the possibility of them. If our souls, our spirits, if you will, are eternal, then maybe the spirit sometimes gets stuck here in this material world and becomes a ghost. How about you?"

"To be honest, I've never given it much thought. I'm probably best described as an empiricist. I started college as a biology major and then switched to art and concentrated in illustration. In both fields I was trained to observe and record, you know? I've never seen a ghost, so I can't say I'm a believer."

"But you don't have to see something to believe in it. You probably took enough science classes to understand that concept." Maddie smiled and raised her eyebrows.

"How so?" Jordan felt like a student being prompted to work through a complicated idea.

"Take the air, for example." Maddie waved her fork around for emphasis. "The oxygen in it fills our lungs. It's invisible. You can't see it, but it keeps us alive. Whether or not you believe in it, it's still there."

"That's an interesting perspective." Jordan wasn't fully convinced.

Good science required experiments to test theories and repeatable results, but she didn't want to argue the point. She might not be a believer, but she liked a good story, and Maddie was a good storyteller. "Tell me more about this haunted campus. Are there any evil spirits?"

"Not that I'm aware of. Some of my colleagues talk about hearing footsteps or doors slamming when they know they're the only person around. A librarian once told me that she hears the voices of children sometimes, late at night, when it's quiet. There's also a residence hall known for its mischievous ghost. I had a student one semester who lost her student ID card five times, and every time she got a replacement, the old one would turn up in an obvious place."

"The actions of a mischievous roommate, don't you think?"

"Perhaps. But my student was convinced it was the ghost." Maddie smiled. "I'm sure you'll hear more stories while you're here. There are lots of them, some grounded in fact and others pure fiction."

"Does Palmer House have a ghost?"

Maddie was silent for a moment before answering, seeming to choose her words carefully. "It does."

"Really?" Jordan stared at her, waiting for her to smile or break into laughter. But she didn't do either. Jordan leaned forward. "Tell me about it."

"Are you sure you want to hear a story about a ghost who haunts the house where you'll be staying alone for the next month?"

"I'm not easily frightened." Jordan sat back in her chair and took a slow sip of her drink. "And I don't believe in ghosts, remember?"

"Okay. You asked for it." Maddie rolled the ice around in her nearly empty glass and then tipped it back, draining what liquid remained. "During the Civil War, the Confederate Army commandeered the house to use as the headquarters for a field hospital. Major Reynold Pettiborn, the commanding officer, was known for his exceptional care, treating the wounded soldiers as if they were his own sons. He refused to leave the hospital for any amount of time until he received a letter from his dying father who said his only desire was to see his son one more time. Honoring his father's wish, he traveled to Atlanta, but the poor man passed before the major arrived, and then, while he was on the way back, the Union troops swept through the area and murdered the defenseless soldiers in their beds. The major returned, doubly devastated, feeling he'd failed his father and his young soldiers. He died a few days later from a fever, but some say it was from a broken heart and spirit. And so—" Maddie locked eyes with Jordan and lowered the pitch of her voice, speaking slowly as she finished the story. "The ghost of Major Pettiborn haunts the grounds around the house to this day. On dark, moonless nights, he wanders through the pecan orchard and shuffles around the edges of the house moaning and wailing in anguish and mourning."

"I'll make sure to pay attention to the phases of the moon," Jordan said. She felt pleasantly tingly from both the spooky story and the timbre of the professor's compelling voice. "I hope he's not looking for some Yankee to finally wreak his revenge upon."

"No. I've never heard such a threat," Maddie said lightly.

"That's good. I'll sleep better knowing that." Jordan laughed.

"Maybe I should have said 'not yet.'" Maddie gave her a lopsided grin. "There's a first for everything, you know."

"Oh! Well, there goes my good night's sleep." Jordan enjoyed the teasing banter, but still, the skeptical scientist in her persisted. "You said earlier that some stories are based in fact and others made up. So, tell me, how much of that one is factual?"

"Not a damn bit." Maddie chuckled. "The Union troops, when they did come through, flew past the town and the mine. They were more interested in destroying ironworks and main rail lines. If the Confederacy couldn't manufacture iron or transport it, then the mines were effectively shut down since there was nowhere and no way to send it. No battles were fought near here, and Palmer House was never a field hospital."

"That was very convincing. You tell a good story."

"Why, thank you."

"I'd like to hear another one."

"And I'd be happy to tell you one," Maddie glanced at her watch. "But, unless you want dessert, we should probably get going."

"Oh, yes. Of course." Jordan gestured to her empty bowl. "That was rich, no dessert necessary." She folded her napkin and placed it on the table. She'd been so caught up in their conversation and Maddie's expert storytelling, she'd almost forgotten she was here for a quick bite to eat before being guided to her temporary residence.

They settled the bill, and Jordan followed Maddie outside. "Where's your car?"

"It's the silver Toyota." Jordan pointed. "The 4Runner across the street."

"Great." Maddie started to cross the street. "I'm parked next to you. Follow me. We'll go past campus, cut through a neighborhood, make a sharp right at the dogleg, then a left and another right, and we'll be there."

Trailing Maddie's mossy green Subaru Outback with a "Save the Cahaba" license plate, they skirted the edge of the stately campus. After several turns, Jordan lost her bearings after they passed through a residential neighborhood that quickly transitioned into densely wooded countryside. When the road zigzagged unexpectedly on the crest of a hill, Jordan knew she'd have gotten lost had she been on her own. After turning on to a gravel lane, they passed through an ornate old ironwork gate and through a deep grove of pecan trees. At the end of the lane stood Palmer House, a two-story, cedar-shingled red-brick building, its windows neatly trimmed in white paint and flanked by dark green shutters. Two tall chimneys jutted out along the sides of the building on each end, silhouetted in the darkening sky. Jordan followed Maddie around back and pulled up next to her in front of a smaller single-story brick building connected to the house by a covered walkway.

"That's the studio," Maddie said, pointing at the smaller building as she got out of her car. "It was originally the kitchen. They were detached from the main house to keep the house cooler in summer and to reduce risk of catching the house on fire. There's a kitchen in the house now. It's small but serviceable."

"I'm sure it's fine for me. I'm not much of a cook," Jordan said. She smiled at the invisible chorus of spring peeper frogs calling from the trees. "If it has a coffee pot and a microwave, I'll be fine."

"It does. Housekeeping comes by once a week to do light cleaning, and they'll restock the coffee service. It's a nice little perk." Maddie laughed at her pun. "You'll find several good restaurants in town."

"Perfect."

"Do you need help carrying anything in?"

"No. I'll be fine. Thanks."

Maddie gestured toward the house. "I'll give you a quick tour and the key, and then I need to get home."

"Oh. I'm sorry if I've kept you from your family or, uh, partner?" Jordan stumbled over the words.

"No girlfriend right now. Just my dog, who needs to go out soon."
Pulling a key from her pocket, Maddie walked to the back door. As she
slid the key into the lock, she rested her palm on the door frame and
lightly tapped her index finger against the painted wood three times
before she turned the lock and opened the door.

Jordan followed her inside, pausing when Maddie stopped in the
center of the hallway and pointed up the stairs. "You'll find the bedroom,
bathroom, and a small study upstairs." She led her through each of
the rooms on the ground floor, showing her the sitting room, dining
room, and the tiny kitchen. On the counter, next to a coffeemaker, was
a basket stocked with packets of tea and coffee, and some granola bars.

"The photos on the website don't do this place justice," Jordan
said, admiring everything she'd seen. Rich heart-pine floors gleamed
against cream-colored walls, on which paintings, darkened with age,
were hung. The furniture, mostly modern, looked comfortable, and
several large bookcases were packed with books.

Maddie glanced at her watch furtively, as if she didn't want to
seem pressed for time. "Would you like me to show you the studio?"

"I hate to keep you longer. You've been generous with your time."

"There's not much to see. But it does have a fireplace, not that
you'll need it this time of year, and a big table and chairs. Some of
our residents have really liked using it for meetings or open studios. It
keeps your living space more private."

"I look forward to checking it out." Jordan rubbed her hands
together.

"That's about it, then." Maddie held out the key between her
thumb and index finger. "Here you go."

"Thanks," Jordan said, taking the key.

"Oh. I forgot to mention we always get complaints about the
air-conditioning being inconsistent. Maintenance can't seem to figure
it out, but if you have any problems, their number is on the fridge."
Maddie glanced at her watch again. "I'd better go. If you need anything
else, you've got my number. Have a good night, Jordan."

"Thanks. You too, Maddie."

Maddie paused as she crossed the threshold, turning to speak.
"I enjoyed our conversation at dinner. If you need a break sometime,
maybe we can continue it."

"I'd like that," Jordan said.

Maddie smiled, the dimples appearing again. Jordan watched her as she crossed the gravel to her car. Maddie moved with a grace and confidence Jordan found attractive. After Maddie left, Jordan remained on the back step, gazing up at the first stars emerging in the orange and blue twilight sky. While she searched unsuccessfully for the moon, a raspy-voiced barred owl called from the darkening woods. She recalled Maddie's description of Major Pettiborn. *On dark, moonless nights, he walks the perimeter, moaning and wailing.* Ghost stories might not frighten Jordan easily, but she was still glad to know that one wasn't true.

Deciding to leave her art supplies in her car until tomorrow, she retrieved her bags and took them into Palmer House. The stairs, rounded and worn smooth from so many years of use, creaked underfoot as she carried her bags to the second floor. When her foot touched the narrow landing halfway up, she suddenly felt cold, like she'd stepped into a walk-in freezer. It was such a shock she stopped and looked around as prickly goose bumps formed on her arms. Then, equally as sudden, the intense chill passed as quickly as it had arrived.

She must have walked into a draft. Old houses weren't designed for modern air-conditioning, and the air circulated strangely, she told herself, and Maddie had already warned her about it. She really hated to waste energy on too much air-conditioning. If it became a problem she'd call maintenance, as Maddie advised. Without giving it another thought she continued up the stairs to unpack.

# CHAPTER TWO

Jordan awoke to her cell phone alarm, an annoying sound she'd selected purposefully because it was difficult to ignore. She reached out and tapped the snooze icon. Rolling over, she pulled the covers up over her shoulders, hopeful for a few minutes more of the sleep that had eluded her most of the night. The bed was comfortable, but she'd slept badly because a mockingbird had sung energetically through the night from a perch in a tree near the light post in front of the house. Cycling endlessly through his litany of songs, he'd stopped only when the sun began to rise.

When the alarm pestered her again, she dismissed it with a groan and rolled out of bed. Pushing aside the curtain, she watched the sun rising above the pecan orchard. The movement of three young squirrels, probably siblings, chasing each other furiously caught her attention. How amazing it would be to navigate a tree like that, running along branches like trails, leaping with a confidence devoid of fear of falling. A robin began to sing, then a blue jay, and then, when the song of a hawk, a chickadee, and a titmouse all followed in quick succession, Jordan realized the mockingbird was still singing.

"Damn bird," she muttered and yawned.

After showering and dressing in khakis and a light cotton button-up shirt, she went downstairs to make coffee. She grabbed a maple-pecan granola bar from the basket while the pot brewed and went into the sitting room to peruse the books on the shelves. She found an eclectic mix of genres. Some looked new and unread, and other books seemed quite old, with faded and cracked spines. Not surprisingly, given what she'd learned about Wilhelmina Palmer's penchant for Shakespeare, she found an entire shelf of his works.

She popped the last bite of the granola bar into her mouth, tucked the wrapper into her pocket, and reached for *A Midsummer Night's Dream*, the play with a character that had inspired the name of the Oberon Coal Company. Opening the old book, she thumbed through the pages back to front, admiring the beautiful color illustrations. She paused to look closely at a whimsical picture of a donkey-headed man sitting dejectedly at the base of a tree, surrounded by laughing fairies.

She continued skimming the book, admiring the feel of the thick pages, the space between the lines of text, and the wide margins. Old books were comfortable in hand and easy on the eyes to read. They just didn't make them like this anymore. A passage underlined in pencil in the first scene caught her eye: *The course of true love never did run smooth.*

"Isn't that the truth," she mumbled to herself. In her twenties, she'd fallen in and out of love a few times, experiences that had left her heart bruised but never broken. Shortly after her thirtieth birthday she met Jessica, a sexy and adventurous health-care cybersecurity engineer, and fell hard for her. It was the first time she'd experienced an all-consuming, thought-scrambling love that she thought existed only in romance novels and movies. She had intended to ask Jess what she thought about moving in together over a romantic dinner. Before she could ask the question, Jess told her she had exciting news: she'd been offered a job on the West Coast and had accepted it. A week later she was gone, leaving Jordan reeling and devastated.

The coffeemaker beeped, snapping her back to the present. Her heart had mended, but the bitterness of the breakup still lingered. She closed the book carefully, placing it on the seat of a wingback chair next to the bookcase before returning to the kitchen. Taking the hot brew to the studio, she sipped it carefully. She'd had worse, but she definitely wanted to find a better source for the duration of her stay.

Outside, the sky was clear, the air cool. No doubt the humidity would rise along with the sun, but for now, it was comfortable. A rectangular white card on the ground next to her car caught her attention. It had a magnetic stripe like a credit card. Picking it up off the gravel, she flipped it over to discover it was Maddie's university ID card, which she must have dropped last night.

She sent Maddie a quick text and carried the card into the studio. The interior was rustic, with plastered walls, terra-cotta tile floor, and brick hearth. A set of louvered doors enclosed a bathroom with a washing machine and clothes dryer. She marveled at the convenience and her good luck. When she'd first investigated the college's artist-in-residence program, she'd wondered if the description of the lodging as "a historic home" was a polite term for something ramshackle. The accommodations here were actually nicer than her two-bedroom apartment in Chattanooga. Her phone pinged, a text alert.

*Thanks! Can I come by in a half hour?*

Jordan immediately texted back saying that would be fine and continued her inspection. The working space in the studio was on the other side of a sliding door. Pushing the door aside, she was pleased at what she found—functional tables and chairs in a brightly lit room with stained-concrete floor, white walls, and skylights with louvers that flooded the room with indirect lighting. It was perfect for painting. Her studio, a bedroom in her Chattanooga apartment, was cramped and dark compared to this. She sat in a comfortable-looking upholstered chair to test it and jumped to her feet, nearly spilling her coffee, when someone yelled outside. Moving to a window, she lifted the blind and peered out cautiously. An old man wearing a blue ball cap and dressed in overalls stood next to her car. Clutching a rope in one hand, he seemed to be scanning the area. She walked back to the door and opened it slowly. The man, seeing her, flinched in clear surprise.

"Can I help you?" she asked. She didn't open the door all the way, ready to slam it shut and lock it if need be.

"Oh…hey," the old man said. His frown shifted into an expression approximating a smile. "Have you seen a little Jack Russell terrier?"

"No, I haven't. Are you missing one?"

"Yep. Darn little bugger." He pointed into the thicket of privet and tall trees behind the parking area. "I live over yonder, and ole Jack likes to take hisself for a run from time to time."

"Jack is the Jack Russell?" Feeling more confident the old man wasn't a threat, she stepped outside.

"Yep," the man said, removing his hat. He scratched his scalp and ran his fingers through his curly white hair before settling the cap back on his head.

"I haven't seen any dogs this morning."

"Huh." The man turned and started to walk away from her. "Well, if you see him, let me know, will yeh?"

"Sure—"

The sound of car tires crunching gravel interrupted them, and they both turned to see Maddie's green Subaru round the corner of the house and roll slowly to a stop. Maddie got out of the car, wearing dark sunglasses and tight black jeans with a light gray blazer over a T-shirt. The professorial attire was stylish; the professor was hot. She slid her sunglasses on top of her head, her gray-blue eyes capturing Jordan's for a moment and flashing a smile before addressing the old man. "Good morning, Douglas. Are you looking for Jack?"

"Yeah." Douglas stretched out the word. "You seen him?"

"No, I haven't. Sorry."

Douglas shrugged and rolled his eyes. Without another word he turned and strode into the privet, which seemed to swallow him in seconds.

"I think I just met the neighbor," Jordan said, laughing.

"That's Douglas James. He's a bit of a curmudgeon."

"You think?"

"He's not as gruff as he seems."

"That's what they always say."

"Let me rephrase that. He's not as unpleasant as he seems. He's a man of few words but considerable talent. He raises goats and is an excellent cheesemaker. He sells it to the farm-to-table restaurants and in farmers' markets in Birmingham. He was even featured in an article in *The New York Times* not too long ago."

"Instead of gruff, he's a diamond in the rough?"

"Something like that." Maddie's smile made her cute dimples reappear.

"Your card's inside. Let me get it for you." Jordan dashed into the studio, returning with the card in hand.

"Thanks again." Maddie took it with a relieved expression. "I didn't realize I'd lost it until I saw your text. I need it to get into my office and my classrooms."

Jordan raised her cup, "Can I interest you in a cup of coffee?"

"I'd love one, but I have class soon. Maybe another time?"

"Sure." Jordan liked the idea.

"What does the rest of your day hold?"

"Drive around, get my bearings, do a little shopping," Jordan took a sip of the now-tepid coffee and made a face. "Get some better coffee."

"Sorry about that." Maddie winced in sympathy. "That's what our food service stocks."

"I've had worse, but I do like a good dark roast."

"Cahaba Coffee downtown is good. They have breakfast sandwiches, too."

"I'll head there soon." Jordan looked skeptically at the dregs of her cup.

"Have any trouble with Major Pettiborn last night?" Maddie asked with raised eyebrows.

"The ghost was very quiet." Jordan laughed. "The mockingbird, however, was not. He sang by the lamp post all night long."

"You know, you can turn off that light. There's a switch by the front door."

"Oh. I didn't look for one." Jordan felt silly for not even thinking to check.

"That reminds me of something I forgot to tell you yesterday. In case of a tornado warning, we have a basement here, but the access is outside. I'll show you." Maddie walked her around to the side of the house, where stairs descended along the side of the fieldstone foundation wall.

"Ghosts or no ghosts, go into a creepy basement of an old house by myself? Are you kidding me?"

"No. I'm not. Don't take a chance." Maddie sounded serious. "You can hear tornado sirens here. Just in case, make sure your phone's set to receive local alerts."

"I have a weather app." Jordan would go down there if she had to. She'd been fortunate not to have experienced a tornado firsthand, but she'd seen the damage they caused—houses that looked like they'd exploded, trees stripped bare or ripped from the earth and vanished. The power of a tornado was almost unbelievable, and it deserved respect.

"I'm sorry if I sounded harsh," Maddie said as they walked back to her car. "Many of our residents don't live in the South, and they don't understand."

"No apology needed. I understand your concern."

Maddie opened the car door but didn't get in. "Do you have plans Friday night?"

"I don't," Jordan said. Was she about to be asked on a date?

"I'm hosting a faculty get-together, if you'd like to come. The biologist I'd like you to meet will be there."

"I'd enjoy that. Thank you." Jordan was happy for the invite and surprised at the disappointment she felt that Maddie's offer wasn't for just the two of them. "What can I bring?"

"Nothing. It's very casual. Just an end-of-the-week get-together. We take turns hosting them."

"I look forward to it. Thanks for the invitation."

"You're welcome. It starts at five. I'll text you my address." Maddie glanced at her watch and pursed her glossy, red lips. "I should have left ten minutes ago," she said as she raised her gaze to meet Jordan's, her lips lifted into a smile extending into her eyes as she slid into the driver's seat. "See you Friday."

Later that morning Jordan relished her second cup of coffee. A smooth, dark roast from the coffeehouse downtown, it was much better than her first cup at Palmer House. She'd ordered an egg-and-cheese cathead biscuit and found a seat at a table by the window, where she took her time mapping out her day. Although her plan was simple—get coffee and breakfast, do a little sightseeing around town, find a grocery store for some staples, and then head back and set up the studio—the day went only partially as planned.

Fortified by the enormous biscuit and strong coffee, and taking two packages of freshly ground coffee with her, Jordan drove through the college campus and looped around the surrounding neighborhoods. The town was charming, and she felt like she was on a vacation, but she wasn't. It was time to start working, to set up her temporary studio and figure out how and when to see the special lilies. After a stop for groceries at the Piggly Wiggly in a strip mall on the edge of town, she arrived back at Palmer House to find a little white-and-brown Jack Russell terrier sitting by the studio door as if waiting for her.

"Hey, pup," Jordan said, getting out of the car. "Are you Jack?"

Hearing the name, the terrier cocked his head and pricked his ears.

"I'll take that as a yes." She smiled at him.

She bent down to pet him and found his coat smooth and clean. He seemed well cared for and was friendly and inquisitive, even following her as she carried the groceries in but stopping several feet away from the back door. She unlocked it, pushing it open with her shoulder and feeling a puff of the cold inside air as it swung open. She turned and looked at the dog, expecting him to be right behind her, but he hadn't budged.

"Do you know you're not supposed to come inside?" She was aware there was a no-pets rule but didn't expect the dog to respect it, though he seemed smart. She took her groceries inside and grabbed a slice of deli cheese to give him. Seeing her return, he barked once and spun in a tight circle. When she held it out for him, he immediately sat and waited patiently for the treat.

"Good boy," she said. He probably came over from the goat farm to charm and beg from every person who stayed at the house. "You ought to go home. Your owner is looking for you, you know." She walked to the studio, and he followed, staying near her feet. She pointed toward the path in the privet and tried a command. "Go home."

Jack looked at her, cocking his head as if he recognized the words but didn't understand their meaning.

She gave the command again, pitching her voice lower, trying to sound serious. "Go. Home."

Jack wagged his tail and panted, open-mouthed, almost looking like he was smiling.

"All right." She sighed. "I'll walk you there."

As soon as she moved toward the path into the woods, he rushed forward to the edge of the thicket, pausing to look back at her as if saying *Come on...this way.*

"If you know the way, why don't you take yourself home?" She emphasized the word *home* while pointing into the tangle of privet and trees. Jack stared at her, unmoving. "Okay, okay. I get the message. I'll take you."

He zipped down a narrow path cleaving the dense privet. She'd first learned about the plant many years ago in an environmental studies class when her professor used it as an example of why invasive species were a problem. Nearly two hundred years ago a nurseryman in Georgia had imported a few plants because their small, dark-green leaves made nice hedges. The vigorous shrubs thrived, and the birds ate their berries and spread their seeds, crowding out the natives that many animals relied on for shelter and food. Although it wasn't so bad for the birds who ate the berries, it didn't help anyone else, and it diminished biodiversity wherever it grew unchecked. No one understood the full impact until the 1970s, and by then it was too late to stop it. The privet had spread all the way over to Texas and up to Maryland. Only the cold winters above the mid-Atlantic region prevented it from establishing a foothold in the North.

Deeper in the woods, where less sunlight penetrated to the ground, the privet thinned, giving way to mature trees with trunks several feet in diameter. She wasn't sure what species they were—elm and hickory maybe. She knew birds better, for they were easier to identify by sight and sound. As she walked the trace, warblers singing from the canopy above reminded her that springtime romance was literally in the air. When the bleating of goats competed with birdsong, she deduced she must be close to Douglas James's farm.

She stepped into a grassy clearing and paused, blinking against the bright sun. Jack bolted straight across the field toward an open door in a small barn. She saw movement through a window, and a girl, maybe twelve or thirteen years old, appeared in the doorway. Her dark hair was pulled back in a ponytail, and she wore a yellow T-shirt with a pattern of daisies, cut-off denim shorts, and tall, white rubber boots. She laughed at Jack as he danced and jumped around her, then looked up at Jordan with a smile and waved.

"Pawpaw!" the girl yelled over her shoulder. "Jack brought somebody with him."

When Douglas James emerged from the barn, Jack's attention immediately shifted to the old man. He petted the terrier, talking to him in a gentle voice.

"He showed up and wouldn't leave," Jordan said as she approached them slowly, feeling like a trespasser.

"He's a rascal." Douglas barely glanced at her.

"I got the sense he knew the way home, but he wouldn't go on his own."

"Yep. He's a stubborn dog." He rubbed the dog vigorously between the ears. "Just like your old man, aren't you, boy?"

"Did you walk over from Palmer House?" the girl asked.

"I did. I'm staying there." Jordan held out her hand. "I'm Jordan, by the way."

The girl took her hand slowly, like she didn't expect to shake hands with an adult. "I'm Ashley. This is my grandpa."

"Yes." Jordan glanced at Douglas. "We met earlier this morning." Douglas grunted an acknowledgment.

"I help Pawpaw milk the goats," Ashley said proudly.

"I hear you make cheese," Jordan said to Douglas.

"Yes, ma'am. Best in Alabama," Ashley replied for her grandfather.

Without saying another word, Douglas nodded and walked into the barn. Jack followed him, tail wagging.

"I hope I'll have a chance to try some while I'm here."

"My mom sells it at the farmers' market on Thursdays. Three to six behind the Baptist church."

"That's good to know. I'll keep an eye out for your stand." Jordan pointed over her shoulder with her thumb. "I'd better go and let you get back to work."

"Aren't you afraid to stay in that house?" Ashley said abruptly, squinting at her.

"No." Jordan shook her head. "Why would I be afraid? Oh, do you mean am I afraid of the ghost of Major Pettiborn?"

"Yeah, him and the other one."

"Other one?"

"The lady in the yellow dress."

"Who—"

"Ashley!" Douglas's voice bellowed out from the barn. "I'm headin' over to the milking parlor."

"I gotta go. Pawpaw needs me. Bye, Miss Jordan. It was nice to meet you." Ashley smiled and gave her a quick wave before trotting off after her grumpy grandfather.

"Nice to meet you, too, Ashley."

Walking back to Palmer House, Jordan speculated about "the lady in the yellow dress." Was she also fictional, like the major? What kind of ghost was she? She considered the ghost stories she knew, realizing that specters seemed to fall into general patterns of behavior. They were often angry, lashing out at the living, or were sad and mournful, wailing their discontent. Some were playfully naughty, pulling pranks on living people from the other side. But they really weren't on the other side, were they? Maybe their mood disorders came from not actually getting to enjoy the afterlife. They hadn't yet moved on and were stuck, a lifeless entity in the world of the living. That had to be frustrating. You never heard stories about happy, contented ghosts. Well, maybe Casper, the friendly ghost. But he was a cartoon character created for kids. No, ghosts were unhappy souls making everyone around them as miserable as they were. If you believed in them, that is.

Without the little terrier's merry company, the woods seemed gloomy. Maybe it was just her ruminating on ghost psychology affecting her perspective, but her surroundings suddenly felt almost spooky. The birds she'd heard singing on the way over were now silent, the thicket eerily quiet. When she heard the low rumble of thunder in the distance, she laughed at herself. How quickly she'd let thoughts of the supernatural get under her skin. As the sky grew darker, the air stilled. The birds knew an afternoon thunderstorm was brewing and were quietly taking shelter. The stillness was perfectly natural and logical. She picked up her pace when she heard the patter of rain on the leaves overhead.

After she arrived back at Palmer House, the light rain became a torrential downpour as soon as she closed the door. Heralded by a lightning flash, thunder rattled the kitchen window as she watched water cascade off the walkway roof like a waterfall. She loved the energy of a storm but was glad to be safely inside and mostly dry. Unpacking her art supplies from the car would have to wait until the rain passed. She made coffee and took a cup into the sitting room, intending to read until it stopped. She couldn't think of a better way to spend time in a thunderstorm. Truth be told, there *was* something better than a book, but it required a romantic partner, flickering candlelight, and some sexy down-tempo music playing softly.

She stopped and stared at the wingback chair by the bookcase. She'd left the copy of *A Midsummer Night's Dream* she'd been looking at in the morning on the seat of the chair, intending to peruse more of the engraved illustrations later, but the book wasn't there. A bright flash of lightning illuminated the room as she stared at the bookcase. She braced for the resounding thunder that followed seconds later. The shelf from which she'd removed it wasn't missing any books. The volume was back in place. As she ran her index finger down its cracked spine, a cold draft brushed across the back of her damp neck, making her shiver and the hair on her arm rise. She must have put it back automatically. It was the only logical explanation.

# CHAPTER THREE

After a good night's sleep, made possible by the soothing sound of gentle rain that had fallen all night after the raucous thunderstorm passed, Jordan awoke refreshed. Peering out the bedroom window, she smiled at the clear cerulean skies. Today she would finally be able to trek to the river to scout around and maybe even draw or paint something. She washed up quickly, dressed in shorts and a T-shirt, and put on her light hiking shoes. Clutching her wide-brimmed straw hat, she headed downstairs for coffee and to pack a lunch for later. After a quick trip to the studio, she picked up her sling pack already loaded with a sketchbook, pencils and ink pens, a small pan of watercolors, and an old water bottle she used for washing brushes in the field.

Pack on one shoulder and coffee in hand, she grabbed a banana and headed for her car. Her destination was the Cahaba River National Wildlife Refuge, a fifteen-mile drive according to the map. While the river was close, about a mile from the town as the crow flies, access to it wasn't direct, as the property flanking the river was privately owned. From living in Tennessee, she had learned that timber and energy companies were the largest landowners in the Southeast, and the locals tended to treat the vast, unoccupied properties as if they were public land. Access roads probably led more directly to the river, but she wasn't a local and felt uneasy crossing private land without permission, especially on unmarked roads. The federal refuge, open to the public and promoting lily viewing, seemed like the best place to start.

The route to the river wasn't particularly scenic, although the curving, two-lane road was a fun drive. The scenery was monotonous, like traveling through Midwestern corn fields except with tall, equally spaced, timber industry-standard loblolly pines, each tree the same height as its neighbor. The only breaks in the green wall were sections where trees had been clear-cut. Tree harvesting, as they called it, seemed to be happening somewhere down the way, given the number of big log trucks that had passed her with their trailers stacked tall with freshly felled logs. She liked the scent of resin permeating the cabin of her 4Runner, but in this context, seeing the trees stripped and piled up like a funeral bier, the terpene odor seemed more like the stench of death.

Seeing a break in the trees ahead and anticipating another clear-cut section, she was surprised by acres of neatly trimmed green grass instead. At first, she thought it must be a golf course until she spotted an enormous house set far back on the crest of a hill, its mansard roof and tower-like façade with a tall archway looking vaguely European. A confusion of French chateau and Italian villa, it communicated one thing clearly—pretentiousness. She'd have gawked longer, but she rapidly approached another tall stand of pines that blocked her view of the mansion. And, really, she needed to keep her eyes on the road, which, having almost no shoulder, didn't allow any room for drift.

A few more miles later she passed a sign announcing the refuge. As the road emerged from the tunnel of trees, the sky expanded, and the road descended to a bridge crossing the river. With no cars behind her, she paused before crossing to catch a view of the river, disappointed to see fast-flowing water murky with sediment the color of dry cinnamon.

It looked nothing like the images she'd seen of blue-green water flowing gently through stands of blooming lilies. Obviously, those photos weren't taken after days of heavy rain, and she reminded herself that this wouldn't be her only visit. She was just scouting today and could come back on a better day. She had time.

Immediately after she crossed the bridge, a large kiosk marked the refuge's entrance. She pulled up and got out to read the information posted, taking a brochure before continuing. The heavily shaded gravel road followed a picturesque stream, with dappled light filtering through the trees and glinting on water trickling over moss-covered rocks. It was pretty and didn't live up to the name, Little Ugly Creek, which she'd seen on the map. The road made a sharp right turn where the creek and the road hugged the river's edge, although trees and shrubs prevented a clear view.

She parked at the first wide stop in the road and walked a few yards to find a break in the vegetation. As she put her hand against the rough bark of a tall pine to steady herself, she leaned forward, looking through branches but able to only glimpse the water. A soft breeze brushed her skin, making the humidity less oppressive. Deeply inhaling fresh air through her nostrils, she parsed out the scents of pine and wet earth, then breathed out slowly through pursed lips. A nearby male chickadee sang his whistling "fee bee" song, either staking out his territory or trying to attract the eye of a female, perhaps both. She continued down the road looking for shoals and lilies, though it seemed they were completely submerged.

She saw only one other car, an SUV with an empty kayak rack on the roof and a back window covered in outdoor-themed stickers, parked near a gently sloping sandy beach. Some daredevil who enjoyed whitewater thrills probably owned it. Beyond the SUV she finally glimpsed the lilies: long, broad green leaves of plants waving in the turbid current. What tough plants they must be to survive regular flooding. She imagined their roots as claws clinging to the rocks below the water's surface. Interrupted, she slapped at an insect that landed on her neck and continued until the gravel road ended at a confluence with another creek. The flow was slower and the water almost clear.

Curious, she walked along the edge of the creek in full sun until her T-shirt was soaked with perspiration and she was ready for a water break. After finding a seat on a boulder under the shade of a tree, she pulled her water bottle from her sling pack and took several long swallows while eyeing a rock face upstream that might be interesting to draw. As she stowed the bottle in her pack again, she noticed a narrow trail along the creek that disappeared into the trees.

While the shade was a welcome relief, she wished she had a walking stick to hold out to break the spiderwebs. She tried to walk around them when she could, but more often she felt them before she saw them. While the thought of a spider crawling on her gave her the heebie-jeebies, she also felt bad about destroying their hard work. Movement in the water below the trail caught her eye. Small, narrow-bodied fish with white spots on their heads darted close to the surface of the shallows. A larger fish, a predatory bass, seemed to have chased them there. The fish rose, seeming to inspect her, and then disappeared quickly into a dark, deep pool.

The path ended when the incline of the hill steepened. Most people must have turned around as soon as the terrain became difficult. She'd paused and considered heading back to the river, when she heard the faint sound of cascading water. Intrigued by the possibility of finding a waterfall, she continued, weaving between the trees but staying close to the creek and being mindful of snakes and where she put her feet as she walked through the leaf litter.

As the sound of rushing water grew louder, the air cooled, a welcome feeling. Pausing to wipe a bead of sweat away from the corner of her eye, she glimpsed water cascading over a wide rock ledge and into a pool beneath, but tree trunks and low branches partially obscured it. She heard a loud splash, and knowing it was probably a turtle, she hoped it might be a river otter. Ducking beneath the branches, she approached slowly and quietly. A woman in the water took her completely by surprise.

"Why, hello there," said a young woman, her body obscured by the ripples in the water. The cadence of her voice was distinctively Southern.

"Uh…hello." Jordan stood upright quickly, thunking her head on a branch and knocking off her hat.

"Did I scare you?" The woman's lips lifted into a smile. She shook her head, as if shaking the water from her blond curls, but her hair seemed dry.

"I wouldn't say scared, exactly." Jordan put her hat back on her head. "Just surprised. I just wasn't expecting to see a person."

"No?" The woman laughed, its sound soft and musical. "What did you think you'd see?"

"A turtle…or maybe an otter."

"I'm not green, nor am I covered in fur." She laughed again. "Did you come here to swim?"

"I was just exploring, and I heard the waterfall."

"This is one of the best swimming holes around. Would you like to get in? I don't want to be a hog."

"I don't have a bathing suit."

"Silly. You don't need a bathing suit to go for a swim." The woman floated backward, her hands fanning slowly back and forth near the surface of the water.

"That's true." Jordan felt light-headed, but she hadn't hit her head that hard. Maybe she was a little dehydrated. The pool really did look inviting. "Another time, maybe, but thanks." She reached for her water bottle and took a drink.

"You're the one staying in the house."

"You mean Palmer House?"

The woman lifted her eyebrows and nodded.

"Yes. I'm the new resident artist." Jordan took another swallow of the cold water. "Are you a student at the college?"

"I was." The woman cocked her head. "For a time."

Jordan didn't press her for details. College wasn't for everyone, and she had friends who had dropped out for personal or financial reasons. "I ought to get going and let you enjoy your swim in peace."

"Thank you." The woman smiled sweetly. "I hope you enjoy your day."

"Thanks. You, too." Jordan waved good-bye and turned to walk back down the way she'd come. After a few steps the woman called to her.

"Hey, watch out for Ol' Red."

"Old Red?"

"You'll know him when you see him," the woman said with a laugh. "Tell him Leda said hello."

"Will do," Jordan called back.

The woman's musical laughter faded, and eventually Jordan heard only the water in the creek and occasional bird calls. Wondering who Old Red was—maybe another grumpy old man—she remained more concerned about snakes and spiders as she focused on retracing her steps to the trail.

When she emerged from the tree cover, the view of the confluence of creek and river struck her as picturesque, a perfect opportunity to make a drawing. Sitting on a flat-topped boulder in the dappled light, she removed her socks and shoes to dip her toes in the cold water, flinching when they touched it. How had that woman, Leda, been swimming so languidly in it as if it were bathwater?

Resting her feet on a dry rock, she began drawing in a new black hardbound sketchbook, using the hard graphite pencil that kept a sharp point and made faint, fine lines. She quickly sketched out her view, cropping it on the page into a traditional composition with trees clustered on either side of the mouth of the creek. She outlined the shape of the boulder near her in the foreground, and when she defined the edges of the creek running at a diagonal toward the river, the image suddenly had a sense of depth. After penciling in the prominent details, she switched to a pen loaded with India ink to complete the drawing with expressive lines. She loved observational drawing and the feeling of being totally present in the moment. She stopped thinking and just looked and drew intuitively, albeit with a confidence and accuracy that came from years of practice.

By the time she'd finished the drawing, the light had shifted, the sun directly overhead now making everything look flat and washed out. She held the sketchbook at an arm's length and squinted at the drawing. Satisfied, she capped her pen and flipped the sketchbook closed. Then she traded the sketchbook and pen for the peanut-butter-and-jelly sandwich in her pack.

While she was eating, mayflies rose around her, dancing in the air. Females skimmed the surface of the water, laying eggs for the next generation. Some rested on the branches of nearby shrubs, allowing for a closer look. She dusted the breadcrumbs from her hands and took out her sketchbook and pen to make a few quick sketches intended not for details, but to capture the dynamic movement of the winged insects with their dragonfly-like wings, elegantly curved bodies, and spiky tails. She covered several pages, each with multiple drawings. As she flipped through them, the mayflies seemed to have emerged from the paper and were living out their one-day winged existence in her sketchbook. The thought hatched an idea, and she jotted a note to make a flipbook of flying mayflies. Always treating her sketchbook like a field notebook, a remnant of her biology training, she dated the pages and noted her location, the time, temperature, and the weather conditions.

Then, lifting her face to the sky, she studied the clouds that had been building. Another afternoon thunderstorm seemed possible. She dusted dirt from her feet and put her socks and trail shoes back on before sliding off the rock. When she reached for her sling pack, she instantly froze when she saw banded salmon-pink and dark Hershey's Kiss–shaped patterns. She remained still as her heart pounded. A very large copperhead coiled in the shadows, under the edge of a rock.

Its chin resting on its thick body, the snake didn't move. She certainly didn't want to rouse it and was thankful she hadn't put her feet on top of it. Feeling threatened, the snake would almost certainly strike first and ask questions later. She watched it, looking for any indication it felt unsafe, and moved her hand slowly toward the strap on her pack, hooking her fingers under it. Slowly, with cool reptilian smoothness, the copperhead turned its triangular-shaped head to face her. The head was the telltale sign it was venomous—those wide cheeks provided space for long retractable fangs and venom glands. It flicked its tongue, tasting the air. Its infrared-detecting pit organs, which looked like a second set of nostrils, were undoubtedly sensing her. Pit vipers, such as copperheads, could see heat signatures. Other than the flicking tongue, it was motionless and seemed untroubled. In one fluid movement she moved back several steps, pulling the pack with her, until she was out of the snake's strike zone. At least she hoped she was. The snake lifted its head a few inches, tilting its nose upward as if curious.

Feeling safe at a distance and emboldened by the jolt of adrenaline, she admired the snake's beauty. Sketchbook still in hand, she took advantage of the unexpected opportunity to draw the magnificent, if terrifying, creature. She'd been this close to a copperhead only in the herpetarium at the zoo. When encountering snakes in the wild, usually all she saw was a tail disappearing quickly in the grass, as they were eager to get away. Statistically, most snake bites came from copperheads, and this fact had given them a bad rap for being aggressive, but it was really just a result of their hunting method. They found a good spot and hunkered down to wait for prey to wander by, ambushing rather than stalking. Usually, copperheads struck people because they'd accidentally stepped on them or put their hands too close, not seeing the snakes because they were so well camouflaged. The Southern species, like this one, were redder than their Northern cousins, having evolved to match the local red-clay soil.

A copper-red copperhead. She smiled at her invented rhyme and stopped drawing, taking in a quick breath. The skinny-dipper's words reverberated in her mind. "Watch out for Ol' Red," she'd said. How could she have known she'd cross paths with this big coppery-red snake?

"Are you Old Red?" Jordan asked gently.

The snake didn't offer any answers. It dropped its head, resting its chin on its back. While drawing the copperhead, she ruminated on her question. Snakes, like many animals, were creatures of habit and had territories. Maybe this spot, with the protection of the rock and a nearby water source, was its preferred place to sit and wait for dinner to amble by. If Leda walked past here on her way to her favorite swimming hole regularly, she might have learned that and, having seen him more than once, given him a nickname. It seemed a logical answer.

Jordan made notes about color, listing the names of pigments she'd use to recreate them in a painting: umber, burnt sienna, cadmium orange, and yellow. Exact color was hard to remember later, and while taking a picture with her cell phone was easy, the images were never quite right. When she had realized that the more she relied on her phone, the less able she was to recall details, she'd weaned herself from automatically grabbing it every time she saw something interesting. She learned more about the thing she was looking at from drawing it than from looking at a photo. She took her time, capturing the form of the snake, its patterns, the light and shadows. Glancing back and forth between the page and the snake, she felt certain she'd make a painting of him. When the drawing was done, she closed the sketchbook slowly and slipped the pencil into the side pocket of her shorts.

"If you are Ol' Red," she said softly to the snake, "Leda says hello." The copperhead flicked its narrow tongue as if in reply.

Leaving the snake in peace, she returned to the river road, being extra careful where she put her feet until she was back on the gravel roadbed. Passing the SUV parked near the sandy beach, she encountered two young twenty-something men, one lanky and bearded, the other shorter, blonder, and clean shaven, dragging kayaks out of the water. Talking and laughing, they exuded the energy of puppies.

She paused and waved to them. "Good day on the river?"

The bearded man waved back. "Great day," he said, his teeth flashing white against his dark beard. The shorter one smiled and nodded vigorously.

"Could I ask you a question?"

"Yes, ma'am."

She smiled at the Southern politeness. She was ten years older than them at most, but they treated her with respect reserved for elders. "Do you know when the Cahaba lilies will bloom?"

The blond kayaker winced and shrugged, seeming unsure. "Maybe a week? Ten days?"

"They'll start pretty soon after the water level drops," the bearded one said.

"And then the river won't be nearly as much fun to run, I bet," Jordan said.

"No, ma'am," he said while wriggling out of his spray skirt. "Not nearly."

"When do you think the water level will drop?"

"Depends on how much it rains," he said with a laugh, dropping the bundle of wet nylon fabric onto the seat of the kayak.

"It's not an exact science, is it?"

"No, ma'am. It's not." He grinned. "But I suspect they'll be in full bloom this side a' two weeks."

"Thanks for your insight. I appreciate it."

"I'm guessin' you're not from around here?"

"I'm from Chattanooga." He looked at her skeptically. She knew she didn't sound like she was from Tennessee, but she didn't offer any additional explanation. A deer fly landed on her arm, and she swatted it away before it could bite.

"Well, if you're around, the Cahaba River Society does guided canoe trips while they're in bloom. You can sign up online." He slipped one arm into the cockpit of the kayak and hoisted it onto his shoulder. His blond friend carried his up to the SUV and tossed it effortlessly onto the rooftop rack.

"Yeah?" She glanced at the swift, murky water. "I'm not sure I'm skilled enough for that kind of canoeing."

"Oh, they'll only go out when the water is calm, not like this. They take kids out all the time. You'll be all right."

She imagined seeing the lilies by floating through them. "That sounds pretty cool."

"It is," he said. Standing in front of her with one arm inside the kayak balanced on one shoulder and gripping the paddle in his free hand, he waited as if expecting to be dismissed.

"Thanks for the information. You guys have a good day."

"Thank you, ma'am. You, too." He nodded and strode to his car.

The men had secured their kayaks by the time she reached her 4Runner and appeared ready to leave. She adjusted the air conditioner to high and waited for them to pass before pulling out into the road, enjoying the cool, dry air blowing on her skin. As she left the preserve, she realized she hadn't seen any other cars. Where had the woman, Leda, come from? Maybe a trail led down to the swimming hole, and if so, where did that trail come from? She'd investigate later. Right now, she could think only about getting back to Palmer House for a cool shower and a fresh cup of coffee.

## CHAPTER FOUR

Jordan lightly touched the tip of a loaded brush to the wet surface of the paper, letting the pigment pool and deepen a shadow under the snake's body. After putting the brush in water, she leaned back in her chair to scrutinize the copperhead snake coming to life on the paper in front of her. It was a portrait of the one she'd seen by the river the day before. Wondering if the snake was male or female, she'd consulted an animal guide. The only visual differences were in size, she'd read, with the females larger, so she decided the big snake was a she. Jordan had nearly finished the painting, but the eye needed a bit more attention. Although she'd done her best to make the snake not look menacing, the flat head and eye ridge made her seem stern and humorless. Snakes smiled only in cartoons, so maybe that was one reason so many people didn't like them. They seemed to lack any sense of mirth that made mammals, humans included, so charismatic.

She stared at the narrow, vertical pupils of the snake's eyes. How could she give the snake an expression suggesting depth rather than malice? She glanced back and forth between the drawing in her sketchbook and the painting, dissatisfied. Van Gogh had written that he wished he could destroy his paintings and keep only drawings. It sounded crazy, but she understood what he meant—the drawing in the sketchbook had a freshness and vivacity that came from her direct experience of observing the snake, and it was difficult to replicate that quality in the painting over which she labored.

She twisted to reach for her phone on the table to take an in-progress photo and felt a rush of cold air, like an ice cube, roll across the back of her neck. She flinched, and her hand abruptly connected with the lid of her open laptop, tipping it off the table. She lunged out of her chair too late to grab it. It landed with a crack on the concrete floor.

"Shit." Jordan spat out the word as she picked it up. A black blob appeared in the corner of the screen, and horizontal lines like a multicolored barcode replaced the wallpaper photo of a misty mountain range. "No, no, no. Damn it!"

Jordan put the laptop on the table and stared at it while she pressed the palm of her hand to her forehead. She couldn't believe she'd just broken her almost-new computer, and all because of the weird air-conditioning. She ran her fingers through her hair, across the top of her scalp, and clutched the back of her neck. The air felt fine now—not cold, no draft. In fact, it was still almost stagnant. "What the hell is up with these buildings?" Jordan huffed.

The painting, distracting her momentarily, looked great. The snake seemed three-dimensional and came alive at a distance. She was satisfied with the painting, but very unhappy with herself for cracking the screen. The files on the laptop were probably fine. She had everything backed up, and it was still under a warranty that included screen replacements for drops, she reasoned with herself. But it was a major inconvenience. The closest store was probably in Birmingham, nearly an hour away, and they would certainly have to send it out for service. She'd be without the computer for a few weeks, at least. Maybe she should just deal with it when she was back home in Chattanooga and could go to her local store.

Unsure what to do, she puffed her cheeks and closed the lid. Her watch caught her eye; it was later than she thought. Not surprisingly, she'd lost track of time, which often happened when she was working. The party at Maddie's would begin in twenty minutes, so she'd have to figure out what to do about her laptop later. With her phone, she took a quick photo of the painting, rinsed the brushes in the corner sink, and placed them, bristles up, in an empty cup to dry before rushing over to the house to wash up and change clothes.

Jordan took a quick shower and surveyed her limited wardrobe while towel-drying her hair. Maddie had said it was casual, but expecting an academic crowd, she wasn't sure what might be most appropriate. She settled on tan denim pants with a light blue, V-neck shirt and slipped a carnelian-bead bracelet on her wrist, clipping the matching beaded necklace around her neck. After quickly applying makeup and finger-combing her hair with gel, she appraised herself in the cheval mirror in the corner of the bedroom. She looked presentable and couldn't help but wonder if she'd look attractive to Maddie.

Maddie had told her not to worry about bringing anything, explaining that there would be plenty of food and drink. Still, Jordan didn't feel right showing up empty-handed. Who didn't like a cheerful bouquet of flowers? Fortunately, she had found fresh-cut flowers at the farmers' market from a woman who turned out to be the grumpy goat farmer's daughter. Seeing the goat's-milk soaps and cheese samples on the table next to buckets of flowers, she'd made the connection and introduced herself as the new temporary neighbor. After a pleasant conversation—mostly about her father's little dog, Jack, who'd visited Jordan every one of the five days she'd been there—she'd walked away from the stall with a log of herbed chevre, two bars of soap, and a beautiful rustic bouquet of delphinium, iris, foxglove, and black-eyed Susans, with fern-frond greenery.

Jordan retrieved the flowers from the kitchen, where she'd kept them in a pitcher of water. Momentarily forgetting about her broken laptop as she rewrapped the cheerful bouquet with the kraft paper and twine she'd saved, she smiled at the thought of presenting them to Maddie when she arrived at the party.

The cars parked along both sides of the street indicated that Jordan had come to the right place. She found a spot down the street and walked back to the neatly landscaped, contemporary ranch-style house. After she wiped the perspiration from her forehead, she pressed the doorbell and heard a sharp bark before the door opened.

Maddie stood on the other side of the threshold holding a margarita glass in one hand and the doorknob in the other, balanced on one leg. Her other leg was outstretched, holding back a bright-eyed black shepherd mix with white toes, a white patch on its chest, and a furiously wagging tail. Maddie's lips lifted into a smile that reached her eyes, her expression matching the gleeful shepherd's.

"I was beginning to think you weren't coming." Maddie tilted her head toward the living room. "Please come in. Are those flowers for me?"

"Yes." Jordan offered them. "Thank you for inviting me. I'm sorry I'm late. I got caught up painting."

"No worries. That's why you're here, isn't it?" Maddie closed the door, taking the bouquet with her free hand. She put her nose into the colorful flowers and smiled, seeming to savor the scent. "These are beautiful. Thank you."

"You're very welcome." Jordan turned her attention to the friendly dog dancing around her. "Well, hello there."

"Chip likes you. First-time visitors usually get a lot of barking and playful feinting."

"Hey, Chip." Jordan squatted to pet the dog. "He's beautiful."

"She, actually. She was a feral puppy. I found her on campus with a chip bag—Golden Flake Flaming Hot Barbecue potato chips, to be precise—stuck on her head. The poor thing was desperate. I called her Chip before I knew her sex, and the name stuck."

Jordan petted her between her upright ears and stroked her thick coat. "Well, Chip, you are one fine and lucky dog." Jordan laughed at Chip's expression. Mouth open with lolling tongue, she looked like she was smiling.

"Do you have pets? You certainly have good dog mojo."

"I do. I mean, I did." Jordan stood up, feeling a pang of sadness. She missed her big, friendly tabby cat. "I lost my cat unexpectedly recently. A blood clot."

"I'm sorry." Maddie sounded sympathetic. "It's hard enough when you know it's coming. Unexpected is worse. Did you have him a long time?"

"He was fifteen when he passed. He was my buddy, who got me through college, grad school, and then some."

"That makes it even harder."

"Yeah…I've been thinking that, after this residency, I'll be ready to look for a kitten or maybe an adult cat who needs a home. Or maybe one will just show up. Sometimes they choose you, you know?"

"I do. I never planned to have a dog like Chip." Maddie smiled at the dog, who turned and looked adoringly at her when she said her name. "Rescuing her and keeping her was the best decision I ever made." She held up the flowers as if suddenly remembering they were in her hand. "Let's take these to the kitchen, and I'll put them in a vase. Everyone is in there or out on the deck. Come on. I'll introduce you."

Jordan and Chip followed Maddie through the living room and dining room to the spacious kitchen. The rooms were open and bright, the decor neat. Jordan noticed a lot of books.

"Do you like margaritas?" Maddie asked over her shoulder.

"I do."

"Good. They're the specialty of the house tonight."

Walking into the kitchen they were greeted by the whir of a blender and people gathered around a granite-topped island covered with platters of finger foods. French doors led to a deck outside, where more people were gathered.

"Everyone, this is Jordan Burroughs, our new artist-in-residence," Maddie said as she grabbed a vase from a shelf and unwrapped the bouquet. She put water and the flowers in the vase and placed it in the center of the island. Then she pointed at each person, naming them, concluding with the margarita maker, Ciera, a plump, dark-skinned woman with a dazzling smile.

Jordan smiled at everyone. "I hope there's not a quiz later."

"The only question tonight is frozen?" Cierra lifted the pitcher and then pointed to a carafe on the counter next to an ice bucket. "Or on the rocks?"

"On the rocks, please."

"Good choice," Maddie said, picking up her glass and shaking the ice in it. "I'll make one for us both."

"More for those of us out on the deck." Laughing, Ciera topped off drinks in the kitchen before heading to the deck, clutching the almost-full pitcher to her chest.

"Oh, wait. Another question—" Maddie held up an empty glass. "Salt or no salt?"

"Salt." Jordan watched as Maddie expertly salted the rim of glass, dropped in ice cubes, and filled it from a large carafe. "Thanks," Jordan said, taking the stemmed glass.

"You're welcome." Maddie peered out the window over the sink and pointed to the darkening sky. "I'll be right back. I need to go lock up the chickens."

"You have chickens? That's so cool."

"Yep. A little flock of six pampered birds."

Jordan took a sip of her drink, the balance of tart and sweet perfect, and the proportion of tequila in it was generous. She watched as Maddie walked to the door with Chip following at her heels, tail sweeping back and forth with each step. She'd almost asked if she could tag along to see the chickens, but now, cocktail in hand, she knew she shouldn't drink on an empty stomach. While the platters looked ransacked, there was still plenty of food, as Maddie had promised. She reached for a pimento-cheese finger sandwich, which was perfect—a layer of spicy cheese spread between two soft white slices of bread, cut at a diagonal with the crust removed. She ate a second one while listening to the conversation between a man and woman seated on bar stools closest to her—Peter and Elana, if she remembered their names correctly. They seemed to be talking about barware.

"It's a collins glass only if it has a Tom Collins in it. Otherwise, it's a highball," Peter said in an authoritative tone. He was pale, trim and middle-aged, with graying reddish-blond hair cut short on the sides but long and wavy on top. The quality of fabric and tailored cut of his shirt and trousers made them seem expensive. Jordan had a habit of mentally imagining people as animals, maybe because she drew them so often. Peter was a rooster.

Elana, delicate and pretty, wore a flower-print sundress. Her chestnut hair, pulled back loosely, was gathered at the nape of her long neck. She raised her margarita glass, narrowing her doe-like eyes as she stared at it. "These are only for margaritas, yes?"

"They have a very interesting history." Seeming to realize Jordan was listening, Peter turned and smiled at her, appraising her with watery blue eyes. He scooted the stool back to open the space to include her in the conversation, though it was really him pontificating. "These are a variant of a French champagne glass called a coupe. Supposedly, the first coupe was made from a mold of Marie-Antoinette's left breast." He slid a finger suggestively down the side of the glass. "But that theory has been discredited. However, she did commission Sèvres to manufacture a porcelain bowl in the shape of a breast supported by three goats' heads. She and her maids at her Hamlet at Versailles drank milk from them."

Jordan took a sip of her margarita, mentally comparing the feel of the cradled glass in the palm of her hand to an actual breast. She wasn't convinced. "Are you a historian?"

"Oh, no." He smiled, his lips thin as they stretched across his teeth. "I teach French language and eighteenth-century literature." He seemed flushed with alcohol, his skin waxy. "You're the new artist-in-residence, eh?"

"I am," she said with a nod.

"Tell me, what kind of art do you make?" He made a face like he'd smelled something rotten. "And please don't tell me it's that nonsense performance-art stuff. The last visiting artist we had here was *terrible*."

"No. I'm not a performance artist," she said.

"Oh, please, Pete," Elana said. "You just didn't like her work because it disturbed your privileged masculine identity."

"That wasn't art." Peter rolled his eyes and huffed.

"I'm so curious. What did she do?" Jordan asked, sipping her drink and reaching for what looked like a spicy, cheesy sausage ball. Southern hors d'oeuvres were heavy and irresistible.

Peter opened his mouth to reply, but Elana waved her hand in front of him to speak first. "She was here during the fall semester and worked with art and music students. She orchestrated a kind of parade of—"

"Female genitalia," Peter said, eyes wide and eyebrows dramatically raised.

"The costumes were rather suggestive. The artist described it as"—Elana paused to make air quotes with her fingers—"'a performative action to disrupt the phallic patriarchal structures dominating campus.' You know, columns. We have a lot of them on campus, if you haven't noticed. It was quite entertaining."

Peter rolled his eyes again.

"So…no parading punani for you," Jordan said with a laugh, gesturing to the glass in Peter's hand as he took a drink. "But you don't seem to mind having a fake breast in your hand."

Peter sputtered as Elana erupted in laughter.

He ignored the comment and changed the direction of the conversation. "What kind of art do you do, Jordan?"

She wanted to say she didn't "do" any kind of art since that phrasing sounded so pejorative, but she refrained. "I'm a nature and science illustrator."

"Ah." Peter's lips formed a thin, cold smile. "Illustration's not really fine art, is it?"

His caustic response took her aback. Sure, she'd teased him, but she meant it in good humor.

Elana scowled and bumped him on the shoulder. "God, Pete. You can be such a troll sometimes." She looked apologetic. "Ignore him. We all do when he gets like this."

Jordan assumed she meant drunk and obnoxious. A tall woman standing behind Peter stared at her. Having caught her eye, Jordan smiled politely. Unfortunately, she couldn't remember the woman's name from the introduction. Mary? Or was it Jenn? Mary-or-Jenn nodded and scooped some roasted pecans from a bowl into the palm of her hand. She was big-boned, bear-like.

"You know there's a long history of artist-naturalists," she said with a friendly smile. Instead of a margarita, she was drinking beer from a bottle. "Until the nineteenth century no one really worried about separating the professions." She glanced sideways at Peter before focusing her gaze on Jordan. "Do you know Maria Sibylla Merian?"

"Of course. She's kind of my artist-hero."

"Or science hero, depending on your perspective." The woman popped a pecan into her mouth.

"She lived in the seventeenth century, traveled the world, and studied insects," Jordan explained to Peter. "She illustrated them in self-published paintings and prints. She controlled her destiny and taught her daughters to be artist-illustrators, giving them a means to take care of themselves, too. She was an amazing woman for the time."

Peter sipped his margarita and didn't seem to be following the new turn in conversation, his gaze focused on the other side of the kitchen.

"And she was the first person to depict them with their host plants, which demonstrated a deep knowledge of what we now call ecology," Mary-or-Jenn said.

"Careful and sustained observation is the best tool for any artist or scientist, don't you think?"

"Absolutely." Mary-or-Jenn grinned.

"I'm so sorry. I've forgotten your name. I really meant it when I said I hoped there wouldn't be a quiz."

"Better there wasn't. You would have failed." Unlike Peter's, her laugh was friendly. "I'm Jenn, and a biology professor, in case you haven't guessed." She smiled and put her hand on Elana's shoulder, sliding it down to the small of her back. "And married to this lovely woman."

"Oh?" Jordan smiled at Elana. "Are you a professor, too?"

"I'm a librarian."

"Some of my favorite people are librarians, including my mom," Jordan said. "I practically grew up in the stacks of the public library where she worked. What department are you in?"

"You are truly the daughter of a librarian. You know what question to ask. Most people think librarians just sit at the reference desk all day and tell people to be quiet." Elana smiled. She had a kind face. "I do acquisitions and cataloging."

"I know a little about that area. My mom was a cataloger before she became the library director." Jordan turned to Jenn. "What branch of biology do you study, Jenn?"

"Ecology. I like to say I'm a muddy-boots biologist. We used to be called naturalists, hence my interest in artist-naturalists."

"I started college as a biology major and then switched to art."

"No wonder you like Merian so much. The artist-naturalist keeps a foot in both worlds," Jenn said, pausing when Peter hopped off the bar stool and, under the pretense of refreshing his drink, excused himself from the conversation. Jenn ignored him. "Maddie mentioned your interest in the Cahaba lilies. Is that right?"

"Yes, very much so. I'm working on a long-term personal project, observing and depicting endangered and threatened species."

"They ought to be blooming by now," Elana said.

"Not yet. I was out at the refuge yesterday, and they were mostly underwater."

"It'll be soon, after the water level drops," Jenn said as she ate the last pecan. She looked up, smiling at Maddie as she returned to the kitchen.

"Oh, good. You're talking," Maddie said. "I thought Jenn might be a good resource for you while you're here."

"You know I love to discuss the local ecology." Jenn picked up a pimento-cheese sandwich. "But form your questions quickly. We're leaving town soon." She ate half the sandwich in one bite.

"I think Jordan will be interested in where you're going," Maddie said. She reached for the pitcher and topped off their drinks.

"The Galapagos," Jenn said.

Elana nudged her gently in the ribs. "And the other part?"

"Oh, yeah. We're taking a luxury barefoot cruise on a sailboat after the Galapagos eco-tour."

"You can tell which part she's most excited about," Elana said with a laugh. "It's our belated honeymoon. A hurricane canceled the trip we planned last summer."

"Congratulations." Jordan lifted her glass in salute. "How'd you get Elana to agree to the Galapagos?"

"We didn't go on any trips last summer, so I argued that we could do two in one this summer to make up for it." Jenn tapped her index finger against her forehead. "Pretty smart, I thought."

"It clearly worked. It sounds like a romantic adventure," Jordan said. "The Galapagos Islands are an ecologist's dream. An artist's, too, for that matter. I know a couple of people who've traveled there. They returned starry-eyed."

"See? I'm not crazy," Jenn said to Elana.

"Crazy for nature." Elana sipped her margarita.

"And you." Jenn grinned at her wife, pointing the neck of the beer bottle toward her.

Elana tapped the rim of her glass against the bottle, the smile on her lips widening. "You know, Pete told us the most interesting little fact about these glasses."

"That they're based on the shape of Marie Antoinette's breast?" Maddie rolled her eyes. "He told me that story years ago."

Jenn studied the glass with an exaggerated expression, as if visually measuring its dimensions, and glanced down at Elana's chest. "Marie Antoinette ain't got nothing on you, babe."

"*Jenn!*" Elana blushed.

Jordan laughed with them—a deep belly laugh—glad she hadn't just taken a sip of her drink. She'd likely have spewed it and embarrassed herself in front of her new acquaintances. She liked these warm, funny women and imagined they could become friends.

"Did I hear you say you were at the refuge?" Maddie asked.

"Yes. The day before yesterday."

"How was it?" Her expression shifted. "Some people go there more to party than to enjoy the great outdoors."

"I saw only some kayakers." Jordan sipped her drink. "And a woman swimming below the waterfall."

"Waterfall?" Jenn asked.

"Yeah. I hiked up along the creek at the far end of the road. There was a pretty waterfall and a deep pool, where the woman was."

All three women looked at her blankly, and Jenn cocked her head like a dog who'd received a confusing command.

"Caffee Creek?" Elana glanced at Jenn.

"I don't know of a waterfall there with a swimming hole." Jenn stroked her chin in thought. "Maybe I've just never been there after heavy rain."

Jordan recalled the color of the water in the creek. It wasn't muddy from sediment in storm-water runoff, like the river. She'd assumed the cold water was spring fed. "Being my first visit, I can't really say. Oh, and I saw a big copperhead."

The eyes of both Elana's and Maddie enlarged, Elana's expression bordering on terror.

"Cool!" Jenn, the biologist, appeared delighted.

"I know they're not endangered, but it was so beautiful. I made a drawing, and now I'm working on a watercolor painting."

"You stood there…and *drew* it?" Elana scrunched her eyebrows. "I would have run."

"I'd love to see your painting," Jenn said.

"It's not finished yet." Jordan pulled her phone from her back pocket and swiped to her photos. "But I have an in-progress photo."

Jordan held up the phone, and all three women leaned forward to peer at the image on the small screen. Elana pretend-shivered before looking away.

"Nice…" Jenn said, nodding. "*Agiskotron contortix contortix*, the Southern copperhead. That's a healthy-looking snake, eating well."

"Beautiful," Maddie said, raising her eyes above the rim of her glasses to meet Jordan's gaze.

"Thank you." Jordan's breath caught in her throat. When Maddie smiled back, her stomach did a little flip-flop. She couldn't help but focus on the perfect curve of her heart-shaped lips, accentuated with lipstick the color of cinnabar and punctuated with dimples. A thought flashed through her mind, a fantasy of what those lips might feel like against her own. The flip-flop turned into fluttering luna moths.

"Do you have a website?" Jenn asked.

"Hmm?" Jordan was distracted by thoughts of Maddie.

"A website…you know, where I can see more of your work."

"Oh, yes." Jordan refocused. "I have one. It's burroughsart-dot-com."

"Cool. I'll check it out," Jenn said.

"Elana," Maddie said. "Don't you think Jordan would be interested in the Cahaba collection at the library?"

Before Elana could answer, a man and woman carrying empty plates and glasses walked into the kitchen, putting them in the sink before saying they were leaving.

"Let me walk you to the door." Maddie reached across Jordan to set her glass on the island. "Excuse me," she said softly. Jordan caught the scent of her perfume and held her breath when Maddie put her hand on her arm. The gentle pressure of her fingertips on her skin felt electric.

While Elana began to describe the library's collection of books and resources on the history and ecology of the local watershed, Jordan's attention lingered on Maddie, so she registered only part of what the friendly librarian was saying. She touched the tip of her tongue to the salt crystals on the rim of her glass before tipping it back to take a deep swallow. "I'm sorry, Elana. Could you repeat that last part, about the maps?"

"Sure," Elana said. A half-smile formed on her lips as her gaze followed where Jordan had been looking.

Jenn lifted her eyebrows and tilted her head forward. "She's single, in case you were wondering."

Jordan felt a creeping blush. "I—"

Elana bumped her wife in the ribs with an elbow and put up a hand, saving Jordan from saying anything more. "The maps," she said, redirecting the conversation. "We have historical maps in our rare book room. Some are more like drawings than cartographic maps, so you might find them interesting. I can show them to you if you like."

"I'd like that very much."

Embarrassed at being caught ogling their host, Jordan mentally chastised herself for ignoring the helpful women she'd just met and refocused her attention. Before they finished their conversation and said their good-byes, she'd made plans to visit Elana at the library and exchanged contact information with Jenn, who had offered to show her the specimen collection in the biology department.

As more guests began leaving, Jordan realized the party was

wrapping up. She finished her drink and went to the living room to grab her bag. Chip, curled up asleep on a dog bed the size of a loveseat, lifted her head and wagged her tail as she approached. Jordan petted her and told her she was a good dog. Her fur was thick but soft. Maybe she'd get a dog *and* a cat. Dogs were such good company. But then she'd have to find a new place to live, as her property manager didn't allow dogs.

She lifted her bag from the coat hook and was surprised when Maddie came up silently behind her, hooking her arm.

"Are you leaving?" Maddie glanced at her bag.

Jordan nodded. "I was just about to find you to say good night and thank you."

"You're very welcome. I'm glad you came." Maddie smiled. "I'm sorry we didn't talk more."

"You've been a wonderful host. It was great meeting Elana and Jenn." Jordan also wished they'd had more time together.

"I'll walk you to your car." Chip leapt to her feet, her eyes bright and expectant. "No," Maddie said gently but firmly. "You stay here. I'll be right back."

Chip followed them to the door but didn't cross the threshold. After they stepped outside, Maddie's hand returned to her arm, her fingers resting lightly on her skin. Outside, the sky was dark, a deep indigo blue—French ultramarine. Jordan had an old habit of thinking of colors in terms of pigments. As they walked down the driveway toward the street, she caught another whiff of Maddie's alluring perfume.

"You smell good." She flinched as soon as the words left her mouth. Her remark sounded so forward. "I mean your perfume, it smells good. What is it?"

"Petrichor." Maddie didn't let go of her arm. Instead, she moved closer and matched Jordan's cadence.

"I've never heard of it. It's nice."

"I'm glad you like it. Do you know what petrichor is?"

"Aside from perfume? No." Jordan smiled at her. "But I hope you'll tell me."

"It's the scent of rain."

"I love how rain smells, especially in the summer. A cool thunderstorm on a hot afternoon is the best."

"I agree." Maddie laughed softly. "That just made me think of one of my grandmother's expressions. When something good and a long time coming happened, she'd say it was 'like rain on hot dirt.'"

"That's quite an expression, summing up feeling parched and replenished in just a few words," Jordan said.

"She had a way with words. She was a storyteller and an author. She published several books of short stories, in fact. Mostly Southern Gothic ghost stories."

"That's very interesting. Considering you're an English professor, I guess she must have influenced you."

"Definitely. She was full of stories, and her house was full of books. And cookies." Maddie laughed. "The cookie jar was always full of homemade ones."

"Books, cookies, and a cup of tea…sounds like a wonderful way to spend an afternoon."

Maddie turned, gazing down at her from half-lidded eyes behind her glasses. The pale orange glow of the streetlight behind cast a warm aura around her head. "Maybe one rainy afternoon you'd like to meet me for tea, or coffee…or a drink?"

"Will there be cookies?"

Maddie leaned forward. Tingling with the anticipation of a kiss, Jordan was surprised when Maddie's beautiful lips skirted along her cheek instead.

"Oh, yes. I make very good cookies," Maddie whispered. Her breath, warm like a gentle spring breeze, tickled Jordan's ear.

❖

While driving back to Palmer House, with the scent of petrichor lingering and an echo of Maddie's seductive voice in her ear reverberating in her thoughts, Jordan smiled the whole way.

As she turned onto the drive leading to the house, the branches of the pecan trees caught in the headlights appeared like monstrous arms reaching into the dark, moonless night. When something big and pale with a large round head flashed across the front of the 4Runner, her mind screamed, *Ghost!* She hit the brakes hard, skidding to a stop on the gravel.

Heart beating rapidly from a rush of adrenaline, she felt her rational brain quickly reassuming control. It was probably a great horned owl swooping down on some small rodent. She'd seen it happen before and had once even narrowly missed hitting one. Why she thought an owl caught in the headlights might be a ghost struck her as odd, though she'd just been thinking about how spooky the orchard looked, and Maddie had mentioned her grandmother's ghost stories.

Arriving at the house, she was glad she'd remembered to turn on the outdoor light and the hallway lamp inside. The owl had unsettled her. Not the owl so much, but her strange reaction to it. Walking in through the back door, she let her mind drift back to Maddie, whose glasses and features she'd initially compared to an owl's.

Wondering if tomorrow was too soon to call about Maddie's suggestion that they meet for coffee or a drink, she walked into the dimly lit foyer. After she tossed her bag onto the seat of the high-backed chair next to the console, she froze in place, surprised. Three stems of black-eyed Susans rested beside a flat fragment of gray rock the size of a deck of cards. Picking up the rock to inspect it, she noticed the dark patterns of fossilized plants. It was exquisite but unsettling. How had it gotten here? Other than the unnerving possibility that someone had been in the house while she was gone, she had no idea.

## CHAPTER FIVE

After two more rainy days and frustrating trips to the river to observe lilies that weren't blooming, Jordan looked forward to doing something productive. She had a meeting with Elana at the college library and then later was meeting Maddie for coffee. A gargoyle leered at her as she approached the front entrance of the library. Smiling, she paused to admire the fearsome-looking creature. Cast in bronze, it crouched on a stone column flanking the entrance of the building that looked more like a medieval cathedral than a modern academic building. The gargoyle's long, claw-like toes curled under, appearing to dig into and crack the stone column, a clever artistic detail. The tops of its feet were shiny and bright, polished by many years of having been touched by passing students, perhaps for good luck while studying for exams. Because the spring semester had concluded, the quiet campus offered few students for the gargoyle to watch over. Following Elana's directions, she entered the library and took the elevator to the offices located behind the stacks on the third floor.

She knocked on the door labeled Acquisitions and Cataloging.

"Come in." She recognized the voice as Elana's.

"Hello."

"Hey, Jordan. Good to see you." Elana greeted her with a warm smile and gestured to her computer screen. "Please have a seat. I'll be with you in a second. I just need to finish this email and send it."

"Thanks." She sat in the chair in the corner, looking around the brightly lit room while Elana tapped at her keyboard. Green-and-white-striped spider plants cascaded out of planters suspended from the tall ceiling in front of narrow Gothic-arch windows. Photos of Elana and

Jenn smiling and looking happy were propped on her desk. The walls were decorated with framed vintage propaganda posters featuring women nurses in heroic settings and entreating patriotic duty.

Elana pushed her chair back from her desk. "You like those?"

"They're interesting, and great illustrations. World War One?"

Elana nodded. "Yes. The era fascinates me. Such a terrible time, but huge advances were made in medicine, and nursing became professionalized. In fact, many of those nurses were suffragists who took the opportunity to show men that they were equally capable."

"Interesting." Jordan nodded. "I didn't know that."

"The history of science and medicine is one of my research specialties," Elana said.

A recruitment poster featuring a curly-haired, coquettish young woman wearing a man's US Navy uniform with her white cap tilted rakishly on her head caught Jordan's attention.

"That one's not about nursing." Elana laughed. "I just think she's cute."

"She is." Jordan laughed as well. "I'm sure a lot of poor closeted lesbians back in the day thought so, too."

"I've no doubt they did." Elana stood, and after walking to the doorway, she turned to crook a finger. "I'm glad you like my posters, but what I wanted to show you is down in the archives. Follow me."

❖

Located in the basement, the archives reminded Jordan of a wine cellar, with arched stone doorways and groin-vault ceilings. After they passed a reception area, they checked in with an attendant, who asked her to leave her small messenger bag in a locker. Posted signs indicated that no photographs could be taken without permission, and no food or drinks were allowed in the reading room.

Dark wooden shelves full of books and stacked, gray archival boxes lined a long, rectangular room filled with sturdy oak tables and chairs. Hidden lighting above the shelves lit the stone-and-plaster ceiling, illuminating the room with bright, but not harsh, ambient light.

"I feel like I've gone back in time," she said, sweeping her gaze across the room. "Or into the world of Harry Potter."

"Yeah. It feels like Hogwarts down here, doesn't it?" Elana

waggled her eyebrows and led her to a table with several books and a wide, shallow archival box. She pointed. "These are some books I thought you'd find interesting. They're nineteenth-century natural histories of our area. First editions." She picked up one book and opened it, turning it to show her a page.

"Oh, nice," Jordan said when she saw a steel-plate engraving illustrating several species of turtles.

"I also made a list of contemporary books we have and will email it to you. I printed a copy for you here." Elana pointed to the printouts on the table. She lifted the lid on the archival box, revealing several old maps, carefully sliding them out of the box and spreading them on the table side by side. "I don't know if these will be useful, but I thought you might find them interesting for perspective."

Jordan glanced between them. The maps were made in the early 1800s. While they recorded place names, many in a language she didn't recognize, mostly they were illustrations of river systems, intricate lines that forked and branched across the surface of the yellowed paper like the fine tendril roots of a plant.

"So, we're around here?" She moved her index finger in a circle above the map in the center.

"Mm-hmm. Obviously, the Oberon mine hadn't yet been established, so it's not marked. If you follow the Cahaba River here…" Elana pointed to a spot above Jordan's hand, her finger hovering a few inches above the map. She traced the line of the river, then stopped over a thumb-shaped bend in the river. "We're right about there."

Jordan squinted, focusing on a dot on the page, and read aloud the name printed next to it, "Ruins of Oschoveo." She looked up at Elana. "What's that?"

"I have no idea. Probably a Muscogee Creek town." Elana pointed at several places on the map marked with small triangles and the words Indian Village. She gestured to the map on the left. "See this earlier map from 1815? Look at all the named Muscogee towns and villages. Then in this one—" She pointed to the map in the center. "The names are replaced with 'Indian Village.' And then this later one—"

Jordan studied the map on the right. "No more Native American villages, just place names in English." Jordan shook her head. "Erasure in less than twenty years."

"And a few years later, the people were erased. The Indian

Removal Act of 1830, better known as the Trail of Tears, forcibly relocated them to Indian Territory in Arkansas."

"Such a brutal, ugly history." Jordan sucked her teeth in disgust. Shifting her focus back to the center map, on the bend in the river with the enigmatic label, she said, "This *Oschoveo* intrigues me. Ruins imply something big and permanent, like maybe a Mound Builder city? Has anyone looked for it? Have you seen any archeological surveys?"

"No." Elana shrugged. "I doubt anything remains, though. Mining companies originally owned this land. It's hard to see now with the timber growth, but many of the mines around here were strip mines. Any evidence of a village has likely been destroyed."

"All this is so interesting." Jordan picked up the printout and skimmed the book list.

"Those books you can check out." Elana pointed at the list in Jordan's hand. "I gave the circulation desk your name for temporary privileges. You just need to fill out a form and show your driver's license. You'll also have access here in the archives anytime the library's open. We're not very busy now, and the books and maps can stay on this table as long as you need them."

"It's so kind of you to go to all this trouble."

"I'm a librarian." Elana smiled. "It's what we do."

The barks and yips of a pack of coyotes, slowly increasing in volume, came from across the room. Elana stared at the puzzled-looking desk assistant, who, in turn, pointed to the lockers behind her.

"Oh! Sorry. That's my cell phone. I think coyotes are cool," Jordan said, rushing to the lockers. She retrieved her bag, and while reaching into it, she spoke over her shoulder. "I set an alarm to remind me that I'm meeting Maddie for coffee." She silenced the phone. "In fifteen minutes."

"Sounds like a date," Elana said with a raised eyebrow and a hint of a smile.

"Actually, I'm hoping it'll be the precursor to one." This wasn't the sort of thing Jordan would normally confess to the friend of a romantic interest whom she'd met only twice, but she felt very comfortable with Elana.

"Don't be late for your pre-date date," Elana said with a laugh. "The library is at your disposal whenever you need it."

"Thanks, again, Elana," she said as she pulled the strap of her messenger bag over her head.

"You're very welcome." Elana grinned. "And good luck."

Jordan arrived at Cahaba Coffee right on time, but Maddie wasn't there. Standing in the order line, she checked her phone, looking for any new messages. She didn't find any, which worried her a bit. The morning after the party, still feeling intoxicated by the near brush of Maddie's lips on her cheek the night before, she had texted to ask if Maddie would like to meet her at the café for a coffee. Maddie hadn't replied until that evening, and then, the messages that followed her responses had been crisp, almost cold.

Jordan reminded herself that the tone of texts could be hard to interpret. But that's what cute emojis were for, right? The professor's text messages contained no smiley faces, only concise, complete sentences. Or maybe Maddie was having second thoughts and wasn't as interested as she'd seemed three days earlier, when she'd been a little inebriated at her party. And why did Elana wish her good luck as she left the library when she could have said "have fun" instead? Her mind racing through all the possible reasons Maddie might not want to meet her, she braced for a last-minute cancellation message.

The line moved forward. Slipping her phone back into her bag, she observed the man in front of her. He wore a crimson-red polo shirt and khakis and was tanned, tall, and broad-shouldered, with an athletic build that indicated he was just a bit past his prime. A wide gold wedding band on his hand glinted. He carried a little extra weight around his waist, the "dad bod" that many straight women seemed to find attractive. He glanced around the room, waving and nodding. Everyone seemed to be trying to catch his eye, including the forty-something blond woman dressed in a fashionable tank top and yoga pants in front of him.

"Barron," the woman said in a low, breathy voice, turning to face him. She gave him an exaggerated side-eye. "Are you sneaking up behind me?" She broke into a smile, but her plump, collagen-enhanced lips resisted movement.

"Hey, Toni," he said, laughing. He looked her up and down. "Been at the club?"

"Silly. You know I don't work out. If I did, I'd break a sweat." She opened her blue eyes wide in mock shock.

Jordan mentally questioned the veracity of Toni's assertion. Not only was her figure clearly the product of a lot of sweat-producing work, but it probably also required the services of an expensive personal trainer. Barron, distracted by a man across the room who waved at him, smiled and gave him a two-finger wave, almost like a salute.

"Barron, darling," Toni said, drawing his attention back to her with her voice. She seemed to add extra vowels to most of her words. "Is there *anyone* here that you don't know?"

Barron put his meaty hands on his hips. They were the soft, manicured hands of a banker, lawyer, or businessman, not the kind accustomed to manual labor. He thrust his shoulders back and surveyed the room with an air of authority. "I know everyone here." Twisting around, he made eye contact with Jordan. His eyes were deep brown, a color so dark the pupils were nearly indistinguishable from the iris. He smiled slowly, deep creases forming in his cheeks as he revealed perfectly aligned, unnaturally white teeth. "Well, everyone except this here pretty lady."

Jordan flinched and blinked.

Toni put her hand on Barron's shoulder, the pink nails of each slender finger pressing into his polo shirt. Tilting her head to see past him, she made eye contact with Jordan. "Don't mind my brother-in-law," she said in a syrupy-sweet voice. "He's harmless. Sweet as a puppy."

"Puppy?" Barron puffed out his chest. He struck Jordan as an alpha male, the kind of man who wanted to be the biggest dog in the room.

Toni laughed and relinquished her grip so she could place an order for a skinny mocha frappé. Barron opened his mouth to speak, but the last man to whom he'd waved interrupted him. The man, wearing a tailored blue suit of fine fabric and holding a file folder, had left his table and was striding toward Barron.

"Hey, Barron. Good to see you," the man said while they shook hands. "I saw your boy last weekend at the lake."

"Oh, yeah? Was he behaving?"

"Seemed like it." The man laughed. "He was taking a flashy red bass boat out of the water. That Skeeter's mighty fine. Birthday present, he said."

"The boy's crazy about fishing." Barron shrugged and raised his eyebrows, wrinkling his forehead with an expression that seemed to say, "What's a father to do?"

The barista interrupted their good-old-boy chitchat, calling out over the loud whirring of the blender. "The usual, Mr. Maxfield?"

Barron answered with a smile and a nod.

The man in the suit held up a thick file folder he clutched in one hand. "If you have a minute, Barron, there's something I'd like to talk with you about."

"Sure, sure," Barron said and followed him to the corner table.

Jordan stepped forward and ordered a cappuccino. Still no Maddie, nor any messages from her. The blond woman, Toni, received her frozen drink with chocolate syrup splashed like a Jackson Pollock painting on the inside of a large, clear plastic cup. Holding it in both hands, she walked past Jordan, closer than she needed to, and brushed her shoulder. When Jordan made eye contact, Toni smiled and winked.

"Have a nice day," she said softly.

"Thanks." Jordan watched her walk away. "You, too." Amused and slightly perplexed by Toni's almost-flirtatious behavior, Jordan laughed quietly to herself while the woman headed to the door with an affected rolling gait that accentuated the curves of her hips.

After Jordan's order was called, she carried the steaming-hot cup carefully to a table near the front window. The foam on the surface of the coffee had been delicately formed into a wispy heart. She blew across the surface of the cup to cool it, the heart re-forming into something unrecognizable before she took a tentative first sip. She hoped it wasn't a bad omen.

She put the cup down as she watched Maddie striding down the street. In her indigo jeans with a white V-neck T-shirt and aviator sunglasses, she looked casually stylish. She paused at the door, seeming to take a deep breath and square her shoulders before reaching for the handle. She slipped off her sunglasses as she stepped through the door of the cafe and scanned the room. The smile she gave Jordan kindled the stirring of desire she'd experienced two nights ago when she'd been hoping for a kiss.

Jordan leaned forward, intending to rise in greeting, but became suddenly unsure of what to do—offer her hand? Reach for a hug? Stand there and gawk? She instead remained seated and returned the smile.

"Hello," Jordan said.

"Hey. I'm so sorry I'm late." Maddie glanced at her watch and raised her eyebrows dramatically while puffing her cheeks. "A chicken got outside the backyard fence, and I had to catch her before I left." She glanced at Jordan's half-full cup and gestured to the counter with her thumb. "Let me get a coffee, and I'll be right back."

Maddie returned, carrying a mug of inky black coffee, and sat across from her.

"Does that happen often?"

"What? That I run late?" Maddie pursed her lips and blew across the top of the mug before taking a sip.

"No. That you chase chickens."

"Occasionally." She laughed. "Every time I think the yard is escape-proof, one of them seems to find a way out."

"I love chickens. At your party, I almost asked if I could go with you when you went to close the coop."

"About the party." Maddie spoke hesitantly and bit her lower lip.

"What about the party?"

"I owe you an apology."

"An apology? For what?"

"My behavior." Maddie winced. "I was inappropriate."

"You were? I didn't think so."

"I wasn't?"

"You weren't." Jordan cocked her head. "Why do you think you were inappropriate?"

"When I walked you to your car, I shouldn't have been so…you know, flirtatious. I was a little drunk."

"Oh," Jordan's heart sank. Maddie was backpedaling, blaming the almost-kiss on a drunken indiscretion. "You mean you regret flirting with me."

"I didn't say that." Maddie spoke quickly.

"Then what are you trying to say?"

"What I just said, that my behavior was inappropriate."

Jordan lifted her cup with both hands and sipped her cappuccino.

She wiped a bit of foam from the top of her lip while observing Maddie over the rim of the cup. "Why do you think that?"

"You were my guest. I was the host…" Maddie sighed. "It's bigger than the party. I'm the director of the residency program, and *you* are our artist-in-residence. I overstepped my bounds."

"Oh…" Jordan suddenly thought she understood. "You're worried that you crossed the line between professional and personal."

Maddie nodded.

"Hmm." Jordan drummed her fingertips on the table and narrowed her eyes. "Well then, that does make things complicated."

Maddie nodded. Eyes downcast, she looked like a scolded puppy.

"If there's a line you don't want to cross, then…" Jordan sighed dramatically, "I guess I won't try to ask you out on a date."

"You were thinking of asking me out?" Maddie, lifting her head, met Jordan's gaze. The pupils of her blue eyes flared, and she blushed, color rising in her checks and on her neck. She seemed so self-assured, but apparently she flustered easily.

Jordan fought the urge to smile. "If you'd rather I didn't ask, then I won't." Jordan couldn't resist teasing her further, amused by her earnest expression, but she didn't wait long before extending her a line. "Look. If you were at all concerned that you were taking advantage of your position as the residency director, please let me assure you that you were not."

"You might think I'm being oversensitive, but far too many people exploit their positions of power. Men are usually the culprits, but women aren't immune. I haven't overseen the program for long. The director before me, an editor for a prestigious literary journal, had a reputation for sleeping with the residents, especially the attractive young writers. One incident almost sank the residency program and forced him into retirement."

"You're being overly sensitive. I'm an artist, and you're an English professor. We don't really revolve in the same circles, and I'm secure in my career." Jordan tried to convey her words in a sincere tone. "We're about the same age, and I both wanted and encouraged your attention." She refrained from adding that Maggie's friends, Jenn and Elana, had provided some of the encouragement.

Movement along the windowsill outside diverted their attention.

A small, chestnut-brown bird with a long, curved beak and short, pert tail had landed on the shallow ledge and was hopping along it, pausing between hops to look around.

"Carolina wren." Jordan smiled at the plucky little bird. "Probably hunting for insects."

"They're so pretty," Maddie said softly.

Jordan watched Maddie's reaction to the bird. Her mouth was open slightly, the sun catching the light on her parted lips. The wren, seeming to sense their presence on the other side of the pane, disappeared in a blur of flapping wings.

Maddie turned her head and met Jordan's gaze. She smiled. "I know them only as 'the little brown bird.'"

"That covers a lot of species." Jordan laughed.

"Indeed it does. There's the little brown bird that scolds." Maddie gestured toward the window, indicating the wren that had just taken flight. "And a little brown bird with a red throat, and another with yellow on its wings, and also the one with a bicycle helmet."

"I think you mean a house finch, a goldfinch, and…I'm not sure what you mean about the bicycle helmet."

"They have black and white stripes on their heads." Maddie ran her fingers through her thick, black hair from her bangs to the crown of her head as if to illustrate. "It always reminds me of a bike helmet for some reason."

"Oh. I think you mean a white-crowned sparrow." Jordan laughed.

"That's a much more elegant name. A naturalist like yourself knows the proper names."

"At least you pay attention to them. Most people don't."

"Speaking of birds and nature, how are things going?"

"Really good. Meeting Jenn and Elana was such an unexpected gift. I'm going to Jenn's zoology lab tomorrow to see the specimen collection. I was at the library earlier today, and Elana showed me some interesting old maps and illustrated natural histories. I know where I'll be spending my time when I need a break from painting."

"That's great." Maddie spoke with enthusiasm.

"It really is. Oh, and yesterday, I discovered a little creek and a trail that runs behind Palmer House and spent the afternoon exploring it with Jack, the neighbor's dog. I tried to tell him to go home, but he

• 70 •

wouldn't listen, so I figured he might as well come along. And I hope to sign up for a guided canoe trip with the Cahaba River Society."

"Wow. Your calendar is full of good things," Maddie said.

"It is." Jordan smiled. "There's one other thing, though."

"What's that?"

Jordan opened her mouth to speak, intending to ask Maddie out on a dinner date, but Barron Maxfield's sudden appearance at their table interrupted her.

"Maddie." Barron spoke her name like a radio announcer.

"Hello, Barron," Maddie said. "How are you?"

"I'm very good. Thanks for asking." He glanced at Jordan.

Maddie took it as a cue for an introduction. "Barron Maxfield, this is Jordan Burroughs, our current artist-in-residence."

"We met in line," Jordan said.

"Yes, but were not formally introduced. You're not from around here." Barron chuckled and wagged his index finger. "That's why I didn't recognize you," he said with a wink. "Nice to meet you, Jordan."

"You, too," she said.

"Well, Jordan, I hope you'll enjoy your time here in Oberon." His tone had a paternal, almost aristocratic quality.

"Thank you. The people I've met so far have been very helpful and friendly."

"You'll find that Oberon is a very special and unique little town, Jordan. I hope both of you ladies have a wonderful day." He smiled and turned to Maddie, revealing the reason he'd stopped by their table. "See you on Saturday at the gala?"

"Yes. I'll be there."

"My wife and I host the annual Oberon Foundation gala," Barron said to Jordan. "If you'd like to attend, I'm sure we could find you a ticket."

"I have an extra one," Maddie said, glancing at Jordan.

"If that's an invitation, sure. I'd love to go."

"Great. I look forward to seeing both of you. Y'all have a nice day." Barron beamed and strutted out of the café.

"If you couldn't tell, he's the cock of the walk around here."

"Ya think?" Jordan laughed and rolled her eyes. "Couldn't have missed that. What's his story?"

"He's new money that married into old money. His wife, Tammi, is a descendant of the Palmer family. A few years ago, they relocated from Huntsville and built the house here on one of her family's local hunting estates. He's the CEO of an aerospace company in Huntsville and a Birmingham-based restaurant group. He's featured in all the advertising, and between his celebrity status and Tammi's family being like landed gentry in the state, you'd think a royal couple had settled in, the way the town behaves. Don't feel pressured to go to the gala, though it will be interesting. A lot of people are usually there, plus a band, big barbecue, open bar, that sort of thing. It's fun, if you can avoid talking too long to Tammi."

"What's wrong with her?" Jordan narrowed her eyes. There was always a catch, it seemed.

"She's pretentious and judgmental, covered in heavy foundation and a thin veneer of sweet Southern sugar. The more bourbon she drinks, the more saccharine she gets. Need I say more?"

"Nope. I know the type." Jordan laughed. "A real Southern barbecue? How can I refuse? Besides, you'll be there. I'll stick close for protection."

"Don't be scared, Yankee-girl." Maddie spoke with an exaggerated accent and laughed.

Jordan smiled. The cozy, romantic dinner she was envisioning would have to wait, but hopefully not for long.

## CHAPTER SIX

How was your date?" Jenn, grinning, waved Jordan into the biology lab, a long room with floor-to-ceiling cabinets and rows of heavy, black-topped tables. It smelled of naphthalene and ethanol. A young man with AirPods hanging down from each ear glanced over at Jenn as he pulled a specimen drawer from a cabinet. He turned to smile at her before carrying the drawer to a table with an open laptop. Jenn flipped a nearby wall switch, and exhaust fans hummed and rattled.

"Elana told you I met Maddie for coffee yesterday?" As Jordan approached, she recognized the insects in the drawer as beetles.

"Yep." Jenn's grin hadn't left her face. "So, how'd it go? Oh, and hi, how are you? Welcome to the Collections Lab."

"I'm doing well. Thanks for asking." Jenn's unfiltered enthusiasm for Jordan's romantic life amused her. "We had coffee, not a date. She invited me to attend a charity barbecue on Saturday, though."

"Oh, yeah. I forgot about the Foundation Gala. Normally, we'd attend, but we'll be packing and getting ready to leave on our trip. Why aren't you counting that as a date?" Jenn narrowed her eyes.

"I sort of fell into it." Jordan summarized how she'd received the invitation from a chance encounter with Barron Maxfield at the café. "If it goes well, I'll ask her out at the barbecue. I sense she's the take-it-slow type." She peered over the shoulder of the young man at the beetles pinned in neat rows by species and size.

"Don't go too slow." Jenn laughed. Jenn tapped the young man on the shoulder, and he pulled an AirPod out of an ear. "This is Garrett, one of my grad students. He's helping me through the summer on a project."

"Hi, Garrett. I'm Jordan, an artist-in-residence."

"Cool. Nice to meet you."

"What are you working on here?" From what Jordan could see of the screen, it looked like a database.

"We're creating a digital catalog of the collection." Pinching a pin with his thumb and index finger, he plucked an iridescent green-and-copper dung beetle from the tray and held it up. Jordan recognized it immediately. She'd illustrated the species for an extension-office publication touting the insect's pest-control benefits for ranchers. "I'm recording each specimen and confirming that the species IDs on the tags are correct."

Jordan squinted at the small square of paper pinned with the beetle. The fine cursive looked like it had been written with a dip pen. "How old is that one?"

Garrett rotated the pin for a better view. "It was collected in 1938."

"If you want to look at any specimens, Garrett can pull them for you," Jenn said. "He probably knows the collection better than me at this point." Garrett nodded as he pressed the AirPod back into his ear and returned to work. Jenn pointed to the cabinets. "Let me give you the quick tour."

Jordan loved natural history collections. To be able to see specimens up close, to view and marvel at the colors, textures, and their intricacies was a privilege. Animals in nature tended to fly off or scurry away quickly. Opportunities to observe them for extended periods of time in their habitat, like that copperhead near the river, were rare. But specimens also made her feel melancholy. Every dry bone, animal fur, and feathered bird skin stuffed with cotton wool that Jenn showed her, no matter how marvelous, was once a living creature that had lost its life in the name of science. She did not forget that sad fact, even while she admired the leaf-like camouflage pattern of a nighthawk, a bird she often heard at twilight when it was hunting insects, but she rarely saw one, and never as clearly as this. When she stroked the dense fur of a beaver skin splayed on a metal tray, she remembered having once witnessed one for a few seconds when she'd been canoeing. With a sharp smack of its fat tail on the smooth surface of the lake, it had disappeared under the swirling water. She'd actually seen only the tips of two rounded ears and a flash of its tail.

When Jenn opened the doors of a cabinet, revealing jars of turtles, frogs, and snakes preserved in clear fluid, the multitude of little faces, beady eyes dull and clouded, gripped her. She whispered to herself, "So many souls."

"Excuse me?"

"So many creatures," Jordan said, not taking her eyes off the jar. "Doesn't it ever make you feel sad?"

Jenn sighed. Jordan suspected she'd answered this question before. "I have a heart, and I love animals, but my scientific training doesn't allow for those emotions here. These specimens have great value. As you saw with the beetle, some were collected decades ago. They've taught innumerable students for generations and will continue to do so indefinitely, as long as we take care of them. I also teach with photographs and computer animations, including augmented reality, but those are all just models. They're not real. All models simplify the complexity of real things. A well-preserved specimen provides the opportunity to see details that you can't easily see otherwise."

"But sometimes simplifying is good," Jordan said. "A lot of my illustration work involves visually simplifying complicated things to help people understand them. But I get what you're saying. Models don't have nuance. Looking at a photograph of a painting isn't the same experience as seeing one in person. It's very difficult to capture the colors and textures accurately, let alone how it feels to stand in front of the work and be impacted by its scale. Something that's really big or really small affects how it makes you feel. Everything on a page or a screen always seems the same."

"Exactly my point." Jenn picked up a jar with a large dark-gray tadpole floating in the clear liquid. The typewritten label, its edges lifted and curled, was yellowed with age. "*Lithobates catesbeiana*, the American bullfrog. Years ago, one of the students in my introductory zoology class became fascinated with frogs, including this one. She's now a research biologist and has revealed the links between an agricultural chemical and reproductive disorders in frogs. Her research was used to make the connection to a specific cancer in humans, and a class-action lawsuit used the evidence in her paper to force the manufacturer to stop using that chemical." Jenn put the jar back on the shelf. "She's making the world a better place for both frogs and us."

"I see your point. I really do," Jordan touched her fingertips to the surface of the jar. "But I feel for that poor tadpole that didn't get to grow up and live out its life as a frog."

"That's probably why you're an artist, not a scientist." The words were blunt, but Jenn's tone wasn't harsh.

"You're probably right," Jordan said. In truth, she loved biology, but she couldn't disconnect her emotions the way scientists seemed to be able to.

"Would you like to see the herbarium and rock collection?" Jenn angled her head toward an open door.

"Yes. Of course." Jordan followed Jenn into a room filled with tall beige cabinets on one side and banks of drawers on the other. In the center stood tables supporting large wooden flower presses and microscopes.

"Geology and botany are outside my area of expertise." Jenn opened a cabinet door, then turned and smiled. "Don't ask me too many questions and reveal the limits of my knowledge."

"I'm sure you know way more than I do."

Inside, the shelves were full of stacked paper folders. Jenn scanned the shelf labels, selected a folder, and carried it to a table. Inside it, mounted to the paper, were several spidery tendrils she recognized immediately as Cahaba lily blooms, each about the size of the palm of Jordan's hand. Pressed, desiccated, and tissue thin, they looked like ghosts of the flowers she'd seen in photographs.

"To me, they're not much to look at, but botanists find them useful," Jenn said.

"Botanists might say the same thing about your skeletons and preserved specimens."

"They might." Jenn lifted her eyebrows and smiled.

"This flower has a strange beauty, though." Jordan pointed to each of the blooms. "And the way they're arranged on the page is nice, too. Do you see the repeating zigzag pattern?"

"Not until you mentioned it." Jenn smiled. "You remind me that art and science play well together."

"They really do," Jordan said. "There didn't use to be such a distinction between art and science. It's a shame people still see them as diametrically opposed. We don't have to approach things from the same mindset. Diversity is good, right?"

"Now you sound like an ecologist," Jenn laughed and closed the folder. While she took it back to the cabinet, Jordan looked around.

"Didn't you say there was a rock collection, too?" She glanced around the room, not seeing any rocks.

Jenn pulled open a drawer and removed a thin glass slide. "Most of what's in here are slides, meant to be used with the microscopes." She held it up, staring at the dark splotch in the center. "Don't ask me how to make sense of these."

"I wouldn't even know where to begin, other than to ask how you can cut a piece of rock paper-thin."

"Thinner than paper, actually." Jenn put the slide back in the drawer and closed it. "All I know is there is a machine, and it makes a lot of noise."

Jordan laughed and noticed a large, framed map attached to the wall behind Jenn. At a distance it looked like an abstract painting— diagonal bands in hues of blue, pink, and orange intersected curving ribbons of green, yellow, blue, and brown. Jenn twisted to see what had caught Jordan's eye.

"Now that, I know something about."

"What is it?"

"The geologic map of the state." Moving closer to it, Jenn effortlessly slipped into the role of professor. "The rich biodiversity of the state is made possible by the geologic formations you see represented on this map. The Appalachian Plateau, the Valley and Ridge formations, and the Piedmont"—she traced the diagonal bands to the wide green ribbon with her fingers as she spoke—"intersect the Coastal Plain that stretches down to the Gulf of Mexico. We have over 4,500 species and sixty-five distinct ecological zones. Mountains, valleys, prairies, plains, coastal regions, and a lot of water—over 130,000 miles of creeks and rivers, in fact—support the animals and plants that live in each of those diverse zones."

"I knew Alabama was biodiverse, but I didn't know why."

"Sadly, few people deeply understand how very special this place is. If you want to know more, there's a really good book called *Southern Wonder*. The library has a copy."

"Yes, I know." Jordan grinned. "Elana put it on a reading list for me."

"That's my girl," Jenn said with pride.

"I checked it out but haven't started reading it. Hey, what's this dark line meandering across at a diagonal? Is that a river?"

"No. It's the fall line. You don't know about fall lines?"

Jordan shook her head. "I confess, the term is familiar, but I couldn't tell you what it is."

"This is the division between the upland region and the coastal plain. It looks like a line here on the map, but it's really a five- to ten-mile band, a transitional zone." Jenn pointed to a spot. "We're here, inside the northern edge. A lot of species live above the line that you won't see below it. And, most interesting, you see the greatest diversity near fall lines. Life flourishes at the edges."

"That's fascinating."

"It is. And it's a very good place for a biologist to be." Jenn moved to the door. "If you'll follow me to the other side of the building, we have rocks in display cases in the hall. There's one case with specimens collected locally. The tour ends there."

When Jenn opened the door, Jordan was surprised that the hallway was dark. The lights overhead flashed and turned on sequentially as they walked.

"Energy-efficient lighting systems." Jenn pointed to the ceiling. "When nothing's moved for fifteen minutes, the lights go out."

"I suppose that takes some getting used to." It was unsettling to walk down a dark hallway with the lights turning on as if an unseen hand were flipping switches.

"It's good for the environment, but to be honest, it's a pain in the ass sometimes. When I'm working in my office, I have to wave my arms around like an idiot at regular intervals to turn the lights back on."

Jordan laughed at the mental picture of Jenn flapping her long arms.

"Do you like barbecue?" Jenn asked as they walked.

"I do." Jordan suspected Jenn was referring to the upcoming gala, her pseudo-date with Maddie.

"Good, because there'll be a lot of it Saturday." Jenn laughed and patted her belly. "I'm a little sorry to miss it."

"You can't be serious. You're going to the Galapagos. Barbecue will be here when you get back."

"I'm kidding, of course. What's your favorite kind?"

Jordan had learned that Southerners were cultish about barbecue.

In most places outside of the South, barbecue meant hot dogs and burgers tossed on a grill. But in the South, barbecue meant meat, cooked "low and slow" over coals, pulled or sliced, and slathered with sauces associated with different regions. Everyone seemed to agree only that it be served with thick slices of soft, white bread. Jordan had quickly learned how to play it safe when confronted with Jenn's question. "Whatever's on my plate."

"Good answer." Jenn directed her to turn left into a wide, intersecting hallway. The lights flickered on, revealing large glass cases lining the walls. They passed historic maps of the Cahaba coal fields and vitrines, containing shale, sandstone, and chunks of shiny, black bituminous coal, the rock that had made Julia Palmer's family wealthy and endowed her with the resources to found and support the college. Jenn stopped in front of a case of fossils. "You might find these interesting. Plus, I actually know some things about them."

As Jenn identified each of the fossilized creatures, Jordan noted how familiar each one appeared. The small, round blastoids looked like sea urchins, the spidery arms of crinoids reminded her of sea stars, and brachiopods and gastropods weren't much different from the mussels and snails you could find in any stream or river if you looked closely. The trilobites looked like horseshoe crabs, but somehow creepier. All those pointy little feet reminded her of centipedes that, for whatever reason, always gave her chills, as if she could feel them skittering along her skin.

There were also plants, ferns, and lycopods, which the label explained as a kind of tree-like moss, and when she saw a dinner-plate-sized flat rock with a pattern that looked like a stem of bamboo, but with long, vertical striations, she sucked in her breath.

"Yeah. That's a really nice calamite specimen, isn't it?" Jenn mistook her shock for admiration. "They were abundant here 300 million years ago, when this area was part of the massive wetlands of Pangea. Calamites were relatives of the horsetail plant, and they grew to the size of pine trees before trees even existed." Jenn lifted her hands and spread her fingers as if imagining a panoramic landscape. "Dense forests of them. The real forest primeval."

"I've seen one of these," Jordan said. The pattern on the rock in the case was the same as the one she'd inexplicably found on the table in the foyer of Palmer House.

"I'm not surprised. They're really common. They're often in the rock near coal seams. I've found them on the ground at old mining sites, which is almost everywhere around here."

"I mean I saw one *in* Palmer House."

"That's what? Good? Bad?" Jenn scrutinized her as if trying to read her emotions. "Strange?"

Jordan nodded and explained how she found the rock and fresh flowers on the foyer table, as if they were put there for her to find.

"The fossil was probably already there, and you just hadn't noticed it. Like I said, calamites aren't uncommon in this area."

"But what about the flowers? I know I didn't put the flowers there."

"Cleaning staff?"

"Why would they leave flowers?"

Jenn shrugged. "Well, someone was there if it wasn't you."

"That's creepy, Jenn."

"It shouldn't be." Jenn spoke in a tone of calm authority. "Do you know Occam's razor?"

"Sounds familiar, but no."

"You probably know the idea: the simplest explanation is probably the correct one."

"Spoken like a true scientist."

Jenn tapped her forehead with an index finger. "Think about it. Who else besides you would have a key to the house?"

"Housekeeping." Jordan paused and recalled the erratic air-conditioning. "And maintenance, I suppose."

"And?"

"I don't know. Who else would have a key?"

"Maddie." Jenn grinned.

"I doubt it. It was the night of her party. And why would she need to go into Palmer House? Besides, she'd probably contact me before just coming in." Jordan stared at the calamite fossil in the case before looking at Jenn, who was nodding. "Out of curiosity, what's the complicated answer?"

"Why, the house ghost, of course." Jenn rolled her eyes, clearly not providing it as a plausible answer.

"You mean Captain Pettiborn? Maddie told me he's not real, that the story is fabricated."

"No, not him. The other one." Jenn dropped her chin and lifted her eyebrows. "Maddie didn't tell you about the house ghost?"

"No. Who is it?"

"Nobody knows. She's one of the lesser-known, just called the Lady in the Yellow Dress."

A chill crept up Jordan's spine. James Douglas's granddaughter had said something about a lady in a yellow dress. "Are we talking friendly ghost or scary ghost?"

"I don't know."

"Does she bring things into the house? Like a fossil and flowers?"

Jenn shrugged. "A ghost who leaves presents only a naturalist would enjoy? Sounds complicated. Like I said, the more complex answer is less likely. Personally, I don't believe in ghosts, so a housekeeper or a maintenance worker left them there, probably accidentally."

"I did call and leave a message with maintenance about the air conditioning."

"There's your answer." Jenn waved her hand as if swatting away the question.

Jenn seemed so confident in probabilities and her logic-derived answer. Jordan wished it would comfort her, but in her experience, life was rarely that simple.

# CHAPTER SEVEN

Holding a tube of lipstick in each hand, Maddie looked at herself in the mirror. She couldn't decide which color to choose.

"Chip, what do you think?"

The black shepherd stood attentively, pricked her ears forward, and glanced at each tube before making eye contact with her.

"Yes. I agree with you completely. Red seems too formal for a barbecue. The natural color is a better choice. You're such a good dog." Chip swept her tail back and forth, seeming pleased with the praise as Maddie put the red lipstick back on the shelf. Clothes were strewn on the bed behind her, all rejected for various reasons—too warm, too light and revealing, too casual, too formal. Finally, she'd settled on a light-periwinkle-blue blouse, tan pants, and sandals. Her indecision had put her behind schedule. She was supposed to pick up Jordan in a half hour. She slid the lipstick out of tube, glancing at the name printed on the bottom. *Nature's Blush.* "Who comes up with these names?" She glanced at Chip. "And why am I having such a difficult time deciding on everything today?"

*Whooh.* Chip responded with a soft bark.

"Right again." She smiled. "You are such a smart dog. You figured out that I'm indecisive because I want Jordan to think I look nice—" Chip's tail wagged faster. "You know Jordan's name already?" Chip's ears pricked forward. "You met her only once."

Chip trotted out of the bedroom, her claws tack-tack-tacking on the hardwood floor as Maddie watched her until she disappeared down the hall. Her dog had liked Jordan from the moment she'd arrived at the house for the party, and that was unusual. Maddie trusted those canine instincts. As she applied lipstick, the tapping of Chip's claws preceded her reappearance in the doorway, carrying her current favorite toy—a plush purple snake with orange dots and comically large, round eyes.

Maddie squatted to pet her with both hands. Chip wriggled with obvious delight. Maddie couldn't stop thinking about Jordan. She seemed a bit younger than herself, but not much. A few years maybe. She was relaxed and an easy conversationalist, traits Maddie found very attractive. While many women had preferred types—hair color, body type, femme or butch qualities, or something on the spectrum in between—Maddie responded to confidence like a moth to a flame. She'd been burned by it, too. Three months after falling crazy in love with Vanessa, a fellow grad student, she'd realized that her breezy confidence masked an ugly arrogance. Breaking up with Vanessa was easy because Maddie had been so angry at her in the end, but Amelia, an English professor from Wisconsin she'd met at a conference, was the one who had broken her heart. They'd attempted a long-distance relationship for nearly three years, but it was just too hard to live so far apart and see each other only during breaks, and neither was in a position to relocate. After Amelia, Maddie had tried online dating, hoping to find romance locally, but she'd stopped trying after a series of first dates fizzled. She hadn't given up completely on love, but she'd resigned herself to believe that it would arrive on its own terms and in its own time. In the meantime, she'd focus on career, friends, and pets. It was enough.

Jordan was the first woman she'd encountered in a long time who piqued her interest. She liked her self-assuredness, intelligence, and passion. Jordan made her curious to know more about her. As her thoughts slipped back to the night of her party, she smiled. Conjuring Jordan's face, she focused on those plump, shapely lips she'd almost kissed and sighed.

Some moments she wished she'd given in to the desire the margaritas had encouraged, but she was also reluctantly relieved she hadn't. Every time she wondered what Jordan's lips would feel like against her own, she reminded herself that Jordan was around for only a month, and then, having ticked the Cahaba lilies off her list of threatened species, she'd be gone. Who knew where she'd focus her attention next, but probably not here in the middle of Alabama. Jordan had made it clear that she traveled to different places every year, so maybe she didn't only chase threatened species. She might have a girl in every glade and a dalliance in every dale. She seemed too good to be true. Maddie's heart sank at the thought of falling for someone, knowing she was just going to leave, and so soon. She really liked Jordan, but maybe they were destined to become friends instead of lovers. The thought made her heart sink deeper.

"We have a good life, just you and me, don't we, Chip?"

A loud squawk outside made Maddie flinch. She stood and lifted the blinds to check on the chickens free-ranging in the backyard. She always worried about hawk attacks during the day but felt strongly that the freedom to roam outweighed the risk. She was glad she'd invested in an automatic door for the coop so she didn't have to worry about being home to lock them in. The hens put themselves to bed before sunset, and the door closed when it got dark, protecting them from nocturnal raiders like raccoons, foxes, and opossums. Peering through the window, she counted heads. All six hens were in sight, scratching around for bugs in a flowerbed of blooming violet salvia and tall pink coneflowers. Nothing seemed amiss. Thelma, one of the bossy bantams, had probably pushed a hen out of the way to snatch a tasty insect. She glanced back at Chip. "Okay. The *eight* of us have a good life." She scratched between Chip's ears.

"What if Jordan became a thing? Like a girlfriend. She lives in another state. That's a lot of driving in the car."

Chip's ears pricked forward on hearing the last word, and she gave the purple snake an enthusiastic shake.

"Oh, right. You love car trips." Maggie laughed. "But we're doing all right. Wouldn't it be better to keep things the way they are? Why complicate our good life?"

She took the plush toy from Chip's mouth and tossed it down the hall. The shepherd bolted after it, claws clattering on the floor, and ducked into the living room, likely to bury it in the couch cushions for safekeeping. Maddie glanced at the clock; it was time to leave.

❖

"*This* is where the gala is?"

"You sound surprised." Maddie turned the car toward the large brick entrance with an ornate black iron gate. Now that they were close,

Jordan could see the names Palmer and Maxfield embossed on a panel attached to the metal bars.

"I've driven past here several times on my way to the river. Every time I've wondered what ridiculously pretentious wealthy person lives here."

Maddie laughed. "That would be Barron and Tammi."

The gate was open, a man holding an iPad standing outside a small gatehouse. "Good evening. May I see your tickets?"

Maddie held up her mobile phone to show him the QR code on the screen, and after he scanned it with the iPad, he handed her two bright-yellow wristbands. "Thank you, Dr. Grendel." He pointed down the road. "Just follow the signs to parking." He looked past her and smiled at Jordan. "Have a nice time, ladies."

Maddie thanked him and did as he said, turning on to a road that led away from the big house. Maddie glanced at Jordan, who was shading her eyes against the low sun, craning her neck to look at the house.

"That's what timber and gas money will buy, I guess," Jordan said.

"And tech. I think I mentioned that Barron is the CEO of an aerospace company with a Department of Defense contract up in Huntsville. This place was a hunting and fish camp until they decided to live here full-time and build that house."

"Monstrous mansion is more like it." Jordan wrinkled her forehead. "Huntsville's what, a couple of hours from here? That's a hell of a commute."

"Not when you have a private jet and your own airstrip."

"Are you kidding me?"

"Nope. Just wait until you see the party barn. It's really a barn-themed event center." The dense tree-lined road opened into grassy pastures, providing a view of the two-story, red and white gambrel-roofed building. Perched on top of the cupola, a copper weathervane in the shape of a pig seemed to glow in the late-afternoon light. Maddie pulled into the overflow parking area, where easily more than a hundred cars were parked.

"Damn. You weren't kidding," Jordan whistled and closed the car door. "This looks like it belongs in a romantic Hallmark movie." She turned her head and winked at Maddie.

Maddie's insides did a flip-flop. "Hallmark? Wouldn't the setting more likely be a New England town at Christmas?"

"In a snowstorm." Jordan laughed. "And my vintage pickup truck would have just broken down outside a quaint village. You'd be the kind stranger offering me a lift into town and some hot chocolate to warm me up."

Laughing with Jordan felt natural and good. "How about a cold beer on a warm spring evening in a fancy Alabama barn instead?"

"I'm parched." Jordan grinned. "Sounds great."

The crowd on the other side of the wide-open barn doors was lively. The gala always attracted an interesting mix of town and gown, and Maddie recognized members of old Oberon families and recently arrived faculty members. The shiny pine floor was dotted with tables covered in red gingham cloth, and the lights strung from the rafters gave the space a festive glow. Glass doors flanking one wall were rolled up, open to the trellised patio outside, where a band played bluesy country music.

Maddie touched Jordan's arm lightly to get her attention and gestured to a break in the crowd. "The bar's that way." Keeping her hand on Jordan's elbow, they wove their way across the room to the back of the long line, where several faculty members and their significant others greeted her.

"Hey, Maddie," said a tall, thin-faced mathematician. His girlfriend smiled and gave a little wave.

"So nice to see you," chimed a cheery Spanish professor. Her husband smiled and nodded. She gave Maddie a quick side hug. "I haven't seen you since the beginning of the semester. How are you?"

"I'm great. Thanks for asking. You know how it goes. Once the students start turning in papers, I become a hermit," Maddie said with a shrug. The Spanish professor nodded, giving a sympathetic look.

"This gala always feels like the official kickoff of the summer break," said a pretty blond chemist. She looked Jordan up and down, smiled at Maddie, and raised her eyebrows in a silent question.

"Forgive my terrible manners." Maddie smiled at Jordan. "Everyone, this is Jordan Burroughs, our current artist-in-residence."

Maddie remained quiet, observing while the group talked and inched closer to the bar. Some people felt awkward around academics, but as she'd previously observed, Jordan seemed comfortable with everyone she met. She fully engaged, answering all their questions enthusiastically and asking a few in return.

While Jordan asked the mathematician if he believed in the Golden Ratio, the chemist leaned close to Maddie, bumping her gently with an elbow and whispered, "She's cute."

Maddie responded silently with a half-smile and soft nod as the conversation circled around to staying at Palmer House.

"Ooh. I don't know that I could spend a night there." The Spanish professor crossed her arms and faked a shiver.

"Why?" Jordan asked.

"Ghosts," said the Spanish professor's husband matter-of-factly.

The mathematician, who was always very logical, rolled his eyes. "If you hear any creaks in the night, Jordan, it's most likely the old house responding to temperature changes."

"The house definitely has temperature issues. But, so far, the only thing that's kept me awake at night is a mockingbird," Jordan said.

As they ordered and received their drinks, they disappeared one by one, heading outside to the terrace. The bartender's back was toward Maddie and Jordan when it was their turn to step up to the bar. After he turned around, a look of recognition crossed Jordan's face.

"Hi! Remember me?"

"Hello," the bartender replied slowly, seemingly confused. He was a tanned, tall, and lanky twenty-something, with a thick, neatly trimmed and combed beard.

"Sorry. I guess you don't. We met at the Cahaba River last week. You were coming out of the river with your kayak."

"Oh." He smiled and nodded. "Yeah. You asked about when the lilies would bloom."

"Have they started?" Jordan asked eagerly.

"I don't know. I haven't been on the river since then. Sorry." He shrugged and pointed toward the selection of hard alcohol, wine, and beer. "What can I get you?"

Jordan eyed the beer taps. "What's local?"

"All of them—Trim Tab, Good People, Cahaba," the bartender said.

"What kind of beer do you like?" Maddie asked.

"Good ones." Jordan smiled waggishly.

The bartender seemed to suppress a laugh, though it was hard to tell from under his bushy beard, but his eyes crinkled into two little half-moons.

"I like the Cahaba Oka Uba myself," Maddie said. "You should try it for the name, if nothing else. It's the indigenous Choctaw name for the Cahaba River."

The bartender poured a little into a cup and handed it to Jordan, who took a sip and made a funny face.

"You don't like it?" Maddie asked.

"No. I do. It's good. Just unusual. It has the aroma of—" Jordan took another sip, emptying the cup. "Cannabis?"

"It's the terpenoids," the bartender said, swiping the edge of the bar with a cloth.

"The what?" Maddie asked.

"Terpenoids. They're in cannabis. Hops are related to cannabis, and some hoppy beers smell very weedy." He smiled, white teeth flashing through his dark beard. "Or so I'm told."

They laughed and ordered two Oka Ubas. Maddie dropped a few bills into the tip jar, and they took their cold drafts outside to the terrace.

"This is quite a place." Jordan gazed across the landscape beyond the wide terrace. The low sun illuminated the wood fences enclosing expansive pastures, ripples on the lake below the barn glinting gold, and dark stands of pine in the distance. Rows of brightly colored booths strung together with strands of lights caught her attention. "Are those carnival games?" Jordan's hazel eyes sparkled. "Want to play?"

"Sure."

After they walked through the mini-midway, scoping out each game booth, Jordan trotted over to the ticket booth and returned, dangling a strip of paper tickets in front of her. "Which one first?"

"How about the milk jugs?"

Jordan tore off a ticket and handed it to Maddie. "You called it. You go first."

"Here." Maddie held out her cup as she took the ticket. "Hold my beer."

"I've lived in the South long enough to know that phrase usually comes right before someone does something reckless." Jordan grinned.

"Standing next to me might be reckless. Watch out. You haven't seen how badly I throw a ball." Maddie wagged her eyebrows and exchanged her ticket for three softballs. She glanced over her shoulder at Jordan. She tossed one ball in the air to test its weight and missed catching it. "You should probably stand back a little farther."

"You don't have to pitch a softball well to earn your lesbian badge." Jordan picked up the ball and gave it to her.

"You'd better hope that's true." Maddie laughed. She didn't mean her words to sound as flirtatious as they came out. She felt her cheeks and the tips of her ears flush.

Jordan, beers in hand and laughing, took two deep steps backward as she gestured toward the stacked metal milk cans. "Do your best, Professor."

Maddie threw the first ball, missing the cans completely. The second ball almost made contact, and the third grazed the can on top, causing it to rock back and forth, but it didn't topple.

"These games are just as rigged as the ones at a county fair." Jordan handed the cups to Maddie to exchange another ticket for the softballs. She closed one eye and stared hard at one set of cans before she threw the first ball. Her pitch was accurate, cleanly knocking over the top can. She hit the second tier of cans squarely with her second and third throws, but they only wobbled. "Definitely rigged." She scowled at the cans. "I think the bottom ones are weighted."

"They must be," Maddie said. "Your aim was true."

"At least it's for a good cause." Jordan shrugged and pointed to the next booth. "Want to try the ring toss?"

Two beers later they'd worked their way down the avenue of booths, having exhausted their supply of tickets by tossing rings at Coke bottles, throwing darts at balloons, spinning roulette wheels, fishing rubber ducks out of a tub, and tossing bean bags in a spirited round of cornhole that ended with Jordan jumping up and down, fist-pumping, and claiming victory. Jordan's enthusiasm and good-natured competitiveness was charming, especially after she took the large teddy bear and a plush green alien with large, black, almond-shaped eyes she'd won to the Toys for Tots donation booth. Maddie hadn't won a thing but didn't care. She couldn't remember when she'd last had so much fun. The evening itself was a win.

"I've worked up an appetite. How about you?" Maddie asked.

"I'm famished. Based on what everyone's told me about this gala, barbecue is what's for dinner." Jordan read the banner hanging above the buffet in the barn. "Maxfield's Whole Hog Natural BBQ—as in Barron Maxfield?"

"The one and only. It's his most recent business venture—farm-to-table barbecue restaurants—and they've been wildly successful. He's buying produce from local organic farms, and the hogs are pasture-raised out here somewhere. I hear it's quite the operation."

"That's good to know," Jordan said as they got into the service line. "I won't feel guilty about eating barbecue tonight. I try not to eat meat from animals that were raised on industrial farms. They use massive amounts of energy and water, and the sheer volume of waste they produce is almost unbelievable. And it all has to go somewhere. It's not good for the environment, waterways especially. Water pollution and fish kills happen all the time, and the big companies just pay the fines—if they even get fined—like it's a regular part of doing business. And I guess it is." Jordan sighed. "It's only about making money. The companies don't care about animal welfare. Most consumers don't care either. They just want cheap meat."

"I can't help but think about the individual animals," Maddie said. "Pigs might have it the worst. They pull out their tusks, chop off their tails, and keep pregnant sows in gestational crates for months. Imagine being pregnant, uncomfortable, and not even able to walk or turn around? And chickens don't fare much better," she said. "They're confined to small cages and pushed to lay eggs at such an unnatural rate, their bones break from calcium deficiencies. When they can't produce any more eggs, the owners gas the whole building—"

"What?" Jordan looked horrified. "Gas?"

"$CO_2$. They say it's humane, but I don't see anything humane about suffocating to death. And then they're trucked off to a landfill or a factory to become pet food. Factory-farmed meat is like eating misery. It's one reason I have backyard chickens."

"You *eat* them?" Jordan's eyes widened.

"Oh, no. I meant that I keep them for eggs."

Jordan laughed when she recognized her misunderstanding. "What're the other reasons?"

"They're good for the garden, and they're funny creatures, very entertaining to watch."

"Sounds like 'cheep' therapy to me." Jordan bit her bottom lip and raised her eyebrows. It didn't take Maddie long to get her joke.

Maggie laughed. "They're cheaper than a therapist, too. Well worth the price of a sack of feed once a month."

"Holy smokes," Jordan said as they approached the long buffet table laden with mounds of pulled pork, ribs glistening with a rich sauce, hearty cubes of corn bread piled high on platters, chopped collard greens, an oil-and-vinegar slaw, and a deep tray of gooey macaroni and cheese. She put a bit of everything on her plate and stopped in front of the dessert table. "Lemon-chess bars or brownies?"

"Why choose?"

"I like how you think," Jordan said.

"How about I get a brownie, you get a chess bar, and we'll share them." Maddie pointed her chin toward an empty table on the edge of the patio. "And then let's go to that empty table over there."

"Good choice," Jordan said after they sat. "This far away from the band we'll be able to hear ourselves talk." A familiar tune blasted toward them. "How many times have they played 'Sweet Home Alabama'?"

"At least three." Maddie rolled her eyes. "I'm sure you'll hear it three more before they're done."

Jordan smiled at her first bite. "This is so good, I can see why so many people want to come to this event. I didn't grow up eating food like this. It's still kind of exotic to me."

"What was Sunday dinner in the Catskills like?"

"Usually my mom's pot roast. She'd make it in a big Dutch oven, and we'd have leftovers for days."

"I'm picturing a large family gathering like those depicted in Norman Rockwell paintings. Do you have a big family?" Maddie broke off a chunk of corn bread and popped it into her mouth. It was tender and rich.

"It depends on how you define big. I have an older brother and sister. I'm the youngest. How about you? Any siblings?"

"Just one, a sister. We're very different."

"How so?"

"She's an attorney at a big New Orleans firm. She's working hard to make partner, so she puts in a lot of hours, and all the superficial things matter—the kind of clothes she wears, the type of car she drives, what neighborhood she and her handsome husband live in, the school her kid attends. It's very different from the environment we grew up in."

"What was that like? New Orleans is mythic to me, a setting for a book or movie."

"The Chalmette neighborhood was rough around the edges, working class, but it had its charm and a sense of community. I liked that. We lived above the small bakery my parents used to own, and it seemed like we knew everyone in the neighborhood."

"You say that in the past tense. Are they retired?"

"No. They lost their business and our home to Katrina. We were fortunate compared to others, though. We evacuated early, before the levees breached. We were safe, but it was an awful time. All we had was what we'd packed into a few suitcases and the car. We thought we'd go back a week or two afterward to clean up the mess and pick up where we left off. Instead, everything changed. We lived in a hotel for a month and then Houston for a year, staying with some cousins. I hated it there."

"Given that sixteen-year-olds tend to hate everything," Jordan's tone was gentle, "I imagine you were a pretty angry teen."

"I'm not proud of my behavior at that time of my life. My parents seem to have forgiven me, but my sister still holds a grudge." Maddie paused. She hadn't talked about this period of her childhood with anyone in a long time. She felt vulnerable but safe with Jordan. "We moved back to New Orleans when my dad got a position at a commercial bakery and became the breadwinner. That's our family joke. But nothing was the same—not the city, or where we lived, or my friends. All of them, including my first girlfriend—first ex-girlfriend by then—were scattered all over the place. I was miserable."

"Is that why you went so far away to college?"

Maddie poked at a fat macaroni noodle and nodded. "Books were my refuge, the one constant in a sea of change. And they were a great way to escape my fucked-up reality, too. I got lost in them and found myself." Maddie looked up to see Jordan watching her with a tender expression that made her chest ache. "School was a refuge, too. I was a very good student and applied to colleges everywhere. The best scholarship offers came from schools in the Northwest. Eventually, I migrated back to the South." She sipped her beer. "Funny how it happened. I didn't really plan on it. Do you think you'll ever live in the Northeast again?"

"Honestly? I don't know. I think about it sometimes, but I do like it down here. It's not just the warmer winters. There's so much to discover in the environment, and so much of it is threatened by development and industry. I feel like my work here can help raise awareness more than if I still lived in the Northeast. Everyone in my family is so busy with jobs and kids. I visit them for the holidays, and we usually rent a big lake cabin for a week or two in the late summer."

Maddie wanted to ask Jordan more about her family, but the band had stopped playing, suddenly derailing her attention. Screechy feedback through the speakers made them both look toward the stage, where Barron Maxfield, dark hair slicked back and dressed in chinos and a red polo shirt, stood center stage clutching the microphone.

"It looks like Barron is going to give a speech," Maddie said.

"Hello, everyone!" His baritone voice boomed through the speakers. "Thank y'all so much for being here tonight and for supporting such a worthy cause. My lovely wife, Tammi, and I are deeply honored to host this annual event." He grinned and wiped a trickle of sweat away from his hairline.

Jordan leaned toward Maddie and whispered, "Do you think he wears makeup, or is that tan real?"

Maddie stifled a laugh.

"And, speaking of my wife, where *is* she?" Barron put his hand to his brow, shading his eyes from the stage lights.

"I'm right here, honey!" The crowd laughed. Two tables over, Tammi stood and waved a rocks glass in the air. She was wearing a floral-print sundress the color of a ripe peach, and the long curls of her expertly highlighted and styled hair seemed especially perfect. Seated next to her was her twin sister, wearing a similar dress, but mint green. She waved and smiled at Barron.

Barron's used-car-salesman grin didn't waver as he leaned into the mic. "Like I was saying, we are mighty blessed to be able to host this event. As you know, Tammi's great-great-great-aunt, Julia Palmer, founded the wonderful institution of higher education that we are dedicated to supporting now and in the future. We thank you from the bottom of our hearts for coming to our little party tonight. Please enjoy your Maxfield's All-Natural Whole Hog Barbecue, and be sure to save room for dessert. I asked my pastry chef to make my grandmother's special lemon chess bars for y'all tonight." Barron paused, clearly enjoying the guests' approving murmurs. "The games in the arcade would be a great way to burn off all those calories. All the game ticket sales go directly to the student scholarship fund. But if you just need to sit and relax, we'll take an online donation. You'll find information cards on the tables." Barron chuckled, and the audience laughed with him. He was smooth, comfortable in front of the crowd, and everyone was smiling at him. "Above all, let's keep putting the fun in fund-raiser! Cheers, y'all!" Barron raised his glass to the crowd, beaming as he absorbed the applause. He gave the mic back to the lead singer in the band, who nodded to the guitar player, who twanged the opening chords of "Sweet Home Alabama." After leaving the stage, Barron worked a meandering line through the tables, talking and shaking hands like a politician at a rally.

"I met the sister at the coffee shop," Jordan said. "She was kind of—"

"Flirty?"

"Yeah." Jordan laughed. "I wasn't quite sure what to make of her."

"Tammi and Toni are both straight as arrows, but their gaydar is good, better than mine probably. They seem to think that flirting with gay men and lesbians makes them cool somehow. It's funny at first but tiresome after the fourth or fifth time." Maddie accidentally caught Toni's gaze before it drifted over to Jordan. Her thin eyebrows shot up, and her heavily mascaraed eyes grew wide. She smiled and waved. Grabbing her wineglass as she stood, she left the table and strode toward them. Tammi, obviously turning to see what had gotten her sister's attention, fell in behind her, rocks glass in hand. Maddie put her hand on Jordan's and spoke through a forced smile. "I'm so sorry, Jordan. I just conjured the demon twins."

## CHAPTER EIGHT

Jordan glanced furtively at Maddie as Toni Palmer marched toward them, her identical twin, Tammi Palmer-Maxfield, several steps behind. Toni, with a toothy smile, fixed her attention on Jordan.

"Hello, again." Toni's voice was sweet as Southern iced tea, the vowels stretched out and soft. She stood so close the cloying scent of her perfume made Jordan's nose twitch. "We met at the coffeehouse."

"Yes. I remember," Jordan said, taking a half step back. "Nice to see you again."

"It appears you've met one of our wonderful professors from the college." Toni, nodding to Maddie, looked prepared for a photo shoot, her hair expertly styled and makeup emphasizing her lips and eyes. Her eyebrows, thin and perfectly symmetrical, seemed unreal. Jordan couldn't help but stare at them.

Tammi edged in, her gaze darting inquisitively among Toni, Maddie, and Jordan. She was a softer version of her sister and spoke in a breathy, gracious voice. "Professor Grendel, thank you for coming to the gala. We admire your service to the college and always appreciate your support for the foundation."

"And I appreciate all that you and your husband do for us at the college."

Tammi and Toni turned to Jordan simultaneously. Toni opened her mouth, but Tammi spoke first. "How kind of you to bring…a friend?"

Jordan sensed that the twin sisters suspected Jordan might be more than a friend and were fishing for information.

"This is Jordan Burroughs, our current artist-in-residence." Maddie pitched her voice slightly lower, giving it an authoritative air.

Jordan found the professorial tenor sexy. Maddie caught Jordan's eye and resettled her glasses on her nose, a nervous habit perhaps.

"Thank you so much for the opportunity to be part of this wonderful event," Jordan said.

"I should thank you, Ms. Burroughs," Tammi said. "It's kind of you to join us, even though you're not from here. May I ask where you are from?"

"Chattanooga."

"You don't sound like you're from Tennessee," Toni said.

"I'm originally from New York."

"An artist from New York City," Toni purred. "How interesting."

"Upstate, actually. The Catskills," Jordan said.

Toni looked disappointed.

"What kind of art do you make, Ms. Burroughs?" Tammi asked.

Jordan answered with her well-honed elevator pitch. "I am a nature illustrator, specializing in watercolor paintings. I also work on contract for scientists, authors, and publishers. I'm involved in my own project right now about endangered plants and animals of the Southeast, all based on direct observation."

"I was hoping you were another performance artist." Toni's face fell, revealing her disappointment. Her plump lower lip pushed forward into a pout.

"I think we've had our fair share of that form of 'art,'" Tammi said dismissively. She rolled the ice in her glass and took a sip of the amber liquid.

Jordan sipped her beer and recalled Peter, Jenn and Elana's friend at Maddie's party, complaining about a recent performance-art project at the college. Normally, Jordan would have argued the merits of performance art and attempted to explain how it was often misrepresented, but she didn't. "I'm afraid I'm rather old-fashioned as artists go."

"Jordan is related to John Burroughs," Maddie said to Tammi. "The highly regarded nineteenth-century writer and naturalist. He was friends with Walt Whitman and John Muir, and he even traveled to Yosemite National Park with Teddy Roosevelt."

"Well, isn't *that* interesting?" Tammi lifted her eyebrows, surveying Jordan with a fresh and approving air after Maddie's name-dropping. "You describe yourself as a nature artist, Ms. Burroughs. Does that include landscapes?"

"Sometimes," Jordan responded guardedly. While Tammi focused intensely on her, Toni scanned the crowded terrace. "Please, call me Jordan."

"Only if you call me Tammi, dear."

"Fair enough, Tammi," Jordan said.

Toni waved to a ruggedly handsome man with a neatly trimmed, grizzled beard who looked like a model in a whiskey ad. Flashing a crooked smile with bright-white teeth, he lifted his chin in greeting. Jordan sensed Toni's interest in her was fading fast.

"I am a proud patron of all the arts." Tammi lowered her voice and spoke as if revealing a secret. "But truth be told, I love landscape painting the most."

"Watch out, Jordan. My sister is about to demonstrate her own special art form." Toni rolled her eyes and stepped sideways, hip first, as if an invisible force was pulling her in the direction of the handsome man, and tittered. "If y'all will excuse me, I need to talk to a man about a man."

Focused on Jordan, Tammi ignored Toni's abrupt exit. "I think my sister was trying to tell you that I'm a collector, and I enjoy acquiring art and curating my collection. It's my art form, so to speak." She turned to Maddie. "If the professor wouldn't mind, I'd like to steal you for a few minutes to show you a painting."

"That's up to Jordan," Maddie said, smiling.

"What do you say, Ms. Burroughs—excuse me, *Jordan*?" Tammi emptied her glass and looked at her from under heavy lids.

Charismatic and politely persistent, Tammi seemed comfortable getting what she wanted. Jordan imagined that the word *no* wouldn't stop her. She opened her mouth to speak, but before she could utter a sound, Tammi grabbed her elbow.

"Wonderful. We'll be back in just a few minutes, Professor Grendel," Tammi said and whisked Jordan away, guiding her through the crowd toward the open barn doors.

Jordan glanced over her shoulder at Maddie, who waved and pointed to the floor, mouthing, *I'll be right here.*

Across the barn floor, down a hallway, through a locked door,

Tammi led Jordan up a flight of stairs to a room that looked like it belonged in a corporate office, with a long, gleaming, polished, wooden table surrounded by leather chairs. An enormous flat-screen television was mounted on the far wall, the room decorated with a trio of colorful abstract paintings, none of them landscapes, Jordan noted.

Tammi flicked her long, pink, acrylic nails in the air as they passed the paintings. "These are not what I wanted to show you. They're here to be decorative, but not distracting. They're just background for Barron's video conferences. He uses this room when he doesn't want to fly up to the Huntsville office, and for corporate retreats when we host his executives. My paintings are in the lounge."

With unfinished wooden supporting beams overhead, the lounge was an orchestration in white. Wood paneling was stained a cool white to complement the pale-gray leather couch and club chairs, which provided a neutral environment for several paintings hanging on the walls, including one large, luminous painting given center stage above the back of the couch. Every painting was perfectly lit by museum-quality light fixtures mounted on the beams. Tammi walked directly to the bar.

"Might I offer you something stronger than that beer, Jordan?" Tammi gestured to the rows of top-shelf liquor behind the bar, flanked by a humidor and a wine cooler. Jordan suspected that Tammi's offer to show her a painting was also an opportunity for her host to refill her glass with some of that fine liquor not being served downstairs. "I'm sure we have whatever you prefer."

Although her words were innocent, her tone implied a double meaning. Was Tammi really flirting with her? Jordan felt awkward, caught between not wanting to insult her host and to not encourage her. Tammi was married, and from what she could surmise, she was at least twenty years older than Jordan. Her skin had a smooth tautness she associated with facial peels and plastic surgery.

"I'm good with what I've got." Jordan lifted her half-full glass of beer and smiled. "Thank you." She took a sip and moved closer to the large painting.

"Have you and Professor Grendel known each other long?" Tammi dropped ice cubes into her glass.

"We met when I arrived in Oberon last week," Jordan said,

glancing over her shoulder to see Tammi tip a heavy pour of Booker's into the glass.

"You look rather cozy together, so I assumed you must have been acquainted longer." She capped the bottle, smiling impishly before placing it back on the shelf. "If I may be so bold, I thought you were a couple."

"No, we're not." Jordan smiled cordially. Tammi was possibly the fifth or sixth person she'd met tonight who'd made that assumption. Perhaps the universe was trying to tell her something. Should she listen? The tingly feelings Maddie roused in her made her want to say yes. Jordan's pocket buzzed, tickling her thigh. It was her cell phone, though it could have been her libido. A quick glance revealed a text from Maddie promising a rescue call if Jordan didn't return in fifteen minutes.

"What do you think?" Tammi pointed to the big landscape.

"It's a very nice painting," Jordan said. It was a masterful painting but formulaic, a knockoff of the American Hudson River School style, with a ribbon of river curving through a landscape of rough-hewn boulders and fluffy green vegetation. The requisite storm-blasted tree in the corner demonstrated the awesome destructive power of nature. It looked a lot more like a river-valley landscape of the Catskills, where the Hudson River School painters worked, than what she'd seen of the local Alabama landscape, though the less-expert eye could confuse the two. The two regions were a part of the same mountain range and shared many characteristics, but their textures, colors, and light were different. "Who's the artist?"

"Carlos Vandercook, an artist-in-residence here many years ago. He lives in New York and is very successful. Do you know him?"

"No. I'm afraid not."

"When I saw his work here, I commissioned him to make this painting." Tammi rested her fingertips on her chest, gazing lovingly at the canvas. "It's a view of the river from our property."

"Oh?" Jordan looked more carefully at the painting. "This is the Cahaba?"

Tammi sipped her drink and nodded, pointing a perfectly manicured fingernail at little smudges of white paint. "Look. There are some lilies in bloom right there."

"Ah. Now I see." Jordan wouldn't have interpreted the brush-strokes as flowers without Tammi's intervention.

"Is your work anything like Vandercook's?"

"Not really," Jordan said slowly, considering how to explain her painting style. "My work is smaller and more precise, not so loosely painted as this. I'm not an Impressionist. I tend to focus on accurate details of animals and plants, though I do sometimes make panoramic views of landscapes for backgrounds or visual notes for myself. But I don't normally sell that type of painting."

"Perhaps I could entice you to show me your paintings of the lilies after you finish them." Tammi tucked her chin and raised an eyebrow. "If I like them…let's just say, I have ample room in the house for my collection."

"I imagine you do," Jordan said. Tammi was in the market for artwork to fill up her mansion on the hill. Although Jordan made her living doing contract illustration work and selling prints through a print-on-demand shop, she'd be dumb to refuse a sale of a painting. Lots of people loved original art, but few were willing or able to buy it. "Maybe you could do a studio visit before I leave." Tammi's expression brightened; she seemed pleased. Jordan pointed to several framed photographs on an accent table. "What about these old photographs? Is this your family?"

"Most of them, yes." Tammi proudly pointed out her grandparents, great-grandparents, and cousins—a litany of Palmers and their offspring.

"They're a handsome bunch," Jordan said. Tammi beamed at the compliment. Jordan recognized a house in the background of a photo of several people standing next to a shiny Ford Model A. "Wow, that's Palmer House, isn't it?"

"Yes, it is. Where you're staying now, correct?"

Jordan nodded and leaned in for a closer look. A rakish young man in tennis whites stood by the driver's side, an elbow on the edge of the door and one foot planted on the running board. A stern-faced, older man in a dark suit flanked the tennis player. Next to them was a young woman with short blond hair, styled in a fashionable wavy bob. Wearing a light-colored, sleeveless, drop-waisted dress with a plunging neckline, she looked confident with arms akimbo and smiling, her mouth open as if she was talking to the photographer the moment the shutter tripped. She looked strangely familiar, like an old movie star, maybe? Jordan flinched with sudden recognition.

"How uncanny…I met someone a few days ago who looks just like her," Jordan said, thinking of the woman swimming in Caffee Creek. "Is she also one of your relatives?"

"Oh, no." Tammi frowned slightly. "The only relative in this photo is my handsome cousin, Bradford Palmer, with his new car. That's Leda Hatchee, the daughter of William Hatchee." Tammi pointed to the older man in a dark suit and hat standing next to her. "Palmer House was the president's house then. Hatchee ran the college in the twenties and thirties. They say that Leda, bless her heart, was a wild child. Poor thing drowned in the river when she was twenty years old, probably not long after this photo was taken. Such a tragedy. They never did retrieve her body."

"What happened?"

"No one knows. They say she used to run off into the woods any chance she got. It could have been an accident." Tammi paused to sip her drink and shrugged. "But she also consorted with the bootleggers who ran a striped pig down by the river. A rough bunch."

"A striped pig?"

"An illegal saloon," Tammi said. "They'd paint a pig black and white, like a zebra, and keep it in the back of the establishment and sell tickets to see it."

"What a strange thing to do."

"Each ticket came with a complimentary drink."

Jordan laughed. "They were selling views of the pig, not the liquor. That's clever."

"When the laws changed and Prohibition made all alcohol sales illegal, they dropped the pretense, let the poor pig go, and kept the place hush-hush."

"But people still knew about it. I mean, we're talking about it now, a hundred years later."

"You haven't been in the South long, have you, Jordan? What people here say in public versus what they do behind closed doors are two very different things. I'm certain the upstanding ladies and gentlemen back then complained high-and-mightily about that immoral den of lugubrious inequity." She waved her glass in the air. "But I bet every single damn one of them had a bottle of bootleg gin hidden in the back of a cupboard."

Jordan laughed, but the thought of the vivacious-looking young woman coming to such a bad end bothered her. "Do you think Leda Hatchee could have been murdered?"

"We'll never know. Like I said, her body was never recovered."

"Then how do they know she drowned?"

"The Methodist pastor, who'd gone out early in the morning to fish, found her. He said her body was caught between two big boulders. He returned to town to tell the police and get help, and when they went back, it was gone." Tammi sighed and shrugged. "Whatever remains of her is still out in the river somewhere, I suppose."

A chill crept over Jordan as she listened to the story and stared at the photo. Leda Hatchee looked like she could have been the woman's twin. The likeness unsettled Jordan. "Maybe I saw a relative of hers. Do any Hatchees still live around here?"

"If any do, I don't know them. I doubt it, though. I know all the old Oberon families. Hell, I know all the new ones, too." Tammi pursed her lips and leaned close, the scent of her perfume making Jordan's nose twitch again. "Even the transients, such as yourself."

The sound of men's voices interrupted them. Barron and three other men who followed him like a pack of dogs sauntered into the lounge. One, a tall, thin man with a long face like a greyhound, had a wheezing laugh. Another was stocky and muscular like a Labrador retriever, and the third man's puffy, sagging face reminded Jordan of a bloodhound.

Barron, seeming surprised to see his wife, smiled. "Oh. I didn't realize you were up here, honey." He gave Jordan a perplexed look. "Hello. I'm sorry. I know we've met, but I've forgotten your name."

"Jordan Burroughs. Artist-in-residence at the college."

"Right. You were with Professor Grendel. Nice to see you again, Ms. Burroughs." Barron gestured to the men with his thumb. "David, Robert, and Daniel. Some of my executive team. Help yourself, boys." Barron spoke magnanimously and waved his friends to the bar. "Hey, Bobby. Make me an old-fashioned with rye."

Jordan nodded and smiled at the men, but they seemed absorbed in making drinks. Barron smiled and gave her an expectant look, as if he thought she might say something, so she uttered the first thing that came to mind. "Dinner was great. Your barbecue is outstanding."

"Why, thank you. I'm glad you enjoyed it."

"And I must say that I'm so impressed that you've committed to pasture-raised meat. Not many businessmen are willing to put ethics over making money."

"I'm just doing things the old-fashioned way, the way my grandparents and their grandparents did." Barron winked at Jordan slowly. "Between you, me, and the lamppost, it's good business. People want pasture-raised meat, and they're willing to pay for it. Raising the pigs out here means that I've cut out the supplier. And being my own supplier keeps my profit margins higher." Bobby returned with the cocktail, and Barron reached for it and took a sip but didn't stop looking at Jordan. "Why are you two up here?"

"I was showing Jordan my Vandercook painting. She is an artist, and she might paint the Cahaba lilies for my collection. I don't have any paintings of just the lilies."

"That's nice," Barron said, using an expression that, in the South, could mean it really was nice or be a subtle insult. Jordan couldn't tell which this was. Tammi's cool expression seemed to imply it was the latter.

"I was just about to invite her to work on the estate, if she'd like." Tammi raised an eyebrow and watched Jordan's reaction, as if looking for a response. "She could use the old cabin. It's not far from a lovely river view."

Barron wrinkled his brow. "Isn't Josh using it?"

"Our son is leaving the country tomorrow, remember? For the fishing tournament in the Bahamas." Tammi sighed dramatically. "I swear, Barron. You don't pay any attention when it comes to family matters."

"Oh, please," he muttered.

Tammi turned her back to him, her angry expression instantly disappearing as she flashed a sugary smile at Jordan. "Joshua is our son. He told me this morning that he saw a few lily blooms."

Tammi's casual mention of the blooming lilies was like casting a lure in front of a hungry fish. Jordan weighed the exchange—private access to the Cahaba lilies for a commission. It wasn't what she'd planned, but it seemed like a good deal. The sale price might even pay for her expenses on this trip. Barron's dark expression didn't give her confidence that he was amenable and would agree to it. Given the palpable rising tension between him and Tammi, Jordan refrained from answering.

"I don't know if that's a such good idea, honey," Barron said, sipping his drink. "The hogs range in that area."

"That's all right," Jordan said. "I planned to see them at the refuge."

"But it gets so crowded on the river this time of year. The people who go out there are so…" Tammi paused as if searching for the right word. "Rough. You know, big pickup trucks and loud music." Tammi's tone implied her distaste. "You'd be able to work on our property and not have anyone bother you. And, of course, I would be honored to support your creative endeavors." She batted her eyes at her husband and spoke in a wheedling tone. "Barron, darling, surely one young woman with some art supplies won't upset your special-needs pigs."

"I know you don't mean any harm, honey," Barron said in a placid tone. "But bio-security is important with free-range animals. And there are liability issues. They're not like your pets. We've talked about this before."

With a roll of her eyes, Tammi spoke more harshly. "You treat those pigs like one of your irritatingly secret defense projects up in Huntsville."

David guffawed, quickly silenced by an elbow to the ribs from Daniel, who gave him a stern look.

"I'll think about it, Tammi. Let's talk about this later, okay?" Barron glanced furtively at Jordan, clearly not wanting to continue the conversation in front of her.

Her phone buzzed in her pocket. She slid it out with a sense of relief, holding it up while stepping away from the bickering couple. "Excuse me, it's Maddie," she said and answered the call.

"9-1-1," Maddie said with a laugh.

"Sure. I can help you with that." Jordan spoke in a cheerful tone loud enough so everyone could hear. "We're just on our way down. See you in a minute, okay?"

Tammi gave Jordan a sidelong glance as she walked toward the bar. "Forgive me, Jordan. I have kept you from the party for too long. I'll just freshen my drink, and we'll get you back to your pretty professor."

Refreshed cocktail in hand, Tammi walked her down the stairs, back into the crowded barn. Before they parted ways, Tammi handed her a cocktail napkin with a phone number written on it. "I'll work on Barron. Call me if you're interested."

❖

"Thanks for the rescue," Jordan said, puffing her cheeks. Maddie's eyes, catching the lights strung across the patio, twinkled. "It came at just the right time."

"You'll have to tell me what happened," Maddie said. She pointed at the dessert table in front of them and grinned. "They just put out lemon meringue pie."

"A third dessert? How very decadent," Jordan said. "I'm up for splitting a piece."

"I have a terrible sweet tooth," Maddie said, as if confessing a sin, and slipped a plate from the table. "Let's take this to that bench under the tree by the lake, and you can tell me about whatever happened in the barn."

They walked away from the loud music and the arcades, down the hill in the cool evening air.

"Oh," Maddie said as they sat down on the rustic bench. "I didn't think to get a second fork."

"That's all right. We can take turns. You go first since it was your idea," Jordan said. Maddie didn't hesitate to slice the edge of the fork through the lofty meringue and custard. Watching her lips engulf the first bite and her eyelids close slowly in pleasure, Jordan felt a quivering, electric thrill. A woman who enjoyed food enjoyed other pleasures.

"It's so good." Maddie held the fork out.

Jordan took the second bite and understood Maddie's reaction. The light, sweet meringue mingled perfectly with the dense, tart lemon custard. "You might have to fight me for the rest of this," she teased, playfully holding it back.

"Oh, I'll wrestle you for my share." Maddie laughed.

"I wouldn't want to deny you this pleasure." Jordan grinned, and even in the low light she saw the tops of Maddie's ears slowly turn red.

"You know I'll gladly reciprocate."

Now that it was Jordan's turn, her cheeks warmed in response. She offered Maddie the plate and fork.

Maddie prompted her after her second bite. "You were going to tell me about the conversation in the barn."

Jordan recounted Tammi showing her the landscape paintings in the luxurious lounge, the offer to let her work on their estate, and the tension she'd witnessed between her and Barron.

"Barron's business execs were creepy. They hardly said a word." Jordan watched a firefly blinking and floating up into the branches before disappearing among the first stars in the indigo sky.

"I'd guess they saw a marital spat coming and know to lay low." Maddie handed the plate back to her with one small piece left.

"You're probably right," Jordan said. She didn't want to take the last bite and halved it, returning the plate to Maddie.

Maddie smiled, seeming to recognize what Jordan had done, and refused the remaining piece. "I took the first bite, so you should have the last."

Jordan accepted it. "I certainly didn't want to get in the middle of it. I felt super awkward. Your call couldn't have come at a better time." She placed the fork on the empty plate. "Thanks again for thinking of the rescue call."

"You're very welcome." Maddie stared at her with raised eyebrows. "So? Are you going to accept Tammi's offer?"

"I will if Barron doesn't object. He didn't seem keen on the idea. He appeared very worried about the security on his free-range hogs. I don't want to cause trouble."

"I understand. I hate drama," Maddie said.

"Really? That surprises me."

"Why?" Maddie blinked, adorable even with a look of confusion.

"Because you're an English professor." Jordan couldn't help but tease her. "I thought you'd like drama. A story would be awfully boring without it."

"You're funny." Maddie's gaze was soft. "I like how much you make me laugh."

"I like making you laugh." She studied the shape of Maddie's lips, following the slight upward curve of the corners of her mouth, and spotted a little white smudge on the edge of her lip. Jordan imagined a sweet meringue-enhanced kiss. Instead, she pointed to her own lip. "You have a little meringue right here."

"Oh." Maddie dabbed her lip with a napkin. "Did I get it?"

Jordan nodded. "Maddie, can I ask you something?"

"Of course."

"Most of the people I've met seem to assume we're together, or they seem hopeful we might get together. Why does everyone seem so eager to hook you up?"

Maddie's eyes widened, the owlish look returning, as if she hadn't anticipated the question. "Most of my friends are in relationships. I guess they wish I was, too."

"You don't want a relationship?"

"It's not that I don't want one." Maddie sighed. "Oberon's a small town, as you know. I don't have many opportunities here to meet other single lesbians. I guess I've resigned myself to a comfortable life alone."

"You guess? Have you tried online dating?"

"I did. I connected with some women and met a few in person, but—"

"But what?" Jordan asked gently.

"I didn't meet anyone I wanted to keep talking to after dessert." Maddie's smile extended into her eyes.

"Even third dessert?"

"There was never even a second dessert. This is a first." Maddie pointed at the empty plate in Jordan's hand. "How about you? From what you've described, Chattanooga sounds like a fun city and big enough to have a datable pool of women."

"I did fall hard for a woman there. I'd started daydreaming about marriage and living in one of these cute little bungalows I'd seen in an old neighborhood, but—" Jordan crinkled her nose.

"Uh-oh, the big but," Maddie said gently.

"Yeah, a really big one. Right when I thought we would take our relationship to a deeper level—I thought she might ask about moving in together—she instead informed me she was taking a job in California."

"And she didn't ask you to go with her."

"Nope," Jordan said curtly. "Didn't even seem to consider it. She seemed more excited about a fresh start out there without me."

"Damn. That's cold."

"It was something." Jordan puffed air in her cheeks. "I went through all the emotions—shock, anger, hurt. Mostly, I felt stupid."

"Why stupid?"

"I totally misgauged us, her especially."

"You were blindsided by love. It happens."

"More like blind to reality."

Maddie cocked and turned her head slightly, squinting at her like she was trying to parse out something that was missing. "I sense you're still bitter, angry maybe."

"I've worked through the anger part, but the bitter taste lingers."

"If you're not careful, that bitterness will affect the flavor of everything else you taste. The poet Maya Angelou said that bitterness is like a cancer that will eat away at your soul. Whereas anger, if you channel it into a creative act, transforms into something good."

"Sounds like alchemy," Jordan said. "How does bad become good?"

"Through love." Maddie spoke as if it was the most obvious answer. "Love is the most powerful thing in the universe. It has no limits. If you want to continue the alchemical analogy, it can even turn leaden hearts into gold."

The flashing lights of the arcade and the voices of hundreds of people having a good time up the hill fell away as Jordan held Maddie's gaze and emotion rose within her, pushing against her chest. The words "May I kiss you?" coalesced in her thoughts. Before she could get them out of her mouth, the opening chords of "Sweet Home Alabama" pierced the air one more time.

"Oh, my God!" Jordan blurted. "That's the fifth time they've played this song."

Maddie burst out laughing, "Welcome to Alabama. You get used to it."

A sudden bright flash of lightning surprised them. They flinched, hunching their shoulders, as if expecting a bolt of electricity to strike them. Several seconds later, thunder boomed and rumbled.

"Thunder sounds different here," Jordan said. "It's like you can hear the shape of the landscape as the sound travels over it."

"Rolling thunder is an expression, but it really does sound like it's rolling, doesn't it?" Maddie said. "When I was a kid, my grandfather used to tell me that thunder was God shoving beer barrels around in heaven."

Jordan visualized a muscular robed and bearded man, a figure like what you'd see on Michelangelo's Sistine Chapel ceiling, pushing oak barrels across a heavy wooden floor. "I like his version of God. He sounds like someone who enjoys his creation. Definitely better than the god who smites everyone."

"Or who turns beloved family members into pillars of salt," Maddie said.

"Godly wrath and theology aside, isn't that biblical story a very human metaphor?" Jordan asked.

"You mean that we shouldn't look back?"

"Yeah. We exist in the present and can only move forward in time. There's no future in the past."

"But the past inspires us, affecting how we live in the present and how we envision our future. You can't realize anything without first imagining it." Maddie gave her a sidelong glance. The breeze picked up, shaking the oak leaves overhead. "Take your distant cousin, John Burroughs, the naturalist, for example. Did knowing about him and feeling a personal connection to him inspire you and impact your path in life?"

"I guess it did." Jordan spoke slowly, pausing. "I always knew about him. My family told stories about him. My grandmother used to say that love of nature runs deep in our blood."

"I daresay it does." Maddie smiled. "Or you wouldn't be here."

Jordan looked up at the sky as a cloud moved across it, dampening the bright glow of the rising moon. "That storm is coming this way."

"I love the energy of a thunderstorm, but we should probably get back to the barn." Maddie stood and held out her hand. Jordan took it, feeling tingly inside, still wanting to kiss Maddie.

As they walked to the terrace, Jordan released Maddie's hand only because she needed to swat a mosquito that buzzed her ear. The band had stopped playing, and as they passed the game booths, the crisscrossing strings of lights swayed in the gusty wind as the attendants closed the structures. She glanced at her watch. The gala was supposed to continue for another hour, but the incoming storm seemed to be dampening all the outside activities. They lingered inside the barn, making small talk with Maddie's friendly colleagues. They and the remaining partygoers left when thunder rattled the windows and the first few drops of rain began to fall.

The storm was wild when they arrived at Palmer House. Maddie edged her car close to the covered walkway that connected the kitchen studio to the back door of the house. Lightning illuminated the yard every few seconds in a purplish-white light, and water poured off the roof in sheets, pounding the hood of the car.

"That's as close as I can make it." Maddie peered through the windshield. "You might get a little wet."

"I haven't melted yet." Jordan grinned.

"Thanks for coming with me tonight. I really enjoyed your company."

"I did, too." Jordan didn't want the evening to end. "Would you like to come in for a coffee or tea? I'd offer you a nightcap, but I don't have anything stronger."

"I would," Maddie glanced at the clock on the dashboard, "but I really should get home. I need to let Chip out, though she's going to hate this rain."

Tomorrow was Sunday, not a traditional date night, but she didn't care. "Would you like to go out to dinner with me tomorrow?"

Maddie's expression brightened, then fell. "I'm driving to New Orleans for my niece's birthday."

Jordan hoped her disappointment didn't show.

"But I'll be back by Friday," Maddie added quickly. "Don't look so sad. Didn't you say earlier you need to focus on your work without distraction?"

"Yeah, but I was talking about unwanted distractions." Jordan laughed. "How about Friday night? That's a proper date night."

"Friday night would be great," Maddie said with a grin.

"Good. We have a date." Jordan unbuckled her seat belt and considered leaning across to kiss Maddie, but she was buckled in, and the bulky console was in the way. It seemed too awkward. Instead, she moved to get out of the car. The rain had let up and was gushing off the walkway roof like a stream instead of a waterfall. "I'm going to make a run for it."

Jordan dashed out into the rain to the protection of the walkway. She waved, and after taking two steps toward the back door, she turned and ran back to Maddie's car. Maddie, giving her a look of concern through rain-splattered glass, rolled the window down, not seeming to care about the splashing water.

"Is everything okay?"

"I forgot to say good night." Before Maddie could reply, Jordan kissed her. Her lips were softer than Jordan had imagined, and Maddie returned the kiss, deepening it slowly and sensuously. Jordan got lost in it, ignoring the pelting rain until Maddie stroked her cheek. Her fingers, warm against Jordan's rain-chilled skin, brought her back to earth. She pulled away, sweeping her rain-plastered hair away from her eyes to see that Maddie's glasses were askew. Using both hands, she straightened the frames on the bridge of her nose. The lenses were covered with drops of rain and condensation. "I'm sorry I got you wet."

"I'm not sorry at all," Maddie said breathlessly. Lightning flashed and thunder cracked. "You'd better get inside."

"See you Friday," Jordan said quickly. "And be careful driving home." She waved Maddie off as the rain came down in torrents.

Energized by the thunderstorm and Maddie's kiss, Jordan stepped into the foyer, grinning to herself and shaking rainwater from her hair. She walked down the hallway, intending to grab a hand towel from the kitchen to dry the water dripping down her neck and arms. The heat building inside her as she savored the memory of Maddie's soft lips didn't offset the chill from the cold rain on her skin. Feeling prickly goose bumps forming, she realized the house was very cold, the crazy air-conditioning working overtime again. Light from the living room crossed the floor of the hallway, but Jordan hadn't turned it on. She hadn't needed to since she'd left the house during the day, and she was always careful to turn off lights to save energy. Stepping into the living room, as she paused and turned in the doorway to look, her blood ran as cold as the rain outside. A woman was sitting in the armchair, glowing.

## CHAPTER NINE

Jordan stood behind the wingback chair staring at the slender arm dangling off the arm rest, the hand cradling a cocktail glass that contained a pale purple liquid the color of amethyst, illuminated as if the lamp were on, though it was clearly off. Jordan flipped the light switch connected to the lamp.

"Good evening, Jordan." The voice was melodic and light.

"Who are—" Jordan stepped forward slowly, craning her neck. When she saw the seated woman, she inhaled a lungful of air so quickly it caught in her throat.

"Did I spook you?"

Jordan nodded and coughed. It was the woman who'd been swimming in Caffee Creek. She appeared exactly like Leda Hatchee, the 1920s flapper in the black-and-white photograph Jordan had seen tonight. Now here she was in Technicolor, wearing a sleeveless dress the color of spring daffodils and embellished with sparkling beads and sequins. She crossed her shapely legs, drawing Jordan's attention to her bare feet. The woman cleared her throat, prompting Jordan to lift her gaze. Short blond hair fell in loose curls around a perfectly painted face, rosebud-red lips, and smoky eye shadow. Thick black mascara drew attention to her piercing blue eyes.

"Maybe you should sit down. You look a little pale." The woman arched a delicate eyebrow. "Like you've just seen a ghost."

"Who are you?"

The woman didn't answer. Instead, she sipped her drink as if she hadn't heard the question and eyed Jordan over the rim of her glass, as if sizing her up. Where had the fancy cut-crystal glass and the purple liquor come from? Maybe she'd brought it with her, although Jordan didn't see any bottles in the room. She didn't see any shoes on the floor, either. Had the stranger wandered in here barefoot? Her feet were perfectly clean, not a smudge of dirt or mud on her toes. It had been raining for at least an hour, and she was dry. Had she been here all evening? Jordan was certain she'd locked the door when she left.

"How did you get in?" Jordan had a chill. Her shirt was wet, and the room seemed to be getting colder. She crossed her arms across her chest, tucking her fingers under her arms, hugging herself.

"You know the answer," the woman said. "Do I really need to spell it out for you?"

"I don't know who you are or how you got in here. Is this some sort of prank?"

"Prank? Hardly." The woman laughed. "Really, you should sit down."

Jordan was too agitated to sit, so she marched across the room and studied the woman from a different angle. "Why won't you answer my question?"

"Because you know the answer, Jordan."

Something about the woman seemed off. She seemed to glow in the lamplight, but her legs cast no shadows on the floor. Jordan stared hard at her face, as if she were a painted portrait. The sight was unreal, almost surreal, her skin seeming to absorb the warm light in the cold room. Impulsively, and without concern for propriety, Jordan reached out to touch the woman's cheek. Expecting solid warmth against her fingertips, she felt like she'd put her hand in ice water. The woman scrunched up her face as Jordan's fingers went through her head and popped out the other side. She was like a cumulous cloud, appearing solid on the outside but composed of vapor. Very cold vapor. Jordan's heart thudded as she retracted her hand. She stared at the woman. *What the fuck was she looking at?* Unable to make sense out of what she was seeing, she felt panic rise from the pit of her stomach into her chest, pushing against her sternum.

The woman spoke in a singsong, teasing voice. "Who am I, Jordan?"

Her throat tightened as her breathing became shallow and fast.

Nostrils flaring, she felt her eyes widen, and she began to hyperventilate. Shaking sensation back into her numb hand, she blurted out, "You're Leda Hatchee."

"Attagirl!" The woman laughed gleefully. "I knew you'd figure it out." Raising her glass as she stood quickly caused the purple liquid to slosh out, evaporating into a pale mist before it reached the floor.

"But you can't be Leda." Jordan's voice cracked. "She died a hundred years ago."

Leda gasped theatrically. "Has it been that long? Oh, my, how time flies," she said, locking eyes with Jordan.

Struggling to grasp the situation, Jordan heard her heartbeat hammer in her ears, and the room began to spin.

❖

Jordan opened her eyes, slowly becoming aware of her surroundings. The ceiling was in front of her. No, it was above her, which meant she was lying down. Something scratched the back of her arms. Spreading her fingers, she deduced it was the coarse texture of the woven rug. She finally gathered that she was lying on the floor staring at the ceiling. Turning her head to the left, she bumped the carved wooden leg of the sofa. Rolling her head to the right, she observed Leda Hatchee, looking like a beautiful silent-movie star, leaning forward on the edge of the chair with her elbows resting on her knees, peering at her.

"Damnation," Leda said gently, her bright-red lips lifting into a smile. "I should've told you to breathe instead of to sit down."

Rubbing her temples, Jordan sat up; she had a splitting headache. "Did I hit my head?"

"No. You passed out into the settee and slid off," Leda said. "I'd offer you a drink," she held up her glass, which was full again, "but I don't think this'll do a thing for you."

"What is that?"

"Sloe gin fizz. Gin is the best spirit." Leda took a sip and giggled. "Next to me, of course."

Jordan leaned back against the sofa, took a deep breath, and let this experience sink in. Could she really be talking to the ghost of Leda

Hatchee? Somewhere between passing out and coming to, she must have lost all reason. She shook her head as if she could fling the idea out of it. "I don't believe in ghosts."

"That's good, 'cause I'm not a ghost." Leda frowned. "I'm a spirit."

"I don't follow you," Jordan said.

"Spirits, like myself, have more freedom. Ghosts, on the other hand, are tortured souls who don't want to be here but can't pass over. They're a pain in the ass, if you ask me. Nothing but a bunch of self-centered wet blankets bumbling around in the dark." She emitted a melodramatic movie-ghost moan. "Woe-oh-oh is me and all that malarky."

Jordan coughed. Her mouth felt dry, her tongue thick. She stared at the ornate blue and red patterns in the kilim rug underneath her as thunder rattled the windowpanes. She'd been so focused on that delicious rain-drenched kiss from Maddie, she must have slipped coming into the house and hit her head. She couldn't really be sitting here, cross-legged on the floor, talking to a ghost, or spirit, or whatever thing had manifested from the deep recesses of her mind, could she? The photograph of Leda Hatchee she'd seen in the barn at the gala, and Tammi's story about her tragic death, must have woven their way into her subconscious like the colorful threads in the rug on which she sat. Could a concussion cause a hallucination? She needed to find out. Maybe she should see a doctor. Should she try to do that now or wait until morning? She ran her fingers through her hair, pressing against her scalp feeling for a tender spot, but found nothing.

"Speak up, Jordan," Leda said. "You're mumbling."

Jordan didn't want to look at Leda. She knew it was faulty logic—the idea that if you can't see something, it doesn't exist—but she avoided making eye contact nonetheless, as she stood and walked unsteadily to the kitchen for a glass of water. Flipping the light switch, she was startled to see Leda Hatchee already there, leaning against the kitchen counter, staring with a fierce expression. Jordan stepped back quickly, almost falling backward and coming to a painful stop when her shoulder blades intersected with the edge of the doorjamb.

"It's not polite to ignore your guest." Leda put her hand to her chin in a thoughtful pose. "Although, if you think about it, you're actually a guest in *my* house."

Jordan met her gaze and pointed at the sink. "I need a drink of water, please."

"That's better," Leda said, moving aside. Jordan filled a large glass and took several deep swallows. "I know what you're thinking, Jordan. I am not a delirium."

Jordan emptied the glass and crossed her arms again. "Why is it so damn cold in here?" She strode into the hallway.

"Adjusting the thermostat won't help," Leda said.

She checked it anyway. It was warmer by the digital thermostat, the screen reading seventy-five degrees. A chill crept up her spine and tickled the back of her neck. She nearly jumped when Leda spoke in her ear. The apparition was standing right behind her, even though she hadn't heard her approach.

"That doesn't make any sense, does it?"

"No, it doesn't," Jordan said.

"I had a conversation with a nice scientist who once stayed here. He explained something about thermodynamics and energy exchange. I confess, I didn't fully understand all the particulars."

"A scientist?"

"Yes, a scientist." Leda widened her eyes for emphasis. "Who believed in spirits when confronted with the facts—well, with me. Let's do a little experiment. I'm going to stand over there." Leda walked toward the living room in a strangely smooth gait, almost like a slithering snake. "And you go back to the sink."

Jordan did as Leda directed.

"How does it feel now?" Leda called out from the far side of the living room.

"It's warmer in here."

"Now come to me."

As Jordan approached Leda, the temperature dropped. Standing in front of her was like being in front of an open freezer door. "Interesting."

"See. I'm just a natural phenomenon, like the wind. You can't see the wind, but you recognize it when it rattles the leaves in the trees or kicks up the dust on a dry summer's day. You believe in wind, don't you?"

"Of course." Uncannily, Maddie had schooled her on the same idea when they'd discussed ghosts at dinner when she first arrived in Oberon. "It was you I saw swimming in the creek that day, wasn't it?"

"It was. And you didn't think I was a figment of your imagination then."

"No, I didn't."

"Then you can believe in me. Trust your senses, Jordan. And trust in me."

"Why should I trust you?"

"I saved you from Old Red, didn't I? You would have stepped right on top of that handsome copperhead. By the way, that's a nice portrait of him you made."

"Him? I thought the snake was a female."

"Nah. Old Red's a big boy snake." Leda grinned. "I've been watching your work. You got the colors and the pattern of his scales just right."

"Thanks," Jordan said weakly.

Leda moved closer. "We're all just bundles of energy, Jordan. You and I are simply different kinds. For you to see me like this, I draw energy from what's around me. I learned that from the scientist." Leda gave her an appraising look. "Now, don't you feel better talking with me and not worrying that you're losing your marbles?"

"Maybe." Jordan wanted to say yes, but she was still in shock, though her heart was no longer pounding in her chest, and the dizziness had dissipated.

"Oh, you're a difficult one. And what a swooner! I didn't expect you to faint." Leda paced the room, throwing her arms dramatically in the air as she spoke. "You're an artist, Jordan," she said, spilling her drink again, the droplets dispersing into little clouds of purple mist. "Aren't you creative types supposed to break the rules, embrace the unknown, run wild and throw caution to the wind?"

"You're thinking of Picasso," Jordan said. "I'm not that kind of artist."

"Well, that's how they were when I was alive." Leda huffed, her tone becoming sarcastic. "Excuse me if I haven't really followed the latest trends in art since then." Putting her arms down, she narrowed her eyes at Jordan. "Wait. Were you trying to be funny?"

"Yeah, a little."

Leda's emotions shifted like the wind. She winked and drained what remained of her gin fizz. "Keep working on that, honey."

Jordan shivered and tugged her cold, damp shirt, pulling it away from her stomach. "I need to put on a dry shirt. And I could really use a cup of coffee. I'd offer you one but—"

Leda held up a hand. "Goes right through me. But thanks for offering."

Jordan went to the bedroom, not expecting Leda to follow her up the stairs. Her silent movement was unnerving. She looked like she had weight and mass, but, evidently, she didn't. Jordan suppressed a nervous laugh, thinking about all that had happened in the last hour. She'd been pulled from the reverie of Maddie's scorching kiss to the shocking appearance of the spirit of a dead flapper. Jordan pulled open a dresser drawer, intending to grab a T-shirt, but, after considering how Leda sucked the heat from around her, grabbed a light hoodie instead. She began unbuttoning her shirt and stopped when Leda didn't turn away.

"You want to give me a little privacy?"

"Why?"

"Because I'm about to take off my shirt."

"Baby girl." Leda threw her a coy look. "I have already seen you in your birthday suit."

"You've seen me naked?" Jordan sputtered. "You've been watching me up here, too?"

"Of course." Leda put a finger to her lips and batted her eyes coquettishly. "Don't worry about me, honey buns. You're not my type. Besides, I know you've got your peepers on the professor."

"What?" Jordan's cheeks grew hot. "How do you know that?"

"Let's see." Leda tapped her fingertips to her thumb one by one as if counting. "After ninety-nine years, five months, and fifteen days, I've become a very good observer. We spirits can't do a lot, but what we do, we do very well." She grinned salaciously. "And we are very good at watching. Running through the rain for a kiss—that was *very* romantic." Leda giggled and moved silently into the bathroom and inspected Jordan's toiletries lining the shelf.

Jordan removed her shirt and quickly pulled the hoodie over her head. "Jeez. I never thought that being haunted would be like dealing with a stalker. I feel kind of violated."

"I'm not haunting you," Leda said from the bathroom. "If I were haunting you, honey, you'd be long gone by now. Trust me." Without warning, Leda leapt through the doorway, launching herself into the air, flying at Jordan so fast, her body was a blur of movement, and time seemed to slow down. Her face stretched into a long, horrible grimace, her mouth twisting into a black, gaping maw that emitted a bone-chilling, high-pitched shriek that made Jordan's ears ring painfully. She threw up her arms to protect herself, bunched her shoulders, and squeezed her eyes shut. *Jesus, she seemed friendly, and now she's going to kill me.* As Jordan braced for impact, the banshee shrieking suddenly stopped, and the only sound in the room was the drumming rain on the roof. Thunder boomed, shaking the house. Jordan opened one eye slowly, tentatively, to peer between her elbows. With both eyes open, she saw Leda standing placidly in front of her and dropped her arms.

"*That's* what a haunting looks like," Leda said, seemingly satisfied with Jordan's reaction.

"Please, don't ever do that again." Jordan put the palm of her hand against her chest. "Unless you want to give me a heart attack."

"My father always told me never to make promises I can't keep."

"Great." Jordan groaned and headed back downstairs to make a small pot of coffee, Leda following her like a stray dog who'd latched on and didn't intend to leave. While the coffee burbled and dripped into the carafe, Leda sniffed the air with a smile.

"You're a spirit," Jordan said.

"I thought we had that settled. Do I need to explain it again?"

"I mean, if you're not alive, you don't breathe. If you don't breathe, how can you smell the scent of coffee?"

"Old habits die hard, even for the dead." Leda sighed. "I used to love a hot cup of strong coffee. I can still smell it, but not through my nose. Don't ask me how it works. Intermingling molecules or something. I don't know. It's not like we get a manual or anything."

Jordan poured herself a cup of coffee while watching Leda float-walk back into the living room. After demonstrating her haunting technique upstairs, she'd stopped mimicking the walking gait of a living person and moved fluidly like an ice skater. Leda was sublimely beautiful to behold.

"Do you talk to people often?" Jordan sat on the sofa, warming her hands against the cup. Leda flicked her hand, and a smoldering cigarette in a long, thin holder appeared in her fingers.

"No. You know, most people are pretty boring." Leda took a long drag and blew it out slowly. Hazy, pale-purple smoke curled around her head. "Ever since they converted my home into a—what do you call it?"

"A residency," Jordan said.

"Since then, more interesting people have been around. Still, most people aren't worth my energy."

"That's true for the living, too."

"You're getting funnier." Leda snorted, causing the smoke to spin into eddying tendrils.

"Why did you reveal yourself to me?"

"I liked you. In fact, I liked you the first time I saw you. I was intrigued that you sensed me."

"I did?"

Leda nodded. "Remember when you went up the stairs the first time?"

Jordan recalled stopping on the landing when she felt cold air and a strange, unsettling feeling washing over her. "That was you?"

"I bumped into you. I didn't expect you to notice. Most people don't."

"I didn't know what I was feeling."

"But you felt something. You were paying attention, and you stopped to think about it. Hardly anyone pays attention to what's going on around them anymore. They're all wrapped up in those little telephones they carry around."

"I couldn't agree with you more." Jordan had a love-hate relationship with her cell phone. It was so useful, but she had to resist becoming tethered to the technology. Mostly, she didn't want to miss out on the world beyond the small black screen.

"I saw a girl get killed by a car because of one of those things. She was looking at it while she crossed the road." Leda pantomimed holding a cell phone in both hands, head down, staring at the screen. "Never saw it coming."

"How terrible," Jordan said.

"It was. She attached to me and pestered me from the day it happened in winter until the first day of spring, when she finally crossed over. It was the strangest thing. She kept saying she needed to tweet. I never before met a ghost who thought she was a bird."

Jordan suppressed a laugh and considered how to explain Twitter. "I think she was talking about something on her phone. It's kind of like a posting a note on a public message board. People share written messages and call them tweets."

"Silly name, but that would explain it. She must have been posting one when the car splatted her. Wasn't pretty."

Jordan winced. The mention of a car reminded her of the photograph she'd seen. "I saw a picture of you, taken in front of this house."

"You don't say?" Leda brightened. "What was I doing?"

"I was told you were with your father and a young man named Bradford Palmer. You were standing by his car."

"Brady and his new coupe." A dreamy look crossed Leda's face. "I sure thought he was swell. He let me drive his car once." Leda floated out of the chair and soared around the room in a circle, cigarette holder clenched in her teeth and hands held up in fists like she was driving a car. "But only once. I liked to drive fast," she said as she passed Jordan.

"I bet you did." Jordan laughed.

Leda stopped in front of a bookcase and rested her feet on the floor. She tapped the spine of a book, pushing it back so it was in line with others on the shelf.

"You can move things?"

"Small things." Leda glided to the couch and settled next to Jordan, crossing her legs elegantly. "I have limits."

"I've been told that some of the campus ghosts are jokers and move things around. But now I'm thinking this house has a *spirit* who's the trickster."

"Could be." Leda wore an expression of feigned innocence. "I'm glad you don't have your ghosts and your spirits confused anymore."

"Did you put the fossil and flowers on the foyer table last week?"

Leda's eruption of laughter answered the question. "You should have seen the look on your face when you found them. You were so flummoxed!"

"What would you expect? I thought some creepy maintenance guy left them." Jordan wanted to tell Jenn that the mystery was solved, and contrary to what she thought, it wasn't the simplest explanation, but the ecologist who didn't believe in ghosts would think she was crazy. "I never considered a paranormal explanation. If I had, maybe I wouldn't have passed out tonight."

"Don't blame me for your lack of imagination."

"I should thank you for stretching my sense of what's possible." Jordan sipped her coffee and put it down on the coffee table. It had already gone cold. She glanced around the room. She'd spent most of her time working in the studio and hadn't been in this room often after her initial exploration of the house. Surrounded by books, the space was comfortable. "You must really love this house if you choose to stay here."

"It looked different then." Leda sounded wistful. "And I did love living here."

"Tell me about your life."

"I was born in St. Louis and was in middle school when my father accepted the position as president here at the college. The city didn't suit me. I liked it much better here."

"How so?"

"It was a magical place to explore. It still is. I had the run of the campus and the woods behind the house. It was much wilder then than it is now. I learned I could follow the creek down to the river and back and had many adventures. Misadventures, too. I was kicked out of middle school before Thanksgiving that first year." She laughed and slapped her knee.

"That doesn't sound like a good thing. Why are you laughing?"

"I stabbed a boy named Billy with a pencil. Oh, don't give me that look. He deserved it. He was mean, a vicious bully. He mercilessly taunted Josiah, the sweetest little boy there ever was. One day I'd had enough. I told Billy, 'William Howard, if you don't let that boy alone, I'll give you a comeuppance!' He laughed at me, so I stabbed him. But that's not what got me expelled."

"No?"

"It was the second and third jabs that did me in." Leda giggled. "Did you know a number 2 pencil will leave a permanent mark?"

"I had no idea." Jordan couldn't help but laugh.

"Truth be told, being kicked out of school was the best thing that ever happened to me. I wasn't good with authority, if you know what I mean. After 'the incident,' as my father called it, he arranged for private tutors from the college. One of them was a student of biology, Miss Mae. Come rain or shine, we spent our recitations in the woods and by the river, sometimes *in* it, chasing after all sorts of creatures. I learned the names of all the things I saw, and she showed me more than I even knew existed, including how the mines were polluting the waters. After she graduated and moved away, I borrowed natural history books from the library and vowed to go to Yale Forest School, though my father warned me they would likely not accept a woman. I started at the college here, intending to transfer." A dark look crossed her face. "I didn't get the chance to try."

Jordan suspected she knew why Leda didn't go to college. She'd died young, before she had a chance to enroll. "You don't have to talk about what happened to you if you don't want to."

"Oh, it's all water under the bridge, as they say. From the look on your face, I can tell that you know I drowned. It was stupid, my own damn fault. I'd been dancing at the cave—"

"A cave?"

"We called it the cave. It was an old mine shaft that had been a striped pig before it was a speakeasy. Everyone knew about it back then. It was pretty swanky, all things considered. There was a long stone bar, and the ceiling of the dance floor was painted to look like a sparkling night sky. That night I'd danced the Charleston and imbibed one more gin fizz than I should have. When I caught my date necking in a dark corner with some floozy, I was as boiled as an owl and spitting mad. I decided to walk home, and crossing the river was a shortcut. When I got there, the moon was rising above the trees, and bats were swooping around catching insects. It was so beautiful." Leda paused as if savoring the memory. "I took off my shoes and navigated to a slab of rock in the middle of the river, where I decided to sit for a while and moon-gaze until this beautiful moth I didn't recognize flitted past. I slipped while trying to catch it and smacked my head before I hit the water. The rest, as they say, is history."

"I'm surprised you still like to swim."

"What's done is done." Leda threw up her hands as if waving off the memories. "And what's not to like?" She grinned. "I don't have to hold my breath underwater anymore."

"I hadn't considered the advantages." Jordan chuckled. Books and movies about the supernatural always made it seem like the goal was to get away from this world, to "cross over," as people said. Leda didn't seem interested in doing that. "What keeps you here?"

"Love," Leda said, her answer giving Jordan a little chill. It was the second time this evening that the power of love had come up. First with Maddie, and now Leda. "And the ever-changing beauty of this place." She floated up to the bookshelf, removed a small book, and dropped it into Jordan's lap before settling next to her. "A wise poet once said that the parlor of heaven would be decorated with common blackberry vines." It was an old edition of Walt Whitman's *Song of Myself,* the edges of the binding cracked and worn down to the boards underneath their cloth cover. Whitman, poet and friend of John Burroughs, Jordan's ancestor. The coincidences were stacking up.

"Section 20," Leda said. "Read the underlined parts."

Jordan opened the book, not surprised to see Leda Hatchee's name written on the inside of the cover in perfect cursive script. She turned to the page as directed, found several lines underlined in pencil, and read them out loud. "*I know I am deathless. I laugh at what you call dissolution. And I know the amplitude of time.*" Jordan looked up. "I'm not sure I understand."

"One of my tutors made me write an English paper on Whitman, but it wasn't very good," Leda said. "I didn't appreciate what he wrote until after I died, when I had some time on my hands and a new perspective. Nature was heaven for him, and it is for me, too. With all the time in eternity to explore and observe, why should I leave? I watch over what I love."

"You're like a guardian angel?"

"Oh, hell, no." Leda cackled. "I'm no angel, honey. But I guess you could call me that. I saw what the planters and mine owners did back in my time, destroying anything that prevented them from making a buck. Greed causes people to do terrible things. It's a slow poison that worms its way through the body, blackening heart and soul. Avarice still thrives here, though it's often hidden from view. Shallow waters can run murky, you know?" Leda stopped speaking, staring at the ceiling as if looking beyond it. "The storm is passing."

Jordan had been so focused on Leda she hadn't realized that the thunder seemed far away, and the rain had eased to a gentle patter. She stifled a yawn, the need for sleep tugging at her. It had been a long day, and with the stimulation from Maddie's kiss and the shock of meeting Leda wearing off, she was feeling spent. "I'm fading."

"Me, too." Leda uncrossed her legs and smoothed the front of her dress. The sequins had grown dull, no longer catching the light, and the cushions behind her were becoming visible. "It's been nice talking to you tonight, Jordan. I don't often get such fine company."

"Wait."

Leda brightened a little. "I can't stay much longer."

"Join me at the river tomorrow if you can. I'll be at Hargrove Shoals."

"I know." Leda was fading again, faster now.

"How did you know?"

"A spirit doesn't give away all her secrets." Leda winked, took a deep drag from her cigarette, and released it slowly, blowing the pale-lavender smoke toward Jordan. When the haze cleared, the room felt warmer, and Jordan was alone.

## CHAPTER TEN

J ordan awoke to the sound of a text alert on her phone. She rolled and reached for the phone, forgetting that she wasn't in bed, and nearly fell off the sofa. She'd stretched out on it after Leda left, intending to lie there for a bit to process the day's events before going to bed upstairs, and must have fallen asleep moments later. The message was a cheery good morning from Maddie, asking if she'd slept well.

"Like the dead," Jordan said to herself with a laugh. She started to text a reply and then decided to call instead.

"Hey, you." Maddie answered on the first ring. "Good morning."

"Good morning." Jordan smiled, imagining Maddie's face. She wanted to tell her about Leda, but how do you tell the woman you're just getting to know, and would like to know much better, that you've not only seen a spirit, but stayed up late conversing with one? Maddie had professed to believe in the supernatural, but Jordan wasn't going to test the limits of her belief. It still seemed unbelievable and a good reason for a woman to reconsider a new romance. "When do you leave for New Orleans?"

"In a few minutes." Maddie paused. "Did my text wake you? You sound a little groggy."

"Yeah. I haven't had a cup of coffee yet."

"I'm sorry."

"No worries. It's okay. I'm really glad you called."

"You called me." Maddie laughed.

"Oh, right." Jordan put her palm to her forehead. Hearing Maddie's voice made her feel giddy. "You texted; I called back. It might sound silly, but I wanted to hear your voice. Text can only do so much."

"That's not silly at all. I woke up thinking about you, wishing I didn't have to wait until Friday to see you again. My sister would kill me if I canceled on her. She's preparing an obnoxiously lavish party for my niece's birthday. And then my mom would be mad at me for making her angry." She sighed. "My niece is turning eight, so I expect toxic levels of pink and glitter."

"And princesses?" Jordan asked.

"Most definitely. And unicorns, too, I suspect."

"Unicorns aren't all bad, not the ones with rainbow tails, anyway. I think of them as the spirit animal of Pride," Jordan said.

"I always thought those were drag queens." Maddie laughed.

"Did you like princesses when you were a kid?"

"Not the Disney kind, if that's what you mean," Maddie said. "I was fascinated by real fairy-tale princesses, the Brothers Grimm stories, and Arthurian legends. I was a total book nerd, obviously. How about you?"

"No princesses for me. I had Smokey Bear everything—plush toys, stickers, coloring books, posters—you name it." Jordan remembered her childhood bedroom decorated like it was a summer-camp bunkhouse. "My grandfather worked for the US Forest Service and kept me well supplied with Smokey swag." Barking in the background interrupted their conversation. "Is Chip going with you?"

"Of course. In fact, she's pacing back and forth between me and the front door right now because I'm not moving fast enough. She loves car trips. Once she sees my suitcase, she doesn't let me out of her sight."

"I'm sorry you'll be out of *my* sight for a while." Jordan spoke softly. Maddie's indistinct murmured reply made Jordan's heart skip a beat and her stomach flutter. "Is it a long drive to New Orleans?"

"It's not bad. About five hours if I don't get stuck in traffic on the causeway."

"Will you text me tonight, let me know you made it safely?"

"Sure. Are you going out to the river today?"

"I am. I hear the lilies are starting to bloom."

"Oh, that's great." Maddie's tone seemed to convey genuine excitement. "It looks like it'll be a beautiful day. If I didn't have to leave, I'd invite myself along."

"If you weren't leaving town, I'd have already invited you to go with me."

"I can't wait to hear about your reaction to them."

"I can't wait to find out what it will be." Jordan laughed. "You be careful on the road."

"Thanks," Maddie said. "You be careful on the river."

"I'll do my best to be safe." Their mutual concern for each other's well-being was charming. "Oh, hey, what about the chickens?"

"They're going with me, of course," Maddie said lightly. "I have a specially designed travel crate for them."

"Seriously?" Jordan couldn't imagine traveling for hours with chickens in a car and taking them to someone else's house.

Maddie chortled. "I'm joking with you, Jordan. I keep my neighbor supplied with eggs, and he keeps an eye on them when I'm out of town."

"I'm so gullible." Jordan laughed at herself. "But you were so convincing. You're really a good storyteller. Hey, speaking of which, you never told me about the Palmer House spirit."

"Spirit? You mean ghost? There's not much of a story to tell other than a few reported sightings of a young woman in a yellow dress. How'd you hear about her?"

"Jenn told me." Jordan spoke truthfully but omitted last night's experience with the spirit. She wanted to continue talking with Maddie but knew she was keeping her from leaving. "We're avoiding hanging up, aren't we?" Jordan's cheeks hurt, and she realized she hadn't stopped smiling since she picked up her phone.

"We might be," Maddie said. Somehow her voice sounded like she was smiling, too. "How about we hang up on the count of three?"

"If you want to get to New Orleans before sunset, we'd better."

"One…two…" They counted together, but on the third count, neither ended the call, and they burst into laughter.

"I'm hanging up now," Jordan said. "For real."

"Me, too." Maddie laughed. "Seriously."

"Okay, okay. Bye, Maddie." Chuckling, Jordan moved the phone away from her ear, hearing Maddie's delightful laughter continue as she ended the call.

❖

An hour later, after having eaten a granola bar and banana for breakfast during the drive, Jordan turned on to the tree-shaded gravel road leading to the Cahaba River. Scanning the river as soon as she saw it in gaps between the trees, she hoped for a view of the lilies. The water level had dropped, and the lilies were no longer submerged, clusters of their long, dark-green leaves visible. She spotted a few white blooms in the distance, but none close to the river's edge.

She parked the 4Runner behind a line of cars in the turnaround at the end of the road near Caffee Creek. Slipping her sling pack over her shoulder, she traveled light, with just a sketchbook, pencils, small pan of watercolors, and a water bottle. As she walked past a group of adults letting their kids play in the shallow water near the river's sandy edge, she noticed a hand-painted sign nailed up high on the trunk of a tree: *Do not leave dirty diapers*. The thought of soiled diapers littering the ground repulsed and aggravated her. If someone had gone to the trouble of climbing the tree to attach that sign, diaper-dumping must have been an actual problem here. The volume of trash she'd seen scattered along the roads in Alabama was appalling, although Tennessee wasn't much better. She didn't understand people's careless disregard of the environment.

The trail to Hargrove Shoals began on the other side of Caffee Creek, a tributary that flowed into the river. Knowing it would require a water crossing, she'd worn shorts and water sandals, expecting to get her feet wet today. The water, surprisingly cold, came up to her calves as she waded across. As she glanced up the creek, she admired the cascade of water flowing through rocks and boulders. Was Old Red still up there, waiting for a meal to amble past? The big copperhead reminded her of Leda. Would Jordan really see her again today?

When she paused on the other side to shake sand and gravel out of her sandals, the confluence gave her a sweeping view up and down the river. Above the mouth of the creek, the river was wide, shallow, and noisy as water rushed through the striated lines of bedrock crossing the river at a diagonal. Below, it was dark and deep, ripples on the deceptively smooth surface indicating the hydraulic power beneath.

Following the shaded and well-worn sandy path, she encountered a small group of middle-aged birders along the way. They pointed to the tree canopy overhead, clutching expensive binoculars and arguing over which species of warbler they'd spotted. She exchanged nods and hellos as she passed, and after fifteen minutes of walking, she quickened her pace when the stand of lilies, known as Hargrove Shoals, came into view.

They were spectacular, stretching as far as she could see, clusters of creamy white blooms resembling a thin layer of snow on top of lush, green foliage. A handful of people already stood there, dispersed among the plants in the water. As she removed her phone from her pocket to take a few photos before wading closer to the flowers, she realized she'd forgotten to bring its waterproof case. Silently cussing, she captured a few images and vowed to be careful while in the water. After putting her phone in her pack, she stepped into the river.

What she'd expected to be an easy stroll through shallow water along the rocky shelf to the lilies turned out to be tricky. The surfaces were slick with algae. Jordan took short, shuffling steps, working her way slowly to the nearest blooms. The rock was also dotted with small aquatic snails that she tried her best to avoid stepping on, slowing her down further. Seeing so many was a good thing, as their presence indicated clean water. She'd read about the Cahaba pebblesnail, a small, light-colored gastropod with a distinctive tan stripe that lived only in this river. It was thought to have gone extinct because of mining pollution. Just a few years ago, a grad student who'd noticed snail populations rebounding since the Clean Water Act went into effect in the early seventies was hopeful that the snails might have survived and went looking for them, finding them in a small section of the river. Although that area was north of where she was, she kept an eye out for their distinctive pattern. Given what was upstream—dense urban areas, industry, mining, and farms—a single catastrophic spill could wipe them out. The author of the article she'd read was optimistic that the populations could rebound. Water quality, in general, was better, and since a small dam on the river had recently been removed, a host of other species was recovering. She'd read with fascination how the tiny larvae of mussels dispersed by catching rides on the gills of fish. Collectively, they grazed decaying plants, filtered water, and provided a food source for other animals. Overlooked and disregarded, snails and mussels having free range were key components of a healthy ecosystem.

As she moved closer to the lilies, at what seemed like, well, a snail's pace, an idea for a painting depicting those interrelated connections began to form in her mind's eye. She tucked the thought away as she approached the first cluster of flowers.

Up close, the shape of the lilies reminded her of amaryllis, the pretty hybridized flowers that bloomed off long tubular stems with leathery dark-green leaves, the bulbs of which were offered for sale during the winter holidays. Unlike the showy garden amaryllis, the Cahaba lily flowers were far more delicate. Seeing them in person now, she was glad she'd read up on the plant's anatomy because it helped her fully appreciate what she was observing. The lily's unpoetic-sounding scientific name, *Hymenocallis coronaria*, meaning "beautiful membrane crown," didn't do it justice. The flower was sensually beautiful, like something Georgia O'Keeffe would have painted. The cup-shaped flower was the crown, a thin, circular membrane with frilled and pointed edges framed by six long, spidery tendrils. Six thin stamens radiated from the edge of the crown, each capped with yellow, pollen-swollen pillows called anthers. A thin, sticky filament, the stigma, emerged from the yellow blush of the flower's throat. Although the flowers relied on pollinators to keep the gene pool diverse, each one was self-contained, with both male and female parts. And it survived only in clean, swiftly flowing water. Jordan respected the inherent wildness of a plant that would wither and die in a domestic garden no matter how carefully tended.

The people in the distance moved among the flowers like the native bees buzzing around her, attracted to the blooms' nectar. She'd noticed that they all had wading sticks, and now she understood why. The bedrock, fragmented and often jagged, sloped down into dark, unknown depths. She reflected on Leda's tragic drowning. She'd known the river well, it seemed, and had still lost her life due to a slip and fall. Imagining her own foot sliding and getting stuck in a crevice encouraged Jordan to be cautious and take it slow.

She paused on a flat, wet rock mid-river in front of a wide channel to wipe the sweat trickling down her forehead. She'd hoped to make it all the way to the other side, but she wouldn't be able to cross here without risking getting her sling pack wet and not without some difficulty. The channel was deep, the flow swift. Water was always more powerful than it seemed. A refreshing soft brush of a slight breeze on her skin felt good and carried with it a subtle, sweet scent. Bending low, she put her nose to the nearest lily bloom and smelled a delicate fragrance reminiscent of honeysuckle. From what she'd read, the flowers bloomed for one day only. Today just a portion of the plants around her were blooming, and they were all heavy with buds, seemingly ripe and ready to emerge.

After taking a long drink from her water bottle, she retrieved her sketchbook and pencil from her pack. She made several quick gestural drawings of the landscape as a warm-up and then a suite of detailed drawings focusing on the lilies. While drawing, she entered an almost meditative state and eased into the flow of translating what she saw into marks on the page. The process also made her more attuned to the variety of textures and colors, and how the water flowed through the shoals. In art school she'd learned about Leonardo da Vinci's fine pen-and-ink drawings of natural forces, like flowing water and violent windstorms, and that he drew from observation as a method of attaining deep knowledge. Drawing helped her appreciate abject things, like spiders and spindly-legged insects. When she illustrated some for a freelance job, they gave her the heebie-jeebies at first, but the more she drew them, the more she felt curious instead of anxious.

Eventually she couldn't make any more marks on the paper without overdoing the drawing, so she stowed her sketchbook and pencil back in her pack and retrieved her phone to take images for source photos. After she captured as many close-ups of the lilies as she could, she set her camera to panorama and held it at arm's length, panning the phone around her. While she shifted her feet to complete the arc, her right foot, closest to the ledge, slipped. Her leg scraped painfully against the sharp edge, and her foot plunged into the fast-moving water, the current tugging it and catching the sole of her sandal like a paddle. She lost traction on her left foot and slipped again, tipping backward. Sensing that she was falling, she instinctively put her hands out to catch herself and watched helplessly as her phone arced through the air, hit the water with a splash, and disappeared into the depths of the river as her butt hit the edge of the rock.

"Fuck!" Unharmed save for a scraped calf, she sat on the wet rock, her legs dangling in the current, staring at the spot where she'd last glimpsed the phone as if she could will it back into her hand. "Fuckity-fuck."

The water-resistant phone could withstand a quick dunk, but it might not survive an extended soak, assuming she could retrieve it. She considered wading into the current to feel around for it, but then she'd risk getting her pack and art supplies wet. She glanced about, looking for an exposed dry rock where she might put the pack, but didn't see one. A small, fuzzy butterfly landed on the front of her shirt, distracting her. It was a silver-spotted skipper flashing its silvery white spots, rhythmically opening and closing its wings. A dainty, seemingly fragile thing, it flitted off effortlessly, as if taunting her with its ability to cross the river with ease.

Movement in the water caught her eye, something dark and shadowy darting beneath her toes. She pulled up her feet and scooted back on the ledge. She wasn't sure what she'd witnessed. Glancing up, she looked for a passing cloud casting a shadow. The sky overhead was clear blue; the only clouds visible were to the north and just beginning to appear over the top of the hillside. The shadow passed again. Something was definitely there, its shape unclear. A big fish maybe? It probably wasn't a turtle; they seldom roamed in rocky shoals and strong currents. Scanning the water, hoping to glimpse whatever it was, she recoiled when a pale hand popped out of the water, clutching her phone.

Leda's head emerged next, covered with a wide grin. "Looking for this?"

"Leda! Oh my God, yes." Jordan reached for her phone as Leda floated to her. "Thank you!"

"You're welcome. You're lucky I arrived when I did."

"Lucky and very grateful." She powered off the phone quickly and grabbed a bandana from her pack to wipe it down.

"What do you think of my little piece of heaven?" Leda bobbed in the water as if there were no current. Water rolled off the surface of her dry hair, and her makeup was perfect.

Jordan puffed air in her cheeks, trying to find the right words as she stuffed the phone into her pack. "It's wonderful. I don't think words can do it justice."

Leda nodded. "Can I see your drawings?"

"Sure." Jordan removed her sketchbook and flipped to the first gestural sketch and held it up for Leda to see, moving slowly through the next few pages. Leda appeared impressed.

"Oh, I like this one," Leda said with exuberance and pointed at the drawing of a lily root grasping a rock. "They look like they're clinging on for dear life, don't they?"

"I guess they are," Jordan said, turning to the last sketch of a snail. "I'm not sure what species this is. I was hoping I might find a pebblesnail. They were thought to be extinct but have survived somehow. I know this isn't one of them."

"The little stripeys?" Leda asked. "They used to be everywhere, and then they all but disappeared. But I've been seeing them again." She pointed an index finger. "I'll be right back." With a grin, she disappeared under the water's surface.

Alone again, Jordan remembered that she wasn't the only person exploring Hargrove Shoals. She glanced over her shoulder to see a few people wading downstream from her, one setting up a tripod and camera with a big lens. She wondered if they, too, could see Leda, or if it looked like she was talking to the river. Hopefully, they weren't paying her any attention.

When Leda returned after a few minutes, she held out a cupped hand with three snails the size of a nickel. The spired shape of the coiled shells and tan stripes was instantly recognizable.

"Oh, wow." Jordan leaned forward to have a closer look, wishing she could use her phone to take a photo. "Do you mind holding them so I can draw?"

"Not at all."

Jordan got out her pencil and sketchbook and made several sketches, some of just the snails and some including Leda's hands, which remained unnaturally still, something a living person in the water couldn't do. Making friends with a spirit was unexpectedly handy. What would have happened if she'd tried to take a picture of Leda? Would she register in the image, or would the photo just show some strange orb or hazy shadow?

"You look very serious when you're drawing," Leda said after Jordan finished and turned the result around to show her.

"I do? I'm not surprised, though. I really focus when I'm working," She stowed the sketchbook in her pack. "I guess you probably ought to get my models back into the water where they came from."

Leda dipped her hands in the water, refreshing the snails. "Something marvelous happens here, but only at night. If you come back when the moon's full, I'll show you."

"I don't know that I can."

"Why not?"

"The reserve closes at sunset."

Leda rolled her eyes while pushing back from the ledge. As she floated away slowly, her form seemed less distinct, as if she were dissolving in the water, her voice taking on a teasing tone. "The river never closes, Jordan."

Leda disappeared completely and didn't return. Jordan shuffled carefully back to the riverbank and found a shady spot with a log that made a good bench. Then she got out her watercolors and sketchbook to add a wash of color to a few of the drawings. As she brought the sketches to life with the dip and swish of the brush on paper, she considered Leda's proposition. What did she want to show her, and, more worrisome, how could she get back to this place at night?

## CHAPTER ELEVEN

On her way back to Palmer House from the river, Jordan stopped by the college library to use a computer. With her laptop useless because of the cracked and bleeding screen, she needed one to find detailed instructions regarding her water-soaked phone. She discovered only that she should wipe it down with a soft cloth, tap out any water accumulated in the charging port, speakers, and microphones, and wait before turning it on again. Some sources said six hours, though others recommended forty-eight. Hopeful it would be fine, she decided to split the difference and try powering it up in the morning.

However, she couldn't text Maddie as promised. Jordan checked their email exchanges. The phone number included with Maddie's signature was for her office. The best Jordan could do was email her, explaining that she had returned from the river safe and sound, but her phone hadn't, and hope Maddie was checking messages.

After that, she looked at online maps as she considered how to reach the lilies at night. By canoe seemed the most direct way. She canoed every summer with her family on camping trips, but most of her experience was on flat water. She could rent one, put in above the preserve, and float down to the stand. With a full moon and clear weather, visibility would be good, but that plan presented problems. She'd have to paddle back up to her car, and going solo wasn't the safest thing to do, especially on a river she wasn't familiar with. Since the only people she really knew here were out of town, no one would realize if she went missing. It was an adventurous fantasy for a few minutes until reality caught up with her.

While staring at the undulating lines of a topographic map on the screen, she thought about Tammi Palmer-Maxwell's offer. She'd mentioned an old cabin near a good view of the river, and she owned that big landscape painting that included a few lilies. From what Maddie had said, her family owned a lot of timber and gas property, as well as local riverfront property. Was some of it near Hargrove Shoals? After searching through more road, trail, and topographic maps, she couldn't ascertain who owned the land around the refuge near the river, so she'd have to ask Tammi directly. Fortunately, Jordan had her number on a cocktail napkin, and Palmer House had a landline. She printed a few maps to take with her before leaving the library to make the call.

"Hello?" Tammi's voice was like golden syrup.

"Hello, Tammi?" Jordan prompted her. "This is Jordan Burroughs. We met at the gala last night."

"Why, Jordan. How nice to hear from you. How are you?"

"I'm good, thanks. I hope I'm not interrupting. Do you have a few minutes?"

"As a matter of fact, I do. To what do I owe the pleasure of your call?"

"I hope it's not too soon, but I was wondering about that offer to paint on your property."

"Oh, good," Tammi said breathily. "Yes. Let's talk about that. Are you available at four today?"

Jordan glanced at her watch. She had just enough time to shower and change clothes. "How about four-fifteen?"

"That will be just fine. Do you mind coming out to the house?"

"Not at all."

"Perfect," Tammi said. "See you then, Jordan."

The gates to the Palmer-Maxfield estate were closed when Jordan arrived. She lowered the window and stared at the call box, finding no instructions, only a video camera and a button. She pressed it, and Tammi answered within seconds.

"My goodness. You are prompt." Tammi's voice resounded through the speaker. Had Jordan violated some unwritten rule about arriving fashionably late? A motor whirred, and the gates slowly opened. "Turn left at the fork and come to the front door."

Jordan followed the smooth, black asphalt road that snaked up the grass-covered hill to the house with its tall arches and cold, almost fortress-like, façade. As she pulled into the wide circular drive shaded by crepe myrtles, Tammi stood waiting for her at the top of the stairs by the door, wearing a floral top, white capris, and sandals.

"I appreciate you seeing me on such short notice," Jordan said, getting out of the 4Runner. "And right after the gala, too. I hope I'm not inconveniencing you."

"Not one bit," Tammi said with a wave of her hand. "The event planners take care of everything. All I have to do is show up and say 'Thank you for coming.'" She laughed. "You got lucky today. My garden club meeting this afternoon was canceled." Tammi angled sideways to peer at something behind Jordan. "Oh, look! Miss Prim has come to see us!"

Jordan turned to see an enormous pink pig emerging from a grove of young trees, trotting across the grass, grunting excitedly and drooling.

"Stay right there, honey. I'll get you a little treat," Tammi said before going into the house.

Jordan assumed Tammi was talking to the pig, who had slowed her pace but was grunting loudly as she neared the base of the stairs. When Tammi returned holding two peppermints, the pig, completely ignoring Jordan, stopped at the base of the stairs to wait patiently for the treat.

"Did you know pigs are as smart as three-year-old children?" Tammi asked while unwrapping the mints. "Miss Prim is a very smart pig, who knows not to come into the house." She tossed the mints onto the ground, and the pig grabbed them greedily, salivating as she crunched the hard candies. "Poor Miss Prim has been all alone since Miss Proper passed last winter."

"That's so sad," Jordan said. "I'm sorry for your loss."

"Thank you." Tammi sighed. "It couldn't have been prevented, the vet said. An undiagnosed heart condition." Tammi scratched Miss Prim behind the ear, making her curled tail wag. "But I feel most sad for Miss Prim here. I'm going to get her a new friend this summer."

"I'm sure she'll appreciate the company." Miss Prim sniffed and bumped Jordan's shoes. "Can I pet her?"

"I don't see why not."

Jordan followed Tammi's lead and rubbed the top of the pig's head, then scratched behind her ears. Her skin felt plump and soft, though her hair was coarse and bristly. "Do they have full run of the place?"

"No. Just up here around the house. Our horse trainer makes sure she's locked up safely in her pen in the horse barn every night. In fact, he gave me the idea after telling me about growing up with 'yard pigs,' as he called them. They were pets instead of for, you know—" Tammi whispered and looked at Miss Prim like she hoped she wasn't listening. "I don't want to say those words in front of her. Barron didn't initially like the idea of me having pet pigs, but he came around. I'm very persuasive." Tammi chuckled. "In fact, I believe I inspired him to start raising swine for his business." Tammi smiled lovingly at Miss Prim as she wandered back toward the wooded area she'd come from.

"It doesn't bother you? You know, what happens with Barron's pigs?" Jordan found it odd that Tammi could love her pigs as pets yet tolerate her husband raising them for slaughter.

"I try not to think about the way they end up and focus on how they live," Tammi said. "I've never seen them. Barron told me that, if I did, I'd have them all up here on the hill as pets. He's probably right about that." She laughed. "He limits any contact with them, anyway. He's always going on about bio-security and how important it is to organic farming."

"It's got to be better than living out your life inside a barn." Jordan watched the pig disappear into the trees.

"Well, Jordan," Tammi said, shifting their conversation. "You aren't here to talk about pigs. You're here to discuss painting. Please, come in." Tammi led her through a bright two-story foyer, a cathedral in white, illuminated with natural light streaming through large windows. Jordan gazed at the wide staircase curving up to the second floor, a colorful, ornate chandelier suspended from the center of the tall ceiling. "Murano glass is pretty, isn't it? Let's go to the courtyard, shall we?"

Jordan followed Tammi through glass double doors into a bright space with a long, rectangular pool. The concrete pool deck, inlaid with rounded river rock, was landscaped with ferns and potted palms, the tropical ambiance heightened by the cabana bar with teak-framed sectional seating at the far end.

"Wow. I never would have guessed this was inside the house. It feels very tropical."

"I find it inspiring." Tammi waved her arm in the air and rested her hand on a pitcher packed with ice and sliced limes. "I just made caipirinhas. I hope you like them."

"I've never had one."

"Well, then, you're in for a treat. They're a Brazilian version of a margarita. I discovered them when Barron and I went to Rio a few years ago. Very refreshing."

Tammi slipped behind the bar and expertly muddled sliced limes in two old-fashioned glasses, then filled them with ice and a pale-green cocktail mixture poured from a glass carafe.

"Here you go." Tammi handed her a glass. "Cheers."

"Cheers." Jordan tapped her glass lightly against Tammi's and took a sip. It was just the right combination of sweet and tart, with a strong kick of alcohol. "It's very good. Thank you."

"You're welcome." Tammi smiled benevolently, gesturing for Jordan to take a seat in the shaded corner. Tammi sat across from her and crossed her legs, seeming at ease. "How's Professor Grendel?"

"She's fine, I think." Jordan wasn't expecting Tammi to bring up Maddie, but she should have.

Tammi frowned slightly at Jordan's tepid reply. "You two *are* getting on well, I hope? It certainly seemed like it." Tammi sipped her drink, not taking her eyes off Jordan.

"Um." Jordan stumbled over her words. "Yes, we are."

"Forgive me for being so forward, but I must say you make a handsome couple." Tammi's big eyes grew suddenly wider. "Oh! Can I say handsome since you're both women? I don't mean to imply that either of you is mannish." Tammi's upper lip twitched, pulling her lips into a half-grin. "Unless perhaps you like that sort of thing?"

"No offense," Jordan said. "Handsome is an old-fashioned gender-neutral term, isn't it? I understand you meant it as a compliment." She felt the need to explain her awkwardness. "My response wasn't about what you said. It's just—" She sipped her drink. "I wouldn't really describe us as a couple."

"Oh?" Tammi smiled, clearly enjoying being in the know. "Perhaps I misinterpreted what I observed."

Jordan wasn't sure what to say. Maddie occupied her thoughts, carnal ones at that, but they hadn't had the chance to establish the depth of their attraction. "It's maybe too soon to tell if we'll be a couple."

Tammi wagged a finger at her. "Dear, the way you're blushing tells me more than what you're willing to confess in words." She clucked her tongue at her. "You Yankees are so reserved." Putting the palm of her hand to her chest, she spoke with dramatic flair. "Love should be unfettered and unrestrained."

Jordan felt light-headed, a giddiness fortified by holding the lithe professor in her mind's eye. Or perhaps it was the alcohol. She lifted her glass. "What's in this?"

"Sugar, lime, and cachaça." Tammi pointed to the elegantly shaped clear bottle on the bar. "It's distilled from sugar cane. The best comes from Brazil."

"This would be dangerous on a hot day. It seems like the kind of cocktail that's so refreshing you want a second one, and by the time you finish the second, you've lost all reason and have a third, which you realize later was one too many."

"I assure you, the danger is real." Tammi laughed. "And I pray to God that the expression about Rio is true."

"What expression is that?"

"What happens in Rio stays in Rio."

"I thought it was Vegas."

"It is, isn't it?" Tammi pursed her glossy lips coquettishly and rolled her eyes to the ceiling. "I hope it's true for both places."

Tammi was funny, and Jordan hadn't expected to like her so much. Wealthy patrons had always seemed unpleasantly pretentious. Jordan reminded herself that most great art would never have been made without patrons supporting its creation. They couldn't all be bad. Jordan steered the conversation toward art. "I don't expect you've had a chance to look at my work on my website—"

"I looked at it this morning, in fact." Tammi raised an eyebrow with an expression of touché.

"I hope you liked what you saw."

"Of course I did. Otherwise, I wouldn't have invited you over," Tammi said archly. "Your work is beautiful, Jordan. Such meticulous detail and lovely colors. I enjoyed reading the little essays that explained what I was looking at." She smiled. "I think I learned some things."

"That's the best compliment I could ever expect."

"Really?" Tammi lifted her eyebrows. "Wouldn't you rather hear that I hope to acquire three paintings from you?"

"Of course, that's very good, too." Jordan laughed. "Which ones?"

"Not from your website. I want to commission you for three paintings of Cahaba lilies. Based on what I've seen of your work, I have no doubt they would be a lovely addition to my collection. Have you seen them in person yet?"

"I have, this morning, actually."

"How wonderful. And what did you think?"

"They're more beautiful than I expected. I'd like to spend as much time with them as I can." Caught up in conversation and flattered by Tammi's attention, Jordan had nearly forgotten why she was here. "While I was there, I was thinking about how nice it would be to have private access and maybe even the amenities of the cabin. I'll be drawing and painting at the river, in the river, really, the whole day, and, well, the refuge doesn't have any facilities."

"I understand you," Tammi said with a look conveying sympathy. "We girls prefer our indoor plumbing, don't we? I'm so thankful Barron gave up years ago trying to get me to go on his hunting trips with him. Even glamping is still camping."

"Being able to use a cabin on the river would be really nice. Is it close to Hargrove Shoals?"

"It is, in fact. There's a trail to the river to a pretty overlook. When I was a child, my family used to go out there for picnics. It's the view in the painting I showed you last night."

"Really? That would be a great place to work."

Tammi beamed. "Well, then, it sounds like you're interested in helping me decorate a room. Say, would you like to see where your paintings will hang?"

"Sure."

"Let's freshen our drinks first." Tammi topped off both their glasses and took her to the second floor, showing off each of the themed rooms along the way. They weren't all to her taste, but the quality of the furniture and furnishings was impressive. It was like a virtual-reality trip through an issue of *Architectural Digest*. After Key West, the Emerald Coast, Cape Cod, and the Rocky Mountains, Jordan had lost her bearings in the rambling house.

"This is one of Barron's favorites." Tammi spoke with pride as she opened the door. "The South Africa Room."

Jordan gasped. The room full of zebra-striped fabrics, wall coverings emulating the look of thatch, and, horrifically, the head and long neck of a giraffe mounted over the bed visually assaulted her. *Who the fuck shoots a giraffe and then puts the poor creature's stuffed head over a bed, for God's sake?* Heat rose in Jordan's cheeks. Taxidermy, even in a natural history collection, unnerved her, but the garish display of dead animals as decor seemed borderline psychopathic.

Tammi seemed to mistake Jordan's reaction as being positive. "Beautiful, isn't it? God's creatures are such a sight to behold, I must say. Barron says the safari fees and the money the hunters spend there in the local communities support conservation efforts in those poor, poor countries. Without the hunters, he says, the big-game animals would be extinct."

Jordan wasn't sure she was hearing Tammi correctly. How incredibly naive to believe that the ruthless killing of animals, many of whom were probably raised and released just to be shot like fish in a barrel, was somehow good for them. But it didn't seem like Tammi was blowing smoke up her ass. She seemed to be earnestly repeating what Barron had told her, and she believed him. Tammi looked at the dead giraffe as just another pretty object.

Tammi seemed indifferent to Jordan's lack of response. "Would you like to see the other safari rooms? Zimbabwe and Namibia are just down the hall."

"That's okay. I think I have the idea." Jordan tried to keep the tone of her voice light. Blood pounding in her ears, she questioned whether she could create work for people who violated her personal ethics. Her art would be just another trophy tacked to the walls. Selling art was good, but maybe it wasn't worth it to sell a piece of her soul in the process.

Jordan stiffened as a rush of cold air swept past her. Leda was nearby. As Jordan looked around the room for any trace of the spirit, a rattling sound pulled her attention to the taxidermized head of the giraffe, which suddenly tilted sideways. The lone screw supporting it held for a moment before giving way. Scraping against the wall as it fell onto the bed, it bounced and landed heads up with a thump on the zebra-striped duvet.

Tammi, who had been pointing out the handprinted curtains made by a women's cooperative in a rural South African village, spun around to face the glass-eyed giraffe staring at her from the middle of the bed. "Lord in the morning!"

Tendrils of cold air brushed Jordan's cheek like icy fingers, and a breathy snicker emanated from the air, confirming Leda's presence. Jordan put her hand to her mouth and coughed to cover up Leda's laughter.

"What did you say?" Tammi asked.

Jordan pointed to the holes in the wall. "Gosh. The weight of the taxidermy must have pulled the wall anchors out."

"We've never had anything like this happen. I'll have to have my man look at that." Tammi quickly regained her composure. "Let's move on and look at the guest room that could become the Cahaba Lily Room, shall we?" Jordan followed her down the long hall to an unfurnished room with white walls, its lack of decor an aesthetic relief. Standing in the middle of the empty room, Tammi swept an arm in the air. "This is my blank canvas."

"You've designed the rooms yourself? I assumed you were working with a professional."

"I appreciate that compliment. I studied interior design at the University of Alabama, but I can't call myself a professional."

"Why not?"

"That's a little complicated to answer." Tammi sipped her drink. "Barron and I started dating in my sophomore year, and I let him sweet-talk me into marrying him right after he graduated. That was the summer before my junior year, and in less than a year, I was pregnant with our son." Tammi sighed. "Being a college student and a young wife *and* a mother slowed me down. I was still in school when Barron started his first business, and we moved to Huntsville before I could finish school."

"I'm sorry," Jordan said, feeling sympathy for her. It was a sadly typical story for so many women; she'd put aside her aspirations for those of her husband. Although outwardly Tammi seemed perfectly happy, the effusive creative effort she put toward the decoration of her house made it seem as if she was compensating for the professional life she wished she could have had.

"Don't you feel sorry for me." Tammi tapped her on the shoulder, reprimanding her lightly. "Even if I didn't finish with a degree, I got a good education."

"I certainly see evidence of that here." Jordan waved her hand to indicate the whole house. While this room wasn't to her taste, she'd seen enough of the house to know that the interior design was well done. Jordan tried to give her an honest compliment without being too specific. "Your sense of design and attention to detail are impressive."

"Thank you, Jordan." Tammi's smile seemed genuine. "That means a lot."

"What will you do when all the rooms are decorated?"

Tammi put her hand to her chest in evident surprise. "Why, no one's ever asked me that." She grinned, wide-eyed, as if an idea had just popped into her head. "I suppose I could buy another house."

Jordan laughed with her and glanced out the window as the movement of a red-tailed hawk flying over the manicured pasture caught her eye. It flapped its wings and then held them in place, coasting toward the trees. "You certainly have plenty of space here. You could add more rooms. Have you heard of the Winchester Mystery House?"

"I've been there."

"Really?"

"Yes. When I was ten or eleven, we went on a family vacation to San Francisco. Have you visited it, too?"

"No, but I saw a movie about it." Originally a farmhouse, the reclusive wealthy owner, an heir to the Winchester firearms company, compulsively renovated and expanded it into an eccentric and sprawling Victorian mansion. "Is it as impressive as it seems?"

"Very much so. Of course, I was just a child, but the quality craftsmanship sticks out in my memory. I was especially fascinated by a flight of polished wood stairs that ran right into the ceiling, seeming to go nowhere. It was the strangest thing."

"It was supposedly built to appease the ghosts of soldiers killed by Winchester rifles. Did you see any when you were there?"

"Ghosts or rifles?"

"Ghosts," Jordan said. "I'd expect they'd have a few rifles on display, considering where the money to build the house came from."

"Rifles, yes. But no ghosts," Tammi said. "The tour guide did tell us spooky stories about visitors bumping into a man repairing a wall and thinking he was a costumed interpreter, or feeling hands tugging on their clothing. Those tall tales gave me nightmares for months. I haven't thought about them in a long time." Tammi put her fingertips to her chin, seeming lost in thought. "You know, we also visited Hearst Castle on that same trip, and each of the rooms there was designed to reflect a different historical era. I never thought about it before now, Jordan—did my love of interior design come from that vacation?"

"Maybe so. I think our childhood experiences influence us more than we realize."

"Do you? What impacted you the most when you were young?"

"Books."

"What kind of books?"

"Pirate stories and illustrated nature books both fueled my make-believe adventures in the woods behind our house. My brothers and I would play hide-and-seek, and I used to pretend I was a pirate running from the British Navy." Jordan fondly recalled the memories. "I was quite good at evading capture."

Tammi gave her an appraising look. "You're an adventurous romantic at heart."

"I've never thought of myself like that." Jordan grinned. "I kind of like the sound of it."

"I bet Maddie would, too." Tammi winked and finished her drink.

Jordan hoped so. She swirled the ice around in her glass, took the last swig, and glanced at her watch. What was Maddie doing right now?

"I'm sure you have things to do," Tammi said. "Let's go to my office, and I'll get you directions to the cabin and the codes to the gate and door locks."

Tammi's tidy office looked like a location for a Martha Stewart photo shoot. Everything—bookshelves, furniture, printer, computer—was a perfectly matched shade of white except for a large vase of fresh-cut flowers on a table, their colorful blooms vibrant against the neutral backdrop.

Tammi printed out directions with the security codes and handed them to her.

"Thank you so much," she said. "Are you sure this is okay with Barron?"

"You're very welcome, and don't you worry about Barron." Tammi laughed. "He's halfway to agreeing to it. He just doesn't know it yet. I look forward to seeing what you create." Tammi walked her to the front door. "I expect you'll let me know when you have something for me to look at?"

Jordan nodded. "I'll show you sketches, and then we can talk about what form the finished work will take."

"How long will it take to finish the paintings?"

"It depends on the medium and size. You can get a sense of my prices from the website, but we can talk specific numbers after I have a better sense of what you want." Based on what she'd seen here, Jordan didn't think price would be much of an issue.

"Fair enough." Tammi stopped by a table in the foyer and gestured to a silver bowl full of wrapped candies. "Care for a mint?"

"Thanks," she said, plucking one from the bowl. "For this—" she held up the mint. "And for the access and opportunity. I do really appreciate it."

"You are most welcome." Tammi affected a magnanimous gesture by putting her hand to her chest and tucking her chin.

Unwrapping the mint as she walked down the steps, she popped it into her mouth and remembered Miss Prim, the yard pig, who'd been here at the base of the steps just an hour earlier. She turned to give Tammi a quick wave and breathed a sigh of relief as she got into the 4Runner. She'd left the house without another reappearance of the mischievous spirit. Sucking on the mint as she drove down the hill, she watched the house recede in the rearview mirror. When she tapped the brakes as she rounded the last curve near the base of the hill near the gate, a late-model red pickup came into view. It was big and shiny, with rugged off-road tires. As their vehicles passed, Jordan glanced over her shoulder to see Barron behind the wheel of the truck, clearly surprised.

## CHAPTER TWELVE

Shaded from the intense New Orleans sun by palms and sweet-olive trees, Maddie sat at a table in the tranquil brick courtyard of the All Saints Café and Bakery, one of her favorites in the French Quarter. Instead of sipping her café au lait and enjoying the rich flavor of the coffee-chicory blend, she stared at her cell phone, tapping anxiously on the marble tabletop while waiting for her sister, Caroline, to return from the inside counter with their beignets. She flipped the phone over. No new messages.

"How many times are you going to do that?" Caroline approached the table carrying a mug in one hand and, in the other, a plate of pillowy squares of fried dough, golden brown and dusted heavily with confectioner's sugar. Caroline now looked so much like pictures of their mother in her younger years. The dappled sunlight caught the highlights in her auburn hair, and like their pretty, round-faced mother, she'd become rather plump as she matured. Maddie, on the other hand, had inherited her father's black hair and lanky physique. She and her sister were so different, physically and in personality, it was hard to believe they'd grown up in the same household. Maddie, unlike Caroline, valued the life of the mind more than the material, which didn't mean she didn't enjoy comfort and like nice things. She just didn't need so much of it or want to show it off so flagrantly. Only a year apart, they had grown up together, alternating between behaving like the best of friends and being each other's worst enemy. Caroline poked and irritated her in the way only a sibling could, but deep down her sister cared about her, and sometimes she even showed it.

"What?" Maddie tried to sound like she didn't know what her

sister was asking as she reached for a beignet before the plate touched the table. Caroline swatted her hand away.

"Have you forgotten our rules? Whoever waits for the order gets the pick of the litter." Caroline plucked a beignet from the plate, tearing off a piece to pop into her mouth.

Maddie slowly chewed her first bite with her eyes closed and moaned softly. "These are so good. I'm glad I don't live here anymore so I'm not tempted to eat them every day." She opened her eyes to see her sister scowling at her. She pointed at her face. "You have sugar on your cheek."

Caroline brushed her skin with her fingertips. "You didn't answer my question." Caroline glanced at Maddie's phone. "What are you waiting for?" Her mouth fell open as her eyes widened. "Are you online-dating again?"

"No," Maddie said truthfully.

"That's an incomplete answer." Caroline narrowed her eyes, scrutinizing Maddie. A trial lawyer, she was very good at reading people. "Why are you checking your phone so often? It's unlike you. You usually rant about everyone being so hung up on their phones, distracted all the time, not paying attention. Yada yada."

"I'm expecting a message."

"Uh-huh." Caroline's lips lifted into a lop-sided grin. "What's her name, and is she cute?"

"She's very cute, and her name is Jordan." Maddie couldn't help but smile.

"Tell me more, the whole story. Don't leave out any details."

She explained how she'd met the visiting artist when she arrived for a one-month residency and been attracted to her immediately but was reluctant to act. Caroline chided her for worrying about taking advantage of her position as director of the residency and expressed concern that Jordan was visiting for only a short time. She pelted her with questions when she thought Maddie was leaving out details and squeaked when Maddie told her that the evening at the gala had concluded with a kiss.

"That's so romantic," Caroline gushed. She cut the last beignet with a knife, took one half, and pushed the plate toward Maddie. "This all sounds promising. Why are you so anxious?"

"Jordan said she was going to the river to see the lilies' first bloom, and she'd let me know when she was back. That was yesterday, and I haven't heard from her."

"Would a resident normally contact you about their day-to-day business?"

"No. I usually just get an occasional question about where to shop or complaints about the air-conditioning."

"You're worried." Caroline pursed her lips. "That's sweet."

"Partly worried." She half shrugged. "The other part, the bigger part, just really wanted to talk with her."

"I know what part of you was talking." Caroline chortled, and Maddie gave her a timid smile. "This Jordan must be something special. I don't think I've ever seen you so mushy after a first date."

"The gala wasn't really a date," Maddie said.

"Didn't you tell me that everyone at the gala kept assuming you two were a couple?"

"Well, yes, but—"

"That means they saw something between you. Hell, she's not even here, and I can see it. And it ended with a kiss—a scorcher, it sounds like. I'd call that a date even if it didn't start out as one."

"She asked me out on a real date—a dinner date—when I get back. I'll count that as the first date." Maddie lifted her cup to her lips.

"You should count it as your second one," Caroline said.

"Why?"

"So you won't violate your dumb dating rule."

She inhaled her coffee and coughed. No sex on the first date was her first rule of dating. She dabbed the café au lait dribbling down her chin with a napkin while her sister laughed at her. "I still think my rule is a good one," she said defensively. "The warning flags aren't always obvious. It's harder to extricate yourself after you've had sex."

"I never had that problem."

"Yeah, I know," Maddie said sarcastically.

"You want to know your problem, Maddie?"

"I'm sure you'll tell me."

"You always look for an exit before you even step through the door."

"I do not."

"Do, too," Caroline shot back. "When was the last time you went on a date?"

"About three months ago."

"That recently?" Caroline raised her eyebrows. "You didn't tell me about it."

"Sophie and Rob were both sick, and you were exhausted."

Caroline made a face. "God, don't remind me. Having my husband and kid sick at the same time was awful. I damn near bleached the whole house before they got well, and I'm still amazed I didn't come down with whatever they had."

"That's why I didn't bother you with the minor details of my life."

"That date didn't go well, I guess?"

"Nope."

"Since what's-her-name, the professor in Minnesota, you haven't had any second dates, have you?"

"Her name is Vanessa, and she lives in Wisconsin." She rolled her eyes at Caroline's feigned poor memory; she was baiting her. Movement in the tree canopy above their table caught her attention. A flock of green quaker parrots landed, the social little birds beginning to chatter as soon as their feet gripped the branches. They were so pretty. Did Jordan know about them? Caroline cleared her throat to recapture Maddie's attention. "Since Vanessa, I've had a long string of first dates," Maddie said.

"Aside from self-sabotage, what keeps you from a second one?"

"I'm not sabotaging myself."

"Are, too."

"Am not," she countered. "I've had good reasons. One woman was intensely allergic to dogs, and I refuse to be with someone who can't be around Chip. That's non-negotiable. I had a coffee date with another woman that extended into dinner, and she got shit-faced drunk. The bartender at the restaurant knew her and told me it happened regularly." She sighed. "Mostly, I just haven't felt a spark with anyone."

"That's kind of vague. What do you mean?" Caroline gestured, asking for more. "You're an English prof. Use your words."

"For the most part, the women I met were nice, but nothing more. Pleasant, agreeable, affable, amiable, likable. Do I need to find more words to describe them?"

"I think I've got the point. Nice, but"—Caroline lowered her voice— "no one you wanted to fuck."

"Caroline!" Maddie glanced around, but no one seated at the nearby tables seemed to be paying them any attention.

"Don't be such a prude. Spark is code for hot, as in sexy, right? Clearly Jordan's got you worked up." Caroline studied her. "What's so special about her?"

"She's very attractive." She paused to consider how to describe her in a way Caroline would understand. "She's an outdoorsy type."

"Granola lesbian?" Caroline made a sour face.

"No. More like L.L.Bean."

"That's better. And?"

"She loves nature passionately. She likes research and learning about the animals and plants she paints, but she's not arrogant."

"Not self-centered. That's good. What else?"

"She seems confident and compassionate. Genuine."

"Well, damn, Maddie! She's got the magic number three—body, brains, and heart. You better set a wedding date." Caroline smacked the table with her palm. "Oh, wait. You need to go on a date first."

"Your sarcasm is not helpful, Caroline."

"It rarely is, but it makes you laugh."

"Sometimes."

"Does *she* make you laugh?"

"Yeah, she does. Oh, there's one other thing."

"What's that?"

"Jenn and Elana really like her, and I overheard Jenn tell her that I'm single."

"Oh my God. She's already met your friends and gotten their approval? And you haven't gone on a date? You're supposed to have some dates and *then* introduce her to your friends."

"I wanted her to meet Jenn, since she's a biologist." Maddie stopped. She knew she was making halfhearted excuses. "I haven't felt like this about a woman in a long time." She sighed and flipped her phone over again, the screen still devoid of new messages. "Not hearing from her is bothering me."

Caroline nodded. "That's just a little obvious."

"Jordan seems to be the kind of person who, if she says she's going to call, will follow through," Maddie said. "If I misjudged her on that quality, what else might I have miscalculated?"

"Jesus, Maddie. Do you hear yourself? You're looking for the exit again."

She winced. "Am not."

"Are, too. For the love of God, give the woman a chance. It sounds like she's interested in you." Caroline took her hand. "Look. I know you think I'm being a bitch—"

"I don't think that."

"Yes, you do. And don't argue with me. You've always thought it. You're the polite, nice sister, and I'm the loud bitch. It's just the way it is. I'm fine with it. It's a good personality trait for an attorney. It's why I'm so damn successful." Caroline laughed, her expression and tone softening as the other version of her, the one who cared about her and displayed her affection, emerged. "Looking at your phone every five minutes won't help make you feel any better. Let's clear the table and get going. Picking up Sophie's birthday cake and the deli trays will keep you preoccupied with something other than the hot artist." She smiled. "And we have to stop by the liquor store, the big one you like. The adults will need something to drink besides pink punch."

Acme Liquor was huge, the size of a grocery store, with entire aisles dedicated to specific types of alcohol and the broadest selection Maddie had seen anywhere. She had become used to living in a state with regressive laws about how and where alcohol could be sold. She surveyed Caroline's cart, surprised at the number of bottles of wine, whiskey, vodka, gin, and mixers. "Exactly how many people are coming to this birthday party?"

"Not that many." Caroline began counting on her fingers. "Mom, Dad, Aunt Charlette, Uncle Joe, two of our neighbors with kids Sophie's age, five of Sophie's friends from school and their parents."

"That's twenty adults and half as many kids." Maddie eyed the cart. "Why so much booze?"

"You've been away from New Orleans for too long." Caroline frowned playfully. "Truth be told, we haven't restocked the bar since Mardi Gras."

Maddie almost jumped when her phone buzzed. She pulled it from her pocket, swiping to answer as soon as she saw Jordan's name. "Hey, you."

"Maddie." Jordan said her name breathlessly. "Did you get my email message?"

"Email? I haven't been checking it since I got here. Did I misunderstand? I thought you were going to text me."

"I was, but I dropped my phone in the river yesterday."

"Oh, no."

"I said something much less polite than that." Jordan laughed. "I was standing on a rock mid-river taking a panorama shot, when I slipped and let go of it. I thought it was gone for good. Luckily, I got it back."

"How?" Maddie asked, but Jordan didn't reply. "Jordan? You there?"

"Yes. I'm here."

"You were telling me about your phone. What happened?"

"I lost it in a deep channel, and it disappeared so fast." Another long pause. "I guess the current took it downstream. A woman found it and brought it to me."

"She probably heard you swearing."

Jordan laughed. "I definitely wasn't quiet. Anyway, when she returned it, I had to turn it off immediately and let it dry out overnight. That's why I tried emailing you. All my contacts are on my phone. I felt bad that I couldn't text you. Other than 9-1-1, I don't have any phone numbers memorized. I knew I could at least email you and hope you'd get the message. I guess you didn't."

"It's okay. You tried. I'm really glad to hear from you now." Maddie had been staring at the floor while they talked and looked up to see her sister smiling, her expression seeming to say, *See? I told you she'd call.* "I know you're an experienced outdoorswoman, but I confess, I was a little worried when I didn't hear from you yesterday."

Caroline silently mouthed, *A little?* Maddie gestured at her sister to keep shopping and walked away from her toward the back of the store.

"I'm sorry I worried you." Jordan's tone grew tender. "If my phone had been working, I probably would have called instead of texting so I could hear your voice."

Jordan emboldened her. "I can't stop thinking about you," she said, then winced, realizing the words might not have come out how she intended. "I don't mean that in a creepy, stalker way."

"I didn't take it that way." Jordan laughed. "I understand. I've been feeling the same. You haven't been far from my thoughts since you dropped me off at Palmer House after the gala."

Maddie smiled, picturing Jordan illuminated by lightning flashes, her rain-drenched hair plastered against her face, her eyes peering out from under her bangs, seeming to burn with desire. "I keep thinking about you in the rain," she whispered. "I can't get it out of my mind."

"Just me getting soaked in a wicked thunderstorm?" Jordan teased her. "Nothing else?"

"And that kiss." Staring at the floor as she walked and talked, she bumped into an end cap of stacked bottles of Herbsaint, a local herbal liqueur. Putting her hand out to steady a bottle, she felt destabilized by Jordan's velvet tone.

"Mmm…that kiss. There's another for you when you get back here," Jordan said brazenly. "And I'm still soaked."

Her heart skipped a beat as desire pulsed deep inside her; and she shivered as goose bumps formed on her skin in the cold, air-conditioned building. "Me, too," she said in the hushed tone of a confession. Feeling self-conscious, she took a deep breath, blowing it out slowly, and glanced sideways down the aisle. Caroline stood at the far end, waving, gesturing to the check-out registers. Maddie lifted a finger and nodded, signaling she'd gotten the message but needed a little more time. "More kisses?" she asked quietly. "I'll hold you to that."

"I'd rather you hold me to *you.*"

If Jordan had been standing in front of her right now, Maddie was certain she would break her first-date rule. "Oh."

The store's intercom interrupted the intimacy of their conversation, a clipped voice announcing that customer service was needed in aisle three.

"Where are you?" Jordan asked.

"At the liquor store with my sister."

"At ten in the morning?"

"It *is* New Orleans," Maddie said with a laugh. "We're shopping for the birthday party tonight."

"You're buying liquor for an eight-year-old's birthday party?" Jordan seemed to be teasing her. "New Orleans is wilder than I thought."

"The liquor is for the adults. The kids get only punch. No worries."

"Has anyone told you that you sound like a sexy female Harry Connick, Jr.?"

Maddie freed her Yat accent. "Now I can't speak for all the tourists who come here to party. But, as for us natives, we may be libertines, but we're not debauched."

"I don't mind a little debauchery, especially if you keep talking to me like that."

She laughed. "I'd love to keep talking with you any way you want, but I have to let you go soon. My sister's almost done here, and we have more shopping scheduled. Tell me about the river. Did you see the lilies?"

"I did. They're beautiful! And they smell good, too. Did you know that?"

"No. I had no idea."

"Their scent is faint, but sweet. I thought it was honeysuckle along the banks. I've been so focused on seeing the lilies, I didn't think about smelling them, too." Jordan spoke quickly in her excitement. "I can't wait to start drawing and painting them when the weather's better. Tomorrow, I hope. We're expecting thunderstorms later in the week. I talked with Tammi yesterday about using their cabin."

"I thought you weren't sure Barron would allow it."

"Tammi says Barron will approve."

"She gave you permission, but he didn't? I thought you said you wanted to steer clear of any marital drama."

"I do, but she convinced me he'll say yes. It seems he never says no to her. And, you know, she's not so bad. The more we talked, the more I realized she's just a stifled housewife, a really wealthy and privileged one, but I felt a little sorry for her. Anyway, there's really nothing at the refuge, and having access to a shelter would be helpful, especially if the weather turns dicey."

Maddie had been out to the refuge many times and understood why Jordan would want the amenities of a cabin nearby, and a cabin owned by the Palmer-Maxfields was probably nicer than average. "Are you going to spend the night, too?"

"I was hoping to see what's out here after sunset. The world is always different after dark, almost magical."

"You're braver than me."

"You wouldn't do it?"

"Not by myself, I wouldn't."

"I won't be—"

"You won't be alone? Will Tammi be there?"

"No. I don't think so." Jordan sounded unsure.

Jordan's awkward response was curious. Before Maddie could ask another question, a smiling store employee, a fey young man with slicked-back hair and a trendy, pencil-thin mustache, strode toward her. "How can I help you?"

"I don't need any help, thanks."

"The woman at checkout said you needed assistance," the young man said, appearing confused. He pointed to the display of the two kinds of Herbsaint. "You need help deciding on which one you need?"

"No. I know the original is the best for a Sazarac." Maddie smiled, pointing to the old-fashioned-looking bottle printed in red and black. "My sister must have called you. She's trying to get my attention and hurry me up. I'm really sorry she bothered you."

Seemingly unperturbed, he waved as if swatting a mosquito. "No problem. If you do need anything, just let me know."

"I will. Thanks." She turned to face the front of the store. Her sister was near the doors, leaning on the handle of the cart, tapping a message on her cell phone.

"I'll let you go," Jordan said. "I feel like I'm interfering with family time."

"No, you're not, but I do need to get back to Caroline and our shopping."

"I understand. Enjoy the party?"

"I will. I hope you enjoy the lilies and painting."

"I plan on it. Thanks."

"Hey." She knew she needed to say good-bye, but she resisted saying the words. "Be careful out there."

"Always. I'll keep you posted."

"Unless you lose your phone in the river again," she said, teasing.

"Never again. I'll remember to put it in its waterproof case next time. You be careful, too. I'm pretty sure a preteen party is way more dangerous than anything I'll encounter."

"Hm." Maddie pretended to weigh the options. "Water moccasins and fire ants versus girls in pink, glitter, and unicorns? You might be right."

Their laughter harmonized as they ended the call. She didn't immediately move the phone away from her ear, as if that would keep Jordan close just a little longer. Smiling to herself, she eyed a bottle of Herbsaint Original on the shelf, wondering if Jordan had ever had a New Orleans Sazerac cocktail. Feeling buoyant and hopeful, she slid the phone back into the pocket of her jeans and grabbed the bottle from the shelf, fantasizing about offering Jordan a special nightcap Friday night. But first, she had to get through her niece's birthday party.

## CHAPTER THIRTEEN

Jordan stood, rolling her shoulders to stretch her tight muscles. She'd been sitting on a dry rock in the middle of the river for hours. When she'd arrived, the water's edge had been at least twelve inches away from her feet, but now it was almost lapping at her toes. As the sun was dropping, the river seemed to be rising. Concentrating on accurately mixing pigments in her pan of watercolors to match those in the landscape around her, she'd been oblivious to the creeping river's edge.

She glanced at the colorful grid of hues on the sheet of heavy paper in her hands. It would be a useful reference when she returned to work in the studio, which would likely be tomorrow, given the slow-moving storm expected to bring severe thunderstorms during the night.

Billowing white clouds peeked above the treetops to the northwest, but the sky overhead was still clear. The last time she'd checked the forecast was while eating breakfast before leaving Palmer House. She had no service near the river and just one bar at the cabin, enough for text messages but no pictures. She used the cabin during the day for convenience and returned to Palmer House every evening so she could catch up with Maddie's messages illustrated with photos, pictures of ridiculous birthday party favors and shots of her sister's baroque house decor.

Jordan hoped the bad weather would hold off long enough for her to meet Leda after sunset. Tonight was the full moon, and Leda had promised to show her something special after dark. She hadn't seen the spirit since she'd retrieved her phone from the river, but Jordan had been finding "gifts" from Leda—a small arrowhead on a tree stump along the path from the cabin to the river, a heart-shaped purple-red rock, and some twigs arranged in the shape of an arrow pointing up the side of the trunk of a tree. Looking up, she spotted a nesting black-capped chickadee peering from the edge of a cavity. It carried bits of dry grass in its beak and disappeared into the hole.

She glanced at her watch. She had several hours before sunset, and she'd been so productive over the last two days, she could afford a break from sketching. Returning to the cabin, she realized how good it felt to be upright and moving.

She dropped off her art materials in the 4Runner, refilled her water bottle from an outside spigot, and grabbed a snack from her pack. Following a trail leading into the woods away from the river, she munched on a granola bar and enjoyed a refreshing breeze. The path was well worn, wide enough for an ATV. Given Barron's proclivity for hunting, she wasn't surprised that, after a half-hour walk, she entered a deer plot, a half acre planted with corn and cowpeas intended to fatten deer during the summer for a hunter's bullet to take them down in the fall.

She studied the deep-green vegetation, looking for meandering lines indicating where deer had crossed the plot. Finding one, she followed it. It was a game she played with herself while hiking alone, following an animal trace, trying to think like the deer or coyote who frequented the path. Where did the trail lead? What tasty foods might be found along it? Where was the best spot to scratch one's rump or antlers on the rough bark of a tree? The ground here was soft enough that she could see the indentations of small, sharply pointed hooves, young deer. Poor babies. It wouldn't be long before they'd be in a hunter's sights. Hopefully they were wary and smart.

When she was midway across the plot, the breeze shifted, bringing a sound that made her cringe. She turned her head to the side, cupping a hand to her ear to catch the elusive metallic screech, coarse and high-pitched. It was followed by the sound of a distressed animal that seemed angry or in pain. The hairs on her arms rose, and a shiver crept up her back. What could possibly make such a sound? When the answer struck, she sucked in a quick breath. A hog! More than one, it sounded like... *Shit.* It was probably Barron's free-ranging ones. He hadn't wanted her out here because of them. Maybe this wasn't a deer plot, after all. It could be green fodder for Barron's hogs on which wild deer had been grazing.

Sure, pigs were cute, like Tammi's yard pig, but that was when they were pets. How friendly were free-range hogs who probably didn't have regular contact with people? If they were anything like their feral cousins, they were voracious, rooting around for tasty things, using their stout muscles to plow the earth with their flat snouts and sharp tusks. Ravenous creatures, pigs would eat *anything*. It was part of what made them so desirable as livestock.

They were easy keepers, as farmers liked to say. Not knowing if she'd be perceived from a porcine perspective as friend, foe, or food, she retreated to the cabin at a quick pace.

Nearing it, she spotted something bright red through the foliage. As she slowed, she saw a big pickup truck. First alarmed by unknown hogs, she now felt a different kind of vulnerability, that of a woman alone. She was rarely afraid of the woods, but the eerie sound had spooked her, reminding her that she was an interloper here.

Distrusting the unknown intentions of a possible redneck visitor, she stepped off the trail, changing the direction of her approach to the cabin, and walked as quietly as she could manage through the undergrowth. She'd learned the skill from years of watching wildlife while trying not to spook the creatures she was observing. The truck, tricked out with tinted windows, oversize off-road tires, and light bars, was parked next to her 4Runner. It was the truck she'd passed when leaving the Palmer-Maxfield estate, and Barron had been behind the wheel.

Approaching the cabin from the side, she saw a man-shaped silhouette on the porch. She paused behind a big pine, watching quietly. Barron was leaning on the porch rail, facing the path leading to the river with his back to her, smoking a cigarette. The pines began to whisper and creak in the stiffening breeze. Standing downwind, she detected an intermingled scent of tobacco and cologne. She lifted her nose like a deer, collecting the odors, and sorted them out. He turned to crush the cigarette on the underside of the railing.

She relaxed slightly, but the adrenaline still buzzed through her. The last time she'd seen him, he was unknowingly about to encounter his wife on a mission to get him to say yes to something he'd already said no to. She assumed Tammi had talked to him, and he'd agreed as she said he always did. But what if she hadn't? Or what if he hadn't agreed, yet Tammi didn't tell her? Clearly, he knew she was out here.

Maybe he'd come to tell her to leave. He'd parked next to her car and was standing there on the porch, gazing into the woods toward the river, appearing to be waiting for her. She was about to find out why he was there.

Maintaining her stealthy approach, she edged up alongside the cabin, emerging quickly alongside the porch. Barron was dressed like a genteel farmer, clad in unsoiled Carhartt dungarees. "Hey, Barron!" she called out cheerfully. He flinched and turned, clearly startled. "I'm sorry. Did I scare you?"

"No. Of course not." He smiled. "I just didn't expect you to come from there." He pointed his thumb over his shoulder in the direction of the river. "I thought you'd be down by the river."

"I was." Jordan walked toward the porch steps.

Barron cocked his head like a dog not understanding what was being said. The tap-tap-tap of a woodpecker drilling into a tree made them both look up. He glanced at the sky beyond the trees. "Beautiful day today."

"Sure has been," she said.

"I hope you've gotten what you need from out here. The weather's about to turn, you know."

"Yeah. The forecast's not looking good. Fortunately, I've done a lot of work in the past few days."

"My wife will be glad to hear that. She's been talking nonstop about your paintings that she expects will decorate her new room. She's already calling it the Cahaba Suite."

"I'm honored she thinks I'll have paintings she wants." Jordan put one foot on the bottom step and hooked her thumb on the strap of her pack. "The cabin's really made working out here easy. I can't thank you enough for your generosity."

"I didn't have anything to do with it. You can thank my wife." With a lackluster smile he nodded and pointed to the path to the river. "I thought you'd be coming up from that way."

"I did and then decided to take a hike. I've been sitting all day drawing."

"You should be careful out here all alone." He spoke slowly, as if to a child. "It's not safe."

"From what?" Truthfully, she felt safer in the woods than on a city street. "You mean from your free-range hogs? I think I might have heard them."

"Did you?" Barron frowned, his expression clouded. "Could be them." He stroked two fingers along the side of his chin as if processing a thought. "Or it could be feral hogs. They're out there in the deep woods, and they get big, like two hundred and fifty pounds. It's spring, and a mean mama protecting her babies," Barron whistled, "is not something I'd want to contend with, especially at night when they're active foraging. They have big appetites and will eat about anything." He paused, looking her up and down, seeming to enjoy her discomfort. "Including a skinny little thing like you." A cold shiver ran up her spine. Barron chuckled. "Are you leaving soon?"

"I was planning on staying to watch the sunset. It'll be the last clear sky for a while if the forecast holds." It was a half-truth. Jordan didn't explain that she intended to stay well past sunset to nightfall.

"Well, enjoy it, but don't get caught out here after dark," he said. "Like I said, you wouldn't want to run into those feral hogs at night."

"Thanks for the warning." She recalled the bone-chilling squeals she'd heard over the hill in the deep woods. "What brought you out here?"

"Just checking fences. As good an excuse as any to escape from the office, get some fresh air, and enjoy God's creation." He lifted his palms to the sky and smiled, flashing his white teeth. "Since I was in the neighborhood, so to speak, I thought I'd come check on you." He walked down the steps, pausing to clap her on the shoulder. "I'll let Tammi know you're all right." He pointed his index finger at her as he passed. "If you want to stay that way, keep out of the deep woods."

"I hear you," she said as he walked to his truck. "Tell Tammi I said hello and thanks."

He gave her a thumbs-up over his shoulder as he climbed into the big truck. After he drove away, the tires of the truck spewing gravel as it accelerated down the drive, an unsettling feeling gnawed in her gut. Something seemed off. But what? Barron checking on his property seemed logical, but didn't he have hired hands to do that sort of work? She climbed the steps, sat in one of the rocking chairs, and sipped water from her bottle. From what she'd seen in his house, he was an avid hunter, and he probably enjoyed scouting his hunting grounds in the off-season. Still, she couldn't shake the feeling that he'd come out to spy on her, and the concern he expressed for her well-being felt more like a threat.

Her phone dinged in her pack, the sound of an incoming text message. Pulling it out, she saw it was from Maddie.

*Ever have a Ramos Gin Fizz?* Maddie asked.

*Nope. What is it?*

*Frothy, sweet, and tart. Very cold. Heavy pour of gin. :)*

*Sounds good! Want to talk?*

*Sure!*

*Give me ten minutes, and I'll call.*

She rushed to the 4Runner, tossed her pack onto the passenger's seat, and drove to the main road, where she turned toward Oberon, pulling over at an entrance to a timber-access road on the crest of the next hill. Checking her phone, she saw enough signal bars for a phone conversation that wouldn't drop.

"Hey, you," Maddie said cheerfully when she answered. "Where are you? I thought you were at the river today."

"I am."

"How are you making this call?"

"I drove to the main road. I'm at the hilltop intersection of a remote country road and clear-cut forest, not the most picturesque spot around here. How are you?"

"I'm spinning." Maddie laughed.

"How many of those delicious-sounding cocktails have you had?"

"Just a few sips of the first one. I'm serious about spinning, though. My parents brought us to the Carousel Bar at the Hotel Monteleone for happy hour. The bar's an actual carousel. It's a slow spin, but still, it's a bit surreal. I've never been here before. I thought it was just for tourists."

"A carousel bar? New Orleans is a strange and interesting place," she said. "Tell me about that drink. Isn't there a story behind everything in New Orleans?"

"That's true for any old place. The longer its history, the more stories there are to tell. About this cocktail? First, it's the happy-hour special. Second, it's a famous local drink invented by Mr. Henry Ramos at the Roosevelt Bar in the 1930s." She paused, evidently taking a sip. "Sweet and balanced with lemon and a hint of orange. The froth comes from an egg white—the bartender worked up a sweat shaking the drink—and it's topped with some club soda. Summer heat arrives in spring here, you know. The cocktail's very refreshing on a hot day."

"I'm hot now," she said slowly, hoping her comment sounded as suggestive as she intended. "I might need more than a drink to quench my thirst."

"I think I can help you with that."

"I hope so." She chuckled, liking the playful, sexy side of Maddie. Perhaps the Ramos Gin Fizz was loosening her up. She couldn't resist teasing her. "How long do I have to wait? When do you get back?"

Maddie laughed. "You know I'll be back tomorrow afternoon. And I'm looking forward to our date. By the way, where are we going?"

"You'll just have to find out," she said, teasing. After doing some online research, she'd made reservations at an award-winning farm-to-table restaurant.

"A surprise? I like that." Maddie exhaled, making a gentle cooing sound. "How was today?"

"Another day in Cahaba lily paradise." She didn't mention Barron's unnerving visit. "I've gotten so much work done that I have time to play."

"Good. I won't worry about distracting you."

"Please, distract me all you want." Jordan laughed.

"Are you heading back to Oberon now?"

"No. I'm staying here longer today. There's something to see after nightfall."

"Are you sure you want to be there by yourself after dark? I know you're comfortable in the woods, Jordan, but why don't you wait until I'm back, and I'll go with you?"

It was a reasonable offer, for which she didn't have a reasonable response. Technically, she wouldn't be by herself—did the spirit of a person count? How could she say she'd "sort of" be with someone without explaining what she meant?

"Jordan? Are you still there?"

"Yes. I'm here. I'm meeting someone—a local—who wants to show me something."

"A local?" Maddie sounded skeptical. "Who?"

"Leda Hatchee." She spoke her name slowly, feeling a rising panic. What if Maddie recognized the name?

"The name's familiar. Is she a student?"

"She took some classes, but I don't think she graduated. She grew up in Oberon, and one of her relatives was a college administrator. But that was a long time ago."

"I should recognize the last name. Leda's not a common name. How old is she?"

"Early twenties, I think. She's older than she looks."

"How'd you meet?"

"She was swimming in Caffee Creek the first time I went out to the refuge. I thought I mentioned her."

"I don't recall you talking about her." Maddie's voice was flat.

"Maybe it was Jenn I told. Anyway—" She paused, trying to find the right words. "Leda's *interesting.* Kind of a self-taught naturalist."

"What does she want to show you?"

"I'm not sure. She's being elusive."

"It's odd she won't tell you." Maddie was quiet for a long pause. "It's probably better you're not out there by yourself. Will you let me know when you're back at Palmer House?"

"Absolutely." She heard jazz music in the background.

"Hey, my sister and mom are looking at me like they want me to get off the phone." Maddie spoke clearly and loudly, like she was talking for their benefit before continuing in a softer voice. "Thanks for calling, Jordan. Be safe, okay? Don't fall into the river again."

"I will. I mean, I'll let you know when I'm back, *and* I'll be careful to not fall in again. You be careful, too. Don't slide off that carousel."

Maddie's laughter made her smile as she ended the call. The phone buzzed as she moved to put it in the console. It was a weather-alert warning of a strong cold front—severe thunderstorms with a chance of hail, damaging wind, and tornadoes. She checked the hourly forecast. The worst of it would arrive in the morning, and she hoped her rendezvous with Leda wouldn't be rained out.

Sitting on the porch of the cabin alone with her thoughts, Jordan waited for sundown. As she nibbled the snacks she'd brought and sipped tepid coffee from her thermos, she observed the light raking through the trees as the color shifted from golden to orange-red. She'd come to terms with having a ghost as a friend. Once she allowed herself to trust her senses, to accept the fact that the world was even bigger and more marvelous than she'd ever thought, it was surprisingly easy. Though immaterial, Leda was as real as the rocks and trees—Jordan swatted a mosquito that landed on her neck—and the insects around her.

Recalling Maddie making a good argument for the existence of ghosts, even if she'd never seen one, Jordan hoped she wouldn't think she was delusional when confronted with the truth about her new local friend. She'd have to tell her eventually; the question was when. If Maddie thought she was crazy, it could be the end of a good beginning. While one kiss in the rain didn't make a relationship, she felt in her bones that they were heading toward something meaningful. Faith and trust were two sides of the same coin. If Maddie truly believed in ghosts *and* if she trusted Jordan, then maybe confessing the nature of her new ethereal friend wouldn't trigger their undoing.

Leda arrived shortly after sundown. Jordan was leaning into the back seat of the 4Runner, looking for her headlamp to take with her in case it was too dark to see the trail later. A cold current of air abruptly wrapped around her, brushing the back of her neck like icy fingers.

"Hey!" She jerked upright, cracking her temple on the edge of doorjamb, and looked around for Leda. Appearing like a reflection in the glass, Leda stood on the other side of the car, making faces at her through the window, transparent and glowing faintly in the fading light. "That's not very nice, sneaking up on someone like that."

"Who said I'm nice?" Leda laughed as she floated up, settling on the roof of the SUV in a reclining pose, propped on one elbow. With a snap of her fingers, a full cocktail glass appeared in her hand. She took a sip before grinning salaciously at Jordan. "Haven't you heard? Naughty girls have all the fun."

She rubbed the tender spot forming on her head. "I don't know about that, Leda. I've been naughty with some real nice girls."

Leda laughed so hard she spewed her drink, the purple liquid evaporating into misty spirals. "You're always funnier than I expect, Jordan. I like you."

"Thanks, I guess." She closed the door. "Is it time for whatever you wanted to show me?"

"It is!" Leda slipped off the car, waving to her to follow as she float-walked down the path to the water.

By the time they arrived at the river's edge, the sun had dropped below the ridgeline, the birders and flower photographers gone. Leda was bright and nearly solid in the quickening dark, though her edges were a little blurry.

"What are you staring at?" Leda asked.

"I'm still amazed by you."

"Why, thank you. That's the nicest thing anyone's said to me in decades." Leda smiled, primping her hair and batting her eyes coquettishly like Mae West, an old movie star. She swiped Jordan's nose with a cold finger. "Good thing your professor's not here, or she'd be jealous. You know, truth be told, I like her, too. She respects the spirits."

"What do you mean?"

"Oh, she does little things, like knocks on the door of my house before she enters, even when I'm the only one there."

"Why haven't you let her see you? She told me she believes in ghosts."

Leda frowned. "I'm a spirit, not a ghost, remember?"

"Sorry. What I mean is, she said she believes in the supernatural, but she's never had proof. If you like her, why haven't you let her know you're here?"

"Honey, I have to be very selective. If I talked to every living person I like, I'd get run out of my house. Visitors are safer. They never stay for long. The more people here who know about me, the more complicated it gets. Ghost hunters show up with irritating equipment. People think they're crazy and run away. Or, worse, other people think they're crazy, and they get hauled off to the nut house."

"I guess you trust me, huh?"

"Just now figuring that out, are we?"

"Why'd you chance talking to me?"

Leda, ignoring her question, pointed to the sky behind her. "Look at that!"

Jordan turned around. The moon, enormous and milky white, peeked above the trees at the crest of the hillside on the far side of the river. Spellbound, they stood in silence for several minutes gazing at it.

"Okay, smarty-arty artiste." Leda swept her arm dramatically, drawing Jordan's attention back to the river. "What do you see down below that looks like what's above?"

Leda watched her while she stared at the river. In the creeping dark, the shoals protruding from the water looked like shadowy islands. Moonlight glinted on the water and illuminated the lilies, the blooms seeming to glow. "Ah, the lilies," she said.

Leda nodded. "They're the same color as the moon. In fact, they're like a bunch of little moons." As soon as the words came out of Leda's mouth, a sweet scent hit Jordan—delicate, but powerfully heady. "Is that the lilies?"

"Yes, the moment they first open," Leda said. "There's nothing like it."

"Wow" was all she could say. It was completely different from what she'd experienced during the day. She drew a breath in slowly to savor the intoxicating sweetness. "I know they're like daylilies—one bloom a day." She paused to take in another lungful of the scented air.

"The flowers are freshest at night. That's why the scent is so strong. It helps attract their special visitors. And I don't mean us."

"Who?"

"Some little friends. You'll see." Leda floated out over the water.

Jordan, grateful for the moon's illumination, followed Leda slowly, shuffling her feet carefully along the wide rock shelf, the inches-deep water seeping into her shoes. Leda stayed a few feet in front of her, giving directions, scouting the easiest wading path to a large group of lilies mid-river.

Leda put a hand up and stopped. "And now we wait—quietly," she advised. "Try not to move."

She didn't say a word, though she wanted to ask what they were waiting for. Instead, she stuffed her hands into her pockets so she wouldn't fidget. She watched the water rolling past, lulled by the sounds—gurgling where the flow moved slowly through clefts in the rock—and the loud shushing of deep, fast channels. Scanning the river from one bank to the other, she didn't see anything happening other than time passing. Stars became visible, dotting the sky; the moon climbed higher, appearing smaller as it rose. She spotted Ursa Major, one of the few constellations she could reliably identify. She knew it oriented her view to the northeast, toward her apartment in Chattanooga and, beyond, to the Catskills of her youth. Right now, she felt very far away from both. The stars blinked in and out as narrow black clouds raced past.

*Psst.* Leda pointed to a cluster of blooms.

Something that looked and moved like a hummingbird darted among the flowers, but it couldn't be a hummingbird. They weren't active at night. The small, winged creature hovered to dip its head into the throat of a flower, unfurling its proboscis for a sip of rich nectar. "A sphinx moth," she whispered.

"Plebian sphinx moth." Leda corrected her.

Now that Jordan's eyes had adjusted to what Leda wanted her to see, she spotted several more moving through the watery field of blooms. "I've seen pollinators all over the lilies during the day, but these guys get first crack at the fresh nectar when the flower opens."

"Watch this one, here." Leda pointed to a nearby flower as a moth descended. "Notice how they work together." As the fuzzy moth hovered and neared to take a drink, the plant's pollen-laden anthers, shaped like little pillows and attached by thin filaments protruding from the edges of the flower, were just the right length to embrace the insect. They were a perfect fit. The moth's delta-shaped wings beating so fast they blurred, the anthers shivered, releasing tiny grains of yellow pollen that covered the moth with a fine sprinkling of genetic material it would carry to countless other flowers during the night. Witnessing the result of an evolutionary dance that produced a symbiotic relationship in which two species helped each other was one of those tiny natural marvels that filled Jordan with joy.

Leda scooped up the moth in one hand, quickly covering it with the other. As Jordan moved closer to inspect it, Leda's hands became transparent, allowing her to better see the fluttering moth trapped within an invisible net of fingers. Unlike the shapely green luna or colorful Polyphemus, its handsome gray-brown patterns looked like tree bark. After a long night feeding on nectar, it probably rested during the day, blending in with its surroundings to avoid becoming another animal's lunch. Leda opened her hands, releasing the moth unharmed.

"Beautiful," Jordan said quietly. "Thank you."

"You're welcome," Leda said, lazily floating backward, dragging her toes in the water.

Jordan watched the moths until, one by one, they disappeared. "Leda," she called out. She seemed restless, moving in the shoals with an ease Jordan envied. "Have you seen any moths in the last few minutes?"

"No."

"They're all gone," she said as Leda floated toward her.

"They know something we don't."

"What's that?"

"The storm's picking up speed." Leda pointed upriver. "I can hear the wind in the trees."

"I can't hear anything but the river," Jordan said. "I guess you can detect things I can't. Why didn't you say something?" The stars were suddenly blotted out, the moon slipping in and out of cloud cover, and the wind gusted.

"You were enjoying yourself." Leda frowned. "But you should get out of the water now," she said sharply.

By the time her feet were back on dry ground, lightning flashed in the distance. Following the thirty-second rule, she started counting, and when she reached twenty-five, the thunder rolled over them, low and sonorous. "It's time to head back to the cabin, Leda. I'd like to be at Palmer House before the worst of this arrives."

"I'll take you back a different way," Leda offered.

"There's another way? This is the only trail I've used," she said, pointing to the path in front of them. The flashes of lightning and rumbling thunder were making her anxious.

"Trust me, Jordan. I won't let anything happen to you."

The words should have been comforting, but Leda appeared troubled. Leda had been good on her word so far, she reasoned. Maybe it was a shortcut. What could go wrong?

## CHAPTER FOURTEEN

Where the hell are we?" Jordan shouted at Leda. The twenty minutes it took to walk to the cabin had become forty. She tugged the hood of her rain jacket forward as rain whipped her face, cascading off the jacket in rivulets. Leda floated ahead of her like a lantern in the dark, seemingly untroubled by the flashes of lightning growing in frequency and intensity. Jordan flinched with every crack of thunder that reverberated through the hollow. Could spirits get lost? She just assumed Leda knew the area better than any living person around here. Following the spirit might have been a mistake. Leda had led her on a meandering route up and down hills that disoriented her. She wasn't sure which way the cabin or the river lay, her only points of reference.

As she trotted to catch up, her foot caught on something unseen, a vine perhaps, and she fell forward so fast she couldn't stop herself from landing in a tangle of vegetation. After wiping mud off her hands on her pantlegs, she readjusted her headlamp. The beam of light danced around as she looked for Leda. "I swear to God, Leda, if I just landed in a patch of poison ivy, I'm going—"

"You're going to what?" Leda suddenly appeared in front of her, hands on hips, the yellow sequins of her dress flickering like tiny candle flames. The rain didn't seem to affect her. In fact, her hair seemed to have a life of its own. It floated away from her head, looking as if she were submerged in water. She appeared the most solid Jordan had seen so far.

"I don't know," she grumbled as she got up off the ground, pulling the hood of her jacket up over her head, though she wasn't sure why she bothered since her hair was already wet. "Are we lost?"

"No."

"Why didn't you let me go the other way? I'd have been back at the cabin by now."

"There's something you need to see."

"Other than the moths?"

Leda nodded.

"You couldn't have waited for better weather?"

"No," Leda said before turning away and zooming up the hill, leaving her no choice but to follow.

Leda stopped next to a large tree and waited for her. Each lightning strike seemed closer than the next, thunder shaking the ground and rolling through the air like a sonic wave. Her anger rose. "This isn't fair," she said, exasperated. "You're dead, so this weather can't hurt you. Personally, I *like* being alive, and I'd really rather not be fried by lightning."

"Calm down." Leda looked at her like a schoolteacher admonishing an errant child. "You're not going to die."

Another flash and crack of thunder reverberating through the woods didn't make her feel better. "How can you know that?" She eyed Leda sideways. "Unless you can control the weather."

"No. I can't control the weather." She chortled. "Lightning doesn't strike me, or even near me. It never does. Lord knows, if it could, I'd have been struck ten times by now. I've been in the middle of countless thunderstorms, three hurricanes, and a tornado—now, that was exciting, let me tell you!" Leda giggled. "I seem to disrupt it. I absorb it like a sponge." Leda took her hand. "It makes me more solid, see?" Leda's touch felt neither cold nor warm, just strangely firm, like Jell-O. She laughed and pointed to her hair, the curls loosened and radiating around her head like a golden halo. "Really messes up my hairdo, though."

"I noticed," she said.

"Yeah? You didn't say anything."

"It doesn't seem polite to tell a woman when her hair is out of place."

"Well, aren't you the well-mannered one! Your mama must have raised you right," Leda drawled, squeezing her hand. "Stay close, Jordan. You're safe with me." She tugged her forward, pointing to the crest of the hill in front of them with her free hand. Approaching the top of the ridge, Leda crouched and gestured, indicating she should do the same. Below them, in a flat, wide clearing, stretched a long, low, white, metal building with large circular fans looking like the nacelles of jet engines embedded in the walls, illuminated by bright-white security lights. A flash of lightning illuminated several shiny metallic silos. The wind blew a terrible stench toward them, rank and sulphureous. It smelled of rot and death. Lightning flashed, pulsing long enough to illuminate the whole area like a strobe light.

"Is that a hog barn, Leda?"

"It is." She scowled.

"I thought Barron said he was raising them humanely, on pasture."

"That's what he says," Leda said. "What people say and what they do don't always match. This is a very bad place, Jordan."

"I'm sure it is." She snorted. "The poor animals in buildings like that never see the light of day. The people who buy their sanitary packages of meat at the grocery store have no idea what life is like in there."

"This place threatens more than people's feelings. I need your help to stop it."

"That's why you diverted me from going back to the cabin? You want me to snoop around here in a storm?"

"Yes. Will you?" Leda asked gleefully. "Oh, thank you, Jordan!"

"Wait a minute. I didn't say I'd go down there. That's trespassing."

"But you have permission to be here," Leda said enthusiastically.

"Tammi said I could use the cabin and go to the *river.* She didn't give me free rein to go wherever I like. And today, Barron told me to stay out of the deep woods. I suspect this is what he actually meant."

"You saw Barron today?" Leda cocked her head, her curls waving languidly.

"Yeah. He showed up at the cabin. It was weird. I couldn't help but feel like he was checking up on me."

Leda narrowed her eyes. "Like he wanted to make sure you weren't here, discovering his big lie?"

"Maybe. I don't know. Like I said, it was weird."

"He doesn't want anyone other than his hired men to know about this. I've been watching him." Leda spoke with confidence and moved forward, seeming to expect her to follow. Leda turned around, staring at her. "Why are you just standing there?"

"It's inhumane to raise animals like that." Jordan pointed to the barn. "And Barron's a fraud if he's selling everyone a story about raising happy hogs for his restaurants on grass and sunshine. He probably concocted the scheme to make more money, knowing people will pay a lot more for pasture-raised meat. And I'm sure he loves being thought of as a good guy. Still, I'm not comfortable with—"

"No one is comfortable standing up against evil," Leda said, her voice sharp, the words stinging like a slap in the face. "When I was a child, the farmland around here was pitiful. Fields that had once been great forests had been worked so hard, the rich soil had washed out, leaving bedrock exposed like bones bleaching in the sun. It wasn't good for much other than grazing cows. By the time I was a young woman, the mines had closed. Once scraping coal from the earth stopped being profitable, the owners closed them, abandoned their workers, and moved on, leaving people here in poverty, scars on the land, and mounds of mine tailings leeching poison. Some things don't change. Greedy businessmen like Barron, they take what they want, discarding it when it's worn out and has no more value to them, and they give nothing back. I believe in something my father used to say, *Veritatem dies aperit.*"

"That's what? Latin?" She recognized one of the words. "Something about truth?"

"You remember that my father was the college president?"

"Yes, of course."

"Every educated person back then knew some Latin, but he loved it. He looked to the ancient philosophers for inspiration, quoting them in Latin ad nauseam." Leda smiled softly as she recalled the memory. "*Veritatem dies aperit* means 'time discovers the truth.'" She paused, as if to let the quotation sink in. "The time is now. The truth needs to be revealed before something very bad happens."

"What's going to happen?"

"Hopefully nothing, if you stop it."

"What do you mean, if I stop it? I don't even know what you're talking about."

"You'll see. I'll show you." Leda moved forward, down the hill toward the building. Jordan hesitated. "Come on. Don't worry. Nobody's going to come out here in the dark in this storm."

"But *we're* here," she said. Leda ignored her, continuing to move toward the building.

She hesitated while considering her options. Follow Leda into the barn, trespass, and risk being caught on security cameras, or try to find her way back to the cabin on her own. A gravel road led to the barn. Surely that would connect to one of the county roads, but she had no way of telling if it would take her toward or away from the cabin. Leda seemed disturbed about something more than just the presence of animals in Barron's barn. She'd been earnest and helpful, and hadn't she described herself as a kind of guardian of this special place? It didn't seem right to turn her back on her now and leave.

The storm was on top of them now, with flashes of lightning and ear-splitting thunder cracking simultaneously. She was edgy. Leda might believe her presence shielded her from being struck by lightning, but she didn't want to find out the hard way that the spirit was wrong. She squinted, struggling to see Leda in the pelting rain. Pale and washed out under a bright white security light, she waited for her outside the barn near a side door. She took a deep breath and hustled down the hill.

❖

Jordan wasn't prepared for the heavy, acrid stench of ammonia and dung that burned her nostrils as she stepped through the door, nor what she saw under the harsh fluorescent lights—scores of hogs, eight or ten crowded together in small metal pens, moving around like fish in an overcrowded tank. It was filthy. Although the slatted concrete floor under their feet seemed designed for the pigs' waste to fall through, excrement was everywhere—splashed on the walls, encrusted on the floor, and smeared on the hogs' pink skin. She pulled the collar of her T-shirt over her nose and mouth, holding it in place with her palm.

Staring in horror at the scars and red gashes on the hogs' backs and shoulders, she wasn't surprised, given their cramped quarters. Like when people were crowded together, the stress of confinement led to fights. She could discern individual voices—low grunts and occasional squeals—but the whirl of fans and constant clanging of motorized feeder doors dispensing food was so loud it drowned out the sounds of the storm outside.

The animals paid them little attention. Pushing each other around in their limited spaces, the hogs seemed more interested in jostling into stanchions for a ration of feed dropped into a narrow steel trough through the tubes of the automated system. Others took turns drinking from water nozzles dangling from the ceiling, and a few rested on the dirty cement floor.

A hog, lying along the edge of a pen near the center aisle, caught her attention. She walked to him, squatting to get close; he was big, easily outweighing her by a hundred pounds. His jowl, the size of a dinner plate, pressed against the metal bars. He was listless, and his dark eyes, ringed by long, pale eyelashes, seemed unnervingly human. "Poor pig," she said.

The hog shifted position, snorting softly to sniff her, his wet snout quivering with a new scent, as his small eyes focused on her. People always said pigs were smart. Hadn't Tammi said they had the intelligence of a three-year-old child? If pigs were comparable to toddlers, then they could most certainly feel emotions. She sank into a pool of despair when she met the hog's gaze. She felt the animal's situation from his cheerless perspective. He was forced to live against his nature and had never been allowed to experience what his species had evolved to do: live in fresh air, root soil in search of food, find cool shade for protection from the hot sun on summer days, fight for a place within the social order, and seek mates to create the next generation. Instead, he lived here with the others, a short, bleak existence in a living hell, all because of greed and gluttony.

Humans had such great capacity for compassion, yet they so easily turned a blind eye to suffering when it seemed inconvenient to do something about it. She briefly fantasized opening the pens and the doors, of turning the hogs loose, but what good would it do? She'd be sending animals unconditioned to the weather into a thunderstorm. They might not even know how to take care of themselves, and Barron, or whoever did his dirty work here, would undoubtedly hunt them down and bring them back. It would be awful to experience fresh air, to feel dirt under your feet and exciting scents in your nostrils, only to be returned to the miserable half-life of the hog barn. These animals deserved a better life. Something needed to be done, but she didn't know what or how to help them.

She held her ears against the sound of scraping metal and moans of suffering. "I want to go, Leda." She stood up, looking around for the spirit. "Take me back to the cabin."

Leda hovered near the door where they'd entered, her hands covering her face. She was pale and translucent under the fluorescent light, and her dress had lost its shimmer. "Leda? Leda! Are you okay?"

Leda lowered her hands, appearing sorrowful. "I followed Barron in here when they brought the first pigs. It was so clean. But this—" She waved her hand, her expression one of anguish. "This is wicked evil." Leda raised her eyes to meet hers. "I didn't know how bad."

"Show me what you wanted me to see outside, and then guide me back to the cabin," she demanded. "We've both seen enough. Maybe I can contact a farm-animal welfare agency or something." As soon as she spoke, an idea struck her. "Give me just a minute." She pulled her cell phone from her pocket to use the camera app. Her phone tried to connect to a wi-fi signal, but it was password-protected. She quickly documented feces-encrusted pigs, chewed ears, swollen red wounds, anything that visually described the situation in the barn. Before she finished taking pictures, she heard a low rumble. It was too regular to be thunder. It sounded mechanical, like an engine. A truck? The thump-thump of doors closing and the muffled sound of men's voices sent her heart racing as adrenaline flooded her veins.

"Leda—"

"People are outside!" Leda finished Jordan's thoughts and disappeared without warning.

"Leda? Where'd you go?" She glanced around. It was just her and the hogs. The sound of metal scraping on metal, a sliding latch, pulled her attention to a roll-up door connected to a chute. As the door slowly moved up, she saw a stock trailer and the legs of a man. She ran toward the corner, to a tall metal box—some kind of housing for electronic controls with gauges and digital screens—and ducked behind it. Crouching between the steel box and the wall, she wrapped her arms around her knees and listened.

"Awright, Darrell. We got one more load to get in the trailer. Barron said to take twenty from these two pens here."

"But what about the pumps, Wayne? I thought we were supposed to check them."

"Are you fucking kidding me? We gotta get these pigs to the processor tonight," Wayne said. "I ain't gonna do shit-else in this storm."

"Shit-else? All's you got here is shit. Pigs are up to their ears in shit." Darrell's laugh was caustic. "Shit. Shit. Shit. Ain't nothing gonna stop the shitting, that's for sure."

"You're not funny, Darrell."

"Ah, you wouldn't know funny if it fell on you, Wayne."

Jordan heard the clangs of gates opening and closing. The grunting and squealing increased, the hogs sounding agitated. The men, too.

"*Gah!* Damn hogs," Wayne growled. "Move!" he screamed, probably confusing the pigs and making them even more anxious.

"What's the holdup?"

"They dun wanna go through the gate into the damn chute."

"I'll go get the cattle prod. That'll make 'em move." After a moment of calm, Darrell spoke again. "Here you go. Use it on that big one in the front. When he goes, the others will follow him into the trailer. It's a one-way ticket, boys." A sharp, dry snap of electricity pierced the air, followed by a raspy screech. "Poke the son of a bitch again, Wayne," Darrell growled. "Harder! Hold it!" Each pulsing electric shock and screech Jordan's teeth on edge. She squeezed her eyes shut and clutched her hand to her mouth to keep from crying out. "Make the sumbitch *move*," Darrell yelled, laughing at every cry of pain the cattle prod caused.

Risking being seen, Jordan leaned forward slowly to peer around the corner of the box. She wanted to know who these men were, but all she could see were denim-covered legs and leather boots through the metal-bar panels, and a large hog, grunting and stumbling, desperately trying to move backward, but lurching forward reluctantly with every shock, his head bobbing as he moved step by step, resisting as if he knew his grim fate. She leaned back out of sight, continuing to listen to the men's callous banter as they pushed and prodded the hogs one by one into the chute leading to the trailer outside. Wayne seemed apathetic to the pigs' plight, but Darrell was something worse. He was a sadistic motherfucker seeming to take pleasure in commanding Wayne's actions. She'd listened to enough true-crime podcasts to know that men like him were dangerous and often misogynists. The reality of what might happen if they discovered her was horrifying. She pressed her forehead against the sheet-metal panel in front of her and silently prayed they didn't find her. After she finished the prayer, she mentally recited another for the hogs. The abuse seemed to take forever.

"That's the last one, Darrell," Wayne shouted over the sounds of slamming gates and sliding latches.

"Awright, Wayne. Drop the door when you're done, and let's get outta here. We got an hour's drive, and this storm ain't getting any better. I don't know why these hogs had to be moved tonight. Seems like it coulda waited a few days."

"I don't never argue with the boss," Wayne said. "Yes, sir. No, sir. Thank you for my paycheck, sir!"

The men's laughter faded into the raging storm as the rolling door closed. She listened for the rumble of the truck engine, hearing it rev a few times, and then silence other than the white noise of the barn and an occasional squealing hog. When she felt safe, she unfolded herself and crawled out from behind the control box.

"Leda? Are you here? Please be here." She scanned the area but found no trace of the spirit. She walked down the aisle to the far end of the barn, past another fifty or sixty hogs, and passed through a swinging door into a narrow room with smooth, white walls, a spigot with a hose attached, and a floor drain in the center. Anger rose in her at the spirit having abandoned her. A second door led into the other end of the barn. "Leda?" she called out as she pulled open the door.

Halfway across the threshold she stopped and gasped, sucking in the fetid air so fast it made her cough. A half dozen sows were confined in gestation crates, pens no bigger than the large animals they contained. She understood what she was seeing. In fact, she and Maddie had talked about gestational crates over dinner when she had first arrived in Oberon. Bonding over their mutually shared ideas about humane treatment of animals, she'd had no idea how prescient their conversation would be. The sows would be confined here for months, unable to turn around, forced to stand or lie down unnaturally, eating, urinating, and defecating until it was time to give birth. Then, they'd be moved to a slightly less restrictive cage that allowed them just enough room to rest on their sides to nurse but keeping them separated from their piglets. It was beyond inhumane. She began to feel claustrophobic, her hands shaking as her blood pressure rose.

"Dammit, Leda! Where did you go?"

Leda didn't respond or appear. One of the sows chewed on a bar, the metal amplifying the sound of her teeth grinding against it, blood-flecked foam dripping from her mouth. Jordan felt helpless and hopeless. These animals were treated like meat-making machines, not sentient living beings who could be driven to compulsive behaviors and probably insanity by these conditions. She had seen enough. Spotting another door, she felt desperate to get out, even if she didn't know how to find her way to the cabin. Thunderstorm or not, she needed fresh air and a clear head. She wasn't a babe in the woods; she could figure out how to get back to the cabin if she kept her wits about her. If she stayed here, she would risk losing them like the mad sow chewing on the bars until her gums bled.

She bolted for the door but stopped dead when she witnessed yet another sign of the neglect these hogs endured—almost a dozen newborn piglets—bloodied, pale, and lifeless—clustered on the cold concrete floor.

Fumbling with the latch on the crate, hoping to release the sow from her confinement, she exploded. "You cruel, heartless bastards!" She tugged on the latch. The sow should have been moved out of the gestation crate before now. What was wrong with these men? Barron himself had a child. He must have seen what Tammi had experienced during pregnancy and how uncomfortable she must have been during the final weeks, unable to get relief in any position. How could he, or anyone who worked in this barn, not have a shred of empathy for these animals?

The latch was stuck. Grabbing it with both hands, she pulled as hard as she could. "Motherfuckers!" she roared, and the latch gave way. She stumbled backward as the door swung open, but the sow didn't move. In fact, she didn't seem to notice anything that was happening around her. She grunted loudly, her sides heaving with heavy breaths. She was still in labor, her sides quivering. Before Jordan fully processed what she was seeing, tiny toes and the nose of a baby pig came into view. Without thinking she bent, stretching her hands forward in time to catch the newborn, wet and wriggling in her hands. Instinctively, she cleared mucus from her nose, mouth, and eyes with her fingers and wished she had a towel to dry her. She improvised with the front of her T-shirt, rubbing the baby-tender skin. The piglet sneezed and head-butted the palm of her hand. She clearly knew she needed to nurse, to get the antibody-rich colostrum that her mother would produce for only a short time. Crawling into the empty stall next to the sow, Jordan reluctantly poked the sow, getting her to shift enough to expose her teats. The piglet latched on, sucking greedily.

She counted the piglets. Number twelve, the one in her hand, was probably the last and only surviving member of the litter. One of the dead piglets twitched and wriggled. It was alive. Wet and cold, but miraculously still alive. She reached for it, dislodging Number Twelve, who wriggled in protest.

"I don't know what number you are, but I'll call you Eleven, for now." Although weak, Eleven reacted when Jordan took her to the sow's side and held her next to Twelve. She began to suckle, slowly at first and then vigorously. When their bodies relaxed, Jordan figured they'd had their fill for the moment. While watching them nurse, she'd reached a decision.

"I'm sorry I can't help you right now, mama," she said quietly, standing up to tuck the little piglets under her shirt to keep them warm. "But I promise you, these baby girls will *never* again see the inside of one of these barns. And they will never grow up to be imprisoned, giving birth to litter after litter."

Looking for a way out, she found that the door at the far end opened into a small room with a boot wash, utility sink, and a cabinet stacked with bottles of iodine and cotton towels. A handwritten note scrawled in all capital letters was taped to the edge of a shelf. FOR FARROWING ONLY. Using the supplies, she dabbed some iodine on the end of the umbilical cord, rubbed them both vigorously with a fresh towel, and then swaddled them together in clean towels before nestling them into her shirt against her skin. Hopefully she could keep them warm enough. With her shirt tucked into her pants and jacket zipped closed, her contraption made a pretty good carrier. She considered giving them one more chance to suckle but couldn't bear the thought of going back into the barn.

"Look at those sweet little babies," Leda said, flickering into form.

"Leda!" Jordan was relieved to see her.

"Are you stealing those piglets?"

"I guess I am."

"Good for you. And good for them!" Leda leaned close to the piglets in her arms, looking at them adoringly, as if she wished she could hold them.

Jordan had been thinking about this as a rescue, but Leda was right. She was stealing towels and baby pigs. She was a pig rustler now. She stifled a nervous laugh. "I need you to get me back to the cabin and my car."

"There is something else you need to see. It's the real reason I brought you here."

"What?" She wasn't sure she could handle one more thing. "I don't have time to look around, Leda. These guys need a warm place and more food soon."

"You'll see it as we go."

"How far away are we?" she asked.

"Not far."

"I mean, how much time will it take to get there?"

"Oh…time. You know, it's all the same when you're a spirit." Leda frowned. "It's hard for me to mark time. I can't really say."

Jordan sighed, impatiently pinching the bridge of her nose. But she needed Leda to get her out of here, so she spoke in a measured tone. "Compare it to the path between the cabin and the river."

"I can answer that." Leda's expression brightened. "A bit longer. But not much if you walk fast."

"Then let's not waste any more time." She flipped her hood over her head and reached for the exit-door handle.

It was still raining, but the storm seemed to have weakened. As they moved away from the barn, Leda began to glow softly, though not as intensely as when the lightning strikes were nearby. The air was still heavy with the sour odor of manure as they rounded the corner of the building. A flash of lightning illuminated the landscape—two flat, dark rectangles in the dark—manure lagoons: containment ponds holding the waste from the barn. The news broadcasts during the last big hurricane on the East Coast had featured tragic stories about millions of chickens and thousands of hogs drowning in barns. Dramatic aerial footage revealed breached hog-farm lagoons, spewing a toxic pink slurry of waste and pathogens into waterways. The news reporters described massive fish kills, which meant not just fish, but anything living in or near the water was sickened or killed. Those factory farms in South Carolina had been negatively affecting people's health for years. The companies had been sued repeatedly and lost every time, but the fines were a slap on the wrist for the mega-corporations, just part of the cost of doing agribusiness, so they continued operating without making changes, creating an environmental disaster ready to happen.

Barron's dirty little secret was a smaller-scale version of one of those massive factory farms, but he was operating under the same principles: too many animals crammed into small spaces for the sake of quick money. And God knows, he had a lot of it.

She put on her headlamp and clicked it on. As she turned her head side to side, the sweep of light revealed the liquified waste very near the edge of the muddy earthen berm containing it.

"That looks awfully close to the top," she said as they walked past. The smell was overwhelming.

"It is. The other side is what worries me. We're going that way, so you'll see."

Before they reached the far side of the lagoon, the rain had stopped, and the milky-white moon peeked through the fast-moving clouds. The piglets grunted and wriggled against Jordan's belly, then settled, nice and warm. They descended the soggy, steeply sloping dam to a small stream below. Being this close to a waterway, the manure lagoon had to violate environmental laws. Barron was a criminal.

Leda pointed across the stream. "The cabin is that way."

"If the lagoon overflows—" She clutched the piglets close as she waded through the shallow water. "God, it stinks worse down here."

"We called this Little Turtle Creek when I was a child. Lots of turtles and crawfish lived here. It's like a sewer now," Leda said.

"You think the dam will fail?" Given their proximity to the river, this creek probably flowed directly into the Cahaba.

"It's already leaking. That's what you're smelling."

"This is an environmental problem waiting to become a disaster." She adjusted the piglets and picked up her pace, wanting to get as far away from the lagoon as she could. Her boots swished in the muck, making her nauseous knowing she was walking through effluent.

"It is," Leda said.

They remained silent the rest of the way to the cabin. After they intersected an ATV trail on the top of the hill and followed the ridgeline, the walking was easy and fast. Keeping one arm wrapped around the waist of her jacket to support her piglets, who couldn't have weighed more than two pounds each, she followed Leda until she stopped by a tall pine tree and directed her to turn downslope, promising the cabin was near the base of the hill.

The sight of the cabin and her 4Runner in the moonlight was a huge relief. She had been running on adrenaline, and it was beginning to wear off. The piglets squirmed again, probably hungry. "Hang on just a bit longer, little piggies," she said gently as she grabbed a beach towel from the back, removed the bundle from under her shirt, and put them on the passenger seat. After starting the engine, she turned on the seat warmer.

"Do you want to ride with me?" she asked Leda, who hovered outside, near the driver's side window. "Can you?"

"I can sit in your car, but when you drive off, I'll still be here." She shrugged. "Some things just don't work for spirits."

"Then I'll meet you back at Palmer House."

"Good. I don't know about you, but I'm ready for a drink. I'll be there before you," Leda said with a wink and disappeared.

Jordan backed away from the cabin and sped down the gravel road. When she patted the towel, the piglets underneath let out excited grunts. That was a good sign. If they were wriggling and vocalizing, maybe they'd be okay.

"Hang tight, little ones," she said. "How do you feel about goat's milk? I hear that all the baby mammals love it. Fortunately for you, I know just the place to get some." As she turned on to the paved county road, she hoped it wasn't too late to stop by the next-door grumpy goat farmer's house for some milk.

## CHAPTER FIFTEEN

Maddie poured a cup of coffee while her sister pulled boxes of cereal from a kitchen cabinet. When she sat at the kitchen bar, Chip waited patiently by her feet, watching her, knowing the rattle of cereal boxes meant she might get a treat.

"Are you sure you want to leave this morning?" Caroline said over her shoulder. "Another bad storm's coming. You can stay longer if you like."

"Thanks for the offer." She grinned over the rim of her cup. "But I have a date tonight."

"You could reschedule. I'm sure Jordan would understand."

"Maybe I don't want to," she said, realizing she sounded like a petulant child. She scrolled through the forecast on her phone. The weather-radar graphic looked ominous, with shaded orange trapezoids warning of severe thunderstorms. Yet another big storm system spiraling up out of the Gulf of Mexico was projected to move across Louisiana, Mississippi, and Alabama, following the same route she'd be driving. The pattern was typical, but with climate change, storms had become stronger—the rain heavier, the lightning more violent, and more tornadoes.

Caroline lined up the cereal boxes in front of Maddie, frowning at the splotches of green, yellow, and red on the weather map on her phone's screen. "If you want to stay ahead of that, you better leave soon."

"You wouldn't mind?"

"Of course not. We weren't going to be able to do much this morning anyway. I have to take Sophie to soccer camp, and it's an office day for Rob." Caroline placed bowls and spoons next to the cereal boxes. "I can't believe you're willing to drive through hell and high water just for dinner."

"I won't be, as long as I stay ahead of the storm," she said confidently.

"Then you better not wait for Rob and Sophie. Go ahead and eat your breakfast." Caroline pushed a cereal bowl toward her.

"It's not just dinner." She grinned while pouring multigrain flakes into a bowl. "It's a date! One that I'm really looking forward to. I have a good feeling about Jordan."

"I have no doubt she gives you good feelings." Teasing, Caroline handed her a carton of milk. "But she lives in another state, so I'm surprised you're interested. That didn't work out so well for you before."

"Jordan's not Vanessa." She sliced half a banana on top of the cereal and poured milk into her bowl. "And Tennessee's not Wisconsin. Chattanooga is just a few hours' drive. Chip likes road trips. Don't you, Chip?" She glanced down at the black shepherd and offered her a thick slice of banana. Her tail thumped the floor as she took it delicately from her fingers with her big, white teeth.

"Look at you, being such the optimist." Caroline shook her head, smiling. "You know, Mom said she noticed a change in you."

"Really?"

"Yeah. Last night at the Carousel Bar. I recall she used the words 'lighter' and 'distracted.'"

"I'm sorry."

"Why be sorry?" Caroline cradled her cup in her hands and leaned back against the counter.

"I'm here visiting all y'all and—" She pointed at her cell phone on the counter. "I've been on the phone talking and texting like a teenager."

"More like a preteen these days," Caroline said. "Fortunately, mine's not quite there yet." As if on cue, Sophie shuffled into the kitchen, sleepy-eyed and hair uncombed. She was dressed in a blue-and-white shirt, shorts, and tall socks, appearing ready for a day of chasing a ball around a field. Chip trotted to her, wagging her tail energetically as Sophie wrapped her arms around her thick neck and patted her head between her ears. "You'd better give Aunt Maddie a hug, too. She's leaving soon."

Caroline whisked away Maddie's empty cereal bowl before she could offer the remaining milk to Chip. Sophie gave her a hug and thanked her again for the birthday books before taking a bowl of cereal to the kitchen table.

Maddie returned to the guest room to gather her things. It didn't take long since she'd packed for only a few days, and she shouted a good-bye to Rob, who was taking a shower. As she carried her bag to the car in the driveway, the sky was the color of wet concrete, the air still and heavy with humidity.

Caroline met her at the front door with coffee in a stainless-steel cup and Chip leashed and ready to go. "You can return the cup on your next visit."

"Thanks." She took the leash and cup.

Caroline patted Chip. "And maybe your mom will bring her new girlfriend when she visits next time."

"Fingers crossed." She laughed. Hands full, she leaned forward to give her sister an air kiss good-bye.

"Be careful," Caroline called from the doorway as Chip jumped into the back seat. Maddie flashed a grin and a thumbs-up at her sister as she got into the car.

The graphic printed on the cup resting in the console caught her eye—a sheaf of wheat in the form of a fleur-de-lis—the All Saint's Bakery logo. She glanced at the clock. A stop at the café wouldn't slow her down too much, and delivering fresh beignets would be an excuse to see Jordan as soon as she got back to Oberon.

She moved at a frustratingly slow pace across the city in the snarled traffic and arrived at the café at what seemed the peak of the morning commuter crowd. While standing in line to place her order for a dozen beignets and a sandwich to eat in the car later, she texted Jordan to let her know she was leaving New Orleans early and asked if she could stop by with a local treat midday. She didn't receive an immediate reply, or by the time she got back in the car, or even three hours later while driving through Mississippi and only two hours from home. Jordan's silence bothered her. She was usually quick to text back. Maybe she'd lost her phone again or was working and not checking messages.

She stopped thinking about Jordan when the storm caught up with her near Meridian, Mississippi. After the color of the clouds took on a greenish pallor and gusting wind buffeted her car sideways, nudging it toward the shoulder, she began to regret leaving New Orleans in slow rush-hour traffic and having stopped for the beignets. If she hadn't made the crosstown detour, she'd be ahead of the storm and just an hour away from home instead of two.

She glanced over her shoulder at Chip, curled up in a tight ball on the back seat, oblivious to the worsening conditions outside and sleeping soundly. She turned on the radio, tuning it to the local NPR station to listen for a discussion of the weather. After a few minutes of bouncy jazz, an announcement interrupted the music—a line of strong thunderstorms expected to produce hail and tornadoes was approaching. The announcer recommended people secure objects outdoors and seek shelter. Almost as soon as the music program returned, the three short, jarring tones of an emergency weather alert interrupted it. With a jingle of her collar, Chip appeared in the rearview mirror, eyes bright and ears pointed forward attentively. The stern robotic voice on the radio calmly stated that a tornado warning was in effect and recited a litany of cities in its path, including Toomsuba, the name of a city on the exit sign they'd just passed. She gasped, and Chip leaned forward, stretching her head and neck forward, sniffing the white pastry bag on the passenger seat.

"Chip, leave it," she said firmly. A pickup truck reflected in the side mirror approached quickly in the left lane. "Asshole," she muttered. Glancing at the truck as it passed her on the left at high speed, she felt her heart skip a beat when she saw a thin tendril of cloud descending from the dark edge of the storm front. The narrow tip rotated and twisted to a fine point as it dropped. Rain fell heavily, hammering the car. She adjusted the wipers to high, and Chip whined and bumped her shoulder with her nose.

"It's all right," she said calmly, repeating the words to Chip, even though she didn't feel calm. Not one bit. She quickly debated the best course of action, speeding forward or pulling over. If she stopped, she'd have to get out and take Chip to the lowest spot she could find, probably the ditch between the roadway and the line of trees. That's what you were supposed to do. The experts said a tornado had very little velocity a foot above the ground, and while staying in the car felt safer, it wasn't. A tornado could easily lift or flip a vehicle. Getting out of the car now was the last thing she wanted to do, but she would if she had to. Alternating between keeping her eyes on the road ahead and watching the tornado, she let out a lungful of air when she realized it would cross behind them. She pressed her foot against the accelerator pedal—continuing forward was clearly the best response.

When the tornado touched the ground it changed color like a chameleon, becoming as dark as mud as it tore across a field of young, green cotton plants before cleaving a stand of pine trees flanking the interstate. As debris churned dark matter into the air, Maddie gripped the wheel tighter with both hands while repeating, "It's all right, it's all right," like a mantra as it cut across the road behind them.

Now slicing through the field on her right, it was heading in the direction of home. She'd never heard any stories about a tornado hitting Oberon, and in the eight years she'd lived there, she'd watched countless ones on weather radar head straight for the town, only to dissipate or veer away just outside of it. The locals believed the geography of the river valley and ridges caused the near misses. Eyeing the backside of the tornado as it rapidly moved away, she hoped it would weaken soon and wouldn't test the theory.

Two hours later, still under cloudy skies, she arrived in Oberon, happy to see nothing but wet pavement and shallow pools of water in low spots while driving through town. Aside from leaves and small branches strewn on the ground, everything seemed fine. Chip whined and paced across the back seat, knowing they were close to home, but instead of turning toward the house, Maddie headed to Palmer House.

She parked next to Jordan's 4Runner and opened the back door to let Chip out, then looked up at the roiling clouds overhead. Chip leapt off the back seat and trotted away from the car to relieve herself, sniffing around the shrubs and the base of the trees. A good dog with strong shepherd instincts, Chip wouldn't go far. Clutching the bag of beignets, Maddie knocked on the door and waited. When Jordan didn't answer, she knocked again. The 4Runner was there, so she should be around. She checked her phone, but she still hadn't received a reply to her text. She walked to the studio and peered through the window. Watercolor paintings were pinned to the walls, and a partially completed painting of a Cahaba lily lay on the slanted drafting table, but Jordan wasn't there.

It didn't seem likely that she'd have gone for a walk in this weather, but maybe she'd decided to take advantage of the break in the rain. Jordan seemed to love the outdoors more than anyone she'd met. Still, Maddie expected she'd have her phone with her. She walked to the back door of Palmer House and knocked one more time. As she turned away, she thought she thought she heard muffled voices and put her ear to the door. People inside were talking. Maybe they hadn't heard her. She turned the knob and opened the door slowly.

Reluctant to walk in without an invitation, she stuck her head through the doorway tentatively. "Hello?" Instead of a response she heard peals of laughter from Jordan and someone else she didn't recognize—a woman's voice, light and musical.

"Stop sucking on my finger." She heard Jordan giggle.

Maddie froze in place in the foyer, her heart sinking, not believing what she was hearing.

"Have you ever seen anything so pink?" cooed the woman.

"Or so soft? My God…" Jordan laughed. "Insatiable! I'm exhausted. You haven't let me get more than an hour of sleep, and now you want more."

Jordan was with a woman? All night? Having sex? And lots of it, from the sound of things. What the fuck? Maddie's heart pounded, her face heated, and her hands trembled. She'd been gone only a few days and been fervently eager to see Jordan. She'd driven back through a raging thunderstorm, had narrowly avoided being killed by a tornado, all the while fantasizing about collecting those kisses Jordan had promised her. And now, unbelievably, here she was, walking in to find Jordan fooling around, giving those kisses to another woman, right before their date.

Jordan had seemed so honest and genuine that nothing about her had sent up any warning flags. Either Maddie had been blind to Jordan's true character, or she was a supremely adept player, and Maddie had fallen for it like a fool. Feeling gullible and stupid, tears welling, she started to leave, but the sounds of low grunting and soft smacking made anger rise faster than her sinking heart. Fury flaring, she couldn't take any more. She turned and strode into the dining room. "What the fuck's going on, Jordan!"

"Maddie?" Jordan squeaked as she appeared in the doorway to the kitchen. A wide, happy grin broke across her face, as if nothing was the matter. "What's wrong?"

"I texted you." She glared at Jordan, dressed in a T-shirt, shorts, and sandals, her hair seeming damp and tangled like she'd recently gotten out of the shower or bed, maybe both, maybe with the woman she couldn't see, the one who liked sucking Jordan's finger.

"I guess I didn't hear it." As Jordan walked toward her, the happy expression fell, shifting to one of confusion. "I got caught up in an emergency."

"Yeah, sure. Some emergency!" she snapped, spitting out the words in a sarcastic tone, pointing to the pretty, young woman who appeared in the doorway behind Jordan. She appeared ready for a night on the town, her blond hair styled in a curly blond bob, makeup impeccable, smoky eyes, lashes thick with dark mascara, and bright-red lips. Curiously dressed in a retro-style yellow flapper dress made from an unusual fabric that sparkled softly, she seemed slightly out of focus. It was like looking at a glamour photograph.

"Are you angry?" Jordan asked.

"Why wouldn't I be?" she snapped.

"Maddie, I don't understand."

"Stupid me. I drove through a thunderstorm and a tornado to get here early. I couldn't wait to see you. I'm so stupid."

"Stupid? Why? I don't understand," Jordan stammered. "I'm excited to see you, too. I just didn't expect you to be here so soon." Jordan looked her up and down appreciatively. "You look really nice." She read the flicker of desire in Jordan's expression, the response she'd hoped for a half hour ago. Now it felt like an insult. "Maddie, I'm really sorry I didn't get your text." Jordan's expression turned serious. "It's been a crazy night. I have a lot to explain."

"I'm not sure I want to hear any explanations."

"Why not?"

"I've heard enough. *She*"—Maddie pointed at the woman—"seems to like sucking on your fingers. I don't want to know what else she likes sucking on."

The woman barked a laugh and slapped her hand over her mouth, convulsing as if trying not to laugh out loud again. Maddie was infuriated.

"Piglets!" Jordan shouted, smacking the palm of her hand against her forehead with a laugh.

"What?"

"Piglets. You misunderstood what you heard, Maddie. We were

talking about the piglets. Come here, look." Jordan waved her around the dining table into the kitchen. In the corner were two tiny pink piglets on a towel, nosing around the edges of an empty shallow bowl. Jordan picked one up. "This is Eleven. She's the one who prefers to suck my finger instead of eat out of the bowl."

"Pigs?" They were the last thing she'd expected to see.

"Piglets," said the woman, stepping closer to Jordan, her movements graceful and fluid, like that of a dancer. She seemed to almost float across the floor. "Aren't they cute?"

"What are you doing with piglets?"

"Trying to feed them." Jordan sighed. "I was up most of the night trying to get them to take the milk from a bowl. The Internet says it's safer than feeding them from a bottle."

"I don't understand."

"It seems they're susceptible to aspirating milk from a bottle into their lungs."

"I mean, why do you have piglets?"

"Oh...that's going to take some explanation." Jordan let out a sigh. Her eyes widened. "But first, I can't believe you thought I was fooling around with Leda."

"Feeding piglets was not at all what it sounded like," she said, staring at the woman. Leda, who remained silent, glanced sideways at Jordan with raised eyebrows.

"Maddie, look at me," Jordan said. Maddie locked her gaze with Jordan's, her dark hazel eyes mesmerizing. "I ought to be the one who's concerned that you don't trust me, but I'm not. The fact that you're a little jealous is kind of sweet." Jordan winced. "That didn't come out right. Jealousy is not a healthy emotion, but it means you like me, Madeline Grendel. And I like you, too." She ran her fingers of her free hand through her hair and resettled the piglet in her arm. She looked tired. "I'm trying to say I'm not interested in anyone but *you*."

"Don't get your bloomers in a twist, Professor," Leda said. "I am not moving in on your girl. Besides, I'm way too old for her."

"Impossible," Maddie said. Leda looked at least ten years younger than Jordan.

"It's very possible." Jordan took a deep breath and puffed her cheeks. "If you died a hundred years ago."

"What?" She wasn't sure she'd heard Jordan correctly.

Jordan scooped up the second piglet, cradling each in the crook of one arm. "I had really hoped to explain Leda before you met her."

"What's to explain?"

"She's a ghost, Maddie."

"Jordan," Leda said and stood tall, pushing up on the balls of her feet for added height. And then her toes impossibly lifted from the floor. With feet dangling in the air, she hovered a few feet over Jordan, her head near the ceiling, glowering at her. "How many times must I tell you? I'm not a ghost, I'm a—"

"Spirit," Jordan said.

The soft, shimmery glow wasn't just caused by the sequins in her yellow dress, Maddie realized. It seemed to be coming from her entire body. Maddie took off her glasses to rub her eyes.

"My apologies," Jordan said to Leda in a tired voice. "Like I said, Maddie, I was hoping to introduce you under better circumstances, but this is Leda Hatchee, the Palmer House ghost—excuse me, the Palmer House *spirit*."

Maddie resettled her glasses on the bridge of her nose. Nothing had changed. Leda was still floating. The dress was still shimmering. Jordan, holding two squirming piglets, acted like nothing was out of the ordinary. This was crazy. Maybe she was crazy. Was she dreaming? Hallucinating perhaps? Heart pounding, she felt short of breath and dizzy, her vision tunneled to Jordan's face. Was that a smile on her lips or a grimace? Suddenly everything seemed surreal.

Leda floated toward her, reaching out with a translucent arm. "Are you okay, Professor?" Her voice sounded tinny in Maddie's ears as her blood pounded and whooshed. Leda looked over her shoulder at Jordan. "I don't think she's taking this well."

"Maddie—" Jordan moved toward her.

"Stop." Maddie put up a hand and threw the bag of beignets she'd forgotten she was holding. The bag hit Jordan in the chest and dropped to the floor. Maddie stumbled backward through the dining room, bumping into the chairs, wanting nothing more than to get away from the house. When her hip slammed against the doorjamb, she turned and staggered out of Palmer House, calling Chip. The dog bounded across the yard and ran with her, tongue lolling happily, seeming to think they were playing a game, then jumped into the car with her.

Maddie sped away, terrified by images of Jordan grinning, pink baby pigs, a golden-haired flapper in a sparkling dress floating in the air churning in her brain like some literary lunacy, a phantasm. But a phantasm was illusory, and whatever she'd witnessed seemed very real. It was too much to process. Her tongue felt thick, like a dry wad of cotton stuck to the roof of her mouth. Turning the air-conditioning on high, she reached for a half-full water bottle in the console and chugged the tepid liquid. She pulled over in the first spot she could find, the driveway of the Epiphany Full Gospel Church. Chip leaned forward, panting hot breath on her shoulder. Maddie petted her as she closed her eyes and rested her head back against the headrest to focus on breathing deeply, slowly in and out, breathing and stroking Chip's soft fur, until her heart rate settled, and her hands stopped shaking.

She'd just seen a ghost. Maddie let the idea sink in. *Leda is a ghost.* A spirit, as she'd corrected Jordan. Maddie herself was a consummate teller of ghost stories. She'd repeated stories of campus ghosts countless times, knowing that, although some were based on real people and actual events, most were complete fiction. Part of the campus culture she loved, the tales were merely spooky entertainment. People enjoyed hearing them, and she enjoyed telling them.

As her rational mind reengaged, she remembered a story about "the woman in a yellow dress" she'd heard only once, from the now-retired public-relations director. She'd said it wasn't much of a story and only the old-timers knew about the occasional apparition of a young woman in a yellow dress who wandered the woods on the edge of campus. She was a ghost without a name, a personality, or a story like the other campus phantoms. Maybe that's why it had faded over time. It wasn't interesting enough to be retold. And now she had seen her, talked to her, even. She took another deep swallow of water and remembered telling Jordan that she believed in ghosts even though she'd never seen one. She was being honest when she said she believed in the possibility of their existence, but now, when presented with evidence, she felt unsteady, destabilized, like the ground had slipped beneath her feet. She just wasn't expecting it, she reasoned. It had been a shock to her system, and she'd reacted instinctually in fear instead of with curiosity.

She began to feel ashamed, not just for running away, but for immediately assuming that Jordan had been making out with another woman. If her sister were here, she'd reprimand her and say, "I told you, didn't I?" And as much as Maddie wanted to deny it, Caroline might be right that she was always looking for an exit, a way out, before a relationship even had a chance to develop. She was allowing fear to drive her actions.

She drummed her fingers on the steering wheel. Not counting the presence of ghosts and the complications of falling for someone who lived in another state, she asked herself what she really wanted. Picturing Jordan in front of her—tousled hair, warm hazel eyes, and shapely lips—she knew the answer was clear. She wanted Jordan. More time with her, more kisses, and more opportunities to explore possibilities. And answers, too. She wanted answers to the many questions now forming. Before she'd tossed the beignets and fled from Palmer House like a lunatic, Jordan had said she had a lot to explain. She most certainly did. Where did those piglets come from? How did Jordan meet the ghost? Maybe the woman in the yellow dress had a story after all. With her curiosity engaged, Maddie regained her courage.

"There's only one way to find the answers, Chip," she said, putting the car in gear. "We go back to Palmer House."

❖

When Maddie pulled up next to Jordan's 4Runner by the back entrance of Palmer House, the door of the house was wide open.

"Hello?" Maddie called into the house from the back steps. "Jordan?" Chip stood behind her, bumping against her leg. Rain began to fall, dripping off the covered walkway between the two buildings. Chip stayed close as she checked the studio. The door was locked, and the lights were out. She walked back to the house and stepped cautiously inside. Chip didn't follow her. Staying outside the threshold, she sniffed the air with interest. The bag of beignets was still on the floor, and chairs were turned over where Maddie had bumped into them. She righted the chairs and picked up the bag, carrying it while she looked around. Strangely, even the sound of the paper sack didn't compel Chip to come in and beg for a treat. The piglets were in the kitchen, burrowed into a blanket, sleeping soundly next to the licked-clean bowl.

The house felt very still. The only sounds she heard were the low rumble of thunder in the distance and rain drumming on the metal roof of the covered walkway. She climbed the stairs. Jordan wasn't up there. Her toiletries were arranged on the bathroom sink, her clothes draped neatly over a chair. She touched a shirt lightly with her fingertips, remembering it as the one Jordan had worn to the gala. Her bag and car keys lay on the dressing table. Nothing seemed amiss, except Jordan, whose absence felt heavy. Something wasn't right.

She went downstairs and walked into the living room. Jordan's cell phone was on the seat of a wingback chair. She picked it up and swiped the screen to find a grid of photos. She expected to see pictures of the river and the lilies, but instead the photos showed a dirty barn packed with pigs. Swiping through the pictures, she was shocked and then disgusted at the condition of the animals the photos captured in crowded, filthy, inhumane conditions. Her stomach churned. Why were these photos on Jordan's phone? There was obviously a connection between the pig barn and the sleeping piglets in the kitchen, but what?

Chip barked outside, and a draft of cold air, like the air-conditioning had turned on high, pulled her attention away from the phone.

"Chip?" She walked to the hallway and turned toward the open front door. Before she could ask why she was barking, Leda flickered into view in front of her, wringing her hands.

"Maddie!" Leda circled her, words rushing out of her mouth, "Thank God, you came back! Jordan is in trouble! You must help her!"

"What? Slow down." Chip drowned out Leda's voice with excited barking, like she'd treed a squirrel. "Chip, no barking. That's a good girl. It's okay." When Chip finally quieted, she returned her attention to Leda. "Where's Jordan? What trouble?"

"Barron took her!"

"Barron? Barron Maxfield?"

Leda nodded.

"What do you mean he took her?"

"He's angry. I think he might hurt her. He knows she saw his hog barn."

Maddie held up the phone, showing Leda a photograph of injured pigs crowded in a pen. "This hog barn?"

"Yes. He is so angry, Maddie."

"This is his barn? This is how he's raising the hogs? It can't be. His farm is—"

"It is." Leda shook her head. "He's lied to everyone. Barron is a cruel and greedy man."

She was appalled. "That lying bastard! He's been telling everyone how much he cares about animal welfare and how his hogs are living the good life. If people knew—" She completed the thought silently. If people knew about this, it would destroy his reputation and his expanding restaurant business. "If Jordan has discovered his dirty secret—" She inhaled sharply at the thought. People killed for a lot less. "Where did he take her?"

"To the barn."

"The barn in these photos?"

"Yes. Oh! This is my fault...all my fault." Leda swooped around the room, saying the words over and over.

"Why is it your fault?"

"I took her there. I wanted her to see those abused animals and maybe do something to expose the cruelty. I didn't think it would end like this."

"*End?*" She turned and rushed out the door. "Come on. You're going to take me there right now."

"I can't," Leda wailed.

"You have to."

Chip growled as Leda followed her, floating over the threshold. "Chip, settle down." The shepherd looked tense, the fur on her back raised. "Look at me," she commanded. Chip obeyed, her big brown eyes meeting hers. "It's okay. Leda's okay." She hurried to her car and opened the back door. "Get in." Chip hopped in, spinning around to stare at Leda. Maddie slid into the driver's seat and rolled down the passenger window. Leda stood still, unmoving. "You, too, Leda. Get in. Hurry up. Let's go!"

"I can't," Leda wailed again.

"Why not?"

"Spirits can't travel that way." Leda pointed to the Subaru and sobbed like she was crying, although her eyes were dry. "I can only guide you on foot. It will take too long for us to walk there."

"Leda." She spoke her name firmly and got out of the car, ignoring the rain pelting the top of her head. "Calm down and come here." She used the firm but gentle tone of voice she reserved for students crying in her office when they'd received failing grades. Leda floated closer.

"Talk to me, Leda. Can you describe where the hog barn is? There must be a road to it."

"It's next to Little Turtle Creek."

"I've never heard of it. Where is it?"

"It runs into the Cahaba."

"Every river, creek, and trickle of water in this area flows into the Cahaba. Where is it in relation to a landmark, something I might know."

Leda squeezed her eyes shut as if concentrating. "There are a lot of trees." She opened her eyes, looking helpless.

"Oh my God, Leda. There are trees everywhere." She lost her composure. "That's not going to help. How am I going to find this barn if you can't tell me where it is?" Maddie waved her arms in exasperation. The weight of Jordan's phone in her hand gave her an idea. "The photos can tell us!" Praying that Jordan had the location setting on her phone turned on, she opened the most recent photo in the preview app, looked for the Show More option, and tapped the GPS button. A map instantly appeared with the location of the photo tagged with a pin. "Aha!" she shouted and zoomed in on the satellite image. "Found it!"

Leda's eyes grew big as she looked at the map. "Wow. Ain't that the cat's whiskers. Can you get there from looking at that picture?"

"I'm not sure. Let me see." She zoomed the map out and saw an unmarked road without state or county numbers. Following it and zooming in, she wasn't surprised to see that the road intersected with the Palmer-Maxfield party barn. It must be Barron's private back-way access to the hog barn. "This looks like the most direct route."

"I'll be there when you arrive," Leda said quickly. Without warning, she disappeared, her voice lingering in Maddie's ears. "Hurry."

Maddie stared at the air where Leda had been standing, blinking as rain dripped down her temples, and her glasses began to fog. Back in the car, she swiped the lenses with the hem of her shirt and resettled the round, plastic frames on her nose, astonished at just how normal it had been to talk with Leda. In fact, the spirit seemed ordinary in comparison to the almost inconceivable situation she faced—that a deceitful and dangerous millionaire restauranteur had kidnapped Jordan, and she was going to rescue her.

"Hang on, Chip," she said as she started the car and sped down the driveway, kicking up gravel. She needed to get through that security gate at the Palmer-Maxfield estate, and she hoped Tammi was at home in the mansion on the hill and would let her in. She had no idea how to explain any of this without sounding like she'd lost her mind.

# CHAPTER SIXTEEN

Jordan opened her eyes and gasped for breath. Lying flat on her back, she winced at the bright industrial lights overhead. Her hands tingled, and the air smelled bad—rotten and fetid like shit. Shit stuck to the slatted concrete floor of the walkway in between the pens in the hog barn she'd been in last night. She closed her eyes to fight the nausea churning in her stomach and focused on the sounds around her—humming fans, grunts and squeals, and dripping water. The animals were nearby. When a fly landed on her nose, she opened her eyes and tried to swat it away but couldn't. Lifting her head to look down the length of her body, she saw her wrists and feet bound with rope. Her heart raced in panic, clearing her foggy mind. She was hog-tied.

The last thing she remembered clearly was Barron striding into Palmer House a few minutes after Maddie left. When she had heard the slam of a car door outside, she thought Maddie had come back, and she'd run to the sound, hoping she'd calmed down and returned to talk, to let her explain everything. Instead, she was surprised by Barron, his expression grim. Without breaking stride or saying a word, he raised his fist as if to hit her. She flinched, but when his hand came down on her shoulder, she felt a sharp pinch instead of a blow. Everything after that was fuzzy, until she woke up here, on the floor in the barn. He must have had a syringe and needle in his hand. Jesus, what had he injected her with?

Panicking, she wanted to get up and run, but that was impossible. She rolled onto her side and bent her knees, pulling them toward her chest and tucking her feet under her butt to take the tension off the length of rope strung between her hands and feet. Twisting, she reached into her pocket for her pocketknife, relieved when she touched the smooth metal of the case. After she carefully gripped the knife in the palm of one hand, she opened it by sliding a fingernail under the notch on the spine of the blade. She used the knife mostly for slicing cheese and apples during her hikes. The smooth, slim blade wasn't designed for cutting rope, but she always kept it clean and sharp. Grasping the knife tightly, she twisted her wrists and jabbed the short blade into the rough fibers of the sisal rope stretched between her hands and feet, then jerked it, severing a few strands. She jabbed and tugged a few more times, each tug pulling her ankles and wrists painfully, but also loosening the rope around her ankles. Barron might be a lot of things, but he wasn't good at tying knots. One more tug and she'd be able to slip it off her feet, but a door slammed, and she kept still.

"You're awake," he growled and ran his fingers through wet hair, pushing the bangs out of his eyes. His red shirt was dappled with dark spots, like he'd been in the rain. "I hoped to keep you out longer, but I only had one dose of ketamine the vet conveniently left behind. I was saving it for a rainy day." He sniggered and shook his head. "I told you it wasn't safe out here."

"I thought you were warning me about feral hogs, not you."

"You're trying to blame your situation on me?" He waved a hand. "You're the trespasser here."

"You drugged and kidnapped me!"

"Only after you trespassed," he snapped back. "Actions have consequences. This is *your* damn fault. I wouldn't have to do any of this if you hadn't trespassed on my property."

"Tammi gave me permission."

"To use the cabin and paint the damn flowers in the river." His cheeks reddened as he pointed at her. "I specifically told you to stay out of the back woods, to keep away from here."

"How can you be so cruel to these hogs?"

"Cruel? They're just dumb animals bred for slaughter. They don't have emotions like we do. The only things they care about are establishing dominance and eating." He chuckled. "I actually kind of respect them for that."

"You're absolutely right," she said. She'd had conversations on this topic before, and her agreement always surprised the person who tried to make Barron's argument. "We cannot hold animals to human standards. But we have ethics, and morality, and choice. We can choose to be decent human beings. I thought you were one, and now I see I was very wrong."

"Don't you dare," he shouted, the veins in his thick neck bulging. "I will not let some nosy, bleeding-heart, liberal dyke lecture me about morality."

"Let me go, Barron," she said.

"Why? So you can tell people what you've seen? Ruin my reputation and my business? I'm not stupid."

"You don't have to do this."

"Just what is it you think I'm doing?"

"Scaring me." She prayed that was all. "So I won't talk about what I've seen."

"You're scared? That's good. You should be. But you don't strike me as the kind of woman who will keep her mouth shut. All y'all damn eco-nuts give me a headache with your constant doom-and-gloom predictions and the-earth-belongs-to-everybody bullshit. News alert: it doesn't. The world belongs to men like me who grab it by the balls and twist hard. Strong men, smart men. *Rich* men." He thumped his chest. "Survival of the fittest—isn't that the rule of nature? If I let you go, you will ruin my life and my wife's life, too. She'd have nothing without me."

"That's because you got her pregnant and she dropped out of college to support you rather than follow her dreams of being an interior designer."

"Trust me, like most women, she's not that bright and has little talent. I did her a favor by knocking her up. She's a very wealthy woman now. After we got married, I took her inheritance and used it to build my businesses. I made her the wife of a multi-millionaire. So, whither I go, she goes. That's straight from the Bible, you know. Now *that's* morality. God helps those who help themselves, Jordan, and you are not helping me. Quite the opposite. You're just one little annoyance getting in my way. And it's pissing me off that I have to deal with it." He grinned wickedly and laughed. "You're nothing but a pest, like a mosquito or a cockroach. You know what we do with pests? We exterminate them."

She shivered and gripped the little open knife hidden in her hand so tightly she risked cutting herself. She needed to keep him talking, to stall for time. If she distracted him, she might be able to slip her feet out of the looped rope and run. It might be the only way to save her life.

"It's not just me, Barron. My friend Leda was here with me. She saw everything, too."

He cocked his head, eyeing her sideways. "You're lying. I saw the security-cam video." He pointed to small white boxes mounted on the ceiling. "You were the only one here."

"You may not have seen her, but she was here." Apparently, Leda hadn't registered on video. She tried a different approach. "You must have seen I was taking pictures. I sent them to several people. They'll come looking for me here and figure out it was you. Kidnapping is one thing, Barron. You can let me go, and we'll chalk it up to a heated argument. But murder? You want to be a murderer? You'll spend your life in prison. In this state you could be executed. You'll never get away with this."

"This is Alabama, honey. You'd be surprised what a respectable, wealthy, and well-connected man can get away with, *especially* in this state. I don't donate to politicians for nothing. I scratch their backs, and they scratch mine." He growled at her, but her words seemed to have unsettled him. It seemed he hadn't considered photographs and that she might have shared them.

"Where's your phone?"

"I have no idea," Jordan lied. "It was in my pocket when you kidnapped me. It must have fallen out."

He paced, and when he turned, she saw something dark sticking out of the back of his Carhartt pants, the handle of a gun in a conceal-carry holster.

*Fuck, fuck, fuck!* The word reverberated in her mind in time with the thumping of his boots on the concrete floor. He ran his thick fingers through his hair repeatedly, seeming preoccupied. He walked back to her slowly and, with hands on knees, leaned over, speaking in a low voice. "Tell me, who the hell is Leda?"

"Oh, so you believe me now?" She goaded him, trying to keep him engaged and trying not to think about the gun.

"Who is she?"

"You wouldn't know her."

"Don't be coy." He lurched forward. With surprising strength, he hooked his hands under her armpits, yanking her into a seated position and pinning her against the bars. The hogs in the pen behind her scattered. "Who is Leda?" he demanded. "What is her last name?"

Knowing Barron couldn't hurt the spirit, she told him. "Leda Hatchee."

"Hatchee? I don't know that name." He pushed her hard, painfully, against the metal bars. The noise frightened the hogs, their feet clacking on the concrete floor behind her as they moved away from them. His face was so close to hers she could see the thin, red veins in his dark eyes and smell the sweet, acrid odor of whiskey on his breath. "She's a local?"

"Yeah, from a real old family."

"It shouldn't be too hard to find her then."

"You can't find her unless she wants to be found."

"Nonsense. Anyone can be found."

"Not this one."

"What makes her so special?"

"She's a spirit."

"A what?" he snarled.

"A ghost."

He dropped her, scowling as he walked away. She heard water running, and when he came back into view, he was carrying a plastic bucket. "That drug must have made you a little fuzzy. You must have been hallucinating," he said as he swung the pail. She closed her eyes and mouth before the cold water hit her in the face, but she couldn't protect her nose. She coughed and sputtered as the water went up her nostrils, stinging her sinuses. "Don't play games with me, girl."

"I'm not." She coughed. It was true. Leda appeared only on her own terms. Where was she? Surely, she must have seen Barron attack her at Palmer House. If Leda was here, maybe she could help. He grabbed her by the hair on the back of her head, turning her to face the hogs in the pen. The bars were thankfully narrow. Otherwise, he probably would have pushed her head into the pen. Several curious hogs rushed forward as a mass, grunting and snuffling the air, the edges of their noses quivering. The bravest hog came close, rubbing his wet snout across her forehead and cheek. He opened his wet, pink mouth, revealing narrow, sharp teeth, as if he might bite. And why wouldn't he? All these hogs knew about humans was that they were abusive and inflicted pain. If they were hungry enough, God knew what they might do to her. She screamed and thrashed. Barron released her, and she pulled away just as the hog chomped the air inches in front of her. He grunted as if surprised to find he didn't have a piece of her between his teeth.

"I told you, pigs are easy keepers. They'll eat just about anything." He laughed. "You know, instead of shooting you, I'm thinking I'll feed you to the hogs. It's an old tried-and-true method of getting rid of the things you don't want. They don't leave any evidence behind. Not a scrap!"

She was breathing so hard and fast she was starting to feel dizzy. She exhaled through pursed lips, trying to force herself not to hyperventilate. Tears began to pool and well in her eyes. She couldn't lose it now. She needed to keep her wits about her if she was going to have any chance of getting out of this barn alive.

"Oh, don't cry. I hate it when women cry," he said with irritation. "You're all so damn weak and manipulative. You cry, and then I'm supposed to figure out how to make you stop, right? You have no idea how hard it is to be the nice guy." He sighed dramatically. "Look, would it make you feel better to know that I'm not going to feed you to the hogs?"

Jordan blinked and sniffed, refusing to let tears break through, trying not to be the weak, emotional woman that Barron seemed to expect her to be.

"No." He spoke slowly and gently like he was calming a child. "Don't worry. I won't do that. It's very messy, it takes time, and these hogs will be going to the butcher soon. I was thinking—" He touched his chin as he shifted his tone to that of a persuasive businessman making a well-crafted pitch. "With all this rain we've been getting, the river's flooding, and you've been working so hard out there every day, painting your little pictures." He smiled and chillingly began talking about her in the past tense. "You weren't from around here, bless your heart. And gosh darn it, you must not have had have the sense to come in out of the rain. You must have stayed out there at the river too long, slipped on a rock, and got swept away. Tragic, but it happens all the time. Hunter goes missing, hiker goes missing, kayaker goes missing.

Sometimes they find the body. Sometimes they don't. My wife's going to be real sad about it. She liked you, and she'll regret not getting those paintings you promised her." He sighed again and lifted his eyebrows, feigning a pained expression. "I'll be a sensitive husband, a good listener, while she whines on and on about it. But she'll get over it. She'll find a new artist to play patron with soon enough." He nudged her with the toe of his boot. "You're a nobody. You're nothing special."

She seethed. "Go fuck yourself, you son of a bitch!"

He laughed. "Now what?" He grunted, his sadistic glee interrupted by the ringing of his cell phone. He pulled the phone from his pocket and looked at it. "Well, speak of the devil. It's my wife," he said with a smirk that effortlessly transformed into a sweet smile. Barron Maxfield was like Jekyll and Hyde. His ability to shift character like a seasoned actor, from nice guy to malevolent asshole, would have been admirable if he were acting. He was definitely a sadistic psychopath. "Hi, honey," he said, answering the phone. "It sure is raining cats and dogs, isn't it? My golf game got canceled. I'm still at the club, though. Having some drinks with the boys. What's up? When will I be home? Oh, a couple of hours, I guess."

A hog rubbed his flank on the bars next to Jordan, giving her an idea. "Sorry, pig," she whispered before poking the hog with the tip of her pocketknife, not hard enough to break the skin, but enough to make him jump forward with a squeal and cause a shrieking upheaval among his pen mates. Barron turned around, frowning. "What's that sound? Oh, that's just the boys horsing around. You know them," he said with a strained laugh as he scurried to the far side of the barn, away from the commotion.

She didn't waste a moment. As soon as Barron's back was turned, she reached forward to pull the sandals from her feet, wriggling them out of the coiled rope and putting them back on. Her hands were still tied, but at least she could run now. She looked around quickly, remembering the doors were in the corners. Locating an exit, she leapt to her feet and, keeping her eyes fixed on the door as she ran to it, pumped her legs as fast as she could. Reaching forward with both hands, she pushed the door open into bracing wind and refreshing cold rain. As raindrops pelted her face, she sprinted like a deer for the safety of cover in the woods.

❖

Maddie lowered the window and jabbed the button on the call box at the gate, trying to smile at the black, circular glass covering the security camera.

"Professor? Is that you?"

"Yes. It's Maddie Grendel. I'm so sorry to bother you unannounced, but I'm here about Jordan Burroughs. She needs your help."

"Well, by all means, come up to the house."

With a warning buzz, the black, ornate gate opened smoothly, sliding open to admit her to the property and closing silently behind her as she passed through and sped up the hill. Tammi, always well put together, wore a flower-print top, white capris, and huarache sandals. She stood under the portico at the front door waiting as she pulled up. Maddie left Chip in the car with the engine and air-conditioning running and climbed the stairs.

"You don't look so good. Are you okay?" Tammi asked.

"I'm not sure I am." She rushed her words. "I have to act quickly, so you'll have to forgive me for leaving out some details. You need to trust me."

"You're scaring me a little, Professor."

"I am scared, and I think you should be, too. Barron's been lying to us all about his business."

"Which one? He has several businesses."

"The barbecue restaurants. The hogs aren't pasture-raised. They're not being treated anything even close to humane. They're hidden away in some God-forsaken barn in horrible conditions out there on your property." She gestured to the trees in the distance. "Jordan found out about it, and he's kidnapped her and taken her to the barn. I think he's going to do something terrible. We need to stop him, and the fastest way out there is from here." She stopped to take a breath and observed Tammi's reaction. Would she believe a word she'd just said?

"You must be mistaken, Professor. My Barron's not that kind of man."

Maddie opened a photo on Jordan's phone, a panoramic view of the inside of the barn crowded with hogs, and held it up for Tammi to see. With thumb and index finger, she zoomed in on one of the sick-looking animals.

"For the love of God." Tammi gasped. "You're saying this is on *my* property?"

"Yes." She opened the map. "Right here. There's a road from the party barn to that hellhole. Barron is there with Jordan right now, and he's going to hurt her." She paused. "I think he might kill her."

"Now you just wait a minute, Madeline. That is quite an accusation! Barron wouldn't…he couldn't…" Tammi rushed inside and returned with a cell phone in hand. "I'm going to call him right now."

"I don't think that's such a good idea—" she tried to say, but Tammi waved her off, glowering while she waited for Barron to answer the call. "Barron, darling. What are you doing?" she asked lightly, nodding while listening to his reply. Maddie could hear his voice but not his words. She fought the desire to run to her car, take off, and not waste any more time. "You're at the club? Rain canceled your game, you say?" Tammi raised her voice and smiled at Maddie as if to say, "See my husband's not a deceitful, would-be murderer."

Suddenly her eyes widened, and her features fell. "Barron, what was that sound? Really? Horsing around at the club? How unusual. They usually expect much more dignified behavior from their members. Yes, I understand. When do you think you'll be home?" A jagged flash of cloud-to-ground lightning caught Maddie's eye. Surveying the sky, she could tell another round of rain was coming soon. Thunder cracked and rolled overhead. Listening to Barron, Tammi narrowed her eyes and pursed her plump lips into a grim line. When she spoke, her voice was flat and emotionless. "Well, don't stay out too late, and be careful driving home. A wicked storm's brewing." She lowered the phone and stared at the tree line in the distance with a dark expression.

"Well?" Maddie asked impatiently.

"Barron is lying," Tammi said coldly. "That thunder we just heard, I heard it on his end a second before, and I heard pigs squealing in the background. He isn't with his buddies at the country club. They don't allow raucous behavior there, and I know what pigs sound like. I have them for pets. They sure as hell don't sound like drunk fifty-year-old business executives. You know, he's never let me see his business hogs, as he likes to call them. He convinced me that I was too tender, that if

I saw them, I'd want to make pets of them all and ruin his business." Tammi turned to face her, looking at her with a steely gaze. "I believe those photos, Professor. Pictures don't lie. And I believe Jordan might have gotten into trouble with Barron, but I do not believe my husband is capable of murder. But he is, sure to God, not telling me the truth. I *hate* being lied to."

Maddie, unconvinced by Tammi's faith in her husband, was anxious to get to the hog barn as soon as possible. "Then you don't mind if I use your private road to get there?"

"Of course not." Tammi looked over Maddie's shoulder at her car. "And it appears to me that you have room for a passenger. Let me get my purse."

The red dirt road was muddy from the recent heavy rains. Maddie was thankful for her Subaru's nimble four-wheel-drive capability. Neither of them spoke as she drove, both hands on the wheel and staring ahead, focused on keeping up her speed as she plowed down the narrow road, pine branches occasionally scraping the sides of the car, windshield wipers thumping, and tires throwing orange, clay-colored water into the air when she hit a dip in the road. Tammi didn't say anything except "Oh!" at every bump, while clutching her purse with her left hand and grasping the handle above the window with a white-knuckled grip. Maddie wasn't sure why she needed her purse, but Tammi was a true Southern lady, and such ladies didn't leave the house without hairspray, lipstick, and a handbag. Chip stood in the center of the rear seat, legs splayed for stability, tail wagging, sweeping rhythmically across the back of the seat like a metronome. From the dog's perspective they were on a fun back-road adventure. She wished that were the case.

At the bottom of a steep hill, the road turned into a level clearing, revealing a long, windowless metal building and silos seated diagonally alongside several ponds containing some kind of carmine-colored liquid. Its pinkish-violet hue looked toxic, and they were full to the brim.

"What is that terrible stench?" Tammi asked, the first thing she'd said since they'd gotten in the car.

"I think it's coming from that." Maddie gestured with her head. "Those are manure lagoons."

"Lagoons?"

"Pig waste. They flush it out of the barns and into ponds like that."

"It's awful." Tammi grimaced and released her hand from the handle to point at a big, red four-wheel-drive truck parked by the barn. "That's Barron's truck."

Maddie's heart thumped. Now what? She'd gotten here without a plan for what to do next. Leda had said she'd meet her here. Would she appear if Tammi was with her, and how would Tammi react? But it didn't matter. She needed to find Jordan and make sure she was okay. But what about Barron?

Pulling up at the barn and stopping, Maddie glanced at Tammi, whose expression was serious but calm. Of course she was calm. She didn't believe her husband was a kidnapper or potential murderer. She probably just expected to give him a thorough tongue-lashing. Maddie, on the other hand, had been convinced by Leda that Barron was dangerous. "I guess we go into the barn?"

"Yes," Tammi said, opening the car door.

The wind and rain didn't dampen the stink from the ponds. They dashed to the barn door and stepped in to discover it was worse inside. Maddie pulled the collar of her shirt over her nose and mouth to try to filter the stench. Standing in the awful reality of it was so much worse than the photos Jordan had recorded on her cell phone.

"I don't see Barron," Tammi said.

"Or Jordan."

"His truck is here, so he must be nearby." Tammi's expression changed from shock, to horror, to anger as she surveyed the expanse of the barn. "That no-good, lying son of a bitch," she snarled. "Barron has some explaining to do."

## CHAPTER SEVENTEEN

Jordan raced up the hill into the woods, darting between tree trunks and ducking under low branches without any sense of where to go or hide. She needed to put as much space between her and Barron as she could. He would undoubtedly come after her. She stumbled and almost fell. With her hands bound in front of her, she couldn't swing them for balance, and she didn't dare take time to pause and try to unbind them. She crested the hill and stopped to scan the area, panting from the exertion. To her left stretched a large mass of craggy, exposed bedrock. On her right, the ground sloped down sharply. A visible, well-worn deer path cut through the undergrowth. If she weren't trying to evade Barron, if she were on a casual hike, she'd probably follow it to see where it went. But Barron was a hunter. He'd notice it, too. Maybe she could use it to throw him off her track. She glanced over her shoulder at the way she'd come. It was hard to wait, with adrenaline coursing through her veins making her jittery and wanting to keep running. But she needed to pause long enough for him to see her, just for a few seconds. A flash of red in the trees, Barron's polo shirt, revealed his position. He was moving below her at a slow trot.

He lifted his head with a jerk. He'd seen her! Like a rabbit, she darted sharply to the right and followed the deer path several yards until she knew she was downhill far enough to be out of his line of sight. Veering sharply left, she stepped off the deer trail and worked her way back uphill, praying she'd make it to the big rock before Barron crested the hill and saw her. If her trick worked, he'd see her heading to the right, and when he spotted the obvious path, he'd assume she was following it. Thinking he was tracking her, he'd be moving away from where she really was—sitting tight, just a few yards above him, hiding behind the big rock.

She made it to the rock before Barron crested the hill. Pressing close to its jagged contours, she took deep breaths, her chest heaving from the sprint uphill. She slowed her breathing, to calm herself. The rope chafed against her wrists, and the palm of her right hand hurt. She looked down to see a trickle of blood. Unbelievably she hadn't dropped the little pocketknife, but she'd gripped it so hard, adrenaline masking the pain, that the blade had cut her. It was a shallow wound, and she could ignore it and the rope for now. She needed to focus on being quiet and listening.

It wasn't long before Barron clumped and shuffled through the leaf litter and then stopped. She could hear him panting. Jordan held her breath. Had he seen her?

"Little bitch. Making me chase you down in this goddamn weather," he muttered. Hopefully he was pausing to figure out which way she'd gone and would see the deer trail as he scanned the hillside. "So you went that way, huh? You're going to be as easy to bag as a stupid young doe." The sound of his feet moving in the leaves began again and tapered off.

He had taken the bait! Elated, she let out her breath quietly. She would sit tight just a little longer to give him some distance. And then what? Where should she go? She tried to visualize the maps she'd studied and correlate the location of the barn in relation to the cabin and the river, but she was too turned around to orient herself in her mental picture. The storm and overcast sky didn't help. She couldn't find the cardinal points from observing the position of the sun. The Palmer-Maxfield property was adjacent to the wildlife refuge and surrounded by timber and gas land, where the few houses were far between and mostly close to roads. If you got lost in the woods, you were supposed to retrace your steps or stay put and await rescue. The last resort was to follow water downstream until you found a road crossing it. None of those options sounded appealing, but getting to the river and following its flow probably gave her the best chance of encountering someone who wasn't Barron.

If he didn't find her soon, he'd come back. He might follow the deer trail and pass the boulder on the way to the hog barn. In that case, staying put would keep her out of his line of sight. But, given this was his hunting ground, he probably knew the topography well, and he might circle around, looking for her. If he climbed the hill behind the big rock, he'd easily see her if she didn't change positions. Moving was best, she decided, and she needed to do it soon, but not too quickly.

She wasn't wearing her watch so didn't have a sense of how much time had passed. It could have been five minutes or fifteen. She waited a little longer, straining to hear any sound that might be him, but the woods were quiet except for the patter of rain in the leaves and rumbling thunder. A flash of lightning was followed by an explosion of thunder a few seconds later. Rain began falling heavier, sluicing through the tree canopy. Normally, she'd be anxious caught outside in a storm like this, but now, being struck by lightning was the very least of her worries.

Soaking wet by the time she felt confident Barron was out of earshot, she shook her head to knock the rain drops off her bangs and inspected the rope wrapped around her wrists. She twisted and tugged but couldn't loosen it enough to free her hands. She suddenly felt cold, as if the adrenaline rush had worn off, but the chill had a recognizably unnatural feel to it.

"Leda?" she whispered. "Are you here?"

"I am," Leda said as she slowly appeared, standing in front of Jordan in her shimmering yellow dress.

"*Shhh!* Get down. Barron's out here looking for me," she whispered and gestured for her to sit. "Can you tone down the sparkle? You look like a fishing lure."

Leda instantly lost her brilliance, becoming translucent. Jordan could see the swaying treetops behind her.

"Can you help me get this off?" She raised her wrists. If Leda could carry small things like rocks, and books, and her cell phone, maybe she could help undo the knot.

"I think so. But I need to be stronger, sorry." Leda's golden glow returned as she pulled at the knot with her fingers, feeling like ice cubes when they grazed her skin. Leda loosened it enough that Jordan was able to slip one hand out.

"Oh, my God…" She breathed and shook her hand and wriggled her bloody fingers. "That feels so good."

"You're bleeding!"

"Just a little cut. I'm okay," she said, pocketing her knife and pulling the rope from her other hand. "Hey, can you tone down the glow again?"

"Of course," Leda said, returning to semi-transparency. "You weren't in the barn when I returned, but Barron's truck was there, and I saw fresh footprints and followed them to the edge of the trees. It took me a while to find you here. You hide well."

"From years of playing hide-and-seek in the woods with my brothers," she said.

"Where is Barron?"

"Down there somewhere." She pointed down the hill. "I threw him off my trail, but I need to get away from here. Which way is the river?"

Leda pointed up the hill. "That way, three hills over. But why don't you wait for Maddie? She's coming to get you," Leda said, keeping her voice low.

"She's coming? You mean to the hog barn?"

"Yes. I found her at my house. I guess she drove back to talk to you. She discovered your little telephone and used the photographs you took to find the barn on a map."

"Clever woman," Jordan said.

"I asked her to help you."

"Did she call the police?"

"I don't know."

"Why didn't she call them?"

"How would I know? I didn't ask. I was in a hurry to get back to you."

"Barron has a gun, Leda. He wants to kill me. If he's willing to kill me, he'll kill Maddie, too. Don't let her walk into a trap. You need to go back to her and tell her Barron has a gun, and she needs to call the police."

"But—"

"Now, Leda! Don't waste any more time."

"I don't feel good about leaving you here," Leda said.

"I'll be okay." She wasn't sure why she said that because she wasn't convinced she would be okay, not one bit, and now she was worried about Maddie running into an angry and armed Barron unawares. "Protect Maddie."

"If that's what you want," Leda said uneasily.

"I do. *Go.*"

Frowning, Leda waved good-bye and disappeared.

Figuring it was now or never, Jordan climbed the hill, and, as she began to descend the other side, she stopped abruptly, stunned by what she saw. Barron, clothes soaking wet, black hair flat and dripping, was traversing upslope, gun in hand. He had his eyes to the ground and didn't see her. She took two steps back and slipped. Her sandals, which were meant for wading, not off-trail hiking, lost their traction, and she slid feet-first, hitting the rocky ground hard. The movement caught his attention, and he raised his head, the frown on his lips lifting into a wicked grin when they made eye contact. He raised his gun.

As she rolled over to push herself up, a shot rang out like the crack of thunder, and the bark on the tree in front of her exploded, peppering her with splinters of wood. She dropped to the ground, covering her head with her hands.

"I didn't miss my mark," he yelled. "Next one's in the back of your head if you get up again," he shouted. "Don't you fucking move."

Something warm snaked down her cheek, and she touched her face. She was bleeding. A piece of bark must have grazed her cheek, but she didn't feel any pain. Her heart pounded, her pulse whooshing in her ears. While he huffed up the hill behind her, she prayed he wouldn't execute her anyway.

"Stupid girl. You really thought you could get away from me?" He spat the words. "Roll over." She complied. Standing over her, he looked like a shaggy, wet dog. "Take off your shoes, and throw them down the hill."

She slowly removed one sandal and thought about throwing it at him, but it wouldn't do any good. It would probably only enrage him more. She tossed the sandal, and it landed with a quiet *thump* in the vegetation.

"The other one! Hurry up!"

She removed and tossed the other sandal. "Satisfied?"

"Shut up and walk that way," he demanded, pointing up the hill, back toward the hog barn. "I don't want to hear another fucking word out of your mouth. Try to run, and, so help me God, even though it will be very inconvenient, I will kill you now instead of later."

He marched her barefoot back toward the hog barn. She only half felt the pain of rocks under her feet and thorny brambles scratching her legs. She didn't want to die, and her mind raced with possibilities for escape, but none seemed possible. If Leda would get Maddie to call the police like she'd asked, they might arrive in time, and she wouldn't die today. She slowed her pace. The slower she walked, the more time the police had to show up.

"Faster," he shouted behind her.

"I can't!" She stopped and turned to face him, breaking her silence and gesturing to her scratched and muddy legs. "My feet hurt. You made me toss my sandals."

"I told you, *shut up*," he barked. "Turn around." He lifted the barrel of the gun in line with her head. "Keep walking."

When they got back to the clearing, the ground was soft and muddy, a relief from the rocks and thorns. The sky was darker, and the rain was so heavy it almost smothered the stench of the manure ponds. She lifted her eyes, rain dripping off her eyelashes, to look ahead. Her breath caught in her throat when she saw Maddie's car parked near Barron's truck by the barn. He saw it, too. Her heart fell when she saw no police cars.

"Fuck," he muttered and grabbed her wrist, pulling it painfully up between her shoulder blades. She started to protest and stiffened when she felt the tip of the barrel of the gun against her temple. "Quiet."

He frog-marched her quickly toward the barn, and when she realized he was pushing her toward his truck instead, her heart raced in panic. She dug her heels into the gravel and pitched her feet forward. Ignoring the searing pain in her shoulder, she leaned back as hard as she could against him, frantically trying to slow him, but he pushed her forward in between his truck and Maddie's Subaru.

She was done being quiet. "Let go of me!" she roared and twisted.

"*WOO-WOO!*" Ferocious barking erupted from Maddie's car. "*WOO-WOO-WOO-WOO!*" Chip, head bouncing with every bark, looked like a hellhound in the back window, the whites of her eyes showing and long, ivory canines flashing against her black fur.

Startled, Barron flinched, releasing his grip on her wrist just enough to allow her to pull free. She leapt toward the car, grabbed the handle, and opened the door. Diving into the driver's seat, she pressed her palm against the steering wheel, sounding the horn in a long, solid blast.

He gripped the waistband of her shorts, pulled her from the car, and then grabbed her by the hair. On her knees in front of him, she balled her hand into a fist and threw her elbow up with as much force as she could muster, connecting with his groin. He bent over, making a sound like the air had been forced from his lungs, but he didn't let go. Chip lurched over the center console, leapt out of the car, and knocked Barron sideways.

Grunting and pressing the forearm of the hand holding the gun against his crotch, he tried to regain his balance, but Chip had sunk her teeth into the back pocket of his pants, tugging and shaking furiously.

Barron's gun discharged into the sodden ground close enough to Jordan's head to make her ears ring.

"Barron!" someone shrieked.

She looked up to see Tammi standing outside the door of the barn. Clutching a handbag, she looked ready for a ladies' luncheon. Maddie, wide-eyed and illuminated by golden light, stood behind her.

Maddie ran forward, screaming at Barron. "Let her go!"

The golden light was coming from Leda, now visible, rising above them, her face a mask of fury.

"Jesus Fucking Christ." Barron's eyes grew wide as he lowered the gun. "What the—"

"Do not take the Lord's name in vain," Tammi snapped.

Leda descended like an avenging angel in a Renaissance painting but wearing a yellow sequined flapper dress instead of a flowing white garment. Barron raised the gun and fired. The bullet passed through Leda, piercing the building, the sound echoing off the metal sheeting. Chip released Barron's pants to run to Maddie, who was calling her. Unfazed, Leda continued her trajectory toward Barron.

"How dare you fire a weapon at an angel!" Tammi shouted.

"Angel?" Barron glanced at his wife, his face contorting in rage and confusion. He let go of Jordan's hair, and she rolled away from him, scrambled to her feet, and ran to Maddie.

"I've got you," Maddie whispered. Keeping a hand on Chip's harness, she wrapped an arm tightly around Jordan's shoulders and led her toward her car, putting it between them and Barron, who remained focused on his wife and Leda.

"Yes." Tammi pointed at Leda. "This beautiful angel appeared to us," she said as she stepped closer to Barron, speaking with the confident fervor of the newly converted.

Jordan looked at Maddie and said, "Leda's not an—" Maddie put her fingers on Jordan's lips, gently silencing her.

"The angel told us all about your wickedness, Barron." Tammi continued advancing on him with Leda by her side. "You horrible, deceitful, greedy man! Lying to me—to everyone—and doing terrible things to these poor animals just so you can make more money. And willing to kill to protect yourself. You make me sick, Barron. I don't know who you are."

"This is some trick," he shouted, his confidence seeming to return. "You're trying to fool me!" He wiped his wet hair out of his eyes and waved the gun at them.

Leda glowed so brightly it was painful to look at her. As he raised a hand to shade his eyes, she shrieked, her face contorting in rage as she swooped toward him. With an expression of terror, he ran. Leda, appearing as solid as Jordan had ever seen her, must have been drawing energy from the storm. She flew at him like a mockingbird attacking a hawk, swooping in for the attack, pulling up and arcing around for another assault, over and over. He ran away from the cars and the barn into the open area, toward the manure lagoons. Jordan couldn't tell if Leda was actually making contact with Barron, but he flinched and flailed his arms as if she were hitting him. When he started to veer one direction, she came at him from the other side, forcing him to redirect. She was herding him toward the big manure lagoon, the one with the dam leaking into the creek. Eventually, he had only two choices: go into the filthy muck of the pond or follow the narrow, muddy, earthen dam.

"Help me!" he pleaded, ducking as Leda dive-bombed him again. Her screams became louder, deeper, and more resonant, almost like the howl of a train. Jordan realized the sound wasn't emanating from Leda. It was coming from behind her.

"Tornado!" Maddie yelled over the wind and, rain whipping them, pointed to the trees beyond the lagoons.

Against the dark sky, the thin, silvery funnel of the tornado snaked toward them. Tammi turned to run into the barn. Chip, ears flat and tail tucked, tried to bolt, but Maddie held on tight to her harness.

"No! Too dangerous!" Maddie shouted, scanning the clearing. "We need a low spot!"

Jordan pointed to a shallow barrow alongside the gravel road and pointed to it. "There!"

"Come on." Maddie dragged Chip with her as they ran for it. "Lie on your stomach and cover your head."

Tammi, looking terrified and pale, threw herself down, putting her handbag over her head, and prayed out loud, the words becoming unintelligible in the moaning wind. Maddie curled into a fetal position, gripping Chip's harness with both hands to restrain her wriggling dog, pulling her against her body. Jordan lay facedown next to Maddie and laid an arm over her, as if she could anchor them, hoping Tammi's prayers would be heard and protect them from being sucked up into the fast-approaching tornado.

A long, metallic screech prompted Jordan to lift her head. She knew she should keep it down, but she couldn't fight the reflex to look. A jagged strip of metal roofing had torn from the rafters and was flapping in the wind, banging wildly against the side of the building. She could just barely see Barron, a gray silhouette, fully exposed to the storm, crawling on his hands and knees across the dam with Leda hovering overhead, effortlessly taunting him, The wind had no effect on her. The muck in the lagoon, swollen by rain and pushed by the wind, lapped over the edge of the dam. Barron tried to stand, slipped, and somehow got back to his feet. With a raised fist, it looked like he was shouting at Leda or maybe the wind.

The tornado was close now, bearing down on them. Whole trees and dark, unidentifiable flotsam were in the air, swirling around the funnel. Jordan felt pressure on her sinuses, a sharp pain in the middle of her forehead. Buffeted by the wind, she gripped Maddie tighter but couldn't look away. The top of the sodden dam quivered and liquified before giving way under Barron's silhouetted feet. Looking like a shadow puppet, he flailed his arms like a drowning man as his legs became mired in the tarry sludge, followed by his torso. He listed sideways, one arm disappearing, then his head. His other outstretched arm flapped, hand jerking before going limp. Then it, too, vanished from sight.

Leda, still glowing brightly in her sparkling yellow dress, rose higher in the sky, spinning and swinging her arms and legs as if dancing the Charleston in the air. As the tornado tore into the clearing, she spun faster and faster, kicking out her heels and her elbows. As she ascended, the tip of the tornado began to retract, its connection to the ground severed.

Jordan's ears popped painfully, and debris that the tornado had churned and pulverized, pine needles and chunks of wood, began to fall on them. She squeezed her eyes shut, tucked her chin to her chest, and didn't look up again until the pressure in her head released and the train-whistle roar of the wind dissipated.

"I think it's passed," she said, sitting up. It was still raining, and thunder rumbled from a distance.

Maddie released Chip, who jumped to her feet and sniffed the ground in circles. Maddie rolled over, looking up at Jordan with a dazed expression. "We made it?"

She nodded and smiled. Even disheveled, Maddie was beautiful. Jordan reached forward and plucked pine needles from her hair.

"Amen! And thank you, Jesus!" Tammi sprang to her feet, still clutching her purse. Her cute floral-print outfit was mud-stained, and her carefully coiffed hair had lost all its loft.

The path of the tornado looked like a freshly cut road through the trees, jagged and raw. The barn was mostly intact, missing only a few strips of metal siding. The manure lagoon was still purple-pink and full, but several feet lower. The middle of the dam where Barron had been standing had a notch in it, like the lip of a pitcher, where it had partially collapsed.

"Where's Barron?" Maddie asked, as if reading Jordan's thoughts.

"Did he get sucked up into the tornado?" Tammi scanned the skies as if expecting to see her husband up in the steely clouds. The rain was coming straight down now instead of sideways.

"The dam collapsed on him," Jordan said, feeling shaky and cold with an internal chill, not Leda's ethereal presence.

"Are you okay?" Maddie touched her arm, her hand solid and warm.

"Yes," she said, although she wanted to say no. She wouldn't feel better until she knew Barron was incapacitated or dead. The thought shook her. She'd never wished anyone dead until today. "I saw him go down, right before the tornado lifted. We need to look for him."

They tottered to the lagoon, which still smelled putrid. Chip ran in front of them, stopping and hopping back when her toes sank inches into the mud near the edge.

"We can't go out there." Jordan pointed to the damaged dam. "It's not safe."

"We have to call 9-1-1!" Tammi said in a frantic voice, pulling her cell phone from her purse and crying, "There's no signal!"

"My car looks okay," Maddie said. "We'll drive to where we can get one."

Jordan volunteered to sit in the back seat with Chip. Maddie had wrapped her in an emergency blanket, and Chip leaned hard against her, panting. She wriggled an arm out to pet Chip and stared out the window as they drove away. Before exiting the clearing, she glimpsed the dam, which looked like a massive logjam. Trees that had been knocked over and uprooted from the tornado were piled up against it, preventing it from failing completely. Barron lay buried somewhere beneath it all.

As the car turned into the woods, she listened to Maddie and Tammi talking about phone calls needing to be made, their voices droning on as she pressed her forehead against the window and closed her eyes. She had never felt so tired.

## CHAPTER EIGHTEEN

Jordan woke up alone in Maddie's Subaru. The windows were rolled down, and the car seemed to be parked in a garage with a lawn mower, gardening tools, and a ladder propped against the wall in front of it. Her T-shirt and shorts were still damp and muddied, dry red dirt was caked on her skin, and blood oozed from scratches on her legs and bare feet. Her cheek was swollen and tender. Touching it carefully, she felt the edges of a bandage.

"Hey, you're awake," Maddie said gently, standing outside the passenger window. "You were still asleep, and I didn't want to wake you. I went in to start you a bath."

"Is this your garage?"

"I brought you home with me." Maddie opened the car door, her hair still wet, her shirt and pants splotched with mud. "You convinced the EMT you were okay and didn't need to go to the hospital, remember?"

"Yeah." Jordan's limbs felt heavy, like she hadn't fully woken up. As she lifted herself out of the car, she ached all over. "I'm just groggy. But I don't remember much after talking to the EMT and the deputy sheriff. I recall just wanting to sit down and get away from all the flashing lights."

"You were exhausted and fell asleep almost immediately. After all you've been through, I wasn't going to let you go back to Palmer House by yourself."

"Palmer House! The piglets! We need to go. They'll be starving."

"The piglets are fine and being cared for." Maddie put a hand on her shoulder as if to assure her. "I told Tammi about them, and she called someone to get them."

She followed Maddie into the house, where Chip waited at the kitchen door adjoining the garage, her claws tapping the wood floor as she pranced and wagged her tail excitedly.

"Hey, Chip." She wished she had a fraction of the happy dog's energy. She crouched to hug the black shepherd, wincing at the pain in her feet and shoulder. "You're such a good dog. A big, brave, hero dog." Chip licked her face and wriggled her joy. "You helped rescue me, didn't you?" It was difficult to believe that just a few hours ago she'd been running for her life through the woods and had nearly been killed by a tornado. Glancing around the clean, bright kitchen, she fixated on the water dispenser on the refrigerator. "I'm so thirsty. May I have a glass of water?"

"Yes, of course." Maddie seemed to have been transfixed watching her and Chip. She quickly filled a large glass with ice and water and gave it to her, surveying her from head to toe with a serious expression. Maddie was treating her gently, as if she were fragile and might break. She took several deep swallows and smiled at Maddie. "You rescued me, too."

"Jordan. I'm so sorry I ran away from you."

"You didn't run from me. You ran from Leda." She took another deep swallow and pressed the cold glass against her cheek. "You saw a ghost, Maddie. It was an understandable reaction. I passed out when I realized Leda was a spirit."

"Really?"

"I did—out cold on the living-room floor. Fortunately, I hit the couch before the floor."

"I still can't forgive myself for leaving Palmer House like that, Jordan." Maddie's blue eyes were watery; she looked like she might cry.

"What's to forgive?"

"If I hadn't left, Barron might not have kidnapped you."

"Or maybe it just would have delayed his plans. Who knows what he would have done if he'd had more time to think about it?" She met Maddie's gaze. "What's most important is that you came back. And, if you hadn't figured out where I was—" She shivered, unable to say what she was thinking: she'd have been dead by now, her lifeless body washed downstream in the floodwaters. "I don't know whether I'm lucky to be alive or if I'm unlucky because it happened in the first place."

Maddie's eyeglasses amplified the tears beginning to spill over her eyelashes.

"Oh, Maddie, don't cry, please." She took her hand, which was warm and solid, making her feel grounded. "You'll make me cry, too."

"I overheard the statement you gave the deputy," Maddie said softly. "Everything that happened, it's all just so awful. If you want to talk about it, I'm a good listener."

"Thank you." She squeezed Maddie's hand gently and took a deep breath, then let it out slowly. "Right now, I'm just shocked to be here in your house. It's like nothing happened." She glanced around the kitchen. "Everything feels a little surreal." Releasing Maddie's hand to drain the glass and set it on the counter, she noticed the dirt under her fingernails and suddenly became aware of how filthy she was after lying on the floor of a hog barn and running barefoot through the woods. "I'm a mess. You said something about a bath?"

"The tub should be full by now. Come with me."

She followed Maddie to her bedroom and the spacious master bathroom with a freestanding claw-foot tub in the corner. The white tile floor was cool under her bare feet. "He made me throw my shoes into the woods. They were new sandals, too."

"Shoes are replaceable. You are not," Maddie said. She pointed out the towels, shampoo, soaps, and a clean bathrobe hanging on the back of the door. "I'm going to shower in the guest bathroom while you soak. Take your time." Maddie gave her a tender, chaste kiss on the lips before she left and closed the door behind her.

Jordan wet a washcloth and wiped the dirt and blood from her arms and legs before stepping into the tub, letting out a quiet moan as she slipped into the warm water. Looking down the length of her body, she saw red scratches crisscrossing her legs and pebbled purple bruises just beginning to show. As the grime lifted from her skin, the reality of the last twenty-four hours crashed down in flashes of memory—Cahaba lilies and moths, crazed hogs chewing on metal bars, newborn piglets dead and alive, herself waking up bound and helpless in the barn, running in the woods until she thought her lungs would burst, then Barron's angry face, him yelling at her, and, worst of all, thinking she was going to die. She really could have. She was that close.

She took a deep breath, held it, and slid deeper into the tub, as if she could drown the noisy thoughts in her head in the silence underwater. She focused on Maddie's beautiful face and the memory of feeling her grab her arm to pull her to safety after she'd gotten free from Barron's grasp. When her lungs demanded oxygen, she sat up and inhaled deeply, drawing up her knees, and burst into tears. Wrapping her arms around her legs, she rested her head on her forearms, releasing the swirl of emotions in tears, allowing the unruly mix of anguish and relief to pour out. When the wave ebbed, she splashed water on her face, washed her hair with Maddie's good-smelling shampoo, and scrubbed herself clean.

When Maddie stepped out of the guest room, feeling refreshed and dressed in clean shorts and a seersucker camp shirt, Chip was standing in front of her bedroom, eyes and ears fixed on the door. "Come, Chip. You can't play with Jordan right now." She spoke firmly, but Chip ignored her. "Do you want a piece of cheese?" The offer diverted Chip's attention, and she trotted to the kitchen for her favorite treat.

Maddie cut a cube of cheese for Chip and then cut more. She glanced at the clock: it was nearly seven thirty. In the chaos of the day, she'd lost all sense of time. Her stomach growled. She was hungry, and no doubt, Jordan would be, too. The grapes in the fridge still looked fresh, so she arranged them on a plate with the cheese and crackers, lamenting the lost beignets she couldn't offer Jordan as originally planned. It was hard to believe she'd left New Orleans that morning. It seemed like days ago.

A half hour later, when Jordan emerged from the hallway into the kitchen, Maddie's heart swelled seeing her clean and wrapped in her fluffy, white terrycloth robe. Jordan seemed deflated, her eyes red and puffy as if she'd been crying. As she walked down the hallway, her body language had changed: her shoulders slumped, she wasn't the confident woman Maddie had become used to.

"Hey, you," she said softly, walking toward Jordan with arms out, inviting a hug. Without saying a word, Jordan stepped into her embrace and wrapped her arms tightly around Maddie's waist. She didn't let go or say a word until she felt Jordan relax. "You okay?"

"Getting there," Jordan said, leaning back to meet her gaze with a half-smile. "Thank you for lending me your bathrobe. It's amazing. I feel like I'm in a cloud."

"It fits you perfectly." Maddie released her and appraised her from head to toe, shocked when she saw Jordan's swollen feet. "Your poor toes. They're bruised! Go into the living room and sit down. I put some snacks on the coffee table. I'll be there in a minute. I have some arnica ointment, which is good for bruises."

She rummaged through her first-aid kit and took the herbal remedy to the living room. Jordan sat on the couch nibbling a cracker and sipping juice. Chip hunkered nearby watching attentively and clearly hoping for a snack from her new best friend.

Maddie sat next to Jordan and showed her the bottle with a hand-written label. "This is made by a local herbalist, and it really works."

"I trust you." Jordan reached for the bottle, but she held on to it.

"Let me do it. You keep eating. Put your feet up here." She patted her thighs. Jordan complied and swung her feet up on to her lap.

"I thought the orange juice would do you good, but I have something stronger, if you want."

Jordan put the empty glass on the coffee table. "That was perfect. Thank you. If I had any alcohol right now, I'd pass out." She leaned back into the cushions as Maddie rubbed the ointment gently into her skin, massaging the oil into each toe in small circles, and then with long strokes on the top and soles of her feet.

"That feels so good." Jordan sighed. "Ooh, it tingles."

"Too much?" She felt tingly, too, but it wasn't from the ointment. Being so close to Jordan, touching her in a way that felt intimate reminded her of the feel of Jordan's lips against her own. They'd shared only one passionate kiss, and she wanted more when the time was right. She glanced at Jordan. Her eyes were closed, a slight smile playing on her shapely lips.

"No. It's just right." Jordan's eyes remained closed. "Can I ask you a question?"

"Of course."

"What was in the bag you threw at me at Palmer House?"

"Beignets." She winced.

Jordan opened her eyes wide. "Those were beignets in the bag?

Real New Orleans beignets?" She nodded. "Damn. One of those would be really good right now with a cup of coffee."

"Rub it in, will you?"

"No. That's what you're doing." Jordan laughed softly, nudging her with her foot.

"I'm glad your sense of humor is intact." Jordan's gentle teasing alleviated some of her embarrassment. Careful not to touch Jordan's scratches, she stroked and kneaded her calf muscles.

"You're incredible," Jordan said. "Even if you did throw a bag of beignets at me."

"That was so childish." She stilled her hands. "Jordan, I swear, I don't normally do things like that."

"The circumstances were anything but normal."

"That's true," she said. "The last thing I remember you saying before I left Palmer House was that you had a lot to explain."

"I do." Jordan sat up, resetting a couch pillow under her back, and regarded her with a serious expression. "I was planning to tell you about Leda when you got back. I should have done it sooner, but I didn't want to risk you thinking I was crazy and not dateable." Jordan smiled sheepishly. "And then everything started happening so fast, I lost control of the situation. Where do I begin?"

"To quote Lewis Carroll, you should begin at the beginning." She rested her hands on Jordan's shins, enjoying the weight of Jordan's legs pressed against her thighs. "Tell me about your first meeting."

"I didn't know who or what Leda was the first time I saw her." Jordan swung her legs off Maddie's to sit facing her. She seemed suddenly brighter. "She was swimming in Caffee Creek when I went out to the Cahaba River the first time. I thought she was some local kid, a college dropout. But something was unusual about her. She even warned me about a big copperhead snake I almost put my hand on later that day. She talked about the snake like it was an old friend, I should have known something wasn't quite right about her."

"But how could you have known? I'm sure you weren't thinking about ghosts."

"I should have been after you'd told me about how haunted the campus is. Anyway, now I realize she'd been watching me for a while, following me around. Sizing me up, I guess, to see if I might be able to help her stop what Barron was doing."

"When did you learn she was a spirit?"

"Remember when you dropped me off after the gala?" Jordan's cheeks reddened, and her hazel eyes seemed to flash a little greener.

"How could I forget the night you gave me the most incredible kiss in the rain?" Her heart fluttered. "It's what inspired me to bring you the ill-fated beignets. They were just an excuse to see you as soon as I got back into town."

"I wish I'd received the message you were coming early." Jordan put a hand on Maddie's knee, and her fingertips felt electric. "Everything at that moment was so wild, the piglets—"

"Wait, slow down. You jumped to the middle of the story. Go back to the beginning."

"Right. When I went into Palmer House, Leda was waiting for me in the living room, sitting in that wingback chair by the bookcase. She didn't introduce herself as much as prod me to acknowledge her. I recognized her from an old photograph I saw in the lounge at Tammi's party barn. Leda admitted she'd been moving things around and had left gifts of flowers and fossils."

"Sounds almost romantic." She raised an eyebrow.

"Don't be jealous." Jordan nudged her playfully. "Leda is quite charming, but I've learned she uses that charm to get what she wants. She built up my trust and showed me all sorts of cool things—trails I didn't know about, endangered river snails and mussels, the nocturnal moth that pollinates the Cahaba lilies. That's why I was out there the night before you came home. The special thing she wanted to show me was the lilies opening at night—they release the most marvelous fragrance, which is so much stronger than what you smell during the day—and the moths arriving to sip their nectar. All of it was amazing. And then the thunderstorm blew in, and she promised a shortcut back to the cabin that wasn't a shortcut at all. Really, she was just luring me to Barron's hog barn, knowing that once I'd seen the abuse and the threat to the waterway, I couldn't not do something. That's pretty sneaky and conniving, when you think about it."

"Are you mad at her?"

"No," Jordan said slowly. "How could I be? That shit needed to stop. Leda might be able to do things we can't, but she has limitations. I don't blame her for tricking me into acting on her behalf. Really, her leading me to expose what was happening there is good for all of us, the hogs and everything living downstream. That reminds me of the piglets. You said Tammi intends to take care of them?"

"When I told her you had rescued two newborn piglets, she got so excited and immediately called someone to get them and the mama pig and carry them to her. She said she'll raise them to keep Prim, her pet pig, company since she lost her sister, Proper, last year. She also said she planned to 'liberate' the hogs from the barn, but I don't know exactly what she meant by that. She was talking about so many things, like she was in overdrive.

"At first, I was thinking, wow, what a trouper for caring so much about the well-being of the hogs when she's just found out about her husband's deceit and attempted murder, and that's he's probably dead and buried in that muck. I would have expected her to be in shock. Instead, she was fired up and taking control of the situation like a professional event planner. Now that I think about it, she seemed a little manic. She was talking a mile a minute, calling people and ordering them around."

"Maybe she's directing her shock into the things she can control. That'll change when they retrieve Barron's body, and she realizes she has a funeral to plan." Jordan frowned. "Any news about him?"

"I checked my phone right before you got out of the bath and didn't have any new messages. One of the firefighters is a former student. I gave him my number, and he said he'd let me know when they find him. Before we left the estate, the fire chief had called in heavy equipment. The search was going to be a slow process because of the rain, and they didn't want to risk the dam or the tornado debris collapsing on their search-and-rescue team. You saw him go down. Do you think he could have possibly survived?"

"How could anyone?" An expression of worry crossed Jordan's face. "Still, I don't think I'll feel safe until they find him."

"You can stay here as long as you want," she said, pressing her palm against Jordan's.

"Thank you." Jordan threaded her fingers between Maddie's. "I feel safe with you."

"Don't forget about Chip. She's the best guard dog around." Hearing her name, Chip pitched her ears forward on high alert, her gaze darting back and forth between her and Jordan.

"What about the tornado—was there any other damage?" Jordan asked. "Did it hit Oberon?"

"Not that I can tell. The town looks fine. It stopped just yards away from the lagoon."

"That's a miracle," Jordan said. "Speaking of miracles, Tammi called Leda an angel. Does she really think that's what Leda is?"

"I'm not sure. Tammi and I were in the barn, shocked and appalled by what we were seeing. Tammi was getting angry at Barron, and POOF! Leda just appeared in front of us, telling us about Barron kidnapping you and that you were out in the woods, in grave danger. She was glowing and magnificent, so I can see why Tammi thought she was an angel. It all happened so fast. We heard the car horn and ran outside to see Barron dragging you to his truck. That's the first time she referred to her as an angel."

"Did she tell the sheriff that?"

"She didn't. Like both of us, she didn't say a word about Leda. Maybe she didn't think they'd believe her. It's why I didn't call the police from Palmer House when Leda said Barron had kidnapped you. They'd have thought I was crazy if I told them the spirit of a woman who died a hundred years ago had informed me that the most respected citizen in town had just kidnapped our resident visiting artist. I would have been wasting precious time."

"I'm glad you didn't waste any time. But I did want you to contact the police once I knew Barron had a gun. I was so afraid you'd show up and get hurt." Tears welled in Jordan's eyes, and she put her arm around Jordan and pulled her close.

"Hey, now. You're safe. I'm safe. We're both okay." She felt Jordan tense and take a deep breath, letting it out slowly, relaxing in her arms.

"If none of us told the deputy about Leda, that she had driven Barron out onto the dam, I wonder if they're questioning why he was standing there alone facing down a tornado?" Jordan asked.

"It could be interpreted as a suicide, don't you think? His house of cards was crashing down fast. It was like he stepped in front of a train."

"He doesn't seem like the type to commit suicide," Jordan said. "Maybe they think the tornado pulled him in. Either way, I hope they're satisfied with our answers and their assumptions." Jordan turned to face her. "I saw something you and Tammi didn't see."

"What's that?"

"Leda disappeared into the tornado as it rose from the ground. I think she stopped it."

"How is that possible?"

Jordan shrugged. "When I was in a thunderstorm with her, she told me not to worry about getting hit by lightning when I was with her. She disrupts natural energy, absorbs it somehow. You saw how she looked."

"As bright as the sun," she said.

"And I swear, it looked like she was doing the Charleston as she disappeared into the funnel cloud. I can't get that picture of her in that yellow sparkling dress, dancing into the clouds, out of my mind."

"The world is strange and marvelous, isn't it?" She smiled, savoring the wonder of it all. "I never thought I'd meet a spirit, let alone a flapper who can dance away a tornado. It's such a fantastic story, it puts a new spin on Pecos Bill."

"Pecos who?"

"Pecos Bill, an old folk-tale character from the American West. He was raised by coyotes and once lassoed a tornado and rode it into the sunset."

"Huh. Too bad he's not real. We could introduce him to Leda," Jordan said. "I bet they'd get along."

"I'm still stunned that Leda is real. I wonder when we'll see her again?"

"I guess that's up to her. I haven't a clue how to get in touch with her. It's not like I can call. She just shows up when she wants to. And sometimes she's around but doesn't reveal herself. She lurks. By the way, if you're ever in Palmer House and feel a cold spot, it's probably her, not the AC."

"Interesting," she said. She'd felt strange cold spots in the historic house but had always attributed them to the quixotic nature of old buildings. "That would explain the complaints from residents about the inconsistent temperatures in the house and the technician's inability to fix the problem. I guess I'll have to make sure I say hello next time I feel a chill there."

"Leda told me you always knock before you enter Palmer House, even when no one is there. She respects you for that courtesy."

"I've always believed it's better to err on the side of caution." She heard her cell phone beep from the kitchen. "That's a text alert. I should check it." She released Jordan and went into the kitchen to find a message from the firefighter on her phone. Barron had been found. When she returned to the living room, Jordan was sitting rigidly upright on the edge of the couch, looking expectant and wary, like someone wanting news but afraid to ask.

"They found his body." She looked up from her phone. "Barron is dead." Keeping her eyes on Jordan, she crossed the room and returned to the couch. Jordan lowered her head and went pale, gulping air like she was trying not to be sick. Maddie wanted to comfort Jordan. She took her hands and remained silent, hoping to give her some mental space to process the new information. After a few minutes passed, she broke the silence. "How are you feeling?"

"Guilty." Jordan's shoulders sagged, and she looked up at her with a pitiful expression.

"I don't understand. Why guilty?"

"I wished him dead. I *wanted* him to die."

"He was not a good man, Jordan. He did a lot of very bad things, including wanting to kill you. You didn't do anything wrong. What happened to him was solely the result of *his* actions. You defended yourself. Besides, you didn't kill him. If anyone's responsible, it's Leda."

"He pleaded for help at the end—"

"When the tornado was almost on top of us, he had nowhere else to go," she interjected. "And we didn't know the tornado would stop where it did. You couldn't have helped him, even if you wanted to. None of us could have, without falling in along with him. You certainly couldn't have intervened without risking your own life." She cupped Jordan's face, gently lifting her chin. Jordan met her gaze, her eyes dark. "How else do you feel?"

"Relieved," Jordan said as a tear slid down her cheek. "Incredibly relieved."

Maddie gently wiped away the tear with her thumb, replacing it with a soft kiss. One kiss led to two, then three, then a trail of gentle kisses traversing the contours of her face. She knew she couldn't kiss away the pain, but she would try. As her lips drew closer to Jordan's, Jordan slid her hand to the back of her neck and drew their mouths together, reciprocating with a kiss that began tenderly and then flared with passion. Suddenly she felt nothing but Jordan's electrifying lips and tongue, and the press of Jordan's body against her own. The kisses lifted her, made her feel light as air, as if she might float to the ceiling if Jordan weren't holding on to her. When Jordan pulled away, she left her breathless and blinking, unable to focus on Jordan, her eyeglasses having been knocked off.

"I want more of that," she said, feeling around for her glasses. "But can we talk about us for a moment?"

"Of course." Jordan looked away and pulled her eyeglasses from between the cushions, where they'd lodged. She slid them back on Maddie's face, settling them behind her ears and trailing her fingers along her jawline, a gesture that felt unexpectedly intimate.

"You'll leave soon, and I haven't been lucky in relationships," she said. "Especially not long-distance ones."

"I'm not like any of your ex-girlfriends." Jordan touched her thigh lightly, drawing an invisible line on her skin with her fingertip.

"Thank God you're not. I'm trying to say that I don't want to worry about past failures. I want to be in the present with you."

"I still have another week here at the residency. Does Chattanooga really count as long-distance? It's only three hours away." Jordan laughed softly. "We need to go on a date soon before something else gets in our way."

"You never told me where you made dinner reservations."

"Cahaba Valley Farm. I wanted it to be a surprise."

"Really? I've heard it's amazing," She was impressed. She'd read stellar reviews of the farm-to-fork restaurant in an old farmhouse, and it had recently won a James Beard Award. "I've heard the food is creative and the atmosphere very romantic."

"I asked for the best table on the terrace for watching the sunset. I wanted to court you over cocktails and the ethically sourced local cuisine they're known for." Jordan sighed. "I'm so sorry we're not having dinner there."

"Are you kidding me? A tornado touched down. I doubt the restaurant is even open tonight."

"I hate to disappoint you. I promised you a romantic dinner."

"Disappointment is the very last thing on my mind."

"What's the first thing on your mind?" Jordan asked eagerly.

"You, silly. I'm so grateful you're here with me, safe and sound." Jordan grinned and tugged at the edges of the bathrobe. "I seem to have done things backward. We should have had a romantic date *before* I ended up naked and wearing your clothes."

"We can fix that." She laughed. "And who says we can't still have a romantic date tonight? In fact, I know a cozy place. It's not award-winning, but it's very exclusive." Maddie patted the couch. "Very local."

"It sounds like the kind of place with a dress code," Jordan said, playing along. "Think they'll let me in wearing this? My wardrobe is a bit limited at the moment."

"I have an in with the owner, so I think they'll make an exception. How do you feel about beer and a pizza delivery?"

"Love it." Jordan took her hand and turned it over. She pressed her lips against the tender skin on the inside of her wrist, creating a delightful shiver that rippled through her entire body. "Truth be told, it's the company that interests me the most." Jordan leaned close to her face, her lips tantalizingly near. "I have just one important question."

"What's that?" she asked.

"How's the service?"

She answered Jordan with a kiss that she hoped would never end.

# EPILOGUE

Waiting for the slices of bread to pop out of the toaster in Maddie's kitchen, Jordan leaned against the edge of the counter, sipping coffee and scratching the top of Chip's head. It seemed like they'd been buddies forever.

Chip shook her head, making her collar jingle. She trotted to the door, then turned and fixed her gaze on Jordan before letting out a sonorous *Woof.*

She was learning Chip's vocabulary; that particular bark meant she needed to go out. "You're a good dog," she said as she opened and closed the door behind Chip.

A long-distance relationship with Maddie hadn't been easy these past six weeks, but they were determined to make it work for now. After she returned to Chattanooga when the residency ended, Maddie visited her the following week. She introduced Maddie to her favorite restaurants and markets in the Southside neighborhood, and when they took Chip for long strolls along the riverside greenway at sunset, their conversations meandered as effortlessly as the curving river flowing slowly beside them.

After that first visit, she had traveled back to Maddie's house several times. Logistically, it was easier for her to make the trip since she didn't have chickens to care for and gardens to tend. With each visit they both confessed to hating saying good-bye, and she was increasingly reluctant to return to her apartment. It didn't quite feel the same anymore. Her things were in her apartment, but her heart wasn't fully there. It was in Oberon with Maddie.

Her phone vibrated on the counter. She turned it over to see a message from Jenn asking if they wanted to have dinner with her and Elana before she returned to Chattanooga. Even her new friends were in Oberon. She sighed at the thought of returning alone to her apartment. After she'd spent time with Maddie in a home buzzing with Chip's boundless energy, the vibrant colors of Maddie's garden flowers that she arranged in elegant bouquets around the house, and the deliciously distracting pleasures that came with a new relationship, Jordan's apartment felt stale and lifeless.

She poured an additional cup of coffee, then slathered the toast with butter and creamed blackberry honey and arranged the slices on a plate to take to the bedroom. Pausing in the doorway of the bedroom, she watched her lover sleep in the cozy bed they'd occupied since she arrived yesterday afternoon. Maddie lay on her back, her short hair adorably disheveled and sticking up in all directions. Jordan felt an aching, fluttery sensation in her chest and a bone-deep sense of contentment. She was falling hard for Maddie.

"Hey, sleepyhead. Wake up." She nudged Maddie gently and put the coffee and toast on the bedside table. "We've got a Fourth of July lunch to attend this morning." Maddie rolled over, smiling sleepily at her. She bent over, expecting a good-morning kiss, but Maddie grabbed the hem of her T-shirt and pulled her on top of her.

"We can't cancel?" Maddie asked with a sly smile, wrapping her arms around her waist.

"No, we can't. We haven't seen the piglets since the day they were born, and that's been well over a month. We promised Tammi we'd come."

"I think you have on too many clothes," Maddie murmured, her hands sliding down Jordan's back into the waistband of her pajama shorts.

"I don't disagree," she said reluctantly. "But we're supposed to be at Tammi's in an hour and a half. And don't forget, we need to stop by Palmer House on the way."

"I haven't forgotten." Maddie rolled away, reached for her eyeglasses, and slipped them on. "How long have you been awake?" she asked, hooking a finger in the handle of the coffee cup.

"An hour or so. I sat on the back deck with Chip and sketched the chickens. They're fun to watch. I'm getting to know their individual personalities."

"You're such an early riser." Maddie sipped the coffee and made a contented sound. "I'm getting spoiled by coffee in bed."

"What? Not me in bed?"

"Nope," Maddie said, teasing. "Just coffee. You make really good coffee."

"I'm going to pretend that's a euphemism for something else."

"You do many things well," Maddie said, looking at her over the rim of her cup, her gray-blue eyes sparkling in the morning light. "Have you showered yet?" she asked abruptly. Not waiting for an answer, she put the cup on the nightstand, gracefully slipped out of bed, and grabbed her hand, tugging her. "You know, we'd be much more efficient if we showered together."

"I never thought the word 'efficient' could sound so sexy," she said as Maddie, naked and irresistible, led her to the shower.

❖

On the drive from Maddie's home to Palmer House, Jordan's cheeks hurt from smiling nonstop. It wasn't only afterglow from the indulgent shower she'd just enjoyed; it was something more, something deeper. She'd never felt like this with any woman she'd dated. Simply looking at Maddie made her a little dizzy. It felt like love.

Maddie glanced at her. "What are you staring at?"

"You have the cutest dimples," she said.

Maddie responded with a dimple-deepening smile. She turned the car on to the drive leading to Palmer House. Leda notwithstanding, the house was currently empty and in between residents, and Jordan was looking forward to seeing the spirit and visiting the historic home for the first time since her residency ended. On her last day here, Leda had materialized while Jordan was packing her art supplies, appearing contrite and swearing she hadn't planned to lead Barron to his death, even though she wasn't sorry about how the events unfolded. She saw no reason not to take Leda at her word and needed to make peace with what had happened. When Leda said she would miss her, Jordan realized that she would miss the spirit, too, and promised to return regularly.

With a new resident coming for a short stay, they couldn't meet at Palmer House, so their next visit took place at Leda's favorite swimming hole in Caffee Creek. Maddie and Chip had joined them, and Leda seemed to enjoy the extra company. When Maddie learned that Leda loved to read but was limited by the stale collection of books in the old house, she'd offered to supply Leda with fresh reading material checked out from the college library. They'd arranged to meet Leda at Palmer House today since it was unoccupied. While Jordan walked up to the back door, Maddie retrieved a heavy bag of books from the back seat.

"Hello? Leda?" she called into the hallway, opening the door after knocking. "Are you here?"

"Hello, ladies," Leda drawled cheerily as she appeared, floating in front of them and smoking one of her ethereal cigarettes using a long, thin holder, the lavender smoke spiraling around her blond curls. Seeing the bookbag, she flashed with excitement. "Hooray, books!"

"When you're done with these, let me know, and I'll exchange them for new ones." Maddie took the bag to the sitting room and pulled the books out one by one. "*Lost Worlds in Alabama Rocks* and *Southern Wonder*, which is a new natural history of Alabama."

"Kippy!" Leda exclaimed, using one of her curious expressions from the twenties. "I love rocks and fossils and natural history."

"Jordan recommended this one," Maddie said as she drew a big hardbound book with a beautiful illustration of a chrysalis and a butterfly on the jacket cover from the bag and placed it on the table by the wingback chair.

"It's about a woman illustrator and naturalist who lived in the seventeenth century and traveled all over the world. She was the first person to understand the metamorphosis of butterflies. She's kind of a hero of mine," Jordan said.

"The cover's pretty," Leda said, inspecting the book but not touching it. "It looks heavy, though."

"Jordan told me you can hold only small things, so I thought I'd put it on this." Maddie took out three flat, notched pieces of finished wood from the bag and assembled them into a bookstand on the table. She placed the book on it and opened the cover. "See? You'll just have to turn the pages to read it."

"You are so thoughtful." Leda clapped. Then, puffing her cigarette, she flipped a few pages before looking back to the bag. "What's the next book?"

"Something a little different from what I think you've been reading." Maddie wagged her eyebrows as she held up a small hardcover book. "A collection of ghost stories by British writers. Let me know what you think."

"Are they scary?" Leda gave it an apprehensive side eye.

"Not terribly. They're spooky and atmospheric."

"If you think I'll enjoy them, I'll give them a try. When is the next resident coming?"

"In three days. She's a novelist from Pennsylvania."

"Maybe the stories will give me some ideas." Leda snickered.

"Please don't scare our residents," Maddie said.

Leda tucked her chin and put her hands on her hips, striking a pose as if she'd just been insulted, making the beads in her yellow dress sparkle. "Maybe I'll *inspire* the writer."

"You'll be an in-house spirit-muse?" Maddie laughed and tapped her chin. "I wonder if we could advertise that? Every residency comes with a muse."

"Ew." Leda screwed up her face. "That sounds like a job."

"I could pay you in books."

"You were going to do that anyway." Leda laughed dismissively. "What else is in that bag?"

Maddie pulled out several dog-eared paperbacks. "Last, but not least, some Nora Roberts and Danielle Steel."

"Who are they?"

"Straight romance writers. They'll catch you up on how modern love works these days." Maddie laughed.

Jordan enjoyed their banter and was a happy spectator when Maddie and Leda talked. They got into deep conversations discussing books or told stories about people from the college, and Leda's perspective on the past fascinated Maddie. Jordan glanced at her watch. Today they didn't have the luxury of time. "We need to get to Tammi's soon. Leda, are you going?"

"Yes. I want to see what she's doing out there. You won't see me though."

"Didn't expect to," she said. "Unless you want today to be the second coming of the angel."

"I've said it before, and I'll say it again." Leda wagged a finger at her. "I'm no angel, honey."

❖

"I'm excited to see the piglets," Jordan said as they pulled up to the gate. Maddie rolled her window down and pressed the call button.

"Hey, girls!" Tammi's voice gushed from the speaker.

"Good morning, Tammi," Maddie said. "Are we still meeting you out at the hog barn?"

"Yes! Come on over," Tammi said.

"See you soon." Maddie raised the window as the gate rolled open to admit them to the estate.

As they passed through the gate, Jordan noticed that the name Maxfield had been removed from it, and *Palmer* had been repositioned to the center of the heavy, black iron bars. Suddenly her stomach churned, her heart raced, and she broke out in a cold sweat.

"Hey, are you okay?" Maddie glanced at her and stopped the car. "You look pale."

"I was just thinking about that day at the barn." She knew she didn't have to be more specific. Maddie understood exactly what day she meant. She took a deep breath. "I thought I was okay. I didn't realize going there would make me feel this anxious."

"I got the sense from Tammi that it's not the same place we saw." Maddie reached for her hand. "If you don't want to be here, I'll turn around, and we'll go back home."

"No. I want to, and you're with me." She squeezed Maddie's hand and forced a smile. "I'll be okay. I really want to see those little pigs."

"They're not so little anymore. Have you been looking at those pictures Tammi's been texting? They must weigh at least twenty pounds now."

"Yeah." She smiled. "They grow up fast, but they're still cute and little compared to how big they'll be when they're adults."

The road to the hog barn had been improved with smoothly graded gravel, and the route seemed prettier now with summer-blooming, yellow black-eyed Susan and puffs of white Queen Anne's lace dotting the sides of the road. When they made the final turn and descended the hill into the clearing, she immediately began to relax, seeing how the place was almost unrecognizable from what she remembered. The barn now had two large windows and was surrounded by newly planted grass sprouting up though a blanket of straw. The manure pond, previously a toxic hue of red, reflected the blue skies above.

They pulled up next to a sparkling white Cadillac XT5 adjacent to a crimson-red BMW coupe. As they got out of Maddie's car, Tammi's twin sister, Toni, stepped through the barn door waving at them before reaching for the dark sunglasses on top of her head. Although the twins were identical, each was easily discernible by her fashion choices. Tammi favored classic styles, while Toni's tastes skewed toward form-fitting athleisure wear. Today she was wearing a white tank top and very short shorts the same color as her peach lipstick.

"Well, Tammi didn't lie about you two." Toni gave them a feathery hug and put her hands on her hips, leaning back to look at them. "Y'all are the cutest couple I've ever seen."

Jordan reached for Maddie's hand and squeezed it. "Thanks."

"Are you having lunch with us today?" Maddie asked.

"No. This is Tammi's show. I was just here to help her set up." Toni strutted to the BMW and reached for the door handle. "I'm heading to Lake Martin for the rest of the weekend. My new man friend has a big boat *and* a bigger—" Toni paused to giggle.

"House?" Maddie asked quickly.

"Yeah, that, too." Toni laughed as she slipped in behind the wheel of the sports car. "It's good seeing you. Y'all have a lovely day."

"You, too!" Jordan and Maddie said in unison.

As Toni zoomed off, Jordan looked at Maddie. "I bet Toni's new boyfriend also has a big wallet."

"Undoubtedly." Maddie laughed.

The barn door opened again, and this time Tammi emerged, wearing a pink-and-yellow sundress. "It is so good to see y'all!" Tammi gushed and trotted over to give them each a heartfelt hug. "Gosh, it's hard to believe we haven't seen each other since…the day."

"You've had a lot to attend to," Maddie said gently.

"If by that you mean arranging a funeral for my lying husband and trying to figure out how to be a better mother so my son, bless his heart, doesn't turn out like his father, then the answer is yes." Tammi, standing defiantly with her hands on her hips, was anything but the portrait of a grieving widow. "I thank God every day for my sister, my therapist, and my attorney."

Jordan couldn't stop staring at the pond. "Everything looks so different."

"Doesn't it, though?" Tammi said. "My aquascaper shored up the dam and pumped out the sludge. I'm working on plans to plant trees, landscape the edges, and stock it with fish in the fall, when it's cooler." Tammi fanned her face with her hand. "Woo. It sure is hot today, isn't it?"

Jordan and Maddie both agreed and commented on the oppressive humidity, a typical preface to any conversation in the South during the height of summer, when no one ever seemed to tire of discussing the weather.

"Thank you for coming all the way out here. Let's get out of the sun before we burn up, shall we?" Tammi waved at them to follow her into the barn. "I have more to show you than just grass and the pond."

As Jordan crossed the threshold, a familiar cold whoosh of air brushed past her. She turned and looked over her shoulder at Maddie, who smiled with raised eyebrows and nodded as if to say, "I felt that, too." Leda was letting them know she was there and entering the barn with them.

What a different place it was now—clean and brightly lit with the additional natural light from the new windows. Instead of concrete slat floors underfoot, there were wide pine planks. The metal panels, gates, watering and feeding stations were gone. And so were the pigs. Before Jordan could inquire about them, Tammi directed them to the center of the room, where three presentation easels covered with sheets stood next to a table set for three that looked like it was ready to be photographed for *Southern Living* magazine. Covered in white and blue linen, it held plates of cucumber and pimento-cheese finger sandwiches with little American flags attached to toothpicks stuck in them, flaky cheese straws, artfully sculpted crudité, and a golden-crusted pie. A small side table held a tall pitcher of lemonade or, knowing Tammi, a cocktail.

"Would you like a cold and refreshing mojito?" Without waiting for an answer, Tammi reached for the pitcher and began pouring drinks, handing out icy cold glasses garnished with a sprig of mint. Tammi held hers up. "Cheers, y'all."

"Cheers," Maddie and Jordan said in unison.

"Wow, this is good," Maddie said.

"Agreed." Jordan wasn't surprised. She knew Tammi made excellent cocktails. "This place is so different. May I ask where the hogs are?"

"Most are out in the woods. Tom, my newly hired farm manager, tells me that's where they want to be on these hot days. I have only twenty of them on the property now. The farm-animal rescues I contacted were able to help find homes for the rest. A few are here in the barn right now, including a couple I know you want to see. Follow me." Tammi strode toward a set of wide doors on the far side, the heels of her sandals tapping the wood floor.

"Holy—" Jordan cut herself off before cursing as they entered the room that had been full of gestational crates and misery. "This isn't a barn. It's a nursery." Now it looked like the interior of a traditional barn, its walls lined with roughly cut wood boards and low-walled pens festooned with red, white, and blue bunting in honor of the holiday. With Maddie by her side, Jordan stepped closer and peered over into the pens to see three mama sows with piglets. Two had big litters of tiny piglets, but one had only two young pigs. "Is that—"

"Meet Willadeene." Tammi beamed. "And her two little babies you saved, Mirabelle and Clarabelle."

Tears welled in Jordan's eyes as she watched the big sow dozing luxuriously, reclining on fresh, clean straw with her two fuzzy pink and plump babies fast asleep between her feet. Doors on the far side of the pens opened to what looked like long outdoor runs. Jordan wanted to jump into the pen to hug and pet the piglets but didn't want to rouse or scare them, or, more likely, get attacked by their protective mama, Willadeene. Content to watch them over the wall of the pen, she felt her throat constrict and didn't think she could speak without releasing her tears in a flood. Maddie put her arm around her shoulders and hugged her tight.

"Mira and Clara are going to stay here and become our ambassador hogs. After they're weaned, Willadeene's coming up to my house to live with Miss Prim."

"Ambassadors?" Maddie asked.

"That's right." Tammi flashed a smile. "Why don't we go back to the other room, and we'll have some nibbles and talk."

Seated around the table with drinks and finger sandwiches, they made small talk for a few minutes. Any remaining anxiety Jordan had felt about coming to the barn had disappeared as soon as she'd stepped through the door. It seemed to be an entirely new building, Barron's presence erased from it as well. Tammi had seemed bitter and angry when she'd spoken about him earlier, but maybe she was channeling that anger into something positive here. She projected the confidence of a steel magnolia, and if she felt any grief for his passing—and how couldn't she?—she wasn't showing it.

Tammi dusted invisible crumbs from her fingertips. "I asked you two to come to the barn because I wanted to show you the changes I've made here so far. This is just the beginning of a far bigger project."

"Which has something to do with those?" Jordan said, pointing to the covered easels.

"Yes." Tammi got up from the table and stood by the first panel to whisk the fabric from the easel, revealing architectural renderings of buildings and natural landscapes. "Welcome to the future site of the Guardian Angel Animal Sanctuary!" Tammi lowered her voice as if she feared someone might overhear her. "I have not told a soul about the angel's visitation. You know how people get about religious things, and Lord knows visionaries and prophets are never treated well and don't live comfortable lives. I'm *not* going down that road. We don't need to discuss what we saw that day, but I know you know that an angel saved us, and those poor hogs."

Jordan stiffened as she felt Leda's invisible icy fingers tickle the back of her neck. She assumed it was her response to Tammi calling her an angel. Trying to hide her reaction, she glanced at Maddie, who flinched seconds later, seeming to have had the same experience. She met Jordan's gaze, owl-eyed in clear surprise.

"I know, Maddie dear," Tammi responded, speaking in a compassionate tone, putting her hand to her chest. "We've all had a lot to process. In those dark days after Barron's funeral, and as I was sorting through his records and getting a fuller picture of his true wretchedness, I thought a lot about the apparition of our angel visitor and realized that I had willfully turned a blind eye to my husband's avarice and cruelty. I was complicit in his moral failures. I concluded that the only way to make amends is to make an amendment." She plucked the fabric from the other two easels and pointed to the drawings and plans on them. "Where we are standing now will be the sanctuary's educational center and café. Here visitors will learn how corporate greed fosters indifference and cruelty. They'll also see how we care for abused animals, and our ambassador animals will be housed in the adjacent room. A safari-style guided Jeep tour will be offered to view the outdoor enclosures and botanic gardens. We'll focus on caring for farm animals, but eventually we will expand to other species, domestic and wild. We will not discriminate. We will be guardian angels of God's creatures. He created them, and any disrespect we show disrespects their creator." Tammi's eyes glistened with her fervor. "This, I believe, was the angel's message to me. The Bible says many are called, but few are chosen." She put a hand to her heart, as if pledging. "I believe I've been chosen."

"Well chosen," Jordan said as she and Maddie stood to look more closely at the drawings. "Did you make these? They're good."

"I did," Tammi said proudly. "I used my interior-design app."

"This is a bold and ambitious project, and you are very talented," Maddie said, looking over her shoulder at Tammi.

Tammi beamed. "Rome wasn't built overnight, and this won't be either. First, I'll need to divest myself of Barron's businesses. My attorney tells me that will take some time to do properly. But the sales will provide more than enough capital."

Tammi sounded like an entrepreneur pitching a new project. She'd clearly done research or had consulted with a business advisor. Jordan eyed her with new respect. If she'd learned anything about Tammi Palmer, it was that she wasn't always what she seemed on the surface.

"And you'll set it up as a nonprofit organization?" Maddie asked.

"That's my goal." Tammi grinned. "What I've done here so far," she said, gesturing around the room, "is to demonstrate the sanctuary's potential. First, we'll need a board of directors to create a mission and vision statement. Then we'll need staff, and volunteers, and donors."

"We?" Jordan asked.

"I'm so glad you asked!" Tammi flicked a pink fingernail at Jordan and clasped her hands, grinning with the bravado of a salesperson. "I wanted you to see my preliminary plans before asking for your help."

She turned first to Maddie. "Would you consider being an advisor to help me create a board of directors? And, Jordan, would you be interested in a long-term position as the sanctuary's official artist-in-residence? I envision you artistically documènting all the changes that will happen on the land over the next few years. I was thinking you could use the cabin by the river for your studio." She paused and batted her heavily mascaraed blue eyes. "And perhaps you both might consider serving on the founding board?"

Jordan had thought they were just coming for a visit and to see the piglets. She hadn't expected to receive a pitch from Tammi about her big plans for an animal rescue or to be offered a role in it. She turned to Maddie, whose expression mirrored her own flabbergasted reaction. Neither of them responded immediately.

"I understand this is a big ask," Tammi said. "But you both would be valuable members of my team. Y'all take some time to think about it and let me know your thoughts in a week or so. If you're amenable to the idea, we'll talk details."

"I'm honored you've asked," Maddie said.

Jordan chimed in. "Me, too."

A door opened, and a tall, dark-skinned man in his thirties walked in. Ruggedly handsome, he looked like the stereotypical farmer dressed in canvas work pants, heavy boots, T-shirt, and ballcap. He nodded to Jordan and Maddie with a smile. "I'm sorry to interrupt, Ms. Palmer, but I got a problem with that new solar system for the hogs' water stations. It's gonna need a little discussion."

"No bother at all, Tom," Tammi said. "Ladies, this is Tom Grady, my new farm manager. Tom, these are Jordan Burroughs and Dr. Madeline Grendel, good friends of mine and maybe future board members of the sanctuary." Tammi winked.

"Nice to meet you," Tom said.

"Nice to meet you, too," Jordan said.

"Same," Maddie said. "Tammi, why don't we let you take care of business with Mr. Grady, and we'll talk more later."

"I'm sorry to have to cut our lunch short, girls," Tammi said. "Who knew I'd be working farmers' hours? Thank you both so much for coming and considering my offer." She pointed at the table. "And why don't you take that pie with you? My personal chef made it with fresh Chilton County peaches. He'll be upset if I bring it back uneaten."

Jordan was more than happy to take the pie but didn't want to be greedy. "Want us to leave you a few slices?"

"I do not need to add any more pie to my thigh." Tammi patted her hip, laughing at her rhyme. "Y'all take it and have a happy Fourth of July weekend!"

"Thank you. You, too," Jordan said, lifting the pie from the table. They said their good-byes to Tammi and Tom, and as she and Maddie walked out of the barn, Jordan had an idea. She stuck her head back through the door. "Hey, Tammi. Would you mind if we went out to the river?"

"Of course not. Go enjoy yourselves. I'm sure you know the way there." Tammi waved them good-bye.

❖

"I should have thought to grab a fork," Jordan said as she sliced through the tender crust of the pie with her pocketknife. She and Maddie were sitting next to each other on a log under the shade of a large sycamore tree on the edge of the Cahaba River. They'd kicked off their shoes to dip their feet in the cool water. Curious little darter fish skimmed the surface of the water, investigating their toes. Overhead, a titmouse family chattered in the tree branches, interrupting the calming burble of the peaceful, hazy, blue-green water flowing through the rocky shoals.

"That pie looks amazing. I have no qualms whatsoever about eating it with my fingers." Maddie turned away suddenly, seeming to focus on something in the river. She waved. "Hey, Leda!"

"Hey, girls!" Leda was floating in the eddy of a deep pool, her head above the surface of the water and a big grin on her lips.

"I wish I could give you a piece of this pie," Jordan said, lifting and tilting the pan to show her.

"Me, too," Leda said. "It looks delicious. How about that Tammi? Isn't it swell what she's doing?" Leda became brighter as she talked excitedly. "You're going to be a part of the animal sanctuary, and Jordan, you'll be here all the time." She spun in a circle. "We'll have so much fun!"

"Whoa, Leda," Jordan said. "I haven't accepted Tammi's offer."

Maddie's face fell. "You're not going to take it?"

"I didn't say that. It's a big decision. I just need to think it through."

"What's to think about?" Leda asked, floating closer. "Jordan, you don't know even half of all the things you haven't seen here yet. I could help you. We could go hunting for rough hornsnails or the Alabama sturgeon that no one except me has seen in decades. And I could help you find rare wildflowers like the Cahaba torch in the glades near here. They look like tiny exploding fireworks. There's more than a lifetime of plants and animals to keep you interested here. Trust me. I know!" Leda's smile flattened as her expression grew serious. "We both know how special this place is. You could make pictures of all the things you care about, and maybe they would help other people care, too."

"Sounds like you could be like the artist-naturalist in that book you wanted Leda to see." Maddie nudged Jordan.

"You two are crazy ga-ga about each other," Leda said, splashing water toward them. "Wouldn't you like to live closer together?"

Maddie looked at Jordan and smiled. "I would like that very much."

Jordan held Maddie's gaze. "I was going to mention that the lease on my apartment is up in August—"

"And you told me you could work anywhere you had a good internet connection."

"It's true," Jordan said. "But that cabin by the river has a lousy signal."

"I have really good broadband at my house," Maddie said.

"Gosh." Jordan feigned innocence. "If I lived here, I might have to go to your house a lot to upload files and stuff."

"Mm-hmm." Maddie bit her lower lip and raised her eyebrows suggestively. "And stuff."

If Leda weren't present, Jordan would have kissed her. She turned to tell Leda she was making a good case for taking Tammi's offer and moving to Oberon, but she'd disappeared. "Hey, where'd she go? Leda? You still here?"

"I think she made her point, and she's giving us some space. Seriously, what do you think about Tammi's offer? You said Alabama's biodiversity is unusual and special. With Leda's help, you might end up with enough illustrations for your own book on its rare plants and animals."

"Professionally, I'd be a fool not to take it. Personally, I'd be a bigger fool not to want to be close to the woman I love." Maddie blinked, clearly not expecting to hear those words. Jordan hadn't expected to say them, but she was speaking from her heart. "You make my heart happy."

Maddie reached out with both hands to cup Jordan's cheeks and kissed her with such passion Jordan almost let the pie slip from her hands into the river.

"I love you, too," Maddie said, breathlessly. "I've been feeling it for a while, but I've been afraid to say it."

"What's to be afraid of?"

"We haven't known each other long, and I didn't want to pressure you to upend the life in Chattanooga you've made for yourself."

"How could I not want to be here?" Jordan smiled at the river. The water cascading over the shoals reminded her that she was in the special place of the fall line, and here, she'd fallen for Maddie. The course of her life was redirecting, and the change felt good. "I'll be moving here for a job, and fortunately, it's also where my wonderful lover resides." Jordan grinned. "What do you think about advising Tammi about a board of directors for the sanctuary?"

"An opportunity to make the world a little bit better? How could I say no?"

"Sounds like we're saying yes to everything."

"Yes, we are." Maddie laughed and cast her gaze to the pie in Jordan's lap. "Did you forget I said yes to that piece of pie you offered me earlier?"

"No. Of course not. I was only momentarily distracted." She lifted the slice from the pan carefully, the sweet peach filling oozing between her fingers. "You, me, the river, and this pie—what could be better?"

"A kiss, perhaps?" Maddie pressed her lips against Jordan's and kissed her until her mind went blank. She barely noticed that half the pastry cleaved from her fingertips and dropped into the water by their feet. She pulled back, holding the remaining bit up to Maddie's lips. Maddie took it and swooned. "Oh…this is the best."

Jordan licked sweet fruit filling from her fingers. "Better than a kiss?"

"Not even close." Maddie leaned forward, offering her lips for another.

# About the Author

Kelly Wacker (www.kellywacker.com), born and raised in the West, currently lives in the Deep South, where she teaches art history at a public liberal arts university on a historic and haunted campus. She advocates for nature and is a proud founding member of the environmental studies faculty council and program. Living on the northern edge of the fall line, she enjoys spending time exploring the local woods and tributary creeks of the Cahaba River. She's inspired by meandering conversations, moments of awe in nature, thoughtful art, stimulating music, and lots of strong coffee.

# Books Available From Bold Strokes Books

**Lucky in Lace** by Melissa Brayden. Straitlaced stationery store owner Juliette Jennings's predictable life unravels when a sexy lingerie shop and its alluring owner move in next door. (978-1-63679-434-1)

**Made for Her** by Carsen Taite. Neal Walsh is a newly made member of the Mancuso crime family, but will her undeniable attraction to Anastasia Petrov, the wife of her boss's sworn enemy, be the ultimate test of her loyalty? (978-1-63679-265-1)

**Off the Menu** by Alaina Erdell. Reality TV sensation Restaurant Redo and its gorgeous host Erin Rasmussen will arrive to film in chef Taylor Mobley's kitchen. As the cameras roll, will they make the jump from enemies to lovers? (978-1-63679-295-8)

**Pack of Her Own** by Elena Abbott. When things heat up in a small town, steamy secrets are revealed between Alpha werewolf Wren Carne and her human mate, Natalie Donovan. (978-1-63679-370-2)

**Return to McCall** by Patricia Evans. Lily isn't looking for romance—not until she meets Alex, the gorgeous Cuban dance instructor at La Haven, a newly opened lesbian retreat. (978-1-63679-386-3)

**So It Went Like This** by C. Spencer. A candid and deeply personal exploration of fate, chosen family, and the vulnerability intrinsic in life's uncertainties. (978-1-63555-971-2)

**Stolen Kiss** by Spencer Greene. Anna and Louise share a stolen kiss, only to discover that Louise is dating Anna's brother. Surely, one kiss can't change everything…Can it? (978-1-63679-364-1)

**The Fall Line** by Kelly Wacker. When Jordan Burroughs arrives in the Deep South to paint a local endangered aquatic flower, she doesn't expect to become friends with a mischievous gin-drinking ghost who complicates her budding romance and leads her to an awful discovery and danger. (978-1-63679-205-7)

**To Meet Again** by Kadyan. When the stark reality of WW II separates cabaret singer Evelyn and Australian doctor Joan in Singapore, they must overcome all odds to find one another again. (978-1-63679-398-6)

**Before She Was Mine** by Emma L McGeown. When Dani and Lucy are thrust together to sort out their children's playground squabble, sparks fly, leaving both of them willing to risk it all for each other. (978-1-63679-315-3)

**Chasing Cypress** by Ana Hartnett Reichardt. Maggie Hyde wants to find a partner to settle down with and help her run the family farm, but instead she ends up chasing Cypress. Olivia Cypress. (978-1-63679-323-8)

**Dark Truths** by Sandra Barret. When Jade's ex-girlfriend and vampire maker barges back into her life, can Jade satisfy her ex's demands, keep Beth safe, and keep everyone's secrets...secret? (978-1-63679-369-6)

**Desires Unleashed** by Renee Roman. Kell Murphy and Taylor Simpson didn't go looking for love, but as they explore their desires unleashed, their hearts lead them on an unexpected journey. (978-1-63679-327-6)

**Here For You** by D. Jackson Leigh. A horse trainer must make a difficult business decision that could save her father's ranch from foreclosure but destroy her chance to win the heart of a feisty barrel racer vying for a spot in the National Rodeo Finals. (978-1-63679-299-6)

**Maybe, Probably** by Amanda Radley. Set against the backdrop of a viral pandemic, Gina and Eleanor are about to discover that loving another person is complicated when you're desperately searching for yourself. (978-1-63679-284-2)

**The One** by C.A. Popovich. Jody Acosta doesn't know what makes her more furious, that the wealthy Bergeron family refuses to be held accountable for her father's wrongful death, or that she can't ignore her knee-weakening attraction to Nicole Bergeron. (978-1-63679-318-4)

**Tides of Love** by Kimberly Cooper Griffin. Falling in love is the last thing on either of their minds, but when Mikayla and Gem meet, sparks of possibility begin to shine, revealing a future neither expected. (978-1-63679-319-1